PASSION'S FIRST TOUCH

Jonathan came forward slowly, the expression on his face intense as if he were in the grip of a powerful emotion. He hesitated, then reached out to touch Katherine's cheek with his hand.

Although she had vowed not to expose her feelings, Katherine had to strive bravely to check the tears that welled up in her eyes at the light touch of his fingers. To contain her emotions, she concentrated on the feel of his hands and emitted a long sigh of delight as they followed the curve of her shoulders. She breathed a little faster, and her pulse beat quickened as she abandoned herself to his deliberate caressess.

A little breathless, she said, "Kiss me, darling," and he bent over to cover her mouth with his own. Her mouth probed and explored his slowly and sensuously.

When he drew back, they looked into each other's eyes — in rapt intoxication. . . .

THE BEST IN HISTORICAL ROMANCE
by Sylvie F. Sommerfield

TAME MY WILD HEART (1351, $3.95)

Fires of love surged through Clay's blood the moment his blue eyes locked with the violet of Sabrina's. He held her bound against him with iron-hard arms, claiming her honeysweet mouth with his own. He had bought her, he would use her, but he'd never love her until she whispered . . . TAME MY WILD HEART!

CHERISH ME, EMBRACE ME (1199, $3.75)

Lovely, raven-haired Abbey vowed she'd never let a Yankee run her plantation or her life. But once she felt the exquisite ecstasy of Alexander's demanding lips, she desired only him!

SAVAGE RAPTURE (1085, $3.50)

Beautiful Snow Blossom waited years for the return of Cade, the handsome half-breed who had made her a prisoner of his passion. And when Cade finally rides back into the Cheyenne camp, she vows to make him a captive of her heart!

REBEL PRIDE (1084, $3.25)

The Jemmisons and the Forresters were happy to wed their children—and by doing so, unite their plantations. But Holly Jemmison's heart cries out for the roguish Adam Gilcrest. She dare not defy her family; does she dare defy her heart?

TAMARA'S ECSTASY (998, $3.50)

Tamara knew it was foolish to give her heart to a sailor. But she was a victim of her own desire. Lost in a sea of passion, she ached for his magic touch—and would do anything for it!

Available wherever paperbacks are sold, or order direct from the Publisher. Send cover price plus 50¢ per copy for mailing and handling to Zebra Books, 475 Park Avenue South, New York, N.Y. 10016. DO NOT SEND CASH.

RAPTURE'S EMBRACE

VALERIE GISCARD

ZEBRA BOOKS
KENSINGTON PUBLISHING CORP.

ZEBRA BOOKS

are published by

Kensington Publishing Corp.
475 Park Avenue South
New York, N.Y. 10016

First printing: May, 1984

Printed in the United States of America

Prologue

England, 1839

The man patted the empty space beside him and said in a deceptively mild tone, "Why don't you sit here with me, my dear? You should be more friendly, you know."

Trying to avoid the gaze of her traveling companion, Katherine Cameron shifted uneasily in the seat of the elegant carriage that was taking her to London at a breathless speed. Her thoughts were chaotic. Still stunned by the sudden turn of events, her mind couldn't yet accept that her aunt had been capable of handing her over to this stranger. The man didn't even bother to conceal the perverse pleasure he was deriving from her acute distress.

At her silence, the thin, bloodless lips of Charles Langford stretched in a sardonic smile. "Very well," he said. "I see that it may take some persuasion for you to come around." His eyes, hard and unrelenting, remained fastened on her. "But you will come around."

Quite intimidated, Katherine shrank back as his malevolent laughter filled the small confines of the coach.

At the moment, however, she had nothing to fear. Charles

was in an extraordinarily good mood. The two months of suffering his father's lectures over his gambling debts were now behind him; moreover, the night spent at the Surrey inn had presented him with a most agreeable surprise in the person of the pretty wench sitting opposite him.

Let other fools spend fortunes on expensive mistresses who demanded to be kept in luxury, he always thought; as for himself, he had discovered not only the way to satisfy his appetite for female flesh, but also an additional source of income whenever his father decided to tighten the purse strings — as he was given to do whenever Charles displeased him.

Since authorities turned a blind eye to the plight of the young women and children who were sold into the city's brothels, white slavery was quite a profitable proposition in London, and this wouldn't be the first time Charles had replenished his dwindling fortunes by selling a pretty wench of whom he had grown weary. There was an abundance of them among the lower classes, many with relatives who were most willing to trade them for a few guineas to spend on drink. Comely wenches brought good prices, and if he played his cards right, he was sure to make an excellent profit from this one — once he had pleasured himself with her, of course.

A good investment, he congratulated himself. The girl was not only very beautiful — perhaps more so than any other he had ever seen — but she had an indefinable quality he had never expected to find among those he considered the dregs of humanity. Once again he let his appreciative gaze roam slowly over the fullness of the young firm bosom that the frayed woolen dress couldn't completely conceal even though it was much too large for her.

He was amused by the way the wench tried to hide her almond-shaped emerald eyes behind a lush curtain of lashes that were surprisingly dark, considering the coppery color

6

of her hair. Her complexion was creamy and unblemished, her face accentuated by high cheekbones and a slightly upturned, delicate nose with finely sculptured nostrils. Her mouth was full and generous, and the sight of her small and white even teeth punishing her lower lip made Charles want to reach for her right then and there. The girl seemed so frightened, however, that he thought better of it. If she was foolish enough to jump from the coach and kill herself, he would lose his investment.

No use having the goods spoiled, he thought. Instead, he decided to spend his time mentally undressing her and imagining the things he'd like to do to her at the end of the journey, when they finally reached London. At least he wouldn't have to waste any time giving her a good scrubbing before taking her to his bed. The wench was scrupulously clean, and this, in itself, was just as rare as her beauty.

That the aunt had been aware of his motives for buying the girl he had no doubt, but she had been too greedy for the purse he had offered.

"A virgin," the old woman had promised. Was it true, he wondered, or had the uncle had her? Charles hadn't missed the hungry look in the man's eyes and the way they had followed the girl the previous evening while she had been performing her chores at the inn. Now that he thought about it, Charles reflected, he wouldn't be a bit surprised if the uncle's lechery hadn't played a more important part than greed in the hag's decision to sell the pretty niece.

A virgin? He would soon find out. They would be in his London townhouse by early evening.

Pale and silent, Katherine stared with unseeing eyes at the fleeting landscape. Shivering with apprehension, she was conscious of the cold, evaluating gaze that made her feel almost naked. Not for a moment had she believed Aunt Harriet's story that she was being sent to London with this gentleman to serve in the household of his parents, and she

7

was more frightened than she had ever been in all of her seventeen years. She had seen lust in men's eyes before; in those of some of the men who came to the inn and in her uncle's, who had tried to corner her whenever Aunt Harriet's back was turned. But there was more than lust reflected in those cold blue eyes; she could sense evil.

At least at the inn her aunt's jealous vigilance had prevented Uncle Thomas from having his way with her; but now, Aunt Harriet wasn't interested in stopping this man.

I'll run away as soon as we reach London, Katherine promised inwardly in an effort to give herself courage. But where could she go? She didn't know a soul there.

I don't care! I'll run away!

One

Amidst the thriving activity of the London docks, a golden-haired giant of a man paused to admire once more the sleek lines of the new clipper ship which had just completed its maiden voyage, her holds filled with a cargo of cotton, sugar, and rum from America. Now that the tall masts bore full canvas, Jonathan Greenfield—a seasoned seaman at twenty-six—thought that to him there was no sight in the world more beautiful than a clipper in full sail.

Shaking his head with a wry inward smile, Jonathan finally made himself turn and walk away. He had invested a great deal on this ship, where at the moment only a skeleton crew remained while he called on the agent who would arrange for the unloading and sale of the cargo. Once this portion of his duties had been concluded, he was free to seek his pleasure. The time at sea had long worn off the effects of the lusty widow he had enjoyed in Savannah, and from tavern wenches to aristocratic ladies, London offered a wide variety to satisfy a man.

Surprised by the early arrival of the ship, Harrison Townsend rose to meet his visitor when Jonathan walked into his office.

"You made excellent time on this voyage, Captain Greenfield," he greeted affably, offering his hand. "I wasn't expecting you for a least another week."

Wringing the proffered hand, Jonathan replied pleasantly, "We had fair weather and good winds, not to mention that the new clipper is faster."

Townsend smiled, and gesturing to a chair near his desk inquired, "How long was the crossing?"

"Sixteen days." Jonathan sat down.

"By George!" the agent exclaimed in admiration. "But that's an unprecedented record! And I understand you're the man responsible for the design of the ship, Captain." At Jonathan's nod of assent, he added, "Then allow me a toast to your achievement."

Crossing his elegant office, the young man went to an oak cabinet that stood in a corner and brought out a bottle of Scotch whiskey and two glasses. He then poured a generous portion of the spirit into each glass and offered one to his visitor. Jonathan accepted the drink.

"To the new clipper," offered Townsend, raising his glass.

Jonathan did likewise. "To the *Mary Beth*," he smiled. "And to many more like her."

They drank, and then Townsend offered a cigar to the American which Jonathan lit up for both of them. Comfortably seated and drink in hand, the two men spent the next few minutes discussing the new ships as well as the ways and means to increase speed even more. Once the amenities were out of the way, Jonathan accepted the agent's assurances that unloading the cargo would be done as quickly as the next day. With the ever-hungry British mills clamoring for cotton, it wasn't unusual for this commodity from America to receive a high priority. Not to mention that perennial favorite of the English: rum.

Another aspect of business Jonathan had to discuss with Townsend was the merchandise—mostly manufactured goods—he would be carrying on his return voyage to America.

It was dusk by the time they had reached an agreement when Townsend inquired, "Have you any special plans for this evening, Captain? I'd be honored to have you join me for supper."

Although Jonathan had met Townsend on previous visits to London and they were close in age, a real friendship had never developed between them. This time, however, the agent seemed eager to hear more about the new clippers, and always delighted to discuss one of his favorite topics, Jonathan had no qualms in accepting the invitation.

Dusk had darkened into night when they left the office and hailed a hansom cab to drive them to Townsend's club, where the agent proved an entertaining host. During the course of the meal, he mentioned his plans to attend a party given that evening by one of his friends and asked if Jonathan cared to join him.

"Charles just came back from the country and is most anxious to make up for lost time," Townsend volunteered. "One thing we must say for him is that his parties are always gay. Although you never know what to expect, of one thing you can be certain: that there'll be beautiful women." Giving his guest a humorous and highly communicative glance, he added, "And I'm sure after your voyage you'll be looking forward to some female companionship, old chap!"

At Jonathan's smiling admission, Townsend continued, "Besides, since Charles is an inveterate gambler, there's sure to be a good game of cards that might appeal to you." Without waiting for a reply, he then proceeded to tell Jonathan of the current gossip on the difficulties Langford was having with his father over the matter of his heavy losses. Even in the country, where he had retired to escape the hustle and bustle of London, the old man had been approached by angry creditors demanding the payment of Charles's mounting gambling debts.

Jonathan listened politely but with disinterest, to Townsend's recital of Langford's woes. During the long weeks and even months at sea, a man has many hours to fill; he had his books, his guitar . . . and cards. At this particular moment, gambling held no special appeal for him. It was the warm, tender flesh of a woman that a young and lusty male such as he needed after a long voyage. About to decline Townsend's invitation, he paused when the agent's words recaptured his attention.

". . . I hear that he has a new wench tonight," he was saying. "And rumor has it that she's quite a beauty, although no one has seen her yet."

Jonathan's interest was immediately aroused at the mention of the wench, and mainly out of curiosity, he decided to accept the invitation.

While finishing their meal and during the ride to Langford's house, Townsend regaled the American with more gossip and a quick rundown of the man's background. Jonathan found nothing of much interest in the story: the scion of a prominent family whose marked penchant for cards, women, and liquor had provoked more than one serious rift between him and his staunch father. Already regretting his impulsive acceptance, Jonathan was finding Townsend rather a bore when arrival at their destination put an end to the agent's gossip. The carriage had stopped in the middle of a narrow semi-circle of buildings which the swirling tendrils of fog made look almost exactly alike.

It was the narrowness of the front that left Jonathan unprepared, at their admittance by the butler, for the spaciousness of the foyer which displayed a majestic carved oak staircase that led to the upper floors, and a huge crystal chandelier which hung from the two-story molded ceiling.

The servant took them through massive double doors that

opened into a sumptuously furnished parlor where paintings in elaborate gilt frames decorated the walls. A number of people had already assembled there, and Jonathan surveyed the gathering with interest. The men were all rather young and elegantly dressed, while the women circulating among them wore low-cut satin gowns of vivid colors and heavily painted faces.

Catching sight of the new arrivals, one of the men detached himself from the group and came forth to meet them.

"Harry, how nice to see you, old chap!" Langford smiled, his hand outstretched in greeting while obliquely surveying Townsend's companion.

Townsend introduced his guest as he shook the proffered hand. "This is Captain Jonathan Greenfield, who arrived this morning from America, Charles. I hope you don't mind my asking him to join us."

"Of course, dear fellow, not at all," Langford replied affably. To Jonathan he said, "A pleasure, Captain Greenfield,"

While the men shook hands, Townsend added, "After his long voyage, he's looking forward to some excitement." And with a conspirator's wink, he chortled, "Especially the company of your lady friends, Charles."

"Of course," Langford nodded, eyeing his unexpected guest with wry amusement. The American — at least four inches over six feet in height — was elegant in light-colored trousers, a well-tailored beige vest and fawn coat over a white silk shirt. To Charles' knowledgeable eye, the gold and diamond pin he sported in his snowy cravat looked quite expensive, although discreet and in good taste. He seemed prosperous enough, Charles thought, delighted at the prospect of a man just out of a ship, probably with his pockets lined with gold and anxious to spend it. With a peculiar

13

half-smile he said, "I trust you had a good voyage, Captain."

Although reading Langford's thoughts loud and clear, the look in Jonathan's blue eyes was open and candid as he replied pleasantly, "Very good indeed."

"And how was the country, Charles?" Townsend inquired then.

Langford heaved a comic sigh of mock exasperation. "Don't even ask, Harry! Two months of the country life while listening to my father's lectures were enough to nearly drive me out of my mind," he chortled. "I can't tell you how good it is to be back in town!"

While the friends conversed, Jonathan discreetly studied his host, whose appearance gave credence to the information Townsend had provided. Langford was approximately his own age, but his complexion had a pasty, unhealthy pallor. The dilated bood vessels visible through his translucent skin, and the bloodshot whites of his eyes combined to give him an air of dissipation beneath his fastidious elegance. Immediately beckoning Jonathan's attention were three deep scratches on his left cheek that were only beginning to heal. It was then that Townsend's remark interrupted his appraisal.

"And tell me, Charles, where's the wench?" the agent was asking. "I hear she's quite a beauty."

"That she is, old chap, that she is." Langford replied. His eyes narrowed imperceptibly as he lifted his fingers to the scratches on his face. "But, unfortunately, she's also quite stubborn. It'll be a while before she's ready to entertain us properly. I'm afraid she needs a little more—persuasion."

The gesture didn't escape Jonathan, but the host turned to him and said, "Come, Captain, I'd like you to meet my friends."

Jonathan was then introduced to the other guests and, as the evening progressed, he was pleased but not surprised to find a brunette hanging on his arm and smiling seductively at him. The girl was very pretty, and the low-cut gown of peacock blue satin she wore displayed her white generous bosom down to the rouged nipples.

In addition to his good looks, Jonathan's charm — whenever he chose to use it — had always made him popular with females of every station. While he had no doubt as to the occupation of his current companion, he was as polite and attentive to the little prostitute as though she had been a lady. Totally unaccustomed to such treatment, the girl became even more anxious to please him. She led him to a corner of the room, and as they sat apart from the others, she let her hand provocatively brush his thigh every now and again while hanging avidly to his every word.

Meanwhile, elsewhere in the salon, the subject of the wench Langford had brought from the country came up again among the other guests, who demanded to see her.

Charles was not pleased by their insistence. He had discovered that a few days of total isolation and hunger would bring the most recalcitrant wench down on her knees. Bringing the girl downstairs for his guests to see would interfere with this highly successful method of persuasion he had developed. Finally, there was so much discussion about the wench, that Langford reluctantly had to agree to their wishes.

"But only for a moment," he warned them. "As I said, she isn't ready to entertain us as yet."

He set down his drink and went out of the room. The men waited expectantly, telling lewd jokes among themselves and laughing noisily until Langford returned pulling with him a beautiful girl dressed in a frayed old frock. Her long coppery hair was loose and tangled; her green eyes were wide with fear. She was immediately surrounded by a number of men who began pawing at her and pinching her while laughing at her futile efforts to avoid their grasping hands.

Now that her isolation had been broken, Langford made no attempt to stop them. Perhaps this was the lesson the wench needed to make her more pliant to his wishes. Consistent bad luck at the gaming tables had depleted his funds, and he had been counting on the price he hoped to fetch for her to replenish his purse. Expecting that by now she would have been sniveling at his feet and doing his bidding as others had before her, the idea of a private auction among his wealthy friends had been the main reason for calling this party. Her refusal to submit to him, however, had changed his mind.

Once again his fingers touched the deep scratches her fingernails had raked on his face, which would probably mark him for life. But that was not all; his groin was still tender from the blow the bitch had given him when he had tried to take her. No, he wouldn't sell her, he had determined. Not until he had taken her and broken that indomitable spirit of hers!

Jonathan's attention, which had been engaged by the brunette, was distracted from his companion by a piercing female scream. It was only then that he became aware of the commotion at the other end of the room.

Getting up briskly, he crossed the room in his long stride. "What's going on?" he demanded as he approached the group.

Before anyone could answer he saw the girl who in vain tried to escape the attentions being forced upon her, and without giving it a second thought he grabbed the two men nearest to him by the scruffs of their necks and pulled them away from her.

The uneasy silence that descended upon the room at his action was only broken by sharp intakes of breath as everyone stood gaping at him in astonishment.

Jonathan looked at the girl. The front of her dress, which had been torn down to her waist, exposed young breasts that

16

were full, firm, and delicately rosy-tipped. This tempting sight had the immediate effect of causing a stirring of excitement in his loins that he mentally pushed aside when he saw the grimace of pain distorting her lovely face; pain caused by the fact that Langford was mercilessly twisting her arms behind her back in an effort to subdue her struggles.

Jonathan's brow contracted as he glared at his host. "Let go of her," he said in a low, but significant tone of voice.

Face colored with mortification at the American's intrusion, Charles reluctantly obeyed the terse command.

Katherine gathered the ends of the tattered dress in an effort to cover herself, and as she did so, Jonathan noticed the rope burns marring the smooth skin of her wrists. Taking a step toward her, he felt anger rising swiftly until it was almost boiling inside him. Involuntarily she flinched as his hand came up to touch her, and she looked up at him fearfully before quickly dropping her gaze.

"Easy now, don't be afraid." Even though his tone had been gentle, the set of his mouth was grim and his eyes sparkled with anger as he tilted up her face to scan her bruised cheek. Glowering at his host, Jonathan asked in a voice that exuded contempt, "Is this your idea of persuasion, Langford?"

Attempting to hide his uneasiness behind a cool, scornful little smile, Langford replied, "She's my property, Captain. To treat any way I please."

Jonathan's frown deepened. "Your property?"

"Bought and paid for," Charles replied with a tight-lipped smile. "And a goodly sum I paid her aunt."

Jonathan had no reason to doubt Langford had spoken the truth. He had been to London often enough not to know that in a society where slavery had long been abolished, young women and children were sold into prostitution without any interference from the law. He had heard of extreme cases where even the parents of abducted victims were impotent to legally rescue their children once they had been purchased by white slavers. "How much do you want for her, Langford?"

Langford's smile became one of silken mockery as he replied, "She's not for sale, Captain. At least, not yet."

"I see," Jonathan drawled. He looked thoughtful for a moment as though considering the situation, and then shrugged rather indifferently. "As you said, she's your property." He grinned at his host and asked amiably, "Well, now, where's that card game I was promised? There's gold burning a hole in my pocket!"

The lightness of his remark served to alleviate the built-up tension, as the collective sigh of relief that followed indicated.

"Now you're making more sense, Captain!" said Langford with a tittering laugh. With eyes shining in triumph, he called a servant and ordered that Katherine be taken away. Then, eager to recoup his loses, he became the expansive host again as the card game was set up and the players began to take their places at the tables.

The servant who had removed Katherine returned while the first hand was being dealt. After placing a key on the table in front of Langford, he proceeded to refill everyone's glasses.

Meanwhile, Katherine had been locked up again in the dismal room where she had been kept a prisoner since her arrival in London. She didn't know how long that was because she had been unconscious for part of that time. The one and only window had been boarded up, and it was so dark in the room that it made no difference whether it was night or day; all she knew was that the time she had spent in that room felt like an eternity.

With the exception of an old bed covered by a thin straw

18

pallet, the room was completely bare. Even the ewer of water which had been left to her in the beginning had been taken away after she had tried to bash Langford's head with it during her first attempt to escape. There had been a second try, and she had almost succeeded when a servant had caught her a few feet away from the front door and freedom. Perhaps next time—

The question was, would there be a next time? She was already feeling so weak not only with hunger and thirst but also the brutality of the man, that she knew that before too long she wouldn't even have the strength to rise from that pallet, let alone fight Langford the next time he came through the door.

As the nightmarish hours had slowly dwindled, Katherine had reached into her mind for memories of other times, happier times, which had helped her retain a grip on her sanity: the lines of a favorite poem; the sound of her mother's voice retelling the story she had never tired of hearing.

Morwenna, her mother, had been the product of the second marriage of a man whose first wife had conveniently died leaving him a prosperous inn. Never allowed to work at the inn, pretty Morwenna had spent her days preening, reading poetry, and painting watercolors which her plain and sour half-sister, Harriet, had disdainfully called silly. Swains came to seek her, but none pleased her, and her father had been in no hurry to find a husband for his youngest and favorite daughter.

Then, one day, Andrew Cameron had made his appearance at the inn riding a tired old nag and looking for work. The youngest son of a good but impoverished Scots family, he had a gift for poetry and a zest for living that combined with his handsome looks had set Morwenna's heart aflutter. He was very tall and had flaming red hair, laughing gray eyes, and a smile that illuminated his boyish, freckled face.

As soon as those two met, they knew they had found the missing part of themselves.

Aware of the ambitious plans her father had for her, Morwenna took pains to keep their love a secret. For a while her hands were quite full trying to restrain Andrew, who wanted to shout it from the rooftops; but it had been Harriet — always envious and jealous of her sister — who had wasted no time in carrying the tale to their father as soon as she had discovered it. In a rage when he had learned that she had fallen for the penniless drifter, Morwenna's father had immediately dismissed Andrew and arranged a betrothal with one of her many prosperous suitors, thereby forcing the young lovers to elope in the night and be married in a neighboring village.

In their wanderings, Andrew and Morwenna had found an old gypsy caravan abandoned in the hedge, grown almost into a copse of saplings and weeds by the side of the road. One of the wheels was off. The former owner must have found the repair too taxing for his skills, or perhaps he had been on the run and had time only to herd his family onto the wagon of another member of his tribe. Andrew had whittled a new spoke, bent and rebent the band that held the outer rim together, and remounted the wheel. The faded, once gaudy cabin protested in its joints when it was turned upright, but it held. Some of the carved decorations that had been nailed to the outside had fallen off, and the leather straps once attached to the wagon tongue were too dry and split to repair, but they made do with bits of leather and rope they carried in their kits. A little cleaning, a little paint, and they were as proud of their little wagon as any lord of his mansion.

In it they journeyed from town to town, stopping wherever work could be found. Young and very much in love, they had lived happily from day to day. Katherine had been born to them a year later, and the three of them had continued their carefree, gypsylike existence.

Never staying very long at any one place had made it difficult for Katherine to find friends her own age, and during her growing years she had spent many hours with her father's books as her only companions. Andrew worked at any job that presented itself, be it as tutor to the children of prosperous country folk or as a farmer's helper, while Morwenna sold her pretty watercolors to supplement their meager finances, because although love had always been plentiful, money had always been scarce.

But not all the memories were happy ones. A tragic accident had put an end to their idyllic existence, and one day an orphaned Katherine had been taken to the low-browed, thatch-roofed collection of buildings that was the inn and her only living relatives: her Aunt Harriet and her husband, Thomas.

It was fortunate that at fourteen Katherine had been a tall, skinny, and long-legged girl with none of Morwenna's beauty. Her large emerald eyes had been her only good feature at the time.

Even her rather educated speech had annoyed her aunt. "Her *ladyship* will have to earn her keep," the aunt had sneered contemptuously when she had put Katherine to work. And there had been plenty to do, for the inn was like a ship at sea, with only the skills and tools aboard to sustain life within its walls. There were long carved tables to welcome the guests in the main reception hall that served as the dining room, and the large kitchen was always filled with the wonderful aroma of bread and meat pasties baking in the brick oven as well as that from the savory racks of meat which basted to perfection over the fire.

Although wine and ale were served, many of the guests staying for a good dinner preferred the strong, rope-smelling tea that put strength and hope back into their parched

21

bodies, dry from breathing dust for miles behind the churning hooves of their horses.

Outside, in the barn, the horses stamped and snorted as they impatiently waited for their favorite drink, a kind of tea made from a bucket of warm water to which the stableman had added a handful of sweet fresh hay. When the hay had soaked for a few minutes, it turned the water into a golden tea the horses loved.

In the spiked, sapling-fenced drying yard, the washerwomen did their laundry in wooden barrels and scrub tubs and a rough smithy attended to the iron parts of the carriages and the shoes of the horses.

With always a shortage of hands, Katherine had been kept busy from dawn until late at night, helping in the kitchen, cleaning the rooms, running errands, tending the chickens, helping with the laundry, and serving the customers. Each night she fell exhausted on her thin straw pallet in the stifling attic room where she froze in winter and suffocated in summer. Her solace during those sad years had been to read Robert Burn's *Poems,* the only book she had managed to hide from her aunt, who had wasted no time in selling the few possessions Katherine's parents had left her. But even her reading had been curtailed by the necessity to prolong the life of the taper her aunt had allowed her; and then, when it was gone, Katherine would lie on her pallet in the dark, thinking of her parents and weeping for the loss of their love and their tenderness.

Katherine was not lazy, and she wouldn't have minded the hard work imposed on her if only her aunt and uncle had shown her some kindness; but Harriet had taken every opportunity to vent on her defenseless niece all the hatred she had accumulated against her half-sister through the years.

The situation became even worse as time went by and Katherine's body began to change, when her skinny figure began to fill up and a rounded softness appeared at her bosom and hips. Her complexion cleared, at first leaving only a smattering of golden freckles that added a special appeal to a face of high, delicate cheekbones, until they completely disappeared. The first to notice these changes, Uncle Thomas had immediately become more "solicitous" toward his wife's niece, but his attentions had not escaped the jealous Harriet for long. A big and burly man, Thomas had always shown a marked propensity for casting his roving eye upon the serving girls, who invariably were found guilty of slovenliness or laziness and summarily dismissed by Harriet. But Uncle Thomas had not been the only one; all of a sudden the patrons also became difficult for Katherine to handle, trying to paw and pinch her bottom and breasts while she served them. Other girls might laugh it off, but Katherine resented being treated in such a crude fashion.

That Aunt Harriet hated her as she had hated Morwenna, Katherine had never had reason to doubt, but to have been delivered into the hands of someone like Langford was something she had never expected. Her eyes narrowed when she thought of her captor. How she had come to hate the man! Although she was frightened and felt lonelier than ever, there was a stubborn streak in Katherine that wouldn't allow her to admit defeat for as long as she drew breath.

To give herself courage she made an effort to square her shoulders, which slowly slumped back in dejection while she again considered her situation.

There had been a glimmer of hope earlier, when Langford had taken her down to the parlor and that golden giant of a man had come to her rescue; but even that hope had faded quickly. She was Langford's property, to do with her as he pleased. She couldn't expect help from any quarter.

What would become of her, she asked herself, feeling the return of her despondency. Langford had already told her that he intended to sell her once he was through with her. Would one of those men downstairs at this moment become her new master and tormentor? Why, they were just as bad as Langford! She shuddered at the memory of those dreadful moments when she had been pinched and pawed as if she were nothing more than a piece of meat to be used and abused. If only . . . Oh, what was the use! Even the tall man who had tried to defend her had backed off after recognizing Langford's claim on her.

Katherine tried to stand up, and the room began to spin so dizzily about her that she had to cling to the bed. An earlier beating, the lack of nourishment, were taking their heavy toll on her. Perhaps it would be better to submit, do whatever Langford wanted her to do, let it happen . . .

"No!" she heard her own voice say out loud. She had been told before that she was too proud for her own good, but at this moment pride was all she had to sustain her, anger to chase her fear away. Lifting her chin in sudden challenge, she vowed, "He'll have to kill me first!"

Downstairs, the card game had continued. The number of players, however, had dwindled with each passing hour until only Langford, Jonathan, and one other man remained at the table. Some of the men had abandoned the game because the stakes had grown too rich for their purses; others because they had become aware of the strain between their host and the American.

With the decreased number of players, the necessary switch to brag had suited Jonathan's purposes very well. For the past hour he had played conservatively and shrewdly, baiting Langford, allowing him small wins only to lose even larger amounts. Right from the start he had been quick to notice that his main opponent played not only recklessly, but also badly. That he constantly kept draining and refilling his glass wasn't helping to improve his skills, either.

The atmosphere in the room was heavy with cigar smoke,

the only sounds heard every now and then were the shuffle of the cards, the occasional clinks of the glasses, the low voices of the players as they placed their bets. The air crackled with tension. A number of spectators had gathered around the table to witness what had become a duel between the two main players. Others watched in stony silence from a distance as the game progressed, aware that Langford's funds were rapidly decreasing.

While Langford had continued to guzzle down his liquor, Jonathan's drink remained untouched before him. The damned American, Charles cursed inwardly, instead of enriching his pockets as he had expected, was winning all the money he had been able to raise through credit only that day. Running an increasingly unsteady hand through his thinning brown hair, Langford watched with impotent fury as Jonathan showed a pair of sevens that beat his two fives and once again reached for the stakes accumulated at the center of the table. All evening he had seen his stack of chips diminish with every round while the one in front of that blasted Colonial grew larger and larger still.

When it became Jonathan's deal again, he shuffled the cards with ease and began to deal the next hand with slow, deliberate movements that irritated Langford to distraction.

Barely able to contain his fury, Charles picked up his cards. He took one look at them, and his heart stopped beating for a split second before it began pounding against his ribs. The nine of diamonds, a high-ranking bragger or wild card, completed a lovely triplet with the ten of clubs and ten of hearts. He couldn't lose this time, not with this hand!

"Cards?" Jonathan inquired.

The third player nodded and took two cards. Langford shook his head, striving to conceal his excitement from Jonathan, who was regarding him with cold, expressionless eyes while waiting for him to place his bet. Charles's confidence wavered a little when the American also decided to retain his hand. Should he discard his tens and try for higher cards? No, that wouldn't be wise, he decided. He placed his bet.

Without hesitation, Jonathan raised. This went on for several turns. After the third player folded, Jonathan met Charles's bet and raised once again, leaving Langford at a loss for his next move, because he was down to his last shilling.

Beads of perspiration surfaced on Langford's brow and upper lip. Playing for time, he reached for his glass and found it empty. With an impatient gesture he motioned to the servant, who immediately rushed to refill his master's glass. Charles's hand was visibly trembling as he drained his drink. He put down the glass and studied his cards again. Slanting a glance at the impassive face of his adversary he deliberated on his move. Only a higher triplet could beat his hand, and be believed the odds were in his favor. The American had to be bluffing.

"I must give you my note, Captain," he said at last.

Shaking his head, Jonathan drawled, "Sorry, Langford, no markers."

"What!" Charles cried with alarm. His pallor had deepened, and defensively he challenged, "Do you question my honor, sir?"

Jonathan remained impassive as he repeated, "I said no markers."

"That's a good sum of mine you have there, sir!" Langford protested indignantly. An increasing tightness in his chest was making it difficult for him to breathe. He had nothing left, he reflected; with a winning hand, he could still lose everything unless he met the American's bet. Suddenly, he wanted to weep.

Jonathan let him stew in his own juice, watching the different expressions that crossed his face until he finally decided the time had come for him to make his move. "I'll tell you what, Langford," he drawled, and lazily pointing at the key the servant had left earlier on top of the table added, "I'll accept the wench."

The sudden realization that his present predicament was the result of the American's strategy, made Langford curse under his breath. The Colonial was no fool, as he had believed. He had known how little were the chances of a foreigner — regardless of how much gold he carried in his pockets — against a member of the English aristocracy. Winning the wench in a card game before so many witnesses, however, would leave Charles no redress on the matter. He had underestimated the man, and that had been a dreadful mistake on his part.

"That wench is worth a lot of money, Captain," he still tried to bargain in an effort to salvage something out of the situation. With affected indifference, he waited while an impassive Jonathan studied his face for a few seconds. Then, without hesitation, the American pushed all his winnings toward the center of the table.

"That's close to three thousand pounds," he drawled indifferently. "Is it enough?"

A vacuum of silence followed his words, and those farther away abandoned their posts to surround the table. With the lust of triumph gleaming in his eyes, Langford licked his lips. Three thousand pounds, a bloody fortune! A broad grin split his face as he nodded and carelessly tossed the key into the pot. Triumphantly he showed his cards and started to reach for the stakes with confidence.

Jonathan's voice froze him.

"One moment, Langford."

Slowly, deliberately, without taking his eyes off his tense opponent, Jonathan placed his cards on the table one by one. Langford's face acquired a greenish tinge as the ace of hearts was laid down, followed by the ace of spades. His eyes bulged out of their sockets as the highest-ranking brag-

27

ger, the ace of diamonds, joined its companions.

An eerie silence reigned while Jonathan picked up the key and rose from the table.

Angry and desperate, Langford suddenly came back to life. Lunging at Jonathan, he snarled, "You tricked me, you ch . . . Ooff!"

He never finished the sentence. Instead, air came whooshing out of him as Jonathan's fist met and sank into his belly. In a reflex action, the same fist came up to smash the contorted face as the man doubled up. Langford stumbled backward against another man who held him up before he could hit the floor. Wavering on his feet he stood clutching at his belly while every person in the room seemed unable to move, watching the incredible scene that was unfolding before their very eyes. What? A common brawl among gentlemen? It was unheard of!

The blue eyes that had seemed so cold only moments earlier sparked now with fire, and Jonathan, legs firmly astraddle, beckoned with his hand, "Come on, Langford!"

Staring at him through eyes that were wild with terror, Charles whimpered piteously when Jonathan grabbed him by the lapels of his coat.

"Come on, you snivelling scum!" Jonathan rasped through clenched teeth, giving one brief, but powerful shake to the trembling Charles. "Or do you beat only defenseless women?"

In the grip of terror, Langford whimpered again, and Jonathan flung him aside with disgust. This time, with no one to stop his fall, Charles crumpled to the jewel-colored Oriental carpet where he cowered, fearful that Jonathan would strike him again.

Jonathan had no intention of wasting any more time on the coward. Instead he demanded, "Where is she, Langford?"

"Up-upstairs," Langford managed through the tremor of

28

his bloody lips. Although the American had refrained from putting all his strength behind the blow, his large fist had caught Charles fully in the mouth, and he could feel that some of his teeth had been loosened.

"Upstairs where?" When Langford didn't reply immediately, Jonathan took one menacing step toward him.

"Th-third floor!" Langford cried in terror. "A-at the end of the corridor!"

Jonathan cast a look of virulent dislike at the fallen Langford before he turned away and leisurely gathered his winnings. He went from the room and mounted the stairs two steps at a time. Once he had reached the top floor, his footsteps resounded heavily on the bare wooden boards of the corridor leading to the rear of the house. There was a small door at the end.

The key he had won from Langford fitted the lock on that door, which he opened cautiously. The doorway into the attic room was low, and Jonathan had to bend down a little to go through it.

"Easy, girl," he said gently to the girl who jumped to her feet and recoiled in terror as he entered. "Easy. I'm not going to hurt you."

He glanced around the small, airless room, taking in the boarded window, the bare pallet on the decrepit bed, and an angry sparkle came to his blue eyes at the sight of the rope still dangling from the crude headpost. "Is this where he has kept you?" he asked in a tightly controlled voice.

Katherine was unable to answer. After the horrors of the last days, a paralyzing terror constricted her throat at the arrival of this new tormentor. Gathering the shreds of the tattered dress to her bosom, she closed her eyes and braced herself for the worst as she heard Jonathan's footsteps advancing toward her.

The touch on her cheek was as gentle as the tone of the

deep, husky voice that said to her, "Don't be so frightened, honey. I'm taking you out of here."

Katherine's eyes flashed open in disbelief, yet she offered no resistance when he took her by the hand. Her mind was completely numb with shock as she followed him out of the room; her bare feet moved down the stairs automatically. Once on the main floor, they paused at the threshold to the parlor.

Slumped in a deep winged chair, Langford was being attended by the same servant who, earlier, had prevented Katherine's escape. Now the man was wiping the blood away from his master's battered face. One side was swollen and beginning to discolor, and Langford still clutched at his abused belly. When he noticed that his friends were staring toward the door, his eyes followed the same path and immediately widened in terror at the sight of Jonathan. Gasping with alarm, Charles cringed in his seat.

"I'm taking her with me now," Jonathan announced to the assembly as though expecting a challenge. When none came, with a gentle pressure on her elbow he escorted Katherine to the front door, where he paused to remove his coat and wrap it around her shoulders. It was only then that he noticed that her feet were bare, and scooping her up in his arms as easily as a feather, he stepped out into the chill, misty night.

The fog—grown thicker in the hours that had elapsed since his arrival at Langford's house—swirled around them, and it was mostly by sound that Jonathan found a hansom cab as it went by. He placed Katherine gently on the seat and, after giving instructions to the driver, climbed in after her.

Huddled against a corner, Katherine kept as far away from him as she could get. By now she was trembling uncontrollably; whether it was from fright, cold, or both Jonathan couldn't tell as he tried to allay her fears by speaking to her in soothing, gentle tones. When she wouldn't answer or stop shaking, he opted for leaving her alone.

Katherine didn't utter a word during the ride. Once they reached their destination, Jonathan paid the driver and gathered her in his arms again to carry her through the docks, which were almost deserted in those early hours of the morning. He reached his ship, climbed the plank and went below.

He put her down only after they had entered a dimly lit cabin, where Katherine stood on shaky legs and in a daze while he poured two fingers of brandy into a glass that he offered to her.

"Drink this, honey," he said. "It'll make you feel better."

When Katherine continued to stand there as in a trance, making no effort to accept the glass, he brought it to her lips. Astonishment replaced the glazed look in her eyes, which widened as the fiery liquid burned its way down to her empty stomach. Sputtering and choking, she pushed the glass away with both hands.

"Come on, love," Jonathan prompted her gently. "The second drink is better, I promise."

Surmounting her feeble resistance, he made her finish the brandy. Since she was still trembling, he sat on a chair and pulled her down on his lap, trying to comfort her.

"It's all right love. Don't be frightened." He stroked her hair, soothing her with little gentle words while he continued to rock her in his arms as tenderly as he would a child.

Little by little, the warm glow the brandy had ignited in the void of Katherine's stomach began spreading through her body. Jonathan's soothing voice, the gentle caresses that accompanied the rocking comfort of his arms, all contributed to chase away the terror that had been her constant companion during the last few days. Unaccustomed as she was to drink, in her state of physical and emotional weariness the brandy Jonathan had practically forced down her throat was making her so lightheaded that she was totally oblivious to the fact that the front of her dress had fallen open.

At that moment, Katherine was at her most vulnerable. Her hunger for comfort and tenderness, for the closeness of human flesh, made her cling to him when Jonathan made to release her because she was in fear of losing the only source of warmth and gentleness she had known in a long, long time. All she was aware of was of being held by strong, protective arms, of warm lips that began tracing gentle kisses on her brow and on her face and then moved to find her own. She tensed up a little when his tongue tentatively touched and parted her lips, but she relaxed again, giving herself to the curious sensations it evoked as it probed and explored her mouth and his hands moved gently to stroke and fondle her naked breasts.

Only semi-aware of what was happening, she dreamed that she was floating through space before she was laid down on a cloud of softness. There was a feeling of unreality as her naked body was pressed against another that was warm, muscular and strong. Then the unreality was replaced by pure sensation, and she moaned softly as Jonathan's lips explored and nibbled the softness of her throat, when they caressed every inch of her that his hands stroked and gently fondled. And she was only dimly aware of a husky voice murmuring words she couldn't comprehend, but it didn't matter; not as long as the caresses didn't stop, as long as she could feel the heat rising inside of her and those sensations her body had never known before, yet seemed to have waited for without her knowing.

Jonathan's mouth covered her surprised gasp at his entry, but even the brief pain caused by that invasion of her body became pleasurable after the first few moments. The pleasure only increased in intensity when he began moving gently at first and then accelerated the tempo of his thrusts, which became more urgent when by their own accord her hips adjusted to his rhythm and she began to writhe in response. Then her loins were shaken by a succession of explosions, and the pleasure was so intense, so overwhelming, that it was almost agonizing. It was as though she were falling into a vortex that was draining her of all her strength, of her will, even of her life, and yet she welcomed it with joy.

Moaning, crying, Katherine clung to Jonathan as his own climax seemed to empty his body into hers. Holding her close he caressed her soothingly, and burrowing her tear-stained face in his chest, she lay quietly in his arms and fell asleep at last.

Sometime during the night, she began to thrash about and woke up crying. Her eyes were wide and dark with fear.

"Hush, love," Jonathan soothed her, gathering her in his arms. "It was just a nightmare."

Katherine wept quietly as he rocked her gently for a while. When at last the weeping ceased, he drew back a little to look at her and smiled.

She had fallen asleep again.

Two

Fidgeting while asleep, Katherine burrowed herself deeply under the warm quilt. At first, the noises that began filtering through her stupor seemed to come from a great distance away; as their volume intensified, however, she became aware that what she heard wasn't part of a dream. The light hurt her eyes when she opened them at last, and this did not help at all the dull throbbing at her temples. She was only dimly aware of her surroundings as her sleepy gaze wandered about the cabin before her mind began to clear a little and register details.

With every inch of space utilized to the fullest, the small cabin was cluttered. The bed, a compact dresser, and a desk and chair seemed to be the only furniture, but there was a small folding table built into the wall. An ewer and a basin were atop the dresser. A sea chest occupied a corner next to the strong box, and there was a guitar leaning against the wall, which was paneled with rich, glowing wood and lined with shelves containing a good number of books and strange-looking instruments. Sunlight coming through the porthole flooded the cabin and shone on the polished shade of a brass lamp hanging from the ceiling on a chain.

It was at this point that Katherine became fully awake,

and she sat up abruptly when suddenly the sequence of events of the previous night came back to her. She remembered being taken away from Langford's house by the tall stranger, but the memories of having been carried by him through the fog were only vague. She thought there had been a carriage ride, and that she had been very frightened because even though the man had kept telling her that she was safe, she had not believed him. She had only a dim recollection of a ship, but after that everything was very fuzzy in her mind except that at last she had felt safe and warm and . . .

"Oh, my God!" She emitted a single short gasp that made her head hurt.

Pressing the tips of her fingers to her temples in an attempt to ease their throbbing, Katherine felt her face flush with embarrassment at the memory of how she had responded to the kisses and intimate caresses of the stranger. How could she have done such a terrible thing?

The sound of approaching footsteps interrupted her self-recriminations and brought forth a surge of panic. Oh, Lord, what was she going to do? How could she ever face the man after she had behaved so wantonly, so shamelessly? With eyes wide with apprehension, she watched as the door slowly opened.

Awed by the tall figure in dark navy trousers and black knee-high boots, her mouth opened a little when Jonathan made his entrance. The front of the white shirt he wore was partially open to reveal a corded muscular neck, and its lawn fabric clung in patches to a broad expanse of chest that she could see was covered with a thick mat of golden fur. The sleeves were rolled up to the elbows and exposed heavily muscled forearms. A lock of tousled silver-blond hair fell rakishly on his forehead when he removed his seaman's cap and tossed it on the dresser.

Jonathan smiled when he saw that Katherine was awake.

"Good afternoon, love," he greeted her pleasantly. His brows rose humorously, and a glint of mild amusement flashed in his smiling blue eyes when Katherine pulled the covers up to her chin when he stood there for a moment waiting for her reply. Then he turned away, and she followed him with wide and frightened eyes as he ambled across the cabin. Towelling the perspiration that was running freely down his face, neck and chest, he faced her again.

Katherine swallowed the lump in her throat in an effort to recover her voice. "Afternoon?" she managed at last.

Carelessly tossing the towel on the chair, Jonathan advanced toward the bed. "It's already well past noon," he nodded. As if it were the most natural gesture in the world, he reached out to brush a strand of hair from her face. Katherine surprised herself by not flinching away. "I didn't wake you earlier because I figured you needed the rest."

The burning sensation she felt on her cheeks told Katherine that her face had turned crimson. Did he have to remind her of their shameless behavior? Avoiding his gaze, she whispered in a choked voice, "I'm so ashamed!"

Jonathan was momentarily bemused before he realized the meaning she had read into his words. "Why? Because you responded to me?" he asked then.

Unable to look at him, Katherine bobbed her head while desperately striving to check her tears.

Jonathan bent forward and crooked a finger under her chin to lift her face. "You have nothing to be ashamed of," he said, sitting down on the edge of the bed.

Katherine still kept her gaze downcast. "But I . . ."

"Look at me, love." His hands were rough and calloused — yet surprisingly gentle — as they framed her face and forced her to look into his eyes. As she did, Katherine couldn't help thinking that they were of the deepest blue she had ever seen. "You were warm, and passionate, and wonderful," Jonathan whispered huskily. Holding her face in his hands, he leaned forward and lightly touched his lips to hers.

Accepting the kiss without responding to it, Katherine was aware of a musky male scent of his sweat.

Apparently aware of her discomfiture, Jonathan drew back. "Say, you must be famished," he said as he rose to his feet. "I'll be right back."

Half-turning a little, Katherine watched him amble away again. This time he stepped outside the cabin, and since he had left the door ajar she heard him talking to someone else although she couldn't make out the words.

Jonathan came back and sat on the edge of the bed again. "Your food should be here shortly," he told her. All of a sudden, he seemed a little startled. "I just realized I don't know your name."

"Katherine," she ventured timidly. Flushing, her eyes downcast, she added, "Katherine Cameron."

"My pleasure, Katherine Cameron," he grinned at her. "I'm Jonathan Greenfield, and we're aboard my ship, the *Mary Beth,* out of Baltimore."

"Baltimore?" Katherine echoed with a blank look.

"That's in the United States of America," he nodded.

It was then that Katherine realized there was a cadence to his speech she had never heard before. She was about to speak when she was jolted by a loud crashing coming from the outside.

"It's all right, Katie," Jonathan reassured her with a smile. At the bemused expression that appeared on her face, he asked, "May I call you Katie?"

Except for her father, who had given her the nickname of *Mouse* because of her predilection for the Robert Burns poem, no one had ever called her anything but by her given name. And here was this man about whom she knew nothing, and yet with whom she had shared the most intimate act between two human beings, who had immediately thought of a more endearing name for her. For some unknown reason, Katherine was no longer ashamed of what had happened between them, although she was still a little bewildered by the situation when she nodded her assent.

"Unless I'm very much mistaken, we just lost a few barrels of rum," he said, and went on to explain, "We've been unloading the cargo all morning. I'm surprised you could sleep through all that racket."

A knock on the door prevented any further comment. Jonathan got up and went to answer. When he came back moments later with a tray, the sight and smell of food made her mouth water. It was only then that she realized how famished she was; she could hardly contain herself while Jonathan smoothed the covers before placing the tray on her lap.

So impatient was she, that in her greedy haste to satisfy her hunger she was mindless of the quilt. In consequence, the covers fell as she reached for the food, and she was exposed in her nakedness. Startled, she looked up at him as she quickly covered herself.

To put her at ease, hiding a wry smile Jonathan went to the dresser. After rummaging through one of the drawers he selected a silk shirt that he handed to her. "I'm afraid your dress was beyond repair, so this is the best we can do for now."

He discreetly turned away while she slipped into the shirt, but when he faced her again, he burst out laughing. The shirt was so large and hung so loosely on her, that it seemed almost like an oversized nightshirt.

Katherine was momentarily mystified by Jonathan's mirth, but when she realized what a comic picture she must present, she saw the humor. In a sudden lighthearted mood she waved her arms, which were totally lost in the long flapping sleeves.

"Here, let me help you," Jonathan chortled when she tried to push the sleeves out of the way. He rolled them up for her before he sat down again to watch her eat her meal with great gusto.

Swallowing a mouthful of the steamy fish stew, Katherine reached for the cup. A look of complete surprise followed her grimace the instant she tasted the scalding, bitter brew.

"I'm afraid I forgot to warn you about the coffee," said Jonathan with a wry chuckle.

"Coffee?" Katherine echoed. She had heard about it, but it was too expensive a commodity for her parsimonious aunt to allow the servants at her country inn. Now that she had finally had a chance to taste it, Katherine wondered if Aunt Harriet had not been right after all. "It's terribly bitter," she said.

A smile worked the corners of his eyes as he said, "Our cook makes it strong enough to stand a spoon in it. You must acquire a taste for it, but I'm afraid we have no tea on board. Here," he added some sugar to the cup. "Why don't you try it this way for now."

Katherine waited until he had finished stirring the coffee and then ventured a taste. The coffee was still not to her liking, but not wanting to offend him, she forced herself to drink some more of it while Jonathan watched her in mild amusement. Then she put the coffee aside and prepared to do justice to the meal.

Food had never tasted so good, she thought with a contented sigh after she had finished.

"For a little girl you certainly can put food away," Jonathan quipped as he retrieved the tray.

Katherine shrugged unhappily. "I—I was famished," she said in a small voice.

A muscle was twitching on his cheek as Jonathan put the tray on top of the desk and turned to her. The good humor had disappeared from his face. "Don't tell me Langford starved you, too."

Katherine's eyes filled with tears as she nodded dumbly.

At the sight of her tears, Jonathan went to her. Making an effort to check the anger he felt, he took her in his arms. "It's all right, love," he repeated over and over while rocking her gently back and forth. "You're safe now, Katie."

Katherine clung to him in a paroxysm of sobbing. "I thought I would never escape him!"

Jonathan held her close, and tenderly stroking her hair he let her cry all the anger and hurt out of her system. "It's over, love. You're safe now."

And as strange as it may seem, Katherine did feel safe in this big man's embrace, enveloped in his comforting warmth. He was so gentle, so tender! She, who had lacked love and gentleness for so long, clung to him desperately, wishing that she could stay in the safe haven of his arms forever.

Jonathan waited until her sobs had begun to subside to draw back a little. "Feeling better?"

Since Katherine had tenaciously clung to him again, her nod was felt rather than seen. Jonathan continued to hold her until the contact of her body served to remind him of how sweet was the taste of her silken flesh. Aware of a reawakening of desire, he reluctantly retreated to look at her.

Even with her face ravaged by tears and her hair all mussed and tangled, she was still quite lovely. Fastening his gaze on her moist parted lips, he yielded to the temptation of kissing her again.

The previous night, when Jonathan had made love to her, Katherine had not been in control of her faculties. She had merely responded instinctively to his kindness. Now that she was fully aware of what was happening, however, she was surprised by the surge of excitement she felt as his firm lips brushed hers lightly. The kiss deepened to make her drowsy and erase every thought from her mind but those of the feel and taste of this man. Before she knew it, her arms had coiled tightly around his neck and she was giving herself to the sensations awakened by Jonathan's exploring tongue as it possessed and savored the sweetness of her mouth.

"Mm," he reluctantly drew back at last, having to disengage himself from the arms that continued to imprison his neck. "I have to get back to work, love."

Amazed at her own boldness, Katherine dropped her arms abruptly. Seeing the flush suffusing her cheeks, Jonathan caught both her hands, and she was at a loss as to what to say or do when he pressed them to his lips and lovingly kissed each finger.

"I really do have to go." He said wistfully as he rose with reluctance. "I promise I'll be back as soon as I can, honey."

A mixture of regret and bewilderment was in the luminous green eyes that followed him until he was out the door. Then, with a sigh of resignation, Katherine lay back on the pillows and absently stared at the ceiling.

She didn't know how long she had resisted Langford, she reflected; but in the space of a few hours, this Jonathan Greenfield had made her feel . . . as she had never felt before. He was a complete stranger, yet he made her feel safe and warm and—loved? How could it be possible, she asked herself with not a little amount of astonishment. But it was true, she had to admit; Jonathan did make her feel loved.

Reveries of their lovemaking were enough to bring back that languid feeling she had experienced at his touch, only this time there was no shame in the memory as Katherine stretched luxuriously and continued to lie abed, thinking of the night spent in Jonathan's arms.

How long she had been lost in her reflections Katherine didn't know before she forced herself back to reality.

"I must be a sight!" she said out loud. With firm determination she pushed back the covers, swung her long legs over the side of the bunk bed and got up.

She filled the basin with water from the ewer, and after removing the shirt Jonathan had given her she washed as thoroughly as she could under the circumstances before donning the shirt again. There was a small mirror on the wall above the dresser, which she used while she tried without success to untangle her hair with her fingers.

Her hair was too long, however, and tiring of her futile efforts, Katherine looked around for a comb or a brush. Since at a glance she couldn't find any of these articles, after a small hesitation she finally dared to open the top drawer of the dresser. Peering inside, she found the brush she needed among items of a personal nature. Next to it was a miniature portrait in a golden frame. Feeling a little guilty about going through Jonathan's possessions without his permission, she tried to ignore the picture; even so, she couldn't help but notice that it was of a blonde young woman of frail, delicate beauty.

She was curious in spite of herself; she wanted to take a better look at it, but fearful of what Jonathan's reaction would be if he came back and found her going through his personal belongings, Katherine commanded her fingers to close around the handle of the brush instead and pushed the drawer shut.

Hoping she would be done with her makeshift toilette before Jonathan returned, she briskly brushed the tangles out of her long hair. She had almost finished when the door opened suddenly. Startled, Katherine swiftly whirled about to find Jonathan standing motionless at the door.

Clad only in his shirt, which came down to her thighs and left her long slender legs bare, Katherine had been caught in the act of brushing her hair. With her arms aloft, her nipples were clearly outlined through the thin silk fabric.

With a guilty shrug of her shoulders she gestured with the brush, "I — I hope you don't mind . . ."

Jonathan made a deprecating gesture. "Of course not, love. Help yourself to anything you need."

Shyly, she dropped her gaze as Jonathan continued to eye

her appreciatively. "You look very fetching in that shirt, Katie," he said at last.

Her blush deepened when she became aware of her near-nakedness.

Jonathan was instantly at her side. "Don't be ashamed of your body, love," he said, capturing her waist. "You're so very lovely, Katie." He drew her into his arms, and his lips descended on hers in a long, searing kiss that forced every thought out of her mind. "Oh, Katie, I want you so much!" he said in a hoarse whisper, hungrily seeking her lips again.

This time there was no gentleness in the kiss, only raw, naked desire. His teeth pulled at her lips as if to devour them before he sucked them into his mouth. Although slightly painful, the hungry caresses were highly arousing. Dizzy with desire, her breathing rapid and shallow, Katherine clung to him. His fingers sought the curve of her breast, and when they found a hardened nipple, her legs were so wobbly that they could barely support her. At the same time his tongue was invading every recess of her mouth and capturing her own. Urgent, consuming, his mouth demanded the responses that she willingly gave. As if to imprint every part of her pliant body into his, he closed his hands on her buttocks and squeezed them to hold her even closer. With a cry of pain Katherine jerked away.

Startled by her cry, Jonathan released her. He, too, was breathing heavily. "Did I hurt you?"

"No," Katherine shook her head. "Not you."

"What's the matter, Katie?"

Katherine looked at him helplessly. "Langford," she wept at last. "He—he," she broke off, covering her face with her hands.

Jonathan regarded her with a bemused expression for a second. Then, as a suspicion formed in his mind, he turned her around and lifted the shirt. Color drained from his face at the sight of the angry red welts marring the fairness of her buttocks and lower back.

"The swine!" he exploded in shocked anger. "I should have killed him!"

Katherine felt as if her bottom were on fire. Docilely she allowed him to take her to the bed and waited while he went in search of a salve to put on her bruises.

"This will help ease the pain, love," Jonathan told her when he came back.

Even the lightest touch of his fingers was so painful that she had to bite her lips not to cry out. When he finished applying the salve, Jonathan kissed the small of her back and tenderly stroked the back of her thighs and her legs.

The cabin was rapidly growing dark, and lulled by the rocking of the ship and the soothing warmth that began spreading through her buttocks and easing the pain, Katherine dozed off.

She didn't hear when Jonathan left the cabin.

It was dark when she opened her eyes again. Turning her head slightly, she discovered the source of the sounds that had awakened her. Standing naked in the circle of light cast by the lamp, Jonathan was washing himself.

How beautiful he is, she thought, admiring the broad shoulders that tapered to waist and hips that were lean and narrow. His buttocks were small but hard, his legs long, strong and well muscled. With every movement he made, sinewy muscles rippled beneath the deeply tanned skin of his back, where drops of water glistened like tiny diamonds as they reflected the dim light cast by the lamp.

The sight of this naked Jonathan brought memories of the interrupted passionate scene that had developed earlier. As she thought about it, the muscles of her stomach tightened, and she felt the warm rush of blood coursing her veins

44

as sensuality surged within her. Suddenly she was filled with the need to touch him and be touched by him. She longed to press her lips to his skin and savor the taste of him. Deep inside her, desire grew hotter still as she imagined the ripple of his muscles under her fingertips as she was being filled by him.

Noiselessly, Katherine rose from the bed and came to stand behind Jonathan, who gave a muted gasp of surprise when she put her arms around his waist and began tracing a pattern of kisses down his spine. He stood still while her hands caressed the broad chest and moved down to his flat hard stomach and her flickering tongue licked the droplets of water from his back, sending waves of intense pleasure through his body.

When her hands ventured further down, Katherine found that he was fully aroused. Wanting to touch her, he turned to face her. After slowly loosening the buttons, he drew the shirt from her shoulders and let it drop to the floor. For a moment they stood motionless, facing each other, and then she went to him.

She could hear the sounds of pleasure purring in his throat as she nibbled his flesh and stood on the tips of her toes to brush her body against his. Cupping his buttocks in her hands, her body tingled with a delicious sense of anticipation as she pressed herself to his pulsating maleness. His mouth seemed to absorb hers completely when they met, and without releasing her lips, Jonathan lifted her in his arms and carried her to the bed.

He lay her down and drew back to let his eyes wander over her with rich possessive pleasure. "You're so lovely," he murmured huskily, gingerly touching her throat and letting his hands glide slowly, sensuously over the soft curve of her shoulder. "Your skin feels like satin."

His hands, so large and powerful, were wonderfully, marvelously gentle on her body; and their texture, roughened by manual labor, exquisitely arousing against the smoothness of her skin as they stroked and kneaded her breasts. He teased her flesh until the engorged rosy crests begged to be consumed, and she sighed with relief and pleasure when his mouth went from nipple to pulsating nipple to suck and nibble, to devour first one and then the other, stoking the flames of desire that were spreading through her with the swiftness of wildfire.

On the brink of madness she cried out to be taken and still he demurred, "Not yet, my love, not yet."

Thrashing her head from one side to another, Katherine moaned as her need for fulfillment mounted with every touch, every caress. Each nerve in her body seemed to have surfaced to the outer layers of her skin to become susceptible to its own delight. Even when she believed she had reached the limits of her endurance, that she couldn't stand another second of such bittersweet torment, Jonathan brought her still to new peaks of pleasure as he found and fondled her most intimate, sensitive places.

Deep in her throat she moaned and clung to him when he plunged into her at last. He moved slowly at first, and as slowly and deliberately he increased the tempo of his thrusts, the tremors that shook her seemed to have no end. He plunged in deeper still, and as his body tensed with the violence of his own release, for a brief instant Katherine was invaded by the strange sensation that her flesh had melted into his flesh, that the beats of his heart had become her own. So moving was the experience that she found herself weeping as she clung to him, unable to hold back the flow of tears as she reached her final climax.

She was still glowing under the influence of the experience when Jonathan gazed into the emerald pools that reflected her languor, and thoughtfully fingered the tears still moistening her cheeks. "You're mine, Katie," he said in a voice that was hoarse and fierce. "You belong to me."

It was hours later when Katherine woke to find the cabin flooded with sunlight. Yawning, she stretched luxuriously and then lay back on the pillow listening to the sounds of the ship. Feeling content and at peace, she reminisced of the hours shared with Jonathan through the long night.

Absently watching a tiny speck of dust drifting in the beam of sunlight, she thought that after suffering Langford's brutality, she had been convinced she could never trust a man or bear his touch. But Jonathan had changed all the ugliness into beauty, the bitterness into such joy as she had never known could exist.

Approaching footsteps cut through her reveries, and when Jonathan came into the cabin she lifted her arms to him and encircled his neck when their lips met in a long, intimate kiss that filled her heart with boundless joy.

"Oh, Jonathan," she breathed when at last the kiss ended. Although he had not yet shaven, oblivious to the prickle of the stubble on his cheeks she pressed her face to his as she sighed, "I've never been so happy!"

Jonathan drew back to look at her and smiled. "Your breakfast should be here any minute. Hungry?"

"Mm, a little," she nodded, surprising herself by adding, "One more kiss?"

"Greedy wench," Jonathan chuckled, dipping his head to satisfy her request.

Eagerly parting her lips, she drank the taste she would never get enough of until a knock on the door put an end to the kisses.

"I'm afraid you can't live on love alone, young lady," he chided her, playfully tapping his index finger to the tip of her nose as he rose to answer. Smiling dreamily, she watched him walk away and then come back carrying a tray with her food. She found herself wanting to touch him again as he smoothed the covers and placed the tray on her lap.

"You need clothes, Katie," Jonathan said once she started

47

eating her meal. "I'll bring something back for you to wear when I go out, and tomorrow we'll go shopping for all the things you need." When Katherine abstained from comment, he continued, "And I guess you must be tired of being locked up in this cabin. There's an inn not too far from here where I'm sure you'll be more comfortable." He paused momentarily, and the corners of his mouth twitched in amusement when she sipped at her coffee without making a face. "I'll be gone for a few hours, so I asked the cabin boy not to wander too far away in case you need him. By the way, his name is Albert."

With that he got up and began discarding his working clothes.

Once Katherine had finished her breakfast, she put the tray aside and sat up on the bed, hugging her knees while she watched him wash, shave, and dress in elegant dove gray trousers, a snowy white shirt and cravat, a pearl grey satin vest, and matching coat. Whether in the rough clothes of a seaman or in this elegant attire, Jonathan Greenfield was the most beautiful man she had ever seen in her entire life, she thought, gazing at him in adoration.

"Is there anything special you'd like me to bring you?" he inquired, hat in hand, as he was ready to leave.

On impulse, Katherine opened her mouth, but quickly closed it again. Unaccustomed as she was to the kindness Jonathan had shown her thus far, she was fearful of what he would think of her if she asked for something as frivolous as a book.

At her hesitation, he gently prompted, "Tell me, love What is it you want?" Coiling a strand of her hair around his finger, he coaxed, "Some ribbons for your hair perhaps? Or maybe a bonnet? Come on, you can tell me."

Katherine swallowed, looking very guilty. "A book," she finally got out.

"A book?" Jonathan repeated, visibly startled.

Suffocating with embarrassment, Katherine curtained her eyes behind her lowered lashes. Had she displeased him? Had she gone too far?

Jonathan surprised her when rather than showing anger, he inquired, "And what kind of book would you like, love?"

Blinking in disbelief, Katherine dared to look at him at last. "You don't mind?"

"Mind!" Jonathan laughed. "Of course not, love. As the matter of fact, I'm delighted."

Katherine gave a sigh of immense relief.

"Now, what would you like to read?" Jonathan inquired.

"Poems, by Robert Burns, if possible," she ventured, still a little diffident. Then, fearful of losing her nerve, she added quickly. "Of course, I'll read anything you'll bring."

"Mm, perhaps I can accommodate you right now," said Jonathan thoughtfully. He went to the sea chest, opened it, and as he rummaged through it Katherine saw that it contained a good number of books. Finally, he found what he was looking for. He came back and handed a book to her with a flourish. "Here you are, my lady."

Katherine's hands were trembling a little as they reached out for the book. It was the same one she had hidden from her aunt years before, her old, faithful companion of so many lonely hours. Her eyes had misted when she held the book to her breast and stroked the well-worn cover.

"Katie?" Jonathan frowned in puzzlement. "What is it, love? What's the matter?"

Momentarily unable to speak, Katherine simply shook her head. "Oh, Jonathan!" she said at last. "This book has been my only friend during the last three years. I think it was the only thing that saved my sanity when I was locked up in that awful room and I thought I would go out of my mind. When I had almost lost all hope, these poems brought memories that helped me regain the courage to fight Langford."

Deeply moved, Jonathan drew the tips of his long fingers along her cheek as he said, "Then it's yours, love."

After Jonathan had gone, Katherine washed and dressed in the shirt again. She managed to contain her curiosity about the portrait, and after she finished brushing her hair set out to tidy the cabin, since her presence there prevented the cabin boy from performing his chores. Only after everything was to her satisfaction did she settle down to read.

This poetry — and her memories — were the only links she had left to her past and her parents; everything else had been stripped away. As her eyes followed the familiar lines, she was again the little girl sitting at Andrew's knee, reading and learning. She could almost hear his voice again, fondly calling her *Mouse*.

She was still immersed in her reading when Jonathan returned hours later.

"There you are, my lady," he said with a grin as he dropped an armful of parcels on the bed. "I hope these will fit you better than my shirt."

Taken a little aback by their number, Katherine put the book down and began to open the boxes. There were slippers and stockings and lovely underthings so delicate that they seemed to have been created by fairies. She had never dreamed Jonathan would buy anything so exquisite for her!

Jonathan frowned in puzzlement when she kept looking and looking at the dress of pale green silk trimmed with velvet, yet not daring to touch it. "What's the matter, Katie? Don't you like it?"

"Like it!" She looked up sharply in surprise. "I — I've never seen anything so beautiful in my life!"

His face relaxed in a good-humored smile. "Then I guess I'll leave you to dress," he said. "I'll be back in half an hour," he called from the door before going out.

Accustomed as she was to the coarse, homespun fabrics of Aunt Harriet's old dresses, Katherine thrilled to the cool caress of the silk against her skin. The dainty camisole and multiple petticoats she pulled on were trimmed with frothy lace; the stockings were so delicate and sheer that she was hesitant to touch them with hands roughened by the work she had performed at the inn.

Jonathan had remembered every detail a woman might want or need: from ribbons to hairpins, to tortoiseshell combs that she used to pin her hair at the crown of her head, letting a little of it fall in curls down her back.

She was buttoning up her dress when Jonathan returned and paused to study the change in her appearance. The dress was of simple, uncomplicated lines, yet elegant and highly flattering to her figure. The tight bodice stressed the fullness of her bosom while emphasizing the smallness of her waist, and the generous sleeves gathered at the wrists by means of narrow ribbons and bows. Peeking out from under the full skirt were the tips of dainty slippers. The ribbon in her hair matched the dress, and her emerald eyes scanned his, eager for approval.

"You look—stunning," he said at last.

The admiration she read in his eyes made her face light up with pleasure. "Everything is so beautiful, Jonathan," she said. "But how did you manage to find such a perfect fit?"

Jonathan's hands captured her tiny waist. "Mm, I'd say that by now I ought to have a good of idea of your measurements, love."

At that moment they were standing so close that she had to tilt her head back to look at his face. The mischievous twinkle she found in his blue eyes made her gurgle with laughter. Throwing her arms around his neck, she rose on the tips of her toes to kiss him. Very soon, what started as a playful kiss became a hungry one.

"Unless we leave right this minute, that dress is coming

51

off again," Jonathan murmured against her mouth.

Katherine wouldn't have minded having to dress all over again, but she sensed Jonathan's impatience when he asked, "Are you ready?"

"I only have to put the boxes away."

"Don't bother, Katie. Let Albert take care of it after we're gone."

He waited until she had put on her bonnet to wrap a velvet cape that matched the dress around her shoulders before they went out.

After so many days of seclusion Katherine was momentarily struck dumb by the sights, the sounds, and the pungency of the London docks. The thriving activity, the deafening noise, the strange smells of tar and other things assaulted her senses and frightened her. In bewilderment, she held fast to his arm, and Jonathan patted her hand, smiling at her reassuringly as he helped her down the gangplank. Once on the docks, they had to skirt the numerous obstacles presented by coiled ropes, barrels, and stacked crates and bales that were being unloaded from a ship. Accompanying the confusion of rattling wagon chains, snorting horses, and shouts, was a colorful parade: hordes of street urchins in filthy rags and dirty faces who roamed through the crowds on the lookout for a chance to separate an unwitty pedestrian from his purse; painted whores who strolled along, seeking to ply their trade among the seamen.

When he raised his hand to hail a hansom cab, Katherine asked, "Couldn't we walk, Jonathan? You said the inn wasn't very far, and it's such a lovely day."

The wistful note in her voice made Jonathan realize that this was the first time in a long while that she had been out in the cool spring air. "As you wish, love." He waved the cab away.

The play of the breeze in her hair and the touch of the sun on her cheeks made Katherine's face light up with pleasure as they strolled along the teeming, noisy streets. Some of the people she saw were elegantly dressed while others wore rags. Carts loaded with merchandise rattled their wheels on the cobblestones, and carriages of all types meandered through the traffic.

For Katherine, who had spent all of her life in the country, London was quite a new and exciting experience. Jonathan was mildly amused by her reactions and the way she looked at everything through wide, startled eyes. In wonder she gazed at the shop windows displaying such wide varieties of merchandise, ranging from bonnets and ribbons to cooking utensils.

Wide-eyed, Katherine paused in front of a bookstore. Jonathan couldn't miss her interest when she demurred, trying to read the titles on the covers, so he took her into the shop. The smell of dust, paper and ink permeated the stale air inside. A small, birdlike man who had a pair of metal-rimmed spectacles perched on his naked pate seemed to appear out of nowhere and amiably invited them to browse.

Katherine was like a child turned loose in a candy store, Jonathan thought, as she walked through the store marveling at the sight of so many books gathered in one place. With so much to choose from, she took her time before settling on an English translation of Victor Hugo's *Notre Dame de Paris*. Afterwards, they found themselves back on the street again.

Jonathan made her feel like a perfect lady when he pinned to her dress a bunch of violets he had bought from an old woman who stood on a corner holding a basket of flowers.

Dusk was darkening into night by the time they arrived at the inn, where they were received by a deferential innkeeper. They were famished and opted to have their supper before going to their rooms. A gray carpet with a pattern of faded yellow roses muffled their footsteps as they followed their host down a long corridor that went past a large room with long tables and benches, and into a smaller and more secluded dining room.

Katherine studied her surroundings with interest while Jonathan ordered their meal. This inn was larger and far more luxurious than the one owned by her aunt, but when a serving girl came with their wine and spilled a little of it on the table, she still had to repress her impulse to wipe it off, reminding herself that she was now a customer.

All the other customers in the dining room were male. Some of them eyed Katherine with undisguised lust, but Jonathan's glare promptly made them quickly turn their attention back to their food. There was nothing to fear as long as he was there to protect her.

They ate and drank and laughed and talked, and when supper was over Jonathan took her upstairs to the rooms he had rented earlier in the day. The furniture in the small sitting room consisted of a settee and two old-fashioned velvet chairs with a butler's table between them. Passing through a draped archway, they stepped into a bedchamber that despite its ample dimensions seemed to be dominated by an enormous four-poster bed covered with a blue satin counterpane. There were also a tall armoire, a highboy, a dressing table with a large beveled mirror, and a high-backed chair facing a hearth where a cheery fire crackled. One of the walls was covered almost entirely by a large tapestry depicting a hunting scene.

The total effect was one of coziness and warmth, and the sight of a large enameled bath which had been placed in front of the fire made Katherine hug herself with joy.

"It's wonderful!" she cried her delight.

"If you want a bath now, I'll send the maid for water on my way out," he said then.

Her eyes flicked warily toward him. Was he planning to leave her? No! her heart and her brain screamed in protest. She would rather stay in that cluttered little cabin on his ship if it meant she could be with him! Trying to keep her apprehension from showing in her voice, she asked, "Will you come back tonight?"

A slow, meaningful grin broke over Jonathan's face as he bent toward her and said, "Just try and keep me away!" accompanying his words with the action of slipping his arms around her waist and drawing her to him.

Heaving a deep sigh of relief, she clung to him and wistfully said, "I wish you didn't have to go."

Since they were standing next to the bed, all he had to do was push her down gently on it as he bent over her. His fingers deftly loosened the row of buttons that ran down the front of her dress, and she shivered with delight when his lips began to explore the softness of her throat, the incipient mounds of her breasts.

"Will you miss me, love?" he murmured huskily.

"Mm, yes!" came her answer, her flesh tingling under his caresses.

With supreme effort Jonathan pulled himself away. Gazing with longing at her parted lips and the dreamy look in her heavy-lidded eyes, he refrained from kissing her, knowing that if he did, he wouldn't be able to tear himself away. "Ah, Katie," he shook his head as if in so doing he could dispel her effect on him. "You make it so hard for a man to walk away from you!" Reluctantly, he rose to his feet. "I'll be back as soon as I can, love."

It was with a deep sense of regret that Katherine saw him go out the door.

Minutes after Jonathan's departure, the same maid who had served their dinner appeared with a boy carrying buckets of steaming water. The boy left as soon as the tub had been filled, but the buxom, rosy-cheeked girl remained behind to help Katherine with her bath. Her name was Rosie, she said, and continued her chatter while she washed

Katherine's hair with the lilac-scented soap Jonathan had bought her on their way to the inn.

Relishing this ultimate luxury, Katherine soaked in the hot water, making the most of it and deriving a pleasure almost sensual. There had been a bathtub very similar to this one at her aunt's inn, which she had learned only by chance that it had once belonged to her mother. But Aunt Harriet had never allowed her to use it. Because of their nearness to London, where the facilities were better, very few of the guests who stopped at their inn required baths, so the tub had mostly gathered dust in the attic while Katherine had been forced to wash in a tub of cold water even in winter, turning deaf ears to the warnings of an early death she received from the well-intentioned cook.

There had been so many times when at the end of a long, arduous summer day she had longed to immerse her weary, overheated body in a cooling bath, because regardless of the customs of the time, Katherine had discovered that there was more physical comfort in personal cleanliness than in the lack of it.

Now that she finally had the chance, she decided to take as much advantage of this luxury as she possibly could for as long as it was available to her; therefore, she luxuriated in her bath long after Rosie had rinsed her hair, until the water had begun to cool. When she finally stood up, she was immediately wrapped in a towel and dried and pampered by the maid, who afterward brought a gossamer gown and told her that Jonathan had brought some of her things earlier that day. Apparently, he had also bought the silver-backed brush Rosie used on Katherine's hair until it was dry.

Sitting in front of the fire, Katherine listened with half an ear to Rosie's prattle while she submitted to the maid's ministrations.

"You're so lucky to 'ave found such a generous gent, miss," Rosie said, as if reading Katherine's mind.

Yes, Jonathan is spoiling me so, Katherine reflected, absently looking at herself in the silver hand mirror that had also been a surprise from Jonathan. All this, the clothes, even the scented soap. He had seen to every detail that would add to her comfort, and this was a totally new experience for her.

"And 'im so 'andsome any gel'd be gladly bed 'im even wit'out being paid for the trouble," Rosie continued. "That's what I told the other gent."

Puzzled by the maid's observation, Katherine looked up sharply. "What other gent?" she asked.

"The one sitting by the window downstairs, miss," Rosie shrugged indifferently. "Couldn't take 'is eyes off you all through supper. Didn't you notice 'im? Gave me a shilling to bring you the message as soon as your gent 'ad gone, 'e did."

Anger and embarrassment surged inside Katherine and flushed her features. Did everyone at the inn take her for a whore? Had that unknown man believed she would sell her favors to him as soon as Jonathan's back was turned? She was about to protest when she realized that even though she felt justified in her indignation, other people could believe no different from her.

Pride again, Katherine chided herself. Perhaps it was foolish to feel as she did under the present circumstances, but she couldn't help it any more than she could stop breathing. In spite of his poverty, Andrew Cameron had been a man proud of his name and his blood, which was the same flowing through the veins of his daughter. "I won't accept any such messages from anyone," Katherine told Rosie evenly.

"Aye, miss."

Rosie was subdued after that, and before she left Katherine asked her to send more hot water for Jonathan's bath later on.

Her exchange with Rosie made Katherine give a great deal

of thought to her situation while she waited for Jonathan's return. Perhaps he would help her find some kind of employment in London, she reflected as she stood in front of the window looking out without really seeing anything of the view. Suddenly, when she became aware of how advanced was the hour, she was fearful Jonathan wouldn't come back to her that night. The anguish that invaded her at the thought of being deserted by him made her realize that she didn't want to be away from him ever again.

How could I feel so strongly about him when two days ago I didn't even know of his existence, she asked herself. Two days ago . . . She shuddered, not wanting to think of that time. How had Jonathan managed to get her away from Langford? Remembering Langford's threats, she wondered. Did she belong to him now because coin had exchanged hands. No, she couldn't believe that; not when she remembered the terror she had seen in the face of her tormentor at the sight of Jonathan before he had taken her away.

The sounds of a door opening and closing broke into her reflections. Her face lit up with pleasure when Jonathan stepped into the bedchamber and dropped the valise he carried to capture her when she flew into his arms.

"Mm, you smell good enough to eat," he murmured. He took the ribbon from her hair, and burying his fingers into the fragrant mass of glossy tresses pulled her head back to claim her mouth.

Katherine gave all of herself in that kiss. Yes, she did belong to Jonathan—both in body and soul—because she loved him. Somehow, she was not really startled by her discovery. Even though she had never put it into words in her own mind, in her heart she had known all along what her feelings for him were.

Without letting her go, Jonathan maneuvered them toward the bed. He had just lowered her on top of the satin counterpane when they were interrupted by a knock on the door.

"Now, what?" he muttered impatiently.

It was only then that Katherine remembered the hot water she had ordered earlier. "It must be the maid bringing the water," she said diffidently. "I thought — I thought you might want a bath when you came back."

"You did, did you?" Jonathan frowned. "So you must think I smell foul." As she opened her mouth to deny such a thing, he added, "Just for that I must think of a suitable punishment for you, wench."

Katherine found it difficult to breathe through the lump that had suddenly developed in her throat. "I-I'm sorry."

"Not as sorry as you'll be after I'm done with you," Jonathan told her before drawing back. He got up and went to answer the door.

While the boy came and went with buckets of water to fill the tub, Katherine dreaded the moment when she and Jonathan would be left alone again. She was frightened. Perhaps he would beat her just a little to teach her not to take such freedoms, but after all the tenderness he had shown her she couldn't believe he would physically hurt her. No, her fear wasn't so much of the punishment Jonathan had promised, but of having displeased him, perhaps to the point that he might want to send her away.

"Come here, wench," Jonathan ordered after the boy had gone.

Gathering her courage, Katherine rose from the bed and obediently came to stand before him. "I'm sorry," she whispered contritely.

It wasn't until she looked up at him that he saw that her eyes were glistening with tears. "Katie!" he exclaimed taking her in his arms. "Honey, don't cry. I'm the one who's sorry, love. I should have known better than to tease you like that."

Crushed in Jonathan's arms, Katherine went limp with relief. He drew back and crooked his finger under her chin to tilt up her face. "Forgive me?"

Deeply moved, Katherine gave him a tremulous smile.

She hoped for a kiss, but instead Jonathan asked, "And are you willing to accept the *punishment* I had planned for you?"

Katherine nodded, without fear now, although the smile she gave him was a little tremulous.

"Very well, wench." A mischievous twinkle sparkled in his eyes as he added, "Then you shall wash me."

"Some punishment!" Katherine burst out laughing. A lighthearted mood took possession of her as she began helping him out of his clothes.

Once he was undressed, he sank into the tub with a contented sigh. His legs were so long that they wouldn't fit into the bath, and he offered a rather amusing sight sitting there with his knees protruding from the water. "These damned things are always too small," he laughed sheepishly with her.

Katherine washed and rinsed his hair, and he submitted to her ministrations while she scrubbed his back with a sponge. When she moved to lather his chest, however, he took the sponge away. "Use your hands, Katie," he said.

It was then that Katherine understood what Jonathan had in mind. This was going to be much more that a simple bath, she realized, excited by the idea as she set the sponge aside.

On the golden fur covering his chest Katherine frothed up a lather that she tantalizingly teased over the flat light brown nipples that rose and peaked under her fingers very much as her own did when Jonathan caressed her. Filled with a heady sense of power at the discovery that she could give Jonathan the same kind of pleasure he had given her, Katherine continued her sensuous assault. He groaned as her hands moved slowly and sensuously over his torso, as they ventured further down to his belly, over thighs and the aroused center of his manhood.

60

She didn't mind a bit getting her hair wet when he reached out and put a hand to the back of her head to bring it down and meet his lips. He drank the sweetness of her mouth, curling his tongue around hers, absorbing her in a consuming kiss that left her breathless when he finally let her go. The gossamer gown was pushed aside to unveil her breasts, and taking one rosy nipple in his mouth he teased it to hardness with his tongue until her legs felt so weak that she had to hold on to the edge of the tub for support.

"Jonathan," she breathed.

He rose then, and before she could finish drying him with the towel she was swept up in his arms and carried to the bed, where the consuming fire of their passion flared hot and bright to fulfill all their longings.

Later, raising herself on an elbow, Katherine propped her head on her hand to dreamily regard the man lying beside her. How she loved to look at him like this, to take in every detail of his beloved face. In the golden glow cast by the fire, the hard-boned rugged looks were more tremendously appealing than ever. His eyes were deeply blue and expressive under brows darker than his light blond hair, which had a tendency to curl at the ends because it was a trifle too long. The sharp aquiline nose, the wide mouth of full and sensual lips, the firm, determined set of his jaw . . .

"You're so beautiful, Jonathan."

The wonder in her voice made his eyes twinkle with amusement. "But men aren't supposed to be beautiful, Katie," he chuckled softly.

"Oh, but you are," she sighed, letting the tip of her finger lovingly trace the contour of his mouth when he smiled.

He took her hand and kissed the open palm, and with another sigh of contentment Katherine lay down again and adapted her body to the length of his.

In minutes, they were both asleep.

Three

Katherine was awakened with a kiss and a hand that moved caressingly over the curve of her hip. Stretching much as a cat would, she yawned and continued to lie abed with a contented smile on her face but without opening her eyes.

"Good morning, Katie," Jonathan's voice said in her ear.

She opened her eyes at last, and sat up abruptly when she saw that he was already dressed and ready to go out.

"Come on, you lazy wench!" he said, grinning. "Get up before I'm tempted to join you back in bed."

Tossing back her long red hair, Katherine laughed as she extended her arms to him.

"Oh, no, wench!" Jonathan resisted, an expression of mock horror on his face. "You're not going to lure me back!"

"But, sire," she argued, pursing her lips in a provocative little pout, "surely a small kiss to start the day can do no harm."

"It's not the kiss, wench, but what follows it," he replied with a comically exaggerated leer.

Katherine pushed the covers aside and swung her legs off the bed in a lithe movement. She made no effort to cover her nakedness as she went to him, and coiling her arms around his neck brought his head down to kiss him fully on the lips.

"Good morning to you, sire!" she said with a smug little grin, openly teasing him with her eyes.

Raising his hand to playfully slap her rump, Jonathan stopped himself in time when he remembered the condition of her bottom. "Ah, Katie," he murmured huskily, drawing her in his embrace to kiss her again—not so playfully this time. Then, releasing her, he gave a wistful sigh. "I think you'd better dress," he said. "We have a busy day ahead."

"Today, sire?" she asked in a teasing tone.

"We're to go shopping, remember?"

"Ah, yes," she nodded, looking at him with a sparkle of pleasure in her eyes.

She turned and, as she walked away, Jonathan noticed that the marks on her buttocks had faded a little. The sight of her parading naked around the room, however, proved a bit too distracting for him. "I'll wait for you downstairs," he tossed over his shoulder as he headed for the door.

Their first stop that morning was at a couturier's establishment where Jonathan was immediately recognized by the proprietress. Her initial curiosity on this point was satisfied when in the course of making her selections Katherine learned that the green dress she had been wearing had come from Madame Solange's shop. He kept finding new things for her, so many, in fact, that by the time they left Jonathan had ordered a complete new wardrobe. Prompted by the generous bonus he offered, the dressmaker agreed to finish four of the gowns as early as the end of that same week, with a fitting session set three days hence. A yellow muslin dress—which had been made for another client and never collected—fitted Katherine perfectly; this, as well as some undergarments, were to be delivered to her that afternoon.

"But Jonathan," she protested as soon as they stepped out

of the shop, "I don't need so many gowns!"

"Nonsense, Katie!" he said in a lighthearted mood. "Of course you do! I plan to take you out on the town, and you shall need gowns befitting of your beauty."

"And a riding habit!" she added with dismay. "Jonathan, I've never been on a horse in my life!"

"Then I shall teach you to ride," he replied cheerfully. "It's very simple, really. As soon as your habit is ready, I'll take you riding in the mornings. You'll love it, I know you will."

He was so full of enthusiasm, that not wishing to dampen his spirits Katherine accepted his generosity without further demur.

They spent the rest of the day visiting shops where he ordered boots, shoes and slippers; hats, bonnets and ribbons; the finest in gloves, stockings and purses; perfumes; a cloak lined in silk; and to store it all, a large leather trunk with brass-bound corners. Although most of their acquisitions were to be sent to the inn, they were laden with last-minute purchases when they returned to their quarters to discover that the packages from Madame Solange's had already arrived.

Since Katherine was weary after such a strenuous and exciting day, Jonathan left her to bathe and rest before dinner claiming that he had to go to his ship for a while. She relished the feel and smell of the new things as she put them away, and although she took a long time about it, she had almost finished when her bath was ready.

After politely declining Rosie's assistance she soaked in the tub, deriving intense pleasure from the lilac-scented foam that she sensuously lathered on her skin. The hot water served to ease a little the cramps she had begun experiencing in her lower back during the afternoon. By the time Jonathan returned, however, she was waiting for him already dressed in her new yellow muslin dress. It was a rather simple dress but very pretty — with very full sleeves and lacy ruffles at the neck—that closed in front down to her tiny waist with a row of tiny pearl buttons.

Still in a cheerful mood, Jonathan ogled her playfully before presenting her with a long strand of pearls that left her speechless. Pushing aside the cascade of curls that she had left trailing to plant a kiss at the back of her neck, he fastened the rope of pearls for her.

During dinner, he told her of his plans to take advantage of his visit to England to look into the progress being made in the building of steamships. When a little bashfully Katherine confessed that she didn't know the first thing about ships—steam or otherwise—Jonathan embarked on a long explanation on the subject. He went on to tell her how the importance of speed in commerce, especially in the China trade, had prompted shipbuilders everywhere to improve the design of their vessels. He spoke of the innovations made on the *Mary Beth,* where in addition to a third mast to provide greater area of sail, the hull had been modified to offer the least resistance to the water—sharp at the bow and widening toward midships to give a concave shape to the waterlines. The result was a ship that in spite of her minimum weight, afforded maximum strength and speed.

At the end of his dissertation, he spoke of the *Savannah,* the first steamship to cross the Atlantic years before on a voyage to Russia that had taken only fourteen days.

"One day the steamships will replace the clippers, and I for one will hate to see those beautiful ships disappear," he reflected rather ruefully. Then, with a small wry chuckle, he added, "But that's a long time away. Ah, Katie, there's nothing like a clipper in full sail! It's poetry in motion, the most beautiful sight in the world!"

Katherine, who listened with interest, became a little subdued as the evening progressed. The cramps she had felt earlier had grown steadily worse, and regretting having to leave

Jonathan to finish his brandy alone, she made her excuses and went upstairs early.

Much later, expecting to find her already asleep, Jonathan entered the room quietly. He was surprised to see her in her white nightgown, curled up in a chair and moodily staring at the fire while an open book lay forgotten on her lap. Sensing a presence, she came out of her trance with a little gasp of alarm and was startled to find him standing at the draped archway. Her eyes were wide and frightened.

"I didn't mean to startle you," he said with an apologetic little smile as he stepped into the room. He came toward the chair she occupied and sat down on his heels beside it. "I thought you'd be asleep by now."

Starting to reach for the hand she had pressed to her breast as though to still the wild beating of her heart he made to kiss her, but she shrank back, crying, "Don't touch me, please!"

A look of complete astonishment froze his features for a few seconds before he recovered from such unexpected rejection. Rising slowly to his feet, he went to stand thoughtfully before the fire, keeping his back to her. When at last he turned to face her again, he saw that although she kept her eyes lowered, her cheeks were still suffused with color. She looked very distressed.

"Katie, I won't keep you with me against your will," he began soberly. "If —"

Before he could continue, however, looking up at him with obvious alarm she uttered a small cry. "No, Jonathan, please! Don't send me away!"

Regarding her quizzically, he saw her pleading eyes swimming with tears. There was an undertone of bewilderment in his voice when he asked, "Then what's wrong Katie? Why won't you let me touch you?"

Her mouth tried to form a reply, but no sound came out. While he waited for her answer, Katherine thought she would die of embarrassment. Swallowing to clear the lump in her throat, she managed to say at last, "It's just that I — I — I'm unclean."

"Unclean?" he echoed in a puzzled voice while she hung her head in shame. Then a suspicion came to mind, and he went back to her side. Crooking a finger under her chin to lift her face, he made her look at him. Although Katherine didn't resist, she kept her eyes lowered. "Katie, are you having your — er — flow?" he asked gently.

Even though it had seemed almost impossible, the flush on her cheeks deepened even more. Then, reluctantly, she bobbed her head at last.

With a small, wry chuckle he leaned over and lifted her from the chair. Her body was stiff with tension as he sat down and cradled her in his arms. "You little fool," he said, warmly touching his lips to her brow. A glint of mild amusement sparkled in the depths of his blue eyes as he regarded her and said, "You should be glad."

"Glad!" she echoed, perplexed. "Why?"

With the tips of his fingers he gently traced her cheek. "Because that means you're not with child, love. Didn't anyone ever tell you?"

Shaking her head, she regarded him in bewilderment.

He smiled and proceeded to explain. Little by little, her body began to relax in his arms. "So you see, love," he said at the end of his explanation, "that's why you ought to be glad. You have nothing to worry about. Let's forget all that uncleanliness nonsense and go to bed, shall we?"

With a slight smile she nodded. Rising from the chair he carried her to the bed, where after depositing her gently on it, he drew the covers over her. Then he undressed, and before joining her in bed, added another log to the fire. In the shelter of his arms, Katherine fell asleep almost instantly.

An hour later, however, Jonathan was still awake as he held the sleeping Katherine. His affairs had always involved women of experience; but the earlier episode had made him realize the extent of her innocence. What will she do when I return to Baltimore, he asked himself thoughtfully. He could not send her back to her aunt, and she had told him she had no other relatives.

At that moment Katherine sighed and snuggled more cozily against him. Remembering her alarm when she had pleaded not to be sent away, he wondered if she was still afraid of Langford. Looking down at her face, so young and lovely, he reminisced of those moments of passion that they had shared in the last days. The bruises he had seen on her body were an indication that she had resisted Langford with all her might; yet, with him, more than compliant she had been willing and eager to please.

Could it be that she really cared for him, he wondered, or was she simply grateful because he had saved her from Langford's cruelty? Suddenly, examining his own feelings toward her, Jonathan recognized that she certainly had touched him more deeply than any other woman he had ever made love to.

"Watch it, Jonathan," he warned himself with a small wry chuckle. The fact that she was beautiful and vulnerable had, perhaps, awakened in him the knight in shining armor who rushes to the rescue of pretty damsels in distress.

Ah, yes, beautiful she is, he reflected; and passionate. And I want her, so I will keep her until the time comes when I must go back home. After I'm gone, I shall see that she's protected, he determined.

In the days that followed, Katherine was content to remain in their room at the inn reading the books Jonathan had given her while he went about his business. Evenings were spent quietly after taking their meals downstairs in the dining room, where they made the acquaintance of a retired professor from the Midlands who was also staying at the inn while awaiting the return from India of his recently widowed daughter.

Appearing always in a rumpled brown coat which had a few careless stains upon it, Professor Stuyvesant was a shaggy old man whose mop of unruly hair was as gray as his bushy mustache. His sparkling blue eyes, which were always genial with friendship, seemed very young in his old wrinkled face. Charming and witty was he, and an entertaining companion who delighted in challenging Jonathan to an occasional game of chess and always managed to include Katherine in their conversations. One evening, when she mentioned that she did not play, he immediately volunteered to teach her the game, an offer she was glad to accept.

When the first gowns arrived, she discovered that the riding habit was among them; true to his promise, Jonathan immediately took her for morning rides in Hyde Park. He was pleased with the progress she made after the first few days. Once she was able to conquer her initial apprehension, Katherine learned quickly and thoroughly enjoyed the sport.

Since it was her first visit to London and Jonathan was well acquainted with it, he delighted in showing her the city. One day, he even engaged a small sailboat in which they tacked back and forth on the Thames, visiting the points of interest strung along the river. Familiar buildings had quite a different perspective when seen from the water, Katherine discovered.

A huge, eerie gate set at the waterline led into the Tower of London, where for centuries the enemies of the Crown had awaited their deaths. After the imprisonment she had suffered while in the hands of Langford, Katherine shuddered at the thought of the poor wretches who had spent their last days in that gloomy tower. A much more pleasant view were the private gardens which, invisible from land, rioted with color as they tumbled down to the water's edge.

At midday, they tied their little sailboat to the flight of stone stairs of an embankment, where they ate lunch from the picnic basket they had brought from the inn. Her laughter while Jonathan played his guitar and sang a medley of seamen's songs, was infectious and carefree.

Later, a full stomach and the langour of the warm spring day lulled her into a quiet doze as they lay on the grass watching the woolly clouds scud across the heavens.

In the afternoon, as they approached the wharves, she was fascinated by the ongoing activity. The men working in unison made her think of a line of ants as they unloaded cargo from the newly arrived ships and carried the bales, barrels and crates into the huge warehouses and waiting wagon vans.

Night had fallen when at last they decided to return to the inn. Visibility in the streets was made poor by the fog rolling in from the river and, because of this, they didn't see the three sinister figures who emerged from the shadows of an alley until it was too late.

"Run, Katie, run!" Jonathan said urgently, pushing her aside when he caught the glint of naked steel.

"Grab the wench!" someone shouted.

Even if Katherine had not been paralyzed by fear at the sight of Jonathan being surrounded by assailants, the fourth man who took firm hold of her would have prevented her flight. Shaking herself into action she desperately tried to twist away from his grasp, but her captor wouldn't let go of her. The hand he put over her mouth muffled her cries for help. Too frightened to notice the smell of the man's unwashed body or the rum in his breath, she watched with dread as an unarmed Jonathan faced the three men bearing long knives.

He had removed his coat and quickly wrapped it around his left arm. With body tense and knees flexed as though ready to spring, he faced his assailants, who continued to close in on him as they threatened with their weapons. In the stillness of the night, the four figures appeared involved in an eerie dance of death.

Blades glistened as the men made short thrusts with their knives that Jonathan parried with his precariously protected left arm; and then, growing impatient, the attackers rushed him boldly.

As the fog continued to grow thicker still, the scene before her eyes became more blurry. Only the sounds were remarkably clear: thumps, gasps, and oaths; and then Katherine saw three forms move away from the tallest one. A flood of relief went through her as she saw that Jonathan was still on his feet after the onslaught; what she couldn't see was that one of the knives had found its mark.

Emboldened by the blood they had drawn, the men rushed him again.

There was the cracking sound bones make when they splinter and shatter, followed by an agonized cry. Suddenly, with a strength born of desperation, Katherine kicked, twisted and tried to pull away from her captor. Hard put to contain her, the man slid an arm around her neck and began to squeeze. Frantically, she clawed at the arm that was choking the life out of her, but the images around her became dimmer still; and through the darkness into which she was falling, she saw one of the figures slump lifeless to the ground.

In a matter of minutes she was dragged away from the scene and pushed onto a darkened carriage, where she was quickly and securely bound, gagged and buried under a blanket.

The clop clop the horse's hooves made on the cobblestones brought her back to her senses. Grief stricken and numb, she continued to lie on the floor of the carriage, not even aware of the tears that were flowing from her eyes. All the fight had gone out of her at the thought that the body she had seen falling before losing consciousness had been Jonathan's.

At last the carriage stopped. She was roughly pulled up and, still wrapped in the blanket, slung over someone's shoulder. Although she could not see where she was being taken, the sound of boards creaking underfoot told her that whoever was carrying her was climbing a flight of wooden stairs.

Unknown to her, a figure stealthily detached itself from the rear of the carriage and found shelter in the gloom of a doorway.

The man stopped. There was a knock on a door, which after a pause opened with a creak of hinges.

"Quickly," a woman's voice said urgently. Once the man had gone inside, the woman closed the door. "You know the way," she said in a flat, nasal tone.

"Aye," a male voice replied.

"Is she conscious?" the woman inquired.

"Dunno. She's quiet now, but she's a devil, this one is. You'll 'ave to tame her first for your gent to 'ave 'is sport with 'er."

"That will be taken care of," the woman laughed in derision. "She's not the first to be displeased with our arrangements, and certainly not the last. In the end, they all learn. Even the most finicky ones."

Katherine was dropped on what she recognized as a bed even though she couldn't see it, and the blanket was pulled away. Lifting her chin she stared at her captors. The man was big and strong. There was a long vivid scar on his left cheek that made his swarthy face even more sinister. The woman had curly bright yellow hair and coarse features. The pallor of her sagging skin was accentuated by two splotches of rouge on her plump cheeks. Both of them were totally unimpressed by the defiance she tried to show them.

"She's pretty," the woman said, examining her with a critical eye. Turning to the man, she added, "Wait. Don't go yet."

Crossing his arms over his chest, the man leered at Katherine while the woman went to a nearby table, where she measured an amount of a whitish liquid from a dark bottle into a glass. As she approached the bed, she told her accomplice, "Remove the gag, will you. And hold her down until she drinks all of this. It ought to keep her quiet until our gentleman gets here."

The liquid the woman forced down her throat while the man contained her struggles was bitter tasting and quickly began to take effect. By the time her captors left her a few minutes later, Katherine was drifting into a drugged sleep.

Shouts and voices raised in anger penetrated into her consciousness. Then she became aware of heavy footsteps. Katherine's mind was spinning as she made an effort to open her eyes, but her lids were so heavy that they refused to obey her weak commands.

"Katie," a beloved voice said near as gentle hands touched her face. "Honey, wake up."

Was it a dream? Was Jonathan really alive? Katherine tried to speak, but her lips would not move.

"Is she all right?" another voice said. She knew she had heard it before, only she couldn't remember where or to whom it belonged.

"She's been drugged," Jonathan muttered savagely. "I'm going to put a torch to this accursed place!"

"Don't do it, my boy," Professor Stuyvesant told him soberly. "These people act as they do because they have connections in high places. If you burn this place down, you and your crew wouldn't stand a chance against them. It ap-

73

pears we were in time, so why don't we just take her out of here and go quickly."

Knowing that the advice was sound, Jonathan lifted the sleeping Katherine in his arms and followed the professor out of the room. At the bottom of the stairs, the occupants of the house—the man, the woman, and three young girls scantily dressed—were being kept in line by five crewmen from the *Mary Beth*.

A faint, pearly light was beginning to brighten the room when Katherine opened her eyes at last. Recognizing the room at the inn, she abruptly turned her head and saw Jonathan asleep next to her. A surge of incredible joy rose within her. It had not been a dream! He was alive!

"Jonathan!" she cried, throwing her arms around him and awakening him in the process. "You're alive!" The tears that came to her eyes then were of sheer relief and pure joy.

With a sleepy little smile, Jonathan put his right arm around her and drew her to him. "Of course I'm alive, honey."

Katherine drew back to gaze at him with eyes that were bright with emotion. "When I thought I had seen you killed, I—" She shook her head, unable to go on.

"Hey," he chortled, giving her a little squeeze, "Didn't you know that I'm a tough nut to crack?"

To her dismay, she noticed that his left arm was bandaged. "But, darling, you're hurt!" she cried, her expression becoming one of deep concern. "How bad is it?"

He gave a deprecating shrug. "It's nothing. The ship's doctor put in a few stitches and said I'll be as good as new in a few days." Suddenly he became serious. "But what about you, Katherine? Did anyone—"

Applying the tip of her finger to his lips, she silenced him.

"No, Jonathan," she said quietly, wishing she could be more sure of what had happened.

His eyes searched hers for the truth as he asked, "Are you sure?"

Although unable to perform the smallest action, she had been able to hear Jonathan and suspected no harm had come to her during that strange sleep. "They made me swallow something, and I fell asleep," she replied, evading a direct answer. "Next thing I knew, you were there with me. I tried to tell you I all right, but somehow I couldn't."

"You were drugged," he told her, apparently accepting her reassurances.

She gave him a curious, inquisitive glance. "How were you able to find me so quickly?"

"We were lucky," he replied. "It seems that Professor Stuyvesant just happened to go by while we were being ambushed. When he saw you being shoved onto a carriage, he managed to climb in the back."

"The Professor!" she exclaimed with surprise.

"Quite an astonishing man, isn't he? Who would have thought, a man his age—" He shook his head with a wry smile. "Anyhow, once he knew where you had been taken, he came back for me. On the way over, we stopped by the *Mary Beth* for reinforcements. I suppose you know the rest."

Katherine lay back on the pillow and snuggled closer to Jonathan. There was a pensive silence. "Who were they, Jonathan? I heard them say something about a gentleman they were expecting. Do you think it might have been Langford?"

"It's possible," he admitted, his expression becoming thoughtful. "However, in a place like this, there are plenty of others who wouldn't hesitate to pay a handsome price for someone as beautiful as you, love."

Katherine was horrified. "And you could have been killed!" she trembled.

Propping himself up on an elbow, he looked at her warmly. "Hush, love. It's over now, and thank God we're both all right." A little wryly, he added. "I was a fool to let them take me by surprise, but I promise it won't happen again." Then his expression became intense, his voice lowering to a husky whisper when he said, "You're mine, Katie, and I'm not going to let anyone take you away from me."

He gazed intensely into her eyes. His pupils were wide and dark, and when his glance touched her mouth, with a small sigh her lips parted invitingly. His strong hand was gentle as it brushed a strand of hair away and smoothed her brow. The growing lassitude of her own longings pervaded every pore of her being as he touched her and caressed her. She closed her eyes as his head came down and felt the warmth of his breath on her cheek. He pressed soft, tender kisses on her lids, and her heartbeat quickened as his lips moved to her cheek and then traced the outline of her own, seductively lingering at the corners of her mouth. Caressingly, the tips of his fingers moved lightly down her throat and slipped beneath her gown to seek the warmth of her breast as his tongue penetrated her willing mouth to savor eagerly given responses.

"Be careful, darling," she murmured. "Your arm."

He lifted his head to look at her. "I've been wounded worse than this before and lived," he said, in his voice a tone of mild amusement. "Right now, not even the lack of an arm would stop me from making love to you, my gorgeous, beautiful wench."

Katherine smiled up at him. She wanted him as much as he professed to want her. Reaching up she stroked his hair, and her fingers entwined in the silver tresses as his mouth covered hers again in a kiss that made her bones melt. She sighed with pleasure as his mouth followed the path his

76

hand had taken. The gown interfered, however; he tugged at it, impatient with the gossamer barrier that kept him from savoring her naked flesh.

"Let me," she said, splaying her hands on his chest. He leaned back a little to give her room, and she sat up to pull the gown over her head. Once she had removed the obstacle between them, she softly pushed him back on the pillow and lovingly bent over him. As she kissed him, she was tightly imprisoned in his arms.

"Make love to me, Katie," he whispered, his voice husky. A little bewildered, she looked into his eyes. His pupils were wide and dark as he sustained her gaze. Not knowing exactly what to do she hesitated briefly. Although she had always responded eagerly to his lovemaking, until this moment Jonathan had always been the aggressor. Except—

A provocative smile played on her lips as Katherine's head came down. Her hands began stroking his throat, his chest, and lingered on the peaked nipples as her tongue sought and caressed his. Her lips traced his face—as he had done to hers before—and continued down to explore his body. She let her hair trail over him, brushing him with light feathery caresses while her flickering tongue sent thrills to his senses as it touched his heated flesh.

She took her time, prolonging his pleasure before she raised herself on her knees above him. Holding her breasts in her hands, she offered them to his lips; first one, and then the other in sensuous abandon. Then, lowering herself on his erect manhood, astride she rode him on the road to passion. Wild, intoxicating rapture pervaded them as their bodies moved in the ancient rhythm and his hands moved sensuously along her spine. She sought his mouth, greedily sucking his tongue as she accelerated her thrusts until they reached the peak of passion and she collapsed on top of him, shaken by the tremors of her climax. Holding her tightly, Jonathan achieved his own.

Lapped by a pleasant languor she dozed off, only to wake a little later to lovingly regard his sleeping face. Trying not to wake him, she kissed him softly on the lips. "Jonathan," she whispered quietly, "I do love you so!"

He had risked his life for her, and again saved her from who knows what horrible fate. I love him, she admitted inwardly. With him I feel safe; he makes me laugh and sets my blood on fire with his touch. He's my friend, my lover, my whole life!

She knew that he desired her, but did he love her? He had yet to say *I love you*; but how could a man make love to a woman the way he did without loving her? Katherine tried to take comfort in the thought that even though he had never spoken the words, his body said them each time he held her.

"I love you, Jonathan," she told him softly, wishing with all her heart that he could hear.

Still suffering a little from the after-effects of the drug she had ingested, Katherine slept so late the next morning that Jonathan had to wake her before going out.

"Bolt the door behind me," he cautioned her seriously. "I'll be back in a little while with someone from my crew." At her inquiring glance, he explained, "From now on, there'll always be someone here to watch over you while I'm away. I want you to keep that door bolted, and don't open it for anyone, is that clear?"

Obediently, she nodded.

"Good. I don't want any more surprises." He kissed her quickly.

Katherine got up and followed him to the door, which she bolted after him as she had promised she would.

Staring at the door after he had disappeared through it, she prayed fervently, "Take care, my love. Please take care."

She washed and dressed, and made herself busy until, true to his word, Jonathan came back with a man from the *Mary Beth* whom he introduced as Joe Flint. In due time Joe would be relieved by someone else, he told her, for she was to be guarded around the clock.

Later in the day, when he took her out, Katherine found herself searching the crowds for the sinister face of her abductor. Although she tried to hide her apprehension, Jonathan became aware of it. He stopped walking, and with his hands on her shoulders made her look at him.

"Stop worrying Katie."

Chewing her lower lip, she looked at him worriedly. "But—"

"Listen," he cut her protest short. "I've already told you, you are safe. I'm armed now, and Joe is only a few paces behind us for good measure."

Katherine thought of the knife she had seen him slip inside his boot and prayed that he would never have occasion to use it. Still she tried to argue, "But—"

"Look, if you're going to wear such a long face, I might as well take you back to the inn. Is that what you want?"

A little shamefaced for being such a coward, Katherine shook her head.

"Then, how about a smile?"

Gradually, her brow cleared. Telling herself that Jonathan was right, Katherine forced herself to comply.

"Now, that's my Katie!" Jonathan grinned, sweeping her up in an exuberant embrace until her feet left the ground. Passers-by glanced at them with amusement.

"Jonathan!" she cried, turning crimson with embarrassment. "Will you put me down!"

Laughing still, he set her down. "As you wish, my lady." A mischievous glint was dancing in the depths of his blue eyes as she accepted the arm he offered. They continued their outing, her apprehension gone.

They returned to the inn after supper, which they had taken at an elegant hotel where she had been very impressed not only by the food that was served, but also by the magnificence of a dining room, the likes of which Katherine had never seen before. While Jonathan remained downstairs to play chess with the professor, she went to their room to read the book she had purchased that day. When he came in, she put the book down and started to get up.

"Don't you want me to change your bandage?" she offered with loving solicitude.

"The doctor changed it this morning," he declined, taking her in his arms. "Right now, there are other things on my mind."

As she was being pulled toward the bed—gently but firmly—Katherine's laughter came forth, free and spontaneous for the first time that day.

A few days later, Jonathan presented her with a delightful surprise: two tickets to a new play—opening the following week—which filled Katherine with eager anticipation for her first theater performance. When at last the evening came, many heads turned at the arrival of the very tall and ruggedly handsome man escorting a strikingly beautiful young woman whose shimmering rust taffeta gown almost matched the color of her hair. Katherine was filled with such excitement that evening, that the sparkle in her green eyes rivaled that of the diamonds at her pure, slender throat. For this occasion Rosie had done her hair, which was parted in the middle and expertly coiffed in the latest fashion.

The orchestra was tuning up as they took their seats. Leaning a little toward her, Jonathan whispered in her ear, "You're the most beautiful woman here tonight." A warm color rose to her cheeks at his comment, which was rewarded with an enchanting smile with a touch of shyness that he found most delightful.

The lights went down, and her hand closed excitedly on his arm as she gave him an ardent glance of expectation. At the end of a short overture, the curtain rose.

During the first part of the performance, Jonathan spent more time watching the purity of her profile than the action on the stage. As she listened attentively — as though afraid to miss any of the lines delivered by the actors — her sensitive features reflected the emotions awakened in her breast by the play.

Her applause at the end of the act was so ebullient, that Jonathan secretly congratulated himself for having thought of something that could bring her such pleasure. It was this one quality of Katherine's — the ability to look at everything with such fresh wonder — that made him unconsciously look for ways to bring it about whether with a silly little gift, and unexpected outing, or a jewel.

During intermission they joined the elegant crowd that had assembled in the lobby to partake of the refreshments. Katherine was experiencing her first taste of champagne when a voice called his name. They turned in unison in time to see a young dandy advancing toward them. A fleeting expression of annoyance crossed Jonathan's face.

"Captain Greenfield," the man said with an effusiveness that Jonathan found a trifle overdone for someone he had met only briefly. At this very moment, he couldn't even remember his name. With a restraining gleam of caution, he shook the hand the other man offered.

"You don't remember me," the young dandy said with a pleasant smile. "Darby, Julian Darby. We met at — "

"Yes, I remember," Jonathan interrupted. With a definite lack of warmth, he added, "Hello, Darby."

Julian Darby nodded in Katherine's direction, and since she had failed to recognize him, his next words caught her totally unprepared. "I see you still have Langford's wench with you," Darby commented. "I say, old chap, her looks have improved tremendously. You must be treating her well."

Releasing a muted gasp, Katherine gave him a startled look for a second. Her shock was so intense that she turned pale.

"She's not Langford's wench," Jonathan replied tersely.

"Of course, old chap, of course," Darby chortled. "No one is disputing that you won her fairly. But let me tell you that Charles is most anxious to get her back."

"I imagine so," Jonathan drawled. "Just let him try and take her."

"Ah!" Darby shook his head and grinned. "He's smarter than that. He knows you'll soon be going back to America, and he's biding his time. But he's not the only one who has an interest in her," he added. "I say, old chap, I do hope you give me the chance to put in my bid before you sail away."

"She's not for sale," Jonathan snapped. His patience having reached its limit, he began to turn away.

Darby, however, was not easily put off. Letting his eyes travel impudently over the generous expanse of bosom that Katherine's gown left uncovered, he licked his lips as he said, "By George, but she's a beautiful wench!"

Jonathan turned abruptly toward him. "Darby—" The angry undertone in his voice as he took one menacing step toward the other man, suddenly hushed the conversation around them.

Darby took one step back, putting a prudent distance between them. Before turning away, however, he called, "Remember, old chap. When the time comes, I'll be delighted to take her off your hands."

Katherine thought she would surely die of shame. Self-consciously, she was aware that they had become the center of attention and that onlookers were whispering among themselves with gleeful malice. Seething with impotent rage, Jonathan clenched his hands into fists as if to keep from wiping the smirks and sneers from their faces. When he looked at Katherine, however, he saw that she was trembling. Conscious of her distress, he took her by the arm and broke through the crowd that had gathered around them.

As he went to collect their belongings, Katherine glanced warily toward Darby's group of friends. They were gesturing toward her, and it was at that moment when the words *"Langford's whore"* drifted to her with their laughter.

So hard was she striving to check her tears of humiliation, that she was almost choking in them by the time Jonathan came back and wrapped her new pelisse around her shoulders.

As they were leaving the theater the bell rang, calling the audience back to their seats.

The return journey to the inn was tense and silent. Once they arrived, neither of them had the heart to acknowledge Professor's Stuyvesant's effusive greeting when they passed him by, on the way to their room.

The words she had overheard, *Langford's whore*, kept tenaciously coming back to haunt her as they undressed, each preoccupied with their own thoughts.

Jonathan knew Darby had been telling the truth. Perhaps it had been Langford who had tried to abduct Katherine. His failure to do so, if that was true, would make him bide his time until he himself went back to America. This conviction made him more determined than ever to find someone who was able to protect her from the man's evil.

He gazed at Katherine then, realizing that she had not uttered a word since their disagreeable encounter with Darby. Her face was still as white as a ghost's. "Katie?" he called tentatively to her.

As though that was all she had been waiting to hear, Katherine flung herself into his arms. The tears she had been fighting until then came forth in full force. "Oh, Jonathan!" she hiccuped, crying in earnest. "I was never his whore, never! He—he tried to make me do things, but I wouldn't, not even when he beat me!"

"I know, darling, I know," Jonathan said, soothingly stroking her hair. "He won't hurt you any more, honey. I promise."

He kissed her and loved her, and even after he had fallen asleep, he continued to hold her.

But Katherine could find no peace in slumber. Jonathan had not said what she wanted most to hear: that he loved her, and that he would take her with him to America. Trying not to wake him, she cried bitter tears.

Was he leaving her, she asked herself in desperate anguish. If only she could bring herself to ask what he planned to do with her! But suddenly she knew she could never find the courage; she was too afraid of his answer.

Four

Although the nightmares that had plagued Katherine in the beginning had become less frequent until they finally disappeared, they began to recur after their unfortunate meeting with Darby at the theater. At those times when she woke up crying, Jonathan would cradle her in his arms and rock her gently back to sleep. His tenderness returned hope to her heart, and the nightmares went away again. But there was always fear in the back of her mind, even though he began spending more time with her than ever before. They spent a good part of the mornings riding in Hyde Park, and then they roamed through the city going in and out of shops, most times buying nothing, just enjoying their being together.

There were also frequent picnics in the country, where away from prying eyes they made love on the grass under the blue canopy of the sky. In the evenings, they would sit in their room to talk or read or simply touch. Sometimes they made love with such tenderness, that she thought her heart would burst with love; at others, with a passion so strong, so overwhelming, that it consumed their bodies like a searing flame. And each kiss, each touch, each magic moment they

85

were together was another link in the invisible chain that bound her to him.

During their long conversations, Jonathan told Katherine of his dreams for the future, of his first voyage as a stowaway at the young age of fourteen. He spoke fondly of his parents, a younger sister and a maternal grandfather who, as a privateer during the War of 1812, had run the British blockade that at the time had choked the American ports. On her part, Katherine told him of her parents and of their life traveling around the countryside in the gypsy caravan; but she was reluctant to speak of the years after their death because she didn't want to spoil those wonderful, intimate moments with memories of her past sorrows.

For many weeks, London buzzed with excitement in anticipation of Queen Victoria's coronation. The event promised to be the most splendid in the history of England, and to make it so, both the government as well as a number of enthusiastic private citizens had spent considerable amounts of money. The newspapers reported that a new Imperial State Crown had been commissioned because the massive Crown of St. Edward used in earlier coronations was far too heavy for the slender young Queen to wear through the long and exhausting ceremonies following the crowning.

As the twenty-eighth of June approached, not even Jonathan, who had traveled so extensively, had ever seen the crowds that flocked to the capital from every corner of the land and invaded their peaceful inn as well as every other hostelry in London. And on that day, when in the small hours of the morning the guns from the Park thundered in salute to the Queen, the crowds camped along the route the procession was to follow stirred to a new dawn, impervious to the showers that fell in prelude to the sun.

It was not until much later that the gilded state coach drawn by eight magnificent cream-colored horses began its triumphant journey surrounded by proud Yeomen of the Guard from the Tower of London. Although it left Constitution Hill at ten o'clock, the crowds made the progress so slow that it didn't reach the Abbey until eleven thirty in the morning. As the Queen alighted from the gilded coach, she was met by the young girls dressed in gowns of white satin and silver tissue who acted as her attendants. The long train of the Queen's crimson robes, which were trimmed with ermine, were carried by page boys dressed in blue velvet jackets, white knee breeches and silver-buckled shoes.

For this memorable occasion only a relative handful of some two thousand were allowed inside the Abbey; since Jonathan had been unable to obtain tickets, he and Katherine had to be content to stand with the crowd who waited outside the Abbey through the long ceremonies. The day grew warmer. Because of the heat and the reek of unwashed bodies Katherine was feeling a little faint by the time the Queen finally emerged wearing her crown and purple imperial robes.

Suddenly, in the midst of the excited, cheering crowd, her hand slipped from Jonathan's grasp as the tide of people pushed and pulled them apart. Jonathan had the advantage of his height; towering over the multitude, he was able to keep his eye on the spot of green that was her bonnet so that he wouldn't lose her while he shoved people aside and anxiously called her name. Swept by the wave of excited humanity, Katherine could barely hear his voice through the din. Confused and disoriented, she was pushed and pulled in all directions until she was grabbed and crushed in the embrace of a sour-smelling man who gave her a smacking kiss reeking of gin. Frightened out of her wits, she cried out until someone pulled the man away from her.

"Jonathan!" She clung to him in panic.

When at last he was finally able to get her away from the crowd, Jonathan surveyed her disheveled condition; the sleeve of her dress had been torn at the seam and she had lost her bonnet, but although very frightened, Katherine appeared unharmed. In the shelter of his protective arms, however, she soon recovered her usually high spirits. After all, not every day has one the occasion to see the coronation of the Queen of England!

Exhilarated by the day's events, they returned to the crowded inn. Anxious for a bath, Katherine went ahead to their room while Jonathan remained downstairs toasting the Queen and discussing the coronation events with a group of other guests.

She was leaving her bath as he came in, and immediately shedding his clothes stepped into the tub. The guileless little grin he wore told Katherine that the toasts to the Queen had been many and hearty. She poured more water into the bath and began scrubbing his back.

"Ah, this is the life!" he sighed in perfect contentment. "A hot bath, and a pretty wench to scrub one's back!"

She laughed, and in a rush of spirits flung the sponge into the tub. His expression of bliss was supplanted by a startled look when water splashed on his face. The picture he presented then was so hilarious — with his knees protruding from the tub and water running down his startled face — that it sent Katherine into such a fit of laughter that her knees buckled and she fell on the bed rolling with mirth.

"I'll get you for that!" she heard him growl. The tone of mocking menace made her look at him. He was standing in the tub, wiping the water from his face.

With a shriek of excitement, Katherine sprang to her feet. In a mood of cheerful expectation she watched him step out of the tub and begin advancing toward her. She waited until he was near to make her escape. Then, with a shriek, she ran behind the chair. Emitting menacing growls, Jonathan chased her around the chair. Katherine made for the other end of the room, but as she was nearing the bed, he dove after her with a bellow, and they fell on the bed in a tangle. Pinned under his weight, she struggled in ineffective attempts to escape him and gave a shriek when he began biting her softly on the side of her neck. They rolled on the bed engaged in playful, lighthearted battle; but soon their romp led to more intimate caresses. Breathless with laughter, she ceased in her struggles when her wrists were captured in his firm grip and held above her head. Her breast was rising and falling as she looked up at him. The exhilaration in her eyes gave way to a soft, intimate glance when she saw that his eyes had grown dark with desire.

"Surrender, wench?" he asked in a husky voice.

In rapt intoxication, they gazed into each other's eyes for endless moments. He released her arms, which coiled around his neck to bring his head down and meet her lips. Her own parted willingly to the invasion of his tongue. As she tasted the warmth of his mouth, Jonathan parted her gown with his hands to seek her naked flesh.

Regardless of how many times they had made love, each one was a brand new experience for her. His touch, his nearness, the taste of him filled her with such sensations that could only find fulfillment in becoming a part of him.

Nothing else existed or mattered as they explored their bodies with their eyes, their hands, their mouths; as they savored each touch and the taste of each other. She turned boneless and melting under his caresses, and the warmth glowing within her spread to every fiber of her being as she received him. As their bodies entwined, they were engulfed in a world of exquisite pleasure and infinite delight. Yielding to the wild swiftness of their passion they clung to each other, hearts pounding in unison as their juices mingled and they became one.

Katherine lived in dread of the moment when Jonathan

would tell her that he was leaving her. Too afraid to admit to such possibility, she had been unable to bring up the subject. She knew she had taken the cowardly way out when she elected to live each day as it came; but just as her love for him had grown so overwhelming, she hoped that his feelings for her would not allow him to abandon her. Although she had never been very devout, there were times—especially when almost two months had already gone by—when she found herself praying that he wouldn't.

Professor Stuyvesant interrupted their game to admonish mildly, "You're not paying attention, Katherine."

Realizing that her thoughts had struck off at a tangent, Katherine forced her attention back to the present. They were alone in the sitting room, she curled on the floor while the professor sat in one of the winged chairs, the chessboard on the table between them. After the attempted abduction, he was the only visitor with whom both she and Jonathan felt confident.

A faint flush suffused her cheeks as she said, "I'm sorry, Professor. It seems I can't concentrate on the game today." Although in a short time she had become a rather adept player, she had made one mistake after another since the beginning of the game.

The professor's gaze betrayed a mild alertness as he leaned back in his chair. "You seemed worried, my dear. Is something amiss?"

Katherine wondered if Jonathan, who had become such good friends with the professor, had mentioned any of his plans to the old man. Afraid of revealing too much, however, she made a deliberate effort to keep her tone—and her expression—detached as she replied, "Oh, I don't know. It's just that Jonathan has been spending a great deal of time at his ship of late. I was wondering if anything was wrong." She paused briefly. When the professor remained silent, toying with one of the pieces on the board she asked casually, "Has he said anything to you?"

"No, he has not," the professor shook his head. In the brief, odd silence that followed, the old man regarded her thoughtfully. "You're not sure whether he'll be taking you with him, is that it?" he said suddenly.

Katherine looked up abruptly, a little startled by the man's perception. Or was she so transparent? The speculation she saw reflected in his eyes made hers fall wretchedly.

"You love him very much, don't you?" the professor asked in a voice full of kindness.

Looking thoughtfully at the table, Katherine nodded in silence.

"But, does he love *you?*"

For a brief moment, Katherine looked at him in helpless silence. Then, taking a deep breath as though to give herself courage, she answered candidly, "I don't know, Professor. I really don't."

She sat quite still, suffering acutely while the old man, rubbing his chin thoughtfully, studied her with a contemplative air. Suddenly, he leaned over and whispered urgently, "Katherine, do you trust me?"

Startled for a second, Katherine gave him a long slanting look from her green eyes. "Yes, Professor, I do," she replied at last, feeling rather foolish once she had recovered from her surprise at such an elliptical question.

"Then, my dear, I want you to listen very carefully to what I'm about to say."

Intrigued by his words, she waited expectantly for him to continue.

"First of all, I must ask for your solemn word that you will not repeat to anyone what I'm about to tell you. That, of course, includes Jonathan Greenfield." He gave a small, wry chuckle at her involuntary gasp. Having assured himself of her increased attention, his shrewd blue eyes appeared younger than ever on his wise old face when with a humorous glance he added, "You see, my dear, I trust you, too. Do I have your word?"

"Yes, of course," she replied, still confused and startled.

"Very well, my dear." A little silence fell as he leaned back in the chair and looked at her thoughtfully, as if considering how and where to begin. At last his face relaxed into a satisfied smile and he said, "First of all, let me tell you that my name is not Professor Stuyvesant, and that this is not my normal appearance."

A look of sheer disbelief illuminated her features. "Who are you?" she asked, apprehension creeping into her voice.

"No, my dear, you need not fear me," he said quickly at her reaction. "I promise you I mean you no harm. On the contrary," he added in a tone that was mild and reasonable, "I may be the only solution to your predicament." He allowed for a pause, and seeing that she still remained unconvinced, he went on. "You see, Katherine, I have been following you for some time now." Turning pale, Katherine opened her mouth to speak, but he raised a hand to forestall her questions. "No, you haven't seen me," he told her. "But then, again, you may have. Only at those times I looked differently. Let me explain," he chuckled at her bewilderment. "Among other things, I am an actor. This Professor Stuyvesant, you know, is only one of my roles, a part I play. I play other parts, too. For instance, I was at Langford's party the night Captain Greenfield so gallantly came to your rescue."

Drawing in her breath, Katherine shrank back. "You were there? Then . . ."

"Don't jump so quickly to conclusions, my dear," he cut off at the apprehension in her manner. He gave a wry shake of his head. "Now, would I be telling you all this if I were working for Langford?" Seeing her eyes widen in fear, he added, "Oh, yes, I know he's after you. That's the main reason why you'd do well to listen to me."

Now that he had her increased attention, he continued. "I got into Langford's house under false pretenses. He's an inveterate gambler, and his parties are quite notorious. I am, also, a professional gambler." He gave a deprecating shrug and smiled a little shamefaced. "I just couldn't resist it."

An undertone of bewilderment was in her voice when Katherine asked, "What do you mean by false pretenses?"

"I forged a letter of introduction," he replied with a pleasant, satisfied smile. "You see, among my other talents, I count forgery." After a brief pause during which Katherine looked at him in astonishment, he continued, "As I said, I forged a letter and went to his party. When I saw what he was doing to you, I decided to help you. Unfortunately," he added wryly, "Captain Greenfield had the same idea, and his method proved effective."

Katherine, who had never brought herself to ask Jonathan what method he had used to rescue her, couldn't resist the temptation to inquire, "How did he do it, Professor?"

It was his turn to be surprised. "He never told you?"

Aware if the warmth creeping into her cheeks, Katherine shook her head. "I'm afraid I never dared to ask," she admitted with a candor he found most charming.

Leaning back a little, he gave her a humorous glance. "Well, it was something to see, let me tell you. Believe me, those who were there that evening won't ever forget what happened." He chuckled at the remembrance. "I was at the table with Langford, your Jonathan, and three other men, but it soon became apparent that the game was not an ordinary one. Your captain is an excellent player," he went on in a mild tone of amusement. "He baited Langford until he had him cornered with what he thought was a winning hand and not enough chips left to cover the bet, so he was forced to bet you."

Katherine literally turned pale as she stared at the professor in shocked disbelief. "What are you saying? That Jonathan won me in a card game?"

"I'm afraid so," the old man nodded. "If it's any consolation to you, he staked more than three thousand pounds and won, needless to say, much to Langford's displeasure. He was so upset at losing you and all his money, that he attacked Jonathan." Obviously relishing the memory of the thrashing Jonathan had given Langford, he chuckled as he added, "I believe you saw the results."

He became serious again. "But, anyway, let me go on with my narrative. After Greenfield took you away, I learned that he had taken you to his ship. I even tried to bribe a member of his crew in order to reach you, but I'm afraid it proved pointless, for they are fiercely loyal to him. I saw my opportunity to approach you when he brought you to the inn, but then I realized that your relationship with Greenfield was a far cry from the one you had with Langford. I could tell immediately that you had fallen in love with him. So, I began to make some inquiries about him, and what I discovered made me decide to stay around for a while. Now, I'm glad I did."

His veiled reference served only to increase her fears. Still, she forced herself to ask, "And what did you discover, Professor?"

Her fears intensified as he hesitated and his gaze became troubled. "What do you know about him?" he asked in turn.

Katherine tried to gather her thoughts as she considered her reply. Except for what he had chosen to tell her, and that he was warm, and loving, and oh, so wonderful, she knew very little else about Jonathan. "He has spoken a little of his voyages and his family," she began diffidently. "But I must admit I don't know much about him, except that I love him."

Katherine shifted uncomfortably, watching a frown form around the professor's troubled eyes. "Then let me tell you about your lover," he said at last. "He's a member of one of Baltimore's wealthiest families; the American aristocracy, you might call it. As a matter of fact, in some distant way he's even connected to our own aristocracy," he reflected, "for one of his ancestors was the youngest son of an English baronet who went to the colonies to make his fortune. Apparently, he succeeded, for today the Greenfields control many interests — mining, building, shipping, a few other things. Your Jonathan is the heir to the family fortune which, as you may have surmised, is quite considerable."

Katherine was having trouble believing her ears. Why had Jonathan never mention any of this to her?

"You thought he was a mere ship captain, I take it," the professor said at her dismayed silence.

Not trusting herself to speak, all Katherine could do was bob her head dumbly.

"You said he mentioned his family."

Again, she bobbed her head. After a small, bleak silence, she finally built up enough courage to look at the professor. Her eyes were frightened as they met his, yet she did not look away. An involuntary shiver went through her limbs at the sight of his worried face. She felt herself turning cold. His reluctance to tell her more was so apparent that her voice shook a little when she said, "There's more, isn't there?"

Heavily, he nodded. "I'm afraid so." His eyes were full of kindness as he leaned over to take her hand in his. "Katherine, did Jonathan ever tell you that he's married?"

A contained expression came to her eyes as she echoed in a near whisper, "Married!" Her mind still refused to comprehend the enormity of the statement. And then, suddenly, it hit her in full force. "No!" she cried, shaking her head wildly, "It can't be true! It can't!"

The professor's eyes were sorely troubled as he held her icy hand and patted it gently in a futile attempt to console her. But nothing could ease the heartache, the terrible weight of desolation that she felt at that moment.

"I'm sorry, my dear. I don't know how to tell you this, but I'm afraid I must."

The eyes she turned to the professor were wild and full of pain. Could there possibly be more? How could it? The man she loved to distraction belonged to another woman! Gradually, the words he spoke penetrated her comprehension.

"He's preparing to leave shortly," the professor was saying. "His wife is expecting their first child soon, and —"

Her heart ceased bounding in her chest and sank slowly. She couldn't hear the rest of it — it didn't matter anyhow. Tears of desolation and pain managed to seep through her tightly shut eyelids and rolled unheeded down her cheeks. She began to weep in quiet despair.

"I realize that this has come as quite a shock, my dear, but you must think of yourself," the professor said then. Realizing that she was not listening, he said peremptorily, "Katherine! Pull yourself together and listen to me! Last night Jonathan had a visitor whom I recognized from Langford's party. Are you listening? His name is Darby."

Looking at him bleakly through more unfallen tears, she echoed faintly, "Darby?"

Growing inpatient with her indifference to his warnings, the professor seized her by the shoulders with urgent hands, "For heavens' sakes, don't you realize what's going to happen if you don't do something about it?"

The import of his words made Katherine come out of her lethargy to look at him incredulously. "Do you think Jonathan is planning to leave me to Darby?"

Her question brought forth a small shrug from the professor. "All I know is that Jonathan won't leave you at Langford's mercy," he said in a cautious tone. "That means he'll have to leave you under someone else's protection.

From what I overheard, Darby seemed very anxious to be that protector."

This new development was even worse than what Katherine had been dreading all along. Deep in her heart she knew that she had been trying to still her fears by telling herself that Jonathan loved her as much as she loved him. What she had just learned about him made her realize that she had been wrong to ignore that warning inner sense she had felt during the last few weeks. In dismay, she asked, "But if what you say is true, Professor, what am I to do?"

"Aha!" the professor said with somewhat exaggerated emphasis. "That's where I can help you, my girl!"

"How, Professor?" she asked in a cautious tone. "How can you help me?"

He gave her an engaging grin. "As I told you before, I am an actor, but if you will pardon my lack of humility, I will confess that I also have many other talents. Now, don't be frightened by what I'm about to say," he cautioned. "Just listen carefully. We don't have much time. As I said, I am an actor, and I already mentioned that I'm also a forger. Now, let me tell you my real occupation." Looking at her levelly he paused briefly for effect. "I am a thief."

Aghast, Katherine gasped, "What!"

He nodded with a smile. "Yes, my dear, a thief. And a gambler. It's not a vice, let me assure you, but a way to make a living. And a very nice living at that," he added with a roguish smile. He leaned forward, and his tone became eager when he said, "Now, the reason why I'm telling you all this, is that I want you to work with me."

Katherine gazed at him in silent astonishment. Then, clearing her throat, she asked, "But—what would you expect me to do?"

"I have studied you very carefully during these past weeks, my dear," he told her pleasantly. "You're a remarkably intelligent girl. With proper training, you could become a very important part of my operation and make a fortune for yourself in the process. Your beauty is a great asset. Use it, as well as that good mind of yours, for your own benefit." He paused briefly, and then, his tone quickening with enthusiasm, he urged her, "Think of it, Katherine. You can make a new life for yourself and become independent of any man."

In the brief ensuing silence, Katherine reflected on his words. "Tell me more about your operation," she prompted, her interest now aroused.

"We work strictly in the Continent, never in England," he began. "This is where I live, where I return after our trips abroad. That's a cardinal rule, my girl. Never trespass in your own backyard."

"You said *we*," she pointed out.

"I said you were quick," he smiled, wagging a finger at her. "Yes, there are other people involved. Unfortunately, however, I've been without a young female partner for more than two years now. The last one married a very wealthy man in Amsterdam and retired to lead an exemplary life, I'm afraid," he said with a mocking little smile. "Her husband is now a good friend and I visit them often. I'm sure you'll have a chance to meet them." His tone became a little wistful as he sighed, "Natalie was an excellent partner. Without her, our operations have not been as profitable as they used to be. However, until you came along, I had not found anyone suitable to take her place." He gave her another one of his engaging grins. "I think you'll do splendidly!"

With quickening interest, Katherine listened as the professor—whose real name was Adam Garfield—went on to explain his method of operation. Apparently, the group of thieves specialized in infiltrating the highest circles of Continental society and made excellent profits gambling with the notables. And if that were not enough, Adam was an expert at appropriating expensive jewels and *objets d'art* that commanded incredible prices when resold. Her part in the overall scheme consisted mostly of serving as a decoy. It sounded simple enough.

"Working with a young female partner is so much better," Adam went on to say. "That's probably because women are not as subject to suspicion as men are. Especially a beautiful and intelligent woman such as you."

Katherine remained thoughtful for a moment. "I don't know if I could do it," she admitted, a little uncertain.

"Perhaps not right now," Adam replied, apparently unconcerned with her reluctance. "But I have confidence that once you're trained in all the arts, you'll be as good, or even better than Natalie used to be. You're a remarkable combination of beauty and brains my dear. You have all the necessary attributes — including the proper motivation." Pausing, he regarded her expectantly. "Well, what do you say, Katherine? I think we could work well together."

A brief, rather blank pause ensued. "I don't know, Professor — er — I mean, Adam," she said then without much enthusiasm. Once the initial shock of discovery was over, the love she had for Jonathan would not allow Katherine to accept such callow betrayal on his part. "I still can't believe Jonathan would leave me to another man." Dropping her gaze, she gave a little shrug of helplessness. "I just can't."

Adam Garfield looked at her gravely. "Then think of it, my dear, but don't take too long." His voice became urgent when he said, "You must find your answer tonight. I believe his ship is scheduled to cast off at any moment."

A little shudder went through her at the thought of confronting Jonathan that evening.

Uncoiling from the depths of the chair, Adam Garfield stood up. "I'll leave you now to think about what I have offered you, my dear. But remember, you must trust me," he said, taking her hand and holding it with strong, compelling fingers. "Whether you accept my offer or not, I will help you. Please remember that."

Sitting quite still, Katherine watched as he slipped out from the sitting room and quietly shut the door behind him.

In the small, bleak silence he left behind, Katherine uttered a heavy sigh that was almost a groan. "Oh, Jonathan!" she spoke his name haltingly. Suddenly struck down by a spasm of swelling despair, she put her head down in her arms and began to cry. Soon her quiet weeping became compulsive as, despairingly, she longed for Jonathan with all her heart.

Tense and overwrought when the tears finally ceased, she paced the confines of the room in a restless, brooding fashion refusing to believe Jonathan would leave her to Darby—yet the doubt was still there. Incessantly, she blamed herself for having been such a coward, as if closing her eyes to the situation would make it go away. But now time had run out and Jonathan would be going back to his wife—

"Oh, God!" she groaned. Jonathan, her Jonathan, belonged to another, and dwelling on her pain, Katherine tried to imagine the woman who bore his name and his child. What was she like? Recalling the miniature portrait she had found in his cabin, she tried to summon the image of the young blonde woman in the painting. She could not, but it didn't matter.

Tormented by memories of their lovemaking, the thought of never being in his warm embrace again was more than she could bear. A wistful thought struck her suddenly. Jonathan didn't love his wife. No, he couldn't. A man doesn't risk his life and make love to another woman as he did and still be in love with his wife. The marriage must have been arranged by their families—a loveless marriage.

A grim determination illuminated her features as she tenaciously clung to that idea. She couldn't live without him. She would beg, on her knees if necessary, that he take her with him. He could keep her as his mistress, anything, anything but leave her!

Reasoning in this wild fashion, Katherine determined to make one last attempt to win Jonathan's affections in the little time left to her. For this she wanted to make herself as beautiful for him as she possibly could, and realizing that she had wasted a good deal of precious time, she went to stand before the mirror. She was immediately dismayed at the reflection it returned. Her lips were colorless and quivering, her eyes red, her face was swollen — it would take ages to repair the ravages caused by her tears even if she knew how, which she didn't.

Suddenly, she thought of Rosie. Surely Rosie would know what to do! Turning away from the mirror, she swiftly ran to the door. On her way out she almost collided with Joe Flint, who was sitting outside the door scrimshawing a piece of bone to relieve his boredom. On an earlier occasion, when Katherine had asked Jonathan about this occupation, he had replied that it was an art Joe had developed during his years on a whaling ship.

Joe looked up, immediately alert. "Is something wrong, miss?" he asked, starting to get up from his chair.

"Everything is fine, Joe," Katherine replied, trying to contain her impatience. "I'm just going for the maid."

"I'll get her for you, miss," he offered.

"Thank you, Joe."

He waited until she had gone back inside and he heard the bolt being drawn. As he started downstairs, Joe shook his head a little sadly. The captain's wench had been crying, of that he was sure. Perhaps he had told her that they would be sailing the next day, as soon as the water barrels were brought aboard. He was glad they were going home at last, although he couldn't help feeling a little sorry for the girl. She was such a pretty thing! The captain surely knew how to pick them. Ah, well, he dismissed the matter with an inward shrug. With her looks, she wouldn't have any trouble in finding someone else to take care of her as the captain did.

While she waited for Joe to return with Rosie, Katherine addressed herself to the delicate task of selecting the dress she would wear that evening. Feverishly going through the contents of the armoire, she discarded one garment after another until she came upon the rust taffeta she had worn to the theater. Of all her gowns, this particular one had the most daringly low decolletage. Although for her there were sad memories attached to the gown, it was the most fitting to the part of seductress she wanted to play for Jonathan's benefit.

Just as Katherine had hoped, Rosie knew immediately what to do to relieve the swelling of her face. While her bath was being readied, Katherine lay quietly on the bed with her face covered by a cold cloth which had been steeped in an infusion of herbs.

Rather than stay to help Katherine with her bath, Rosie left, taking with her the taffeta gown which needed a little pressing.

A little later, Katherine removed the cold cloth from her face and went to the mirror to examine the results. The swelling had considerably gone down, and she hoped that in the half-light of the dining room Jonathan wouldn't notice that her eyes were still a little red.

With a certain amount of alarm, she noticed that the room was beginning to grow dark. She had previously thought of washing her hair but now discarded the idea. She would have to hurry if she was to be ready by the time Jonathan returned, although in the last few days this had been rather late.

On that particular evening, however, he arrived much earlier than she had expected and surprised her while still in her bath. So immersed was she in her own musings, that she didn't hear when he came in. Suddenly becoming aware of another presence, she paused in the act of lathering her leg. Looking up abruptly, she was startled to find him standing there, raptly watching her from the doorway. The way he was looking at her caused a little stirring of excitement deep inside her. Perhaps this was even better than what she had planned, she told herself wistfully.

Without taking her eyes off him, she began to lather her shoulders. The glistening globes of her breasts drew his gaze for a moment before he met her eyes again. In wordless invitation, she offered him the cake of soap.

Jonathan came forward slowly, the expression on his face intense as if he were in the grip of a powerful emotion. He held out his hand and accepted the soap. Then, sitting down on his heels, he took on the task of lathering her skin. Closing her eyes, Katherine threw her head back and offered the arch of her white swelling throat.

Although she had vowed not to expose her feelings, Katherine had to strive bravely to check the tears that welled up in her eyes at the light touch of his fingers. To contain her emotions, she concentrated on the feel of his hands and emitted a long sigh of delight as they followed the curve of her shoulders. She breathed a little faster, and her pulse beat quickened when her breasts seemed to acquire a life of their own under his fondling hands. Her rosy nipples hardened and peaked and little noises of pleasure gurgled in her throat as she abandoned herself to his deliberate caresses.

A little breathless, she said, "Kiss me, darling," and he bent over to cover her mouth with his own. Her tongue probed and explored his slowly and sensuously.

When he drew back, they looked into each other's eyes in rapt intoxication for a few moments. Then she stood up, and wrapped in a towel she was carried to the bed. Laying her down on it, he bent over her. He towelled her slowly, tracing, as he did, sensuous kisses on her fragrant skin, rosy from her bath.

Her hands crept up the front of his chest and entwined behind his neck as she sought his mouth. Tremulous with desire, she said in a husky voice, "I want you, Jonathan."

She undressed him herself, tracing his body with her lips as she uncovered his flesh. He pulled the ribbon from her hair, and burying his fingers into the tumbling copper tresses tilted her head up to kiss her eyes, her nose, her cheeks, her chin. He claimed her mouth at last with a compelling, searing kiss that made her head spin and her limbs grow weak.

She received him hungrily, devouring him with her passion, consuming him with her love. But Jonathan's need for her that night could not be sated. He took her time and time again before spent and languid they lay quietly in each other's arms drifting into a pleasant slumber.

She woke up in the small hours of the morning. As she lay quietly on her side of the bed staring at the ceiling with eyes remote and wistful, Katherine thought of the strange note in Jonathan's lovemaking. Had it been goodbye? Then the scene with Adam Garfield came to mind. She turned her head a little and noticed that although Jonathan's eyes were closed, his breathing was a little irregular. He was awake.

I must ask him, she kept telling herself and lacking in courage to face the truth she only suspected. Finally, gathering herself, she decided that it was better to know the truth than to lie there waiting for the ax to fall.

She turned slowly to regard him. "Jonathan?" she called softly.

"Humm?" Still he didn't open his eyes.

"You are leaving, are you not?"

It seemed like an eternity had passed before he turned to her. There was a note of regret in his voice when he answered, "Yes, Katie. Tomorrow."

She managed to keep her expression even, although she had to clear her throat before speaking her next words. "And you're not taking me with you."

His eyes looked troubled as he replied, "I wish I could, Katie, but I can't."

A contained expression came to her eyes as she studied his face. Was it her imagination, or had he looked sad for just a second? She hoped her eyes did not reflect the heartache she felt as she regarded him and asked her next question. "Have you a wife, Jonathan?"

He gave her a frowning glance before he looked away. "Yes," he said finally.

With nerves painfully on edge, Katherine forged ahead with the question that would decide her fate. "Do you . . . love her?"

"Yes, I do." There had been no hesitation.

Suddenly, all her courage deserted her. She turned away, afraid that if he looked at her again she wouldn't be able to sustain the stolid facade she was striving to preserve. But, she wouldn't cry; and she wouldn't beg. She wouldn't even let him see how much she was hurting. She felt hollow, as if her heart had been ripped out of her breast. Her pain was so unbearable that she wanted to scream in agony.

"You won't have to worry about Langford, Katie," she heard Jonathan say over the pounding of her own heart. "I've seen to it that you're protected."

Sick at heart, Katherine felt herself turning cold. Now, in addition to her sorrow, a sharp disappointment gripped her. Adam had been telling the truth!

"Katie?" Jonathan called to her.

She didn't stir. She couldn't answer. She lay stiff and cold, her emotions in turmoil.

Katherine was barely aware when Jonathan eased himself out of bed and ambled across the room. She heard the clink of glass on glass as he poured a drink from the bottle of brandy they kept in their room. Suddenly, there was an explosion as the glass he had hurled across the room shattered against the mantel.

Startled, Katherine sat up abruptly and blinked in confusion.

"Damn you," he muttered savagely, fixing her with a glare in which she read such fury that it made her tremble.

She opened her mouth to speak as he advanced menacingly toward her, but no sound came out. Suddenly, she was being seized by the shoulders and his fingers dug painfully into her tender flesh. He shook her as if she were no more than a rag doll, her head bobbing up and down until she thought that her neck would snap at any moment. His eyes were blazing as he pushed her back. Realizing his intentions, Katherine started to cry out, but his mouth covered her protest. Impervious to her flailing arms and the small fists pounding his back he kissed her savagely, robbing her of her breath. In spite of her fear, Katherine's body responded to his assault with a will of its own. Little by little, her struggles became weaker and ceased; all resistance had left her when he parted her thighs with his knee and penetrated her.

"Damn you!" he groaned as his body tensed and shuddered with the force of his climax.

The hatred she heard in his voice made her tremble. Inert and cold she lay on the bed with her eyes closed as Jonathan rose and began to dress. A few minutes later, she heard the door slam shut behind him.

As though that had been the signal they had been waiting for, hot and bitter tears sprang from her eyes. Her entire body shook with the intensity of her sorrow and a convulsive weeping took possession of her. Then, when there were no more left to shed, she felt numb, spent and cold.

How long was she in that trance Katherine didn't know. She only knew that when it was over, something inside her had died.

Yet she had to go on living. Forcing herself out of bed, she crossed the room on leaden feet. She filled the basin, splashed cold water on her face, and still pressing a cloth to her face went to stand before the open window. Looking moodily into the night, she began taking stock of her situation.

For too long she had been a pawn in other people's games; first her aunt, then Langford, and now Jonathan, she reflected. Langford had tormented her body, but Jonathan — Jonathan had given her hope and encouraged her love only to crush all her expectations in one fell swoop with his ruthless betrayal. And that she could never forget — or forgive.

Suddenly, Katherine's shoulders, which had been drooping in dejection, began to straighten up as a dark, sobering change of mood began to overtake her. Langford had failed to defeat her; she could not — and would not — allow Jonathan to do so. She would take control of her life, and she would survive.

Adam was expecting her when she walked into the dining room early the next morning and seemed to know her answer even before she spoke. "I'm sorry, Katherine," he said at her appearance. Her lips were colorless, her eyes red and still a little swollen.

"I have decided to go away with you." Although she had spoken without emotion, her features were set in grim determination. "I've already packed a few things, so we can leave as soon as you're ready."

"Just one moment, my dear," he said, trying not to look too pleased with her decision. "You don't really believe we can just walk out of here, do you? Look around you, Katherine." Discreetly, he nodded his head toward Joe Flint, who was sitting across the room eating his breakfast while keeping watch on them. "Do you think he'll let you walk out of here with me?"

Katherine looked askance in the direction he had indicated and shrugged her shoulders in a gesture of indifference. "He's here only to protect me," she said flatly.

"And he will stop you if you try to leave," he reminded her.

Katherine realized it was the truth. After a brief, but definite pause during which she considered the situation, she looked up at her companion. "What can we do?" At the malicious expression that came over Adam's face, she rushed to add, "I don't want him harmed, Adam."

"There's one thing you must learn about me, Katherine," he told her, adopting a slightly injured air. "I loathe violence. And besides," he added, his expression beginning to show amusement, "it's much more challenging to use one's wits." Suddenly, his expression became serious. "Now, listen carefully and do exactly as I say. But remember, you must hurry. We don't know how soon Jonathan will return." He leaned forward and murmured to her in a confidential tone of voice, "Last night, my *widowed daughter* arrived with her maid. They're in the room adjacent to yours. I want you to go upstairs quickly and unlock the connecting door between the rooms." At the look of surprise that came to her eyes, he added, "It's hidden behind the large tapestry on the wall. The women are waiting for you. They'll help you with your costume and with the packing." Leaning back in his chair he added, "I'll remain here, where I can keep an eye on the stairs. If Jonathan happens to come back before you're ready, I'll try to detain him for as long as possible."

"I don't want any of the things Jonathan gave me," Katherine shook her head. "I've already packed all I need."

Rolling his eyes heavenward, Adam heaved a sigh of exasperation. "That's a very gallant gesture my dear, but highly impractical. Tell me, what would it accomplish? Not to mention that in your new profession, you'll be needing all those elegant clothes that he bought you, as well as the jewels." Lifting a hand to forestall the protest she was about to make, he added, "Please do as I said. See that everything is packed, and don't forget to bolt the connecting door again. As soon as you're ready, you and the girl posing as your maid must leave from the other room. I'll ask the innkeeper to send someone for your luggage." He gave her a swift but searching glance before asking, "Are there any questions?"

"What of the other woman?" Katherine asked, a little bewildered by such an elaborate plan. "How will she get away?"

Shrugging his shoulders in a deprecating gesture, Adam smiled. "Who's to notice a serving girl leaving the inn? "Becoming serious again, he urged, "Now go. And do hurry!"

Katherine went to her room and followed Adam's instructions. Just as he had said, there was a connecting door hidden behind the tapestry. As she drew the bolt, she wondered how Adam had known of its existence when she had been unaware of it even after having inhabited that room for almost two months.

Once the door was open, she stepped into the adjacent room. The two women there had been expecting her and quickly started to pack her belongings. They moved so quickly and so efficiently that the task was finished in much less than half of the time Katherine had expected it would take. Then, the three of them went to the other room, where Katherine was helped out of her dress and into the widow costume. After placing a heavily veiled hat on her head, Katherine and the girl posing as her servant followed the grooms carrying her luggage out the door.

Even though the heavy veil concealed her features, Katherine's heart fluttered with apprehension as she approached Joe Flint and he looked up from the newspaper he was holding in front of him. Expelling a long sigh of relief when he didn't recognize her, she walked briskly down the hallway toward the stairs.

Although Adam appeared confident while the grooms loaded her trunk and valises onto the carriage he had engaged, Katherine felt unsettled and ill at ease. Once the luggage was secured, Professor Stuyvesant and his *widowed daughter* boarded the carriage and departed from the inn without incident.

Just before the coach reached the corner, however, a hansom cab stopped in front of the inn. Both she and Adam turned in unison to look at the passenger who alighted from it. It was Jonathan.

"Just in time," Adam said with a wry chuckle as he faced front again. "Just in time."

Five

While the carriage traveled through the teeming streets of London, Katherine began to entertain second thoughts as to the wisdom of her decision of running away with Adam. In the role of Professor Stuyvesant he had been most charming, witty, and she had liked him tremendously; but, what kind of man was he, really? Although he had assured her of his help whether she agreed to work with him or not, as yet he had not even asked for her decision, she meditated darkly.

Looking out the window, the shabby section of town they were traversing did little to still her qualms. Turning to him, she asked in a cautious tone, "Where are we going?"

Adam's gaze was speculative—as if trying to gauge her reactions—as he replied, "Our final destination is Polperro, a small fishing village in Cornwall."

"Cornwall!" she echoed almost in a whisper, giving him a look of astonishment.

At the note of dismay in her voice, an ironic twinkle appeared in his eyes. "It's my home," he replied pleasantly. "First, however, we'll be stopping at a friend's house."

A small frown bit into her brow. "A friend?" she repeated warily.

"Now, don't be alarmed," he said, giving a wry little sigh. Then, with exaggerated patience, as if addressing a recalcitrant child, he explained, "We'll stop there only long enough to change our costumes and our conveyance."

Troubled, yet peevish, Katherine gazed at him defensively. Her face had colored with mortification, and in the tightness that came to her mouth he saw the irritation the condescension in his tone had caused her.

Although he could not refrain from smiling, Adam dropped his mocking tone when he said, "I realize that your past experiences may have made you wary, my dear, but let me assure you once more that I mean you no harm. I told you I would help you and I will, whether or not you decide to work with me. However, I don't expect you to rush into anything. I won't ask for your answer until you've had a chance to think things over. At any rate," he went on agreeably, "it will take us a few days to get to Cornwall, where my sister lives. You may stay with us whilst you decide what to do. Fair enough?" Before Katherine could reply, he looked out the window and exclaimed, "Ah, here we are!"

Once the carriage had come to a halt, she gathered the voluminous skirts of the widow' weeds and alighted with Adam's assistance. The driver remained on his perch while with a gentle pressure on her elbow Adam led her toward the front door of a dwelling that, although unpretentious at best, seemed better cared for than those around it. The front door opened before he had had a chance to ring the bell.

In addition to having a very plain and ordinary face, the bespectacled little man who stood before them had lost most of his mousy brown hair. Only a fringe of it remained on his rather rounded head. "Come in, come in," he said, punctuating his words with spasmodic gestures. "I've been expecting you." With a little trepidation, Katherine stepped in, followed by Adam. While they were still standing in the small foyer, the little man squinted his pale myopic eyes as though to pierce the heavy veil that concealed her features. "Is this the girl?" he asked.

"Yes, of course," Adam replied. This brief exchange caused the swift return of her earlier apprehension, and Katherine felt herself grow rigid. Apparently unaware of her increasing suspicions, turning to her he added, "Katherine, my dear, this is Daniel Sutherland, who's been dying of curiosity since I told him about you." He gave her one of his engaging smiles. "Why don't you lift that veil and give the poor man a chance to see your pretty face, eh?"

Still a little uneasy, Katherine disclosed her face.

"Ah," Daniel smiled, apparently pleased by what he saw. Offering his hand, he said, "Delighted, my dear. Adam wasn't exaggerating a bit when he said you were very beautiful." The small hand he took in his not much larger one, was trembling a little. To her immense surprise, Daniel Sutherland bent from the waist in a courtly gesture and kissed her hand.

"Your costumes are in the bedrooms upstairs," he said, addressing Adam. "First door to the left for this charming young lady, and yours at the end of the hallway." He turned to Katherine with an apologetic smile. "If you will excuse me, my dear, I shall see to your luggage whilst you change."

"Thank you, Daniel," Adam said, making no attempt to conceal his impatience. "I do want to get under way as soon as possible."

While Daniel Sutherland went out, Katherine followed Adam further into the house. The elegance of the furnishings she saw there—quite in contrast to the apparent modest facade of the dwelling—made her wonder about Daniel Sutherland's reasons for deliberately appearing far less affluent than he actually was.

At the top of the stairs, Adam paused at the first door their host had indicated.

"You may change in there," he said.

The sight of a key in the lock reminded Katherine only too well of the room where Langford had kept her prisoner, and, instinctively, she backed away.

"It's all right, my dear," Adam said with a rather rueful little chuckle. He removed the key from the lock and handed it to her. "I promise I had no intention of locking you in."

Katherine felt her cheeks suffuse with color as she accepted the key. "I'm sorry," she said, looking quite stricken with remorse at her suspicions.

"It's all right, my dear. I understand," he said, smiling at her without apparent rancor. "Whenever you are ready, I'll meet you in the parlor downstairs."

He turned, and Katherine's puzzled glance followed him as he walked away. Even though he still wore the face of the old Professor Stuyvesant she had known, he seemed quite different now. It took her a moment, before he disappeared at the end of the hallway, to notice the metamorphosis in his manner. Now his voice had a younger sound, and he walked erect and tall, no longer with the little stoop at the shoulders the old professor had worn. Shaking her head in bemusement, she opened the door and entered the bedchamber.

On the half-tester bed she found the costume she was expected to wear: a rather nondescript gray woolen dress, an old-fashioned bonnet of the same color, a mousy brown wig that somehow reminded her of Daniel Sutherland's remaining hair, and a pair of wire-rimmed spectacles. While divesting herself of the widow's weeds and adopting her new costume, in spite of her somber mood Katherine couldn't help being a little amused by the charade she was about to play.

The dress was padded, she discovered, and made her appear quite stout. Next, she had to coil her hair around her head in order to put on the wig, which was too tight and felt very uncomfortable. Standing before the dresser mirror she laced the bonnet, and after putting on the spectacles smiled at her reflection. The transformation was so complete, that she believed not even Jonathan would be able to recognize her if he passed her on the street.

Once she had finished, Katherine went downstairs to meet Adam. The parlor was empty, however; so sitting down in a Chesterfield settee of pale blue damask, she prepared to wait for him.

A few minutes later a tall, slender man dressed as a vicar came in. His brown hair and the spectacles he wore were very similar to her own. "All set?" he asked her.

Recognizing only the voice, she looked at him a little startled. Diffidently, she asked, "Adam? Is that you?"

"Reverend Barlow," he grinned, apparently delighted by her mystified expression. "And you are my dear sister Henrietta. Keep that in mind, because that's who we'll be for the next few days." He paused briefly to examine her appearance and then added, "Our coach is waiting, dear sister. We must leave immediately if we're to get to Surrey by this evening."

"Surrey!" she cried, bouncing to her feet. "You're not planning to spend the night at the inn, are you?"

"Yes, of course," he replied in a cautious tone.

Katherine shook her head emphatically. "I can't go there!"

"Why not?"

"The inn belongs to my aunt," she said with an involuntary shudder. Haltingly, she told him the whole story.

"I see," he reflected thoughtfully when she finished, studying her worried face. "Come over here, Katherine," he said then, and taking her by the hand made her stand in front of a mirror that was hanging on the wall. "Look at yourself. Now tell me, do you believe your aunt will be able to recognize you?"

Intently, she studied the image the mirror returned. "I guess not," she admitted, heaving a wry little sigh. Then, turning to him, she squared her shoulders and tipped her chin. "I'm ready," she said.

An hour later, the new carriage was retracing the same road she had traveled with Charles Langford only two months before. So many things had happened to her during that brief period of time that, somehow, Katherine felt like a completely different person. No longer was she the innocent, frightened young girl who had left Surrey, she reflected, absently looking in a distant, detached fashion at the green countryside beyond the window. That girl had been sold and abused; she had known the joys of love and passion; the heartbreak of disenchantment; the agony of betrayal.

The new Katherine was no longer a girl, but a woman; and a woman in control of her own life, of her own destiny. Yes, she would work with Adam, she determined at that very moment. She would learn all he had to teach her, and she would gamble and steal if she had to; but one day she would find Jonathan again, and when she did, it would be on equal terms—no longer as a supplicant—and he would know the force of her wrath. He would suffer as she herself had suffered. Only then would she be free of the memory of his treachery.

Turning her gaze to Adam, who had occupied his leisure with a book while she had been busy with her thoughts, she tipped her chin in that peculiar gesture of hers when faced with a challenge. "I've decided to accept your offer, Adam," she announced suddenly.

This decision, coming sooner than he had anticipated, made Adam look up from the book to give her a speculative glance. Closing the book, he studied her expression carefully for a few seconds. "Are you sure?"

"Yes," she nodded with assurance. Once her decision had

116

been made, there were no regrets lingering in her mind. "You said I could make a fortune and never be dependent on another man again. That's exactly what I want, Adam. To be free."

"You realize, of course, that there'll be risks involved," he told her carefully.

"I realize that," she replied, smiling a trifle wryly. Then, crooking a sardonic brow, she added with thin humor, "But I haven't exactly led a very sheltered life of late, have I?"

Adam looked a little startled by the swift change of her mood and then, throwing his head back, he burst out in a hearty roar of laughter.

With a wry look on her face, Katherine waited until his mirth subsided. With a half-shake of his head, he held out his hand, "Then I think we're going to have a very profitable association, partner."

Katherine shook the hand he offered without hesitation. "I hope so, Adam," she said with a little grim smile, "because what I'm going to need is a fortune."

It was almost midnight when they arrived in Surrey. In spite of the earlier assurance she had shown, Katherine still felt a certain amount of trepidation when she walked into the inn. Her confidence soon returned, however, for neither Aunt Harriet nor Uncle Thomas recognized her; in fact, she even enjoyed the experience of being served by the woman who had made a living hell of the last three years of her life.

Although she had imagined she wouldn't be able to sleep that night, Katherine did so soundly, and early the next morning she and Adam took to the road again. It was a long journey to Cornwall. After riding through the days, nights were spent at other inns along the road.

During that time, Adam spoke of his sister with fondness. Agatha was a widow, he told Katherine; her husband, a seaman, had been lost at sea many years before. Following the death of their infant daughter, she had returned to their parent's old home—now Adam's property—a cottage on the outskirts of the village where for the last several years she had served as a midwife.

Traveling with Adam became quite an experience for Katherine. Having been an actor in his youth, during the long hours they spent together he kept her entertained with stories of his days in the theater. Before reaching the London stage, there had been an arduous and poorly remunerated career with second-rate companies in small towns, some of which Katherine herself had visited with her parents. Since he had also learned a little bit of magic during that time, he performed card tricks for her and even insisted on teaching her a few of the simpler ones. He was so entertaining that, before she knew it, they had left Devon behind.

Katherine was glad when at last Adam allowed her to abandon her disguise. The increasing heat of summer made wearing the padded dress terribly uncomfortable, and, in addition, the tightness of the wig made her head ache. And when he also reverted then to his own appearance, she was very surprised at how different it was from what she had imagined.

A very attractive man in his middle to late thirties, Adam was tall and slender, had sandy blond hair and an engaging smile. The only feature that remained the same—his clear blue eyes—often twinkled with mischief during his telling of tales, which she imagined were a trifle embellished for her amusement.

As Professor Stuyvesant, he had appeared as a small old man in a rumpled coat; but it was all illusion, for he was nearly six feet tall, and now—as himself—quite elegant and dapper; a master of disguise, as she had discovered, who adapted himself so well to the role he happened to be playing that even physical characteristics seemed to change. As he wryly told Katherine one day, the stage had lost one of its greater assets when he had taken to a life of crime. "Humility," he grinned with engaging impudence, "is not counted among my flaws, my dear."

A sudden access of longing for Jonathan came over Katherine as she and Adam approached the Cornish cottage on foot. For her, there had been a feeling of unreality to the days of constant travelling; but now that they had reached their destination, she was struck down by the realization that a part of her life—the most important part, perhaps—had definitely ended.

An involuntary shiver went through her limbs, and despite the warmth of the afternoon, she felt herself turning cold. Her pace slackened, imperceptibly at first; then she stopped completely.

Adam turned slowly to regard her. "Are you all right?" he asked when he saw her shrink back.

Such was her desolation that for a moment she couldn't answer. Then, making a valiant effort to shake off her despondency, she tried to set her features into a semblance of composure. "Yes, of course," she murmured faintly.

They resumed walking.

The afternoon sun sparkled on the small windows set in stone walls that were several feet thick and weathered by age. In the small but well-kept garden in front, flowers added bursts of color here and there while their perfume filled the soft, gentle air.

The woman who answered the door a few minutes later was slender and petite, and the kindness of her face served to quiet a little the lingering fears in Katherine's breast.

"Adam!" she cried, her face cracking in a wide and spontaneous smile at the sight of her brother. "You're finally home!"

While they embraced, Katherine looked away a little self-consciously.

After such an effusive greeting, Adam introduced his companion, and following a warm welcome on Agatha's part, they were led into a parlor that although rather small, was furnished with elegant pieces and a beautiful rug in pastel hues on the meticulously scrubbed floor. There was a faint, pleasant scent of pine and beeswax in the air.

A few minutes later, a pretty blonde girl of about fifteen came rushing in to hug and kiss Adam and became a little subdued when introduced to Katherine. Her name was Jenny. Since Adam had already told her that Agatha had no living offspring, the unexpected appearance set Katherine to wonder about the girl's relationship to Adam and his sister.

"Jenny, won't you show Katherine to her room?" Adam asked after a few minutes. "I'll have her trunk taken upstairs later."

"Yes, of course," Jenny replied quickly. Turning to Katherine, she said in a low voice, "This way."

Realizing that perhaps Adam wanted to explain her presence to his sister, Katherine rose to her feet a little self-consciously and followed Jenny from the parlor.

"I'm afraid we'll be sharing a bedchamber," Jenny said as they climbed the stairs to the second floor. Politely, but with some reserve, she added, "I hope you don't mind."

"Of course not," Katherine rushed to answer. "I'm only sorry to put you to such trouble, Jenny."

"Trouble?" They had arrived at the top of the stairs, and Jenny turned to look at Katherine. "Sharing the room with you won't be any trouble at all," she said, eyeing the newcomer with wry amusement. "Before Adam found me and brought me here, I had to sleep in a room full of people — and believe me, it wasn't even half as nice as this one is."

A little bewildered by her manner and such cryptic sort of explanation, Katherine followed the younger girl into a small, but quite charming bedchamber with a double bed.

"I'll make room for your things," Jenny said, going to the armoire standing in one corner. She paused and turned to Katherine. "Adam didn't tell you about me, did he?"

"I'm afraid not," Katherine confessed, a little shame-faced.

"I thought so," Jenny said. Turning away, she threw open the doors of the armoire. "I suppose that if you brought a trunk, there won't be enough room for your clothes here. I guess I'll have to move mine."

"No, Jenny. I won't hear of it," Katherine protested quite sincerely.

Abruptly, Jenny swung around to face her. "You're going to be working with Adam, aren't you?" she asked suddenly.

A stirring of tension started within Katherine as she regarded the other girl. There was a silence, an uneasy shifting as she tried to gauge Jenny's emotions. Jenny's face was a little pale, and the anxiety she read in the expectant blue eyes made Katherine feel rather uncomfortable while she ruminated on her reply. "Well, I—"

"I knew it," Jenny murmured faintly. Her frail shoulders drooped as she shook her head in somber disappointment. She turned away again and started to take some of her dresses out of the armoire and lay them on the bed.

For the next few seconds Katherine stood there watching, a little bewildered by the situation and unsure as to what to do about it. Why was Jenny so disappointed to learn that she'd be working with Adam, Katherine asked herself. It didn't take her long to realize the obvious answer, that Jenny had expected to fill the vacancy left by the mysterious Natalie.

Going to Jenny, Katherine put her hands on the young girl's shoulders and made her stop what she was doing. "Jenny," she said quietly. "Please, let's talk about it."

Without facing Katherine, Jenny stood staring moodily

at the floor. "What's there to say?" she said with a slight shrug of her shoulders.

"You and me, for one thing," Katherine replied quietly. "I'd like us to be friends, Jenny, but that cannot happen unless we're honest with each other."

There was a pause during which Katherine waited for the other girl's response. Then, when she was beginning to think she had failed to reach her, Jenny half-turned and unexpectedly met her gaze.

"Do you really mean that?" she asked cautiously. "You want us to be friends?"

"Yes, Jenny," Katherine replied, sustaining her gaze. "I really do."

Jenny's gaze was challenging as she asked pointedly, "Why?"

Katherine made a deprecating gesture. "I have nowhere else to go," she admitted quite frankly.

To her surprise, Jenny smiled and shook her head. "I think I'm going to like you, Katherine," she said, going to sit on the edge of the bed. Patting the space beside her for Katherine to sit, she asked, "Where did you meet Adam?"

"In London," Katherine replied, and went on to tell her story to her new friend.

"Bastard!" Jenny said of Jonathan at the end of the narration. Katherine was surprised and a little taken aback by the anger in her eyes when Jenny looked up at her. "You were daft to believe that American gent would care for you. All men are bastards," she muttered savagely, although her tone became gentler when she added, "All except Adam."

Quite astonished, Katherine gazed at her in silence. What could have happened to Jenny to make her so bitter, she wondered. She didn't have to wonder much longer.

"You were lucky Adam found you before you 'ad to sell yourself on the streets," Jenny said, "as I 'ad to do since I was nine. That's where 'e found me." Seemingly unaware that she had slipped into the lowly speech of London, she went on, " 'e asked about me parents and when I told 'im that they would beat me if I didn't bring back enough coin to buy their gin, 'e asked me to take 'im to them, and so I did. I was scared when 'e offered a w'ole guinea to take me with 'im. I thought he was one of those fancy gents who like to 'urt girls like me, and even after 'e told me about 'is sister, I didn't believe 'im. But everything 'e said was true," she reflected. "Agatha 'as been better to me than me own mom ever was, and wit'out 'er and Adam, I'd probably be dead by now. I was sick, you see."

Jenny looked up then, and her cheeks flushed when she saw the pity reflected in Katherine's eyes. "We're just like a real family, Katherine," Jenny said in a voice that shook a little with emotion. "Now you can be a part of that family, too."

Katherine's eyes were suspiciously bright as she reached for Jenny's hand and covered it warmly with her own. Looking at this pretty girl with her rosy complexion, soft shiny blonde hair and healthy young body, she couldn't believe anyone would have guessed that only a short time before, she had been one of those pathetic little creatures who populated the streets of London. "You expected to work with Adam, didn't you?" she asked gently.

Heaving a wistful sigh, Jenny nodded heavily. Then, giving a little shrug, she looked up at Katherine and smiled sadly. "I wanted to help him, but except for picking pockets, I guess I've always known I'd never be smart enough — or beautiful enough — like you and Natalie."

"Oh, Jenny!" Katherine sighed with regret as she embraced the young girl. "Perhaps we should talk to Adam . . ."

Jenny drew back to look at her seriously. "No, Katherine. Adam knows his business. If he chose you, then he must believe that you'll be better at it than I." Shaking her head, she added in a wry tone of voice, "Besides, I still forget to talk like a lady when I get nervous or upset, 'though both Agatha and Adam have been trying to teach me for years. Perhaps I'll never learn."

"Don't say that, Jenny," Katherine protested. "Of course you will."

There was no sadness in Jenny's smile when she said, "I'm glad you're here, Katherine."

Since Adam immediately put Katherine to work, she had little time left to brood about her problems. There was a great deal to learn, and the sooner they began, the better. Soon her hours were filled learning card skills, improving her speech, learning French and German and experimenting with makeup and costumes. She learned dancing, etiquette, and to roll the dice; Jenny instructed her in the fine art of picking pockets. With such an endless list, she spent every waking hour learning her new profession.

The long hours were fascinating, but exhausting, and a few weeks later her health seemed to be on the decline. Her appetite became poor, and she suffered from constant dizzy spells. And mornings were the worst; there were times when even the sight of the hearty breakfasts Agatha served made her nauseated.

One morning when she was unable to leave her bed, Agatha came to see her.

"What's wrong, my dear?" the kind woman inquired. "Are you ill?"

Katherine's answer was a groan. The entire room seemed to spin all about her whenever she opened her eyes.

Sitting on the bed's edge, Agatha put her hand to Katherine's brow to feel her temperature. "You don't seem to have a fever," she said, looking a little puzzled. "How long have you felt this way?"

"A few weeks, I guess," Katherine finally got out. "Some giddiness and nausea, but it's never been as bad as today. It's terrible, ooh!"

Agatha's eyes were full of thought as she studied Katherine for a few seconds. "Katherine, when did you last have the curse?" she asked then.

"The curse?" Katherine echoed faintly, a furrow deepening her brow as she searched her memory. Closing her eyes when another wave of dizziness came over her, she groaned, "I can't remember."

"Was it in London?" Agatha insisted.

"I think so," Katherine admitted miserably as she waited for her discomfort to ease. "Yes, I guess it was." The import of Agatha's questions struck her suddenly as she remembered Jonathan's explanation. She gave a gasp of alarm, and the eyes she turned to Adam's sister were wide with apprehension. "You don't think I may be . . ." She couldn't bring herself to voice her suspicions.

Thoughtfully returning the look, Agatha studied her worried face for a few seconds. "I think so, my dear," she said at last. "I believe you are with child."

Katherine was startled for a second. Then, in a tense expulsion of breath, she cried "No!" A look of sheer disbelief illuminated her features as she shook her head. "It can't be!"

Agatha's face was full of kindness as she reached for Katherine's hand and said, "I'm afraid so, my dear."

There was a small, bleak silence while Katherine tried to assimilate the enormity of this new development. "What am I going to do?" she asked in dismay at last.

"Why, have your child, of course," Agatha replied, reinforcing her words with a reassuring squeeze of her hand.

The face Katherine turned to the older woman was pale and taut at the cheekbones when she asked, "And where will I go?"

Her question brought forth a deprecating shrug and a lifting of Agatha's brows. "Why would you have to go anywhere when you can stay here with us?" she asked.

"But I'll have to!" Katherine said bleakly. One of the tears that had been burning in her eyes slid slowly down her pale cheek as she dropped her gaze in misery. "What will Adam say when he finds out?"

"He'll probably be a little disappointed," Agatha said calmly.

"Won't he send me away?" Katherine asked in a hopeful tone.

Mildly astonished, Agatha gazed at her. "Of course he won't!" she exclaimed. "How can you believe that? What kind of a man do you think he is that he would send you away in your condition?"

"But you know I came here to work with Adam," Katherine replied, her color beginning to return. "We made so many plans, and now—"

"There's no reason to change your plans, my dear," Agatha said in a matter-of-fact tone. "You'll just have to wait a little longer, that's all."

"And what of the child?"

"Jenny and I will care for him—or her." Agatha's smile conveyed her reassurance. "Don't fret, Katherine. I will speak to Adam, and I'm sure he will agree. But whatever he decides to do, believe me, he wouldn't even think of sending you away."

Fervently, almost as in prayer, Katherine said, "I hope you're right."

Agatha dismissed her doubts with a wave of her hand. "I know I am, but . . ." she hesitated, "what of the child's father, Katherine? Won't you let him know?"

Katherine's pallor returned. "No!" she denied swiftly. "He . . . he has a wife. I was nothing to him, nothing!"

After a constrained pause, Agatha said gently, "You must have loved him very much."

"With all my heart," Katherine admitted, feeling her eyes again fill with tears. Bleakly, she added, "But he was leaving me to another man."

The desolation of her young friend prompted Agatha to wrap a comforting arm around her shoulders. "I am truly sorry, my dear, but you must be strong. Remember you are carrying a new life within you now. Promise me that you will take care and not distress yourself."

Lifting her swimming eyes to Agatha's kind face, Katherine attempted a tremulous smile. "I'll try," she said.

Agatha smiled. "Good. You rest now, and do try not to worry. I'll speak to Adam." She rose, and after giving Katherine another thoughtful look, she went from the room.

Once she was alone, the valiant facade Katherine had tried to present crumpled at the thought of Jonathan's child growing inside her. A bastard! The child of a man who had used her and discarded her after breaking her heart.

"I don't want his child," she wept bitterly. "I don't want it!"

She hurriedly tried to dry her tears when Adam came to see her a few minutes later.

"What's this?" he asked, coming into the room. "Tears?"

With a growing sense of expectation, Katherine watched him pull a chair closer to her bed. "Did you speak to Agatha?" she asked at last.

"Quite a surprise, eh, pet?" he replied, smiling a trifle wryly as he sat down.

Katherine nodded, not trusting herself to speak.

"It's all right, Katherine. We'll have to make some changes in our plans, but that may even work to our advantage."

Katherine blinked, her pupils dilating in disbelief. "You're not upset?" she asked, mildly astonished.

He made a wry, deprecating gesture. "I'd be lying if I said I wasn't, but let's look at the bright side. Since it's obvious

127

we won't be able to do as planned, you'll have more time to learn and perfect your craft. Ergo, you'll be better prepared when the time comes." He paused to give her a calm, confident smile. "When is the child due?"

Katherine took a moment for a quick mental calculation. There had been another flow after the one that had prompted Jonathan's explanation. "April, I think," she said a little uncertainly.

Adam concealed a small sigh. "Well then, we shall have a cozy winter at home perfecting your skills, and after allowing you some time to recover, we could be on the Continent in the fall." With a smile of encouragement, he added brightly, "It's the best time there, anyway."

"Oh, Adam!" Katherine began to weep quietly and with relief.

"Come now, pet," Adam said with affectionate irony, "There's no need for that. Besides, I hate to see a pretty woman cry."

His slightly mocking tone made Katherine smile through her tears. "How can I ever repay you?" she said in a tremulous voice.

"Before you start fitting me with a halo," he said, tipping his head slightly, "let me remind you that I've been looking for someone like you for almost two years without much success."

Refusing to be taken in by his humorous reproach, Katherine regarded him fondly. "You could have had Jenny. She wants to work with you, you know."

"Jenny?" His brows rose humorously as he eyed her with wry amusement. "I'm perfectly aware of her expectations, but as I've already told her as gently as I can, she's not the girl I need."

"But she's so pretty, Adam."

"I'm not arguing that," Adam replied, leaning back on the chair. "But just being *pretty* is not enough." After a brief pause, he went on, "Do you realize the kind of men we'll be dealing with? Rich, spoiled, jaded—" He shook his head. "No, Katherine, it takes a special kind of woman to make a man like that not only sit up and take notice, but to keep him so enthralled with her charms that he'll be unable to notice what the rest of us will be doing."

"Adam!" Katherine gave a startled gasp. "You're not saying that I shall have to—to—" she broke off, suffocating with embarrassment.

"Bed them?" he finished for her. "Not unless you want to, but my advice is that you don't. It's the lure of the chase more than the actual capture of the prize that keeps their interest."

Suddenly intimidated by the magnitude of her undertaking, Katherine looked at him in dismayed silence. At first blush, her role had seemed simple enough; now that she knew more of what it entailed, she wasn't so sure she could live up to Adam's expectations.

"There's no doubt in my mind that you'll be perfect," he said, as if able to read her doubts.

"What makes you so sure?"

"Because of a special and rare quality you have, my dear, that goes beyond beauty itself." At the quizzical expression that came to her face, he smiled a trifle wryly and shook his head. "And what makes it so charming is how unaware you are of it. We must strive to preserve the appearance even after you become aware of it, and you will."

Katherine found herself frowning slightly. "I don't understand," she had to admit, not having an inkling of what he was saying.

"I'll try to explain," he said, concealing a small, wry sigh. "There's something about you, Katherine—a certain allure, an innocent sensuality—that makes any man who sees you want to possess you." The mystified expression that came to her face made him smile. "It's true, you know. I've seen it in the faces of the men who saw you at the inn, even now that you are still — shall we say, unpolished? I can just picture how you will affect them once you've learned the fine arts of seduction."

Gradually, her brow cleared. In spite of her desolation, Katherine was fascinated by Adam's convincing argument as he spoke of his plans.

"You're tired," he said with an understanding smile when some time later she tried to hide an enormous yawn behind her hand.

She tried to protest, although her eyelids felt so heavy that she was finding it difficult to keep her eyes open.

Adam rose from the chair. "I'll leave you to rest now, and we'll continue with the lessons when you're feeling better."

He started to leave. He was almost at the door when he half-turned and looked down at her seriously. "Katherine, Agatha told me that you won't tell Jonathan about the child," he said, his voice troubled. "Don't you think he ought to know?"

As if by magic, the question dissipated the growing lassitude, the languor that had threatened to engulf her moments earlier. Now fully alert, Katherine tipped her chin slightly as she gave him a swift glance of indignation. "He wouldn't be interested," she said, her tone suddenly chilly.

His eyes were faintly brooding as he looked at her across the room. "In all fairness, I think you should let him know."

Dismissing the shade of reproach in his voice, she gazed at him defensively. "Why? He didn't care about me. What makes you believe he'd care about his bastard?" she said with a touch of asperity.

During the ensuing brief but intense silence, a contained expression came into his eyes. "As you wish, my dear," he said at last, shaking his head dolefully. "We won't mention it again."

Sitting quite still, Katherine watched him go.

She tried to sleep once she was alone, but anger and resentment mingled with her pain to keep her awake. She couldn't even rest. Then, growing impatient, she got up and began pacing the room in a restless, brooding fashion. In her mind's eye she could see Jonathan's child, with Jonathan's face, his blond hair, his blue eyes, mocking her through all of her remaining years. Suddenly, she wished she would lose the child.

"I don't want your child, Jonathan Greenfield," she repeated over and over. "I hate you, and I will hate your child. I will!'

As the weeks passed and her symptoms lessened, Katherine was better able to concentrate on her studies and on honing her newly acquired gambling skills. She was quickly becoming so proficient, that even Adam began to find it difficult to detect when she dealt from the bottom or palmed a card. Jenny taught her to pick pockets with such degree of finesse that he had to laugh with a certain amount of pride when on occasion Katherine would return to him articles she had lifted from his pockets without his notice.

In a short time her speech became as that of the most refined high-born lady, and to complete the image her work-roughened hands received a great deal of special attention. The callouses were subjected to frequent treatments with a pumice stone, and what remained of them began to disappear with constant applications of rich creams that softened and whitened the skin.

The progress she made with French and German pleased Adam greatly, who said she had a natural ability for languages and assured her that she would become quite fluent once she spent some time in France and Austria. In the meantime, she was made to spend many hours reading only those languages. To improve her conversational skills Adam forced her to use them at all times except when Agatha and Jenny took part in their conversations. In the beginning, Katherine was terribly self-conscious of the mistakes she made; but Adam corrected her patiently, and little by little, with his encouragement, she was able to converse more freely.

Her natural beauty was an advantage not to be minimized, but as Adam had warned, she would need much more than a pretty face to attract the attention of men of sophistication and jaded tastes. Adam was surprised to discover that, in spite of her humble origins, Katherine seemed to possess a natural sense for elegance and beauty. Since clothes played a very important part in her new role of seductress, she now learned the use of color, style and texture to enhance her own sensual appeal.

She was carefully drilled in the subtle arts of flirtation and seduction: a certain smile, an inviting glance, the way she moved, the tone of her voice; a myriad of fascinating details that were rehearsed over and over until they became a second nature without her having to make a conscious effort. And she learned them all, knowing that those were the weapons she would one day use against Jonathan. After all, he was only a man!

Six

The breeze coming in from the sea was cool when Katherine left the cottage in the early evening. Now in her fourth month of pregnancy, she felt a little restless and in need of exercise after having spent the day indoors. Adam had gone to London as he did on occasion, and although she still had Agatha and Jenny, she missed the stimulation of his company.

During the time she had spent in Cornwall, Katherine had discovered that Adam's love for acting was satisfied by the different roles he played and was mildly amused by this facet of his engaging personality. His enthusiasm, however, was contagious, and there had been great fun in creating new personalities for her. She had been amazed at his transformation from Professor Stuyvesant, but as she had grown to know him, she had learned that his imagination knew no boundaries. He was a chameleon; he could adopt personalities whose presence was not even felt and others that would dazzle. His range was unlimited. And with care and patience, he had instructed her in the art he had mastered; a change in the shape of her nose, the arc of her brows, a different hairstyle, and she could barely recognize her own image.

His collection of costumes, wigs, and other accoutrements was quite imposing. After his occasional trips to London, he usually came back with costumes and wigs for her that she was delighted to try on. The wigs looked perfectly natural and fitted her comfortably. Since her experience with the first one she had worn had made them realize that her waist-long hair was much too bulky under the wigs, they had trimmed some eighteen inches that Adam had saved and taken with him on this last trip to have hairpieces fashioned from it.

As she walked across the little meadow, out on the corner of her eye Katherine caught sight of a vixen carefully loping her way across the field toward the cliff. As though sensing the presence of the predator, a band of long-tailed tits took off from the ground and flitted away toward the blackthorn of the bluff.

It was at that precise moment that she became aware of a little stirring inside her—something akin to the fluttering of bird's wings—that made her stomach contract a little. With a look of mild astonishment on her face, Katherine stopped abruptly.

Once the early symptoms of her pregnancy had eased, she had sought refuge in her activities refusing to even think of the life growing within her body. At those times when she did, she was unable to find fondness for the intruder in her womb and referred to it as *Jonathan's child*. Until then it was a symbol, a constant reminder of Jonathan's deception and betrayal. Now, however, standing transfixed in the quiet meadow, without stopping to analyze her impulse Katherine slowly ran her hands over her swollen belly. Another little stirring followed the first, as though the child could feel the mother's touch and responded to it in his own fashion. For some reason she couldn't fathom at the moment, she found herself smiling and wishing she could see the tiny babe's face. Suddenly she knew with almost certainty that it was a male child, and that in spite of how much she had vowed to hate him, his presence would be a solace to her wounded soul.

"Jason," she whispered, her conscious mind responding to the overwhelming wave of tenderness that surging from deep within her began to spread until it pervaded every fiber of her being.

Mentally, she reviled herself for having wished the loss of the babe. No, he was not an intruder, but a child conceived in love; on her part if not Jonathan's. Unconsciously, she began to walk, slowly at first, then a little faster as she was filled with a sense of well being for having come to terms at last with the fruit of her love.

The sea, the sky, nothing but space and silence were all around her. Especially pleased by the moment of privacy, she stood at the cliff's edge watching the gulls floating into the sky from the rocks until she was distracted by a small fishing craft returning to port, foam trailing behind it as it slid through the waters.

How many times the sight of a sailboat, the sound of laughter and song—so many other little things—had brought back the pain she was trying to hard to forget! Even after all this time, the memories had failed to grow dimmer. Often during the night, while listening to Jenny's gentle snores, she still yearned for the contact of Jonathan's body and longed for the tenderness and the passion she had known in his arms. She had to remind herself time and again that although she had given him all the love she had to give, she had been no more than a plaything to him, a possession, a receptacle for his lust. She had vowed to never make that same mistake again. Not ever.

"Katherine!"

Swiftly she turned, and her face lit up in welcome at the sight of Adam's approach.

"Adam!" she cried, rushing to him and throwing her arms

135

around him with considerable eagerness when they met. "I'm so glad you're back!"

Adam returned the embrace. Then, when he took one step back and held her away from him to look at her, she was suddenly filled with an unaccountable desire that he would kiss her.

"Agatha told me you had gone out for a walk along the cliff," he said, gazing at her a little startled. "Are you all right?"

The sense of guilt over her sudden desires made a blush rise to her cheeks. Dropping her gaze, she murmured faintly. "Yes, of course."

Still without releasing her, Adam continued to look at her a little perplexed. "You seem — different, pet," he said at last in a puzzled tone.

Unable to restrain her mind from reverting to her earlier thought, Katherine attempted to disguise her uneasiness with a smile. "The child moved today for the first time," she said with an almost imperceptible shrug.

Adam looked pleased, and wrapping an affectionate arm around her shoulders started walking toward the cliff with her. Standing on the edge, for a few moments they stood looking down at the sea in pensive silence.

"You do want that child, don't you, pet?" he asked quietly then.

"Yes, I do," she admitted in a low voice.

After a few seconds of silence had elapsed, he suddenly asked, "Have you thought of what you'll tell him when one day he asks about his father?"

With a sharp intake of breath, abruptly, almost violently, she pulled away and swung around to face him. A terrible expression came to her face as she stood there clenching her hands into impotent fists of rage.

Adam held up his hand to forestall the explosion of her anger. "Listen to me, pet," he said in a calm and reasonable tone. "Please believe that I'm not trying to be unnecessarily cruel, but what you're doing is wrong. You're not only denying a man the right to know his child—"

"Jonathan has no right!" she broke in, staring at him reproachfully before angrily turning away.

Wrinkling his forehead, Adam shook his head in disappointment. Then he went to stand behind her and put his hands on her shoulders. "Two wrongs don't make a right, Katherine," he said in the same soft, reasonable tone of voice. "Regardless of what he may have done, a man has the right to know that he has created life."

"No!" she shook her head emphatically.

Realizing that there was no reasoning with her in such a state, he gave up trying. "Very well, Katherine," he said, expelling a wistful little sigh. "I only hope—" Shaking his head again, he broke off.

He started to walk away.

"Adam," Katherine called after him with a certain amount of hesitation.

He paused and turned to look at her with an attentive air. What a beautiful, warm and vivid creature she was, he thought, watching her in silence as she slowly came to him, her hair flowing in the breeze.

"Please don't be angry with me," she said haltingly, looking up at him with pleading eyes. "I—I couldn't bear it."

Staring at her for a few seconds he seemed to wonder. Then the hint of a smile appeared at the corners of his eyes as he said in a curiously reflective voice, "I could never be angry with you, pet."

Her expression relaxed and she tried to smile. The result was only half-hinted. She slipped her arm through his and together they started back toward the cottage. After a few minutes, she digressed in a conversational tone, "You came back earlier than I had expected. Is everything all right?"

"Daniel and Ronald are getting a little restless, but otherwise everything is fine."

She remembered Daniel, but the other name was new to her. "Ronald?" she inquired with curiosity.

Adam explained that although they would be the principal characters during their journeys, there were other minor, but no less important members in their cast. Daniel Sutherland, the self-effacing little man she had briefly met in London, was, in addition to his other talents, a highly skilled jeweler. Since on occasion Adam favored replacing a stolen jewel with a paste duplicate, Daniel's expertise was extremely valuable.

There were also Angelique and Lazarus Brissard, a married couple who would pose as their servants and care for their costumes. At one time they had been members of the *Comedie Francaise;* he a retired actor now, she a former wardrobe mistress. And, lastly, Ronald Lambert, a painter who had never been able to gain recognition for his own creations but who could produce remarkable copies of the masters. Even experts were hard pressed to distinguish between the originals and Ronald's reproductions, especially when it came to his Rembrandts and Vermeers. Another one of his useful qualities was his great physical strength.

And that was the entire cast, except for those who stored and fenced the stolen items. These were a number of people — mostly respectable merchants — in different countries who had proven most reliable and trustworthy.

Katherine also learned that aside from obtaining the costumes they needed, Adam's trips to London were intended to gather intelligence on their future adventures. Using the names of people of importance who had connections on the Continent, he forged letters of introduction that would give them access to the most restricted circles as well as letters of credit to provide them with ample funds for their operations. When after some hesitation Katherine expressed her scruples about these actions, Adam listened to her objections and then presented his arguments.

"I understand, pet," he said. "But you must remember that we'll be dealing with people who use their wealth and power for their own pleasure without regard to others who are less fortunate. What we do is take advantage of their greed, their lust, for our own purposes."

"I don't know, Adam," she countered thoughtfully. "It still doesn't seem right."

"Right?" he repeated, arching a mocking brow. "And tell me, Katherine, what is right?" After a brief, but definite pause, he added with frustrated anger, "Was it *right* for Jenny to be forced to sell herself on the streets at the age of ten to pay for the drunkenness of her parents? Or, for that matter, that your aunt sold you to Langford? Is it *right* for young children to slave their lives away in sweatshops for starvation wages? Is it *right* that the law turns a blind eye to the Langfords of this world who purchase other human beings to satisfy their dastardly pleasures? Young children, Katherine, are being bought and sold every day for men like him to use and abuse—even mutilate. What is *right*, Katherine?" Breathing heavily, he paused in his impassioned speech at her expression of horror and gathered himself for a moment. When he continued, he did so at a normal conversational level. "What we take is just a drop in a bucket for those people. The only damage is to their pride, and God knows they can use it!"

Weeks passed; winter came, and while the elements roared and screamed outside tearing at the old granite walls, the atmosphere inside the cottage was safe and cozy and warm. Katherine's relationship with Adam and the others had become very close during this time. Clumsy and heavy with child, as Jenny had predicted, she had a new family to

139

celebrate her birthday by the end of February. She was eighteen.

The first labor pains started in the small hours of the morning in the middle of March. Since the child was not expected for a few more weeks, Katherine tried to ignore what she thought to be cramps. The discomfort, however, became pain that continued to increase not only in intensity, but also in frequency. By the time she decided to call Jenny, who was sleeping quite soundly next to her, Katherine's brow was beaded with perspiration.

"Jenny!" she called. When Jenny went on sleeping, she sat up and began shaking the other girl by the shoulder. "Jenny, wake up!"

At long last, Jenny began to stir, "Mmm, what?" she mumbled sleepily. She looked at her bed companion for a moment, and had started to turn away to go back to sleep when the pain of another contraction made Katherine whimper. "The child!" cried Jenny, sitting up with a start.

Still a little disoriented, she regarded her friend as though now knowing what to do. Then, apparently having gathered her wits about her, she bolted from the bed crying, "I'll fetch Agatha!" Without pausing to put on her robe and slippers, she ran from the room.

Panting a little under the strain, Katherine lay back on the pillow. "Oh, God, Jonathan!" she murmured, wishing with all her heart that he could be there with her to hold her hand and to tell her that he loved her and their child. Suddenly, she was very frightened. Every day, women died in childbirth. What would become of Jason if she did? Perhaps she had been wrong in not listening to Adam in telling Jonathan about their child. No, she brought herself up short. Making a deliberate effort to control her fear, she said out loud, "I will not die!"

The sound of hushed voices approaching gave her a measure of comfort. Jenny and Agatha entered the room.

"It'll be a while yet," Agatha said calmly after examining her with nerveless efficiency. "Do try to conserve your strength, my dear." Turning to Jenny, she gave instructions as to what was needed.

Although the babe was a bit early, they had been preparing for some time and now waited in readiness. Agatha and Jenny took turns at sitting with Katherine and wiped the perspiration that surfaced to her brow as contractions came closer and closer together.

"Does it always take this long?" Katherine asked between waves of pain.

The question brought an indulgent smile to Agatha's face. "It hasn't been that long, my dear," she replied gently. "It only seems that way."

Hours passed. By dawn, the agony was becoming quite unbearable. Clenching her teeth, Katherine held on to the bedpost with all her might.

"My dear, you don't have to be stoical," Agatha said when she saw Katherine biting her lips to hold back a scream of agony. "Go ahead. Scream and yell all you like."

Katherine waited for the pain to subside to say, "Agatha, if anything happens to me, will you . . ."

"Hush, child," Agatha interrupted. "Nothing is going to happen to you. You're young, strong and healthy, and I see no reason why you should be talking like this. Just be calm. The babe will come when it's ready, you'll see."

Jenny was scurrying to the kitchen when Adam came out of his room.

"Where are you going in such a hurry?" he inquired curiously. A piercing scream answered him before Jenny could. He turned visibly pale. "By George! What was that?" he inquired with dismay.

Jenny paused only to reply, "Katherine is in labor." She turned and ran to the kitchen, where Adam followed her. After having checked the fires and made sure that the water in the cauldron was boiling, she turned to him. "Would you like some breakfast?" she asked calmly.

The expression on Adam's face was one of incredulity as he shook his head. "I couldn't eat a thing."

He turned ghastly pale when another scream came from the room upstairs. Seeing how profoundly upset he was, Jenny went to the cupboard and brought out a bottle of brandy. She poured a generous amount into a glass that she offered to her benefactor. "Here, Adam, you'd better drink this."

Adam's hand was shaking when he took the glass. With a little wry smile on her face, Jenny watched as he—usually so fastidious—downed the brandy in one gulp.

More screams brought an anxious question from Adam. "Is there anything we can do?"

Jenny gave a little shrug of helplessness. "You wait here," she said starting for the door. "I'll see if Agatha needs help."

Once he was alone, Adam went to the small parlor, where he began pacing the floor with all the anxiety of an expectant father.

Usually, he never smoked in the mornings, but this one was an exception. Not knowing what to do with himself, he lit one cigar after another while straining to hear any sound that would indicate the end of Katherine's ordeal. Shortly before midday, when at last the lusty cries of the babe rang throughout the cottage, every ashtray in the parlor was filled to overflowing. He ran up the stairs.

Jenny ran into him when she came out of the bedchamber. "Oh, Adam, he's beautiful!" she smiled dreamily at him.

Adam blinked. "He?"

"Jason," Jenny nodded. "He's the most beautiful babe I've ever seen!"

With some exasperation, he demanded, "And Katherine? How is she?"

"She's well, just a little tired."

Looking quite relieved, he emitted a long sigh. "When can I see her?"

"Soon." Starting to turn away, Jenny added, "I must get back inside and help Agatha."

She disappeared through the door, and he resumed his pacing, pausing every now and then, straining to hear what was going on inside the bedchamber. A short while later, the door opened and Jenny allowed him into the room.

As he looked anxiously around the room, his face clouded slightly. Wan and pale after the ordeal of giving birth, Katherine was lying quite still with her eyes closed, as though she lacked the strength to open them. Her hair, damp with perspiration, was plastered to her brow.

"Katherine?" he called tentatively.

Slowly, her eyes opened. "Adam," she murmured faintly with a wavering smile.

Adam approached the bed with hesitation. "Hello, pet," he said with an effort to keep his uneasiness from showing in his voice. Studying her face carefully for a few seconds, he noticed that her eyes seemed a little glazed.

Wearily patting the edge of the bed in invitation, she asked almost in a whisper. "Have you seen him?"

"Not yet," he replied, taking her hand and holding it in his. With gentle humor, he added, "Agatha is now dressing him for the formal introduction. How do you feel?"

"Tired," she sighed softly.

"You're entitled," he said. In a wryly humorous tone he added, "You did all the work and *I'm* exhausted."

With a melting softness in her gaze she smiled at him and said, "Oh, Adam!" To his enormous surprise, she pressed her lips to the back of his hand. "Dear, dearest Adam!"

Face colored with embarrassment, he gave a little sigh of relief when Agatha chose that precise moment to approach them with a small bundle in her arms. "Meet Master Jason," she told them, beaming.

Awkwardly he held the babe when she placed him in his arms. Looking down with a mystified expression, all he could see of him was a red and wrinkled tiny face and the light fuzz covering his head. "He's so tiny!" he said with an undertone of bewilderment in his voice.

Agatha gave a snort of annoyance. "Tiny! He's at least eight pounds!"

Adam chuckled when the child shook a tiny fist at him, and looked up at the new mother. "He's beautiful, Katherine," he said, sounding not entirely sure.

"Let me hold him," Katherine said, trying to sit up.

Rushing to help her, Agatha plumped the pillows to support her before Adam handed over the child.

All of Katherine's weariness was dissipated by the thrill of holding her child for the very first time. Jason had fallen asleep, and continued to do so while she counted every finger, and every toe, and examined the details of the minute body. Her face was radiant with happiness as she looked up at her friends. "My son!" she said fervently, "My very own son! Isn't he beautiful?"

Agatha and Adam smiled and offered agreeing murmurs.

"You must get some rest, my dear," Agatha said a moment later.

Adam rose to his feet. "Yes, Katherine, do."

"Please, let me keep him just a little longer," Katherine pleaded when Agatha made to take the child away. With immense tenderness, she kissed her son before laying him down by her side.

Adam bent over her to kiss her brow. "Sleep now, pet," he said gently. As an afterthought, he added, "You do have a beautiful son."

Yes, Katherine said inwardly after they had gone. I do have a beautiful son, Jason Cameron. But it should be Greenfield, she thought with anguish. Suddenly, she felt like crying. Regardless of what Adam said, Jonathan did not deserve their child. Jason was hers, hers alone.

She touched a finger to the tiny hand, and immediately the small fingers closed tightly around it. A tear slid quietly down her cheek as she looked down at her son.

"Yes, darling," she murmured sadly. "You *are* mine."

As spring turned into summer, Katherine began to see the signs that her son would bear a strong resemblance to his father. His eyes were bright blue, his hair so light that it looked almost white. And holding her child to her breast, she tried not to think of Jonathan. Still, the unbidden question came to mind. What would Jonathan do if he knew of his son? She reminded herself that he had planned to turn her over to someone else without a second thought; no, she told herself, he probably wouldn't care for her son, either. By now his wife must have had presented him with a child— a legitimate child. There would be no room in his life for Jason—his bastard.

Time slipped away so quickly that summer was almost over. Treasuring each moment with her child, it was with mixed feelings that Katherine began her preparations for her first sojourn into the Continent with Adam. They had been preparing for this moment for over a year, but now that the time was at hand, the thought of leaving Jason behind filled her with desolation.

"Agatha and Jenny will take good care of him, and besides, we'll be back before you know it, pet," Adam tried to console her one September afternoon when he found her almost in tears.

"I know, Adam," Katherine replied with a musing, distant air. With eyes full of tenderness she looked down at the child in her arms and said in a wavering voice, "It's just that it's so hard to leave him."

Adam's face expressed concern. After a moment's silence,

he put his hands on her shoulders. "We'll all be counting on you, Katherine," he said very seriously. "You must concentrate on the task at hand and remember everything I've taught you."

Not trusting herself to speak, she gave an affirmative sign.

"Good," he nodded. His eyes were probing when he added, "We shall be leaving the day after tomorrow."

Katherine went ghastly pale as she raised her head to look at him. "So soon?"

At his shuttered expression, an inner sense told her that Adam's patience was beginning to run out. But he had kept more than his end of the bargain he had made with her; now the time had come for her to pay her debt. In an effort to conceal her distress, she pushed herself erect, and with that gesture that was so peculiar to her, she tipped her chin slightly when she said with dignity, "I shall be ready, Adam."

Seven

Daniel Sutherland and Ronald Lambert had already joined the Brissards by the time Katherine and Adam arrived in Vienna, and the reunion of the friends — a lively group of people who immediately strove to make Katherine welcome in their midst — was a gay event for them.

She took an immediate liking to the Brissards. Angelique was a handsome woman. Although well into her forties, her hair was still as black as a raven's wing, and she had the darkest eyes Katherine had ever seen. Her husband, Lazarus, was a distinguished-looking man whose brown hair had turned silver at the temples. Of medium height and build, his figure was slim and youthful; he was charming, witty, and quite devoted to his wife of many years.

On the surface Daniel Sutherland seemed such an insignificant little man, that in the beginning Katherine had a little trouble remembering what he looked like. It didn't take her long to discover, however, that beneath such plain exterior lived a warm and intelligent human being.

Although Adam had already mentioned Ronald Lambert's physical strength, Katherine was quite startled by his appearance. Somewhere in his thirties, he had tawny eyes and a mane of unruly light brown hair that reminded her of the lions she had seen illustrated in one of her father's books. His body was so muscular that it strained against the seams of his clothes until he seemed about to burst out of them. More than the artist he was, Ronald resembled an athlete, but this rough appearance concealed a rather shy and gentle disposition, as well as a delightful sense of humor.

Katherine could tell that after such a long period of idleness, everyone was anxious to embark on new adventures.

In preparation for their arrival a house had already been secured for their use, as well as a separate flat to store the accoutrements of their profession. As Adam had already explained to her, this was part of their usual procedure; a house afforded far more privacy for their doings than a hotel, and the second location — or what they called a safe house — served another purpose in addition to storing a portion of their luggage: a place they could use as a hideout in the event they had to run from the law.

In spite of her unhappy state of mind over having left her young son behind, Katherine couldn't help but fall under the spell of Vienna. She found the roses in the Volksgarten were still in bloom, and that music filled the air with light and teasing tunes in a city where baroque buildings were painted in yellows and ochres, green, soft pink and white. Even the stern censorship imposed by Prince Metternich's secret police had failed to dampen the fun-loving people crowding the streets and coffee houses of the irrepressible, importunate capital.

With the aid of a special makeup Adam had created for her, Katherine's debut in her new profession was to impersonate a mysterious beauty whose olive complexion and raven black tresses contrasted quite vividly with her emerald eyes. To her annoyance, however, she discovered that not only did it take a long time to apply the coloring with silk sponges, but that coming home after a night of dancing and

148

gambling she had to soak in a tub of soapy water in order to remove it from her skin. But she was dazzling, and soon after their arrival they were besieged with invitations to parties and balls that lasted until dawn.

Before long, Katherine found herself surrounded by a crowd of gay young blades vying for her attention, but it was Baron Heinrich von Traub whom they selected as their mark. He was handsome, charming—and very, very rich. His main attraction, however, consisted of a celebrated collection of jewels that had been in his aristocratic family for generations.

At Adam's suggestion—and properly chaperoned by Angelique as corresponded to a lady of her class—Katherine allowed the Baron to squire her around the city and graciously accepted the valuable gifts he showered upon her as tokens of his affection. Such assiduous attention from the confirmed bachelor toward the beautiful young foreigner couldn't escape attention for long; soon, their budding romance became a favorite topic of gossip in the fashionable drawing rooms of Vienna.

Waltz madness was running rampant through all of Europe, but in the Austrian capital it had become a way of life. People gathered every night at the numerous sumptuous ballrooms like the Sperl, where they swirled until dawn to the music of Johann Strauss and his orchestra of more than two hundred musicians. At the von Traub palace a special room had been designed for the sole purpose of the dance; mirrors on the walls reflected the dancers into infinity while intricate, airy chandeliers hung dizzily from the ceiling to lend a romantic glow to the sparkle of jewels and satin whirling below.

For Katherine, this particular evening had a strange feeling of unreality. As in a dream, she followed the baron without conscious effort, but was troubled by the vibrant message in his eyes and in the pressure of his hand holding

149

hers. She could sense in his manner that Heinrich von Traub was about to take a step forward in their relationship—which until then she had adroitly managed to maintain at a platonic level. A little frightened, she told herself that the aristocrat she was impersonating would be treated very differently from the tavern wench she had once been; ladies were seduced while wenches simply used.

At the end of the dance, when Heinrich led her out on the terrace and put his arms around her, Katherine had to remind herself once more that she had to avoid his advances without discouraging him entirely. Her first reaction when she saw his intention was to reject him, but keeping in mind the purpose of her mission, she allowed the kiss. To her surprise, she found it rather pleasant.

"My darling," he whispered huskily, tightening his arms around her. Again he tried to kiss her, but she turned her head a little and his lips only grazed her cheek. *"Liebling,"* he murmured, leaning forward to trace kisses along the curve of her bare shoulder.

"Heinrich, please," she said, fear gnawing at her breast. "Let's go back inside."

He felt her trembling and loosened his hold on her. "Why are you so afraid, *Liebling?*" he asked softly. "You must know how I feel about you."

She didn't have to feign the quiver in her voice when she replied, "It's too soon, Heinrich. Everything is happening so quickly that I can't think clearly."

"What is there to think?" he asked with a soft laugh. He started to reach for her again, but at that moment a group of people came out on the terrace and their conversation and laughter served to quell his ardor—at least momentarily. To Katherine's great relief, he offered no protest when she asked again that they go back to the ballroom.

Meanwhile, Adam had been careful to change dancing partners often throughout the evening; therefore, when he finally slipped away, he did so unnoticed by any particular damsel. He had wandered through the sumptuous palace appraising the paintings and sculptures that abounded mostly in the lower levels. He found it difficult to decide which items—in addition to the jewels—he wanted to take when there was so much to choose from.

But why choose, he asked himself then. Why not take all? Until that moment they had never attempted such an ambitious robbery, but with careful planning there was no reason why it could not be accomplished. The servants' quarters were a good distance away; if only they could keep the baron occupied elsewhere, they could slip into the palace and walk away not only with the jewels, but with *objets d'art* as well.

The celebrated von Traub jewels were very much in Adam's mind as he continued his investigation. In the deserted study he searched for the strong box where he expected to find them. Obviously not much imagination had been used to conceal it, for he found it almost immediately, imbedded into the wall and concealed behind a large painting in a massive gilt frame. His quick, but methodic search of the mahogany desk was fruitless; as it was to be expected, the key was kept somewhere else.

Satisfied with his findings, Adam returned to the ballroom before his absence could be noticed. Once there, he scanned the dancers without finding a trace of either Katherine or the baron. Imagining they must have stepped outside for some fresh air, he directed his steps to the terrace. At that moment, however, the couple was returning to the ballroom and he immediately noticed that Katherine seemed a little unsettled. The baron must be getting overly romantic, he told himself wryly, deciding to go to her rescue.

"Ah, there you are, my dear," he said cheerfully as he went to meet them. To Heinrich, he asked with good humor,

151

"You don't mind if I take a turn around the floor with my sister, do you, old chap?"

"Of course not," Heinrich replied with a polite, but stiff little bow of his head.

Katherine rewarded Adam with a smile of relief as she accepted his arm, and Heinrich's eyes followed them as they joined the dancers.

"The strongbox is in the study just as I thought," Adam told her while they moved with the music. "We must assume that the key is kept hidden somewhere in this house, perhaps in his room, or that our friend carries it on his person. Let's work on the last assumption for now. Has he said anything to you about the jewels?"

"Nothing at all," she replied. Unable to keep her apprehension from her voice, she added, "Adam, I don't know if I can keep up the pretense. I'm so frightened!"

Adam regarded her intently. "Now listen to me," he said, "The only way to succeed in this business is by keeping our heads. So far, you're doing just fine."

Looking at him almost fearfully she murmured in a dismayed tone, "I don't want to hurt him, Adam. He's been so nice to me—to both of us."

A spark of anger flashed through Adam's eyes. "For heaven's sakes, Katherine, don't be such a fool!" he said sharply. In a gentler tone he added, "Look, pet, I know this is difficult for you, being your first time, but trust me. I know his reputation. Behind that charming facade, Heinrich is a womanizer as ruthless as Charles Langford." The change in her expression was so immediate, that he mentally congratulated himself for his choice of words to prod her into action.

"Now, listen, pet," he went on in a reasonable voice. "We've got to find out where he keeps the key to the strongbox. I've been watching Heinrich, and it seems to me that he's about to make his move." He paused briefly, as though expecting a comment from her. The tinge of color that rose to her cheeks as she looked away with embarrassment was an eloquent enough answer. "Don't be afraid of him," he told her in a persuasive tone, stressing his words with a slight increase in the pressure of his hand. "Remember I'm here to protect you."

The warmth in his voice made Katherine revert her eyes to his face, and his affectionate gaze served to restore her confidence. "I know," she said, offering an apologetic little smile.

She wished that he would hold her closer but, instead, a cold gleam came to his eyes as he said thoughtfully, "I know the jewels are here. I can feel it." Refocusing his eyes on her, he went on to say, "I also have a feeling that Heinrich might try to impress you with them tonight, Katherine. Admire them if he does, but don't act too eager."

At the end of the waltz, they were immediately joined by the baron again.

"What a beautiful ballroom this is," Katherine commented pleasantly. "Even more so than those lovely rooms we passed on the way."

"Would you like to see the rest of the palace?" the baron asked immediately, anxious to be alone with her. Although the question had been addressed to both of them, the invitation was implied for Katherine alone.

"That would be lovely, my dear Heinrich," she replied with a seductive smile. "But what of your guests?"

"They won't even notice that we're missing," Heinrich shrugged, and taking her hand added, "Besides, there's something I would like to show you."

Katherine turned to look at Adam, who nodded benignly, "Go ahead, my dear. A very enchanting lady promised me the next waltz."

"Very well, then," she smiled at the baron, who tried not to look as pleased as he felt that Adam had declined the invitation.

That Heinrich took enormous pride in his possessions was evident to Katherine, who acted duly impressed as he showed her the many artistic treasures he had accumulated. The tour ended in the study, where the baron reached into his pocket to bring out a key.

"And now, *Liebling,* I will show you something that no visitor ordinarily ever gets to see."

He pushed aside the large painting to reveal the strongbox behind it, and after unlocking the door, he pulled a tray lined in black velvet. Katherine had to bite her lower lip to suppress a gasp of astonishment. There, against the dark cloth, was the sparkle of diamonds and rubies, emeralds, sapphires, iridescent pearls, deep purple amethysts and many other precious stones in the form of rings, necklaces, earrings, pins, brooches, bracelets and pendants.

The sight of such magnificent display left Katherine speechless. Even in her wildest dreams had she ever imagined anything like this existed.

Obviously pleased by her reaction, Heinrich paused before he brought out the next object — larger and also wrapped in velvet. "And now, *la piece de resistance,*" he announced proudly.

With ceremony, he placed the object on the desk and slowly unveiled the treasure, a magnificent tiara worthy of a queen that held Katherine's gaze hypnotically. "Beautiful, are they not?" he asked, encompassing the collection with a gesture of his hand.

Forgetting Adam's instructions and feeling all tangled up inside, Katherine finally managed, "I've never seen anything so — magnificent."

Picking up an emerald brooch, the baron held it close to her face. "These match your eyes, *Liebling,*" he said in a seductive voice.

Suddenly faced with the enormity of Adam's plans, all Katherine could think of at the moment was to get away.

Still, she forced herself to remain when the baron began showing her the individual pieces. A cabochon ruby on a platinum chain in itself was worth a king's ransom.

"Which one is your favorite, my darling?" he invited. At his prompting, Katherine selected a ring with a large, translucent green jade that was surrounded by smaller diamonds. The baron came to stand close behind her, and placing his hands on her bare shoulders whispered in her ear, "One word from you is all I need to put all this at your feet." His lips touched the curve of her shoulder as his arms went around her waist. "Say you'll be mine, *Liebling*."

Although Katherine's hand was somewhat tremulous when she returned the ring to the tray, she was in complete control of her role when she sighed, "Not yet, Heinrich." Turning around to face him, she looked up into his eyes. "Please give me a little more time."

Hearing the veiled promise in her voice, Heinrich von Traub gave her a confident smile. "Very well, *Liebling*. We'll get to know each other better, and then you'll say yes." Caressing her bare shoulder with one hand, he used the other to tilt her head back and gazed deeply into her eyes. "I won't accept any other answer," he murmured huskily as his head came down.

This time, when his lips covered hers, Katherine had to make a supreme effort not to push him away. Still, she did not allow him more than a chaste kiss, moving away before it could become more intimate.

The baron released her with a sigh and began to return the jewels to the strongbox.

"Shouldn't you keep them in a safer place?" she inquired casually as she watched him.

He locked the box and slipped the key back into his pocket. "They are perfectly safe there, *Liebling*. Anyone who tries to steal them, will find a big surprise."

Her brows rose quizzically. "What do you mean?"

"It's a secret," he replied, giving her an oblique half smile.

The glance she bestowed on him then was playful and co-
quettish. "Really, Heinrich, you can't tell a woman you have
a secret such as that, and not expect her to ask what it is."

He smiled only with his lips. "Perhaps one day I will tell
you."

"That's not fair!" she pouted prettily. "You're only teasing
me, Heinrich. I won't breathe a word, I promise."

When he still refused to tell her, she thought it prudent
not to insist. Her voice grew husky and full of promise when
she said, "As you wish. But one day, you will."

He started to reach for her. "Ah, *Liebling,* you're driving
me wild!"

She evaded him when he tried to capture her by the waist,
and laughing and teasing him with her eyes she let him catch
her at the door, where she allowed him another brief kiss
before returning to the ballroom.

The ball lasted until dawn, and before leaving the party
Adam accepted the baron's invitation to spend a few days at
his country estate.

Daniel was left behind to conduct the investigation
prompted by Katherine's report when three days later they
found themselves riding through the Wienerwald en route to
the baron's estate. There, the huge peaks of the Alps diminished into cozy hillocks that spread in the shape of a cres-
cent east of the city. Once the carriage had breasted that last
slope, the passengers alighted to stretch their legs and admire the sweeping panorama far below.

The sun was shining, yet there was a hint of frost in the
pine-scented air. The city was enveloped in a soft haze that
made it appear like a vision in a dream; beyond it, the
Danube was like a gleaming silver ribbon.

The scenery filled Katherine with a kind of exhilaration
that momentarily made her forget her fears. Pushing aside
the feelings of guilt that had plagued her until then, she told

herself that Adam trusted her to carry on with her role, and she would do so to the best of her ability. She owed it not only to him and the others, but to herself as well.

And so she played her role to the hilt. While the baron dedicated all his attention to her during the following days, Adam was free to accumulate the information on the workings of the estate that he needed as part of the plan he was formulating.

Although to her the baron continued to be the same charming, devoted admirer, during those days Katherine had ample opportunity to familiarize herself with his true nature. To begin with, Heinrich was kinder to his animals than to his people. He was self-centered and petty; he became so petulant when his orders were not instantly obeyed, that his servants were in such awe of him they almost ran to do his bidding. She was greatly upset—but managed to conceal her feelings—when in her presence he soundly slapped a servant over a trifle. His attitude in general toward those who worked on his lands was one of contempt—the same contempt he would have for her if he knew her true identity. Adam was right she reflected; Heinrich was no better than Langford.

She was impressed, however, by the knowledge of herpetology he displayed when one day during their ride her horse was startled by a snake he identified as an adder. But since this did not serve to improve her opinion of him, she was immensely relieved when the time came to return to Vienna.

Daniel's investigation had failed to provide any new clues to the riddle, except that in order to enter the palace at night they would have to find a way of avoiding the dogs guarding the grounds.

"It can't be just the dogs," Adam reflected, trying to bring to mind something he had seen in the study that had barely caught his attention at the time he had been searching for the strongbox. If only he could remember . . . Perhaps if he returned to the study he could find it again, he suggested, and it was left up to Katherine to arrange the visit.

The invitation was not difficult for her to obtain, but even after another careful examination of the room Adam was no closer to the answer than he had been before.

Keeping Heinrich at arm's length while Adam figured out the solution to the puzzle was beginning to wear Katherine's nerves to a frazzle. "I feel just as skittish as the horse was that day when the snake popped out of the ground," she was telling Angelique one evening after they had returned from the opera.

On his way to his room, Adam stopped short when he heard her comments. Whirling about, he asked suddenly, "What did you say?"

She turned toward him. "That Heinrich is . . ."

"No," he shook his head emphatically, seizing her by the shoulders. "Something about a horse."

"A horse?" Puzzled by his intensity, for a moment Katherine stared at him in astonishment. "Oh," she said then, "that one day when I went riding with Heinrich, a snake popped out of the ground and frightened the horse."

Uttering a sigh that was almost a groan, Adam smote his forehead and exclaimed, "That's it!"

Much to her bewilderment, he turned away and rushed down the stairs.

Angelique and Katherine exchanged a puzzled glance and then, unable to contain their curiosity, decided in unison to follow him. Pausing at the door of his study, they found Adam rifling through a sheaf of papers.

"What is it, Adam?" Katherine inquired. "What did you find?"

"Aha!" he cried triumphantly, pulling a slip of paper from the rest. Shaking it in his hand, he looked at them with undisguised satisfaction and said, "Heinrich collects snakes. Poisonous snakes, mostly cobras."

Katherine and Angelique looked at each other as if he had lost his mind. Suddenly, Katherine began to follow his reasoning. "You don't think he keeps a poisonous snake *inside* the box, do you?"

"What else could it be?"

"But he opened it in front of me, and there was nothing but the jewels inside," she argued.

"Of course," Adam nodded. "He had planned on showing you his collection, so he took the snake out earlier in the evening."

Katherine remained unconvinced. "How do you know?"

Looking very pleased, Adam replied, "Because what I saw there and didn't register at the time, was a long pole that was hidden behind the drapes. It wasn't there the second time when I went into the study, but it was there the first time." He came to her and gently seized her by the shoulders. "Can't you see? Anyone who opens the box not knowing that there's a cobra inside would be bitten and die in a matter of minutes."

Katherine looked badly frightened. "It's too risky, Adam," she said, much agitated. "Forget about the jewels, please!"

"There's no danger once you know what to expect," he replied in a reassuring voice. "We can take the snake out of the box just as easily as Heinrich does himself."

"But there are still the dogs," Angelique reminded him.

Katherine seized on this to try to dissuade him. "That's right, Adam. How do you intend to go past them without being torn to pieces?"

"We'll take care of them, don't you fret," Adam assured them with a confident air.

Katherine's heart was thumping with apprehension. "You're not going to kill them, are you?"

Adam looked pained. "I told you once that I abhor violence, Katherine, even to animals," he said, in his voice a

159

veiled reproach. "No, we won't harm them."

"Then, how?" she demanded, her face tight with worry.

He gave her a mischievous smile. "We'll just provide a little diversion for them."

When he didn't clarify his intentions, Katherine inquired with acid sweetness, "Are you going to tell me, or do I have to guess?"

"My dear," Adam smiled at her tolerantly. "Heinrich seems to have more faith in animals than in humans." He gave a wry shake of his head. "And in a way, he may be right, since animals are not susceptible to bribery. However, there are other things . . ."

"Such as?"

His blue eyes twinkled merrily. "The basic instincts good old Mother Nature provided."

A couple of days later their visit to the baron's palace was interrupted by the delivery of an urgent message from the manager of his country estate requesting his immediate presence. The baron disliked the idea of leaving Vienna, but when Katherine expressed her desire for a return visit, he encouraged her to meet him there the next day.

While kissing him goodbye, Katherine lifted the key from Heinrich's pocket and deftly passed it on to Adam, who left them alone for a moment under the pretense of granting them privacy for their farewell. It took him only a few seconds to make a clear imprint of the key on a piece of softened wax while Katherine delayed the baron. Once he had the print, Adam returned the key to her, and after one last goodbye kiss the key was safely back in Heinrich's pocket.

In the wee hours of the morning, four men dressed in dark clothes emerged from a carriage that was stationed outside the iron fence surrounding the baron's palace. Alert to the intruders, the guard dogs appeared immediately bar-ing their fangs. However, they were soon distracted by the scent of the bitches in season the men had brought with them. The men unlocked the gates, and after releasing the bitches quietly congratulated each other at the sight of the fierce guard dogs running down the quiet street in hot pursuit of their prospective mates.

Protected by darkness the thieves crossed the grounds and forced their way into the palace through a window; once inside, they made short work of removing the canvases from their frames.

While Ronald and Daniel took care of the paintings and sculptures, Adam and Lazarus ventured into the study armed with a long pole and two bags. The key produced by Daniel was a perfect fit, and Adam had no difficulty in unlocking the safe. Holding the pole firmly in one hand, he cast a warning glance at Lazarus, who held the bag at ready, and they quickly stepped back to avoid the cobra that shot out of the safe as soon as the door was opened. With the aid of the pole Adam captured the elusive reptile before it could slip away, and once the cobra was safely inside the bag, he prudently explored the inside of the box with the end of the pole before reaching into it for the jewels.

The sacking of the baron's palace was accomplished in less than an hour, and that very same morning the thieves were on their way out of Austria under different disguises.

Katherine was anxious to be with Jason again, but when Adam proposed a brief visit to Natalie van Doorn and her husband, her curiosity to meet the woman she had replaced in Adam's organization was too strong to resist.

At their arrival in Amsterdam, they were warmly welcomed by the most striking woman Katherine had ever seen. Tall, slender and beautiful was Natalie, whose blue-black hair vividly contrasted with her porcelain complexion and deep blue, almost violet eyes. Her lovely face reflected her contentment with her new life. Her husband, Bernard, was a handsome man with light blond hair and clear blue eyes who appeared totally captivated by his charming wife.

It was not until late that evening, when after supper the men were involved in a chess game, that the women had a chance to exchange confidences. It was Natalie who opened the conversation.

"I'm so glad Adam found you, Katherine," she began. "I've been terribly worried about him since Bernard and I were married."

"It was my good fortune that he did," Katherine replied without a second's hesitation. "He came to my aid when I had no one else to turn to."

"He's wonderful, isn't he?" Natalie commented.

The affection in Natalie's voice sparked a twinge of jealousy within Katherine's breast. "Yes, he is," she said quietly. Telling herself then that she was being rather foolish, she made an effort to put more cordiality in her voice when she added, "And so is Agatha. She and Jenny are caring for my son."

Natalie regarded her with surprise. "You have a child?"

"A little boy," Katherine nodded with a smile.

During the ensuing hour, the women heard each other's stories. Like Jenny, a drunken father had forced Natalie to sell herself on the streets of London when she was still a child. She had been almost fifteen when Adam met her, and as he had done with Jenny, he had taken her to his sister in Cornwall, where they had restored her in body and soul. Afterwards, they had worked together for six years until Natalie had fallen in love with Bernard.

"I was in a terrible quandary," Natalie confessed while Katherine listened with attention that by now went beyond mere politeness. "I loved Bernard, and I believed that he returned those feelings, but there was always the fear that he would despise me if he knew of my past. Besides, I couldn't tell him the truth without betraying Adam's secret. I didn't know what to do. I was so unhappy, I just wanted to die." She remained thoughtful for a moment and then went on, "But as things turned out, it was Adam who took matters into his own hands, and we were married with his blessings. We've been so happy, Katherine," she smiled with melancholy. "Bernard is the most wonderful man in the world. If only I could give him a child . . ." Her voice faded as sorrow clouded her lovely countenance.

"And you will, Natalie," Katherine encouraged her new friend, her jealousy now forgotten. "You're both young."

"You don't understand," Natalie replied, her voice tinged with sorrow. "I've already had several miscarriages, not only after our marriage, but even before Adam found me. I pray that one day . . ."

"Oh, yes, Natalie!" Katherine said with unfeigned compassion as she reached for Natalie's hand. "I'm sure you will have Bernard's children, just wait and see."

Shaking the despondency that threatened to engulf her, Natalie began asking Katherine about her experiences in Vienna.

"You did well and Adam is very pleased," Natalie said when Katherine finished her recount. "It's dangerous work, but quite exciting once you get used to it. Adam loves it, especially now that you're working with him. He never was fond of operating alone."

"I was so frightened!" Katherine confessed with a rueful little laugh. "But I must admit that I found myself actually enjoying it, too."

Three days later, when they left Amsterdam for England, Natalie and Katherine had become close friends.

Ensuing years were fraught with the exhilaration of high

adventure, romance, riches . . . and danger. The band of thieves traveled through the European Continent leaving behind little of what they set their goals upon. Paris, Vienna, Rome, Budapest, Warsaw, Florence, Milan; these and other fabulous cities saw them often under different disguises, but always welcomed them with open arms.

Between capers, Katherine and Adam continued to visit their friends in Amsterdam before returning to Cornwall for periods of rest. More than ever, it was at those times — when Katherine saw how Jason had grown and changed during her absence — that she realized how much of his childhood she was missing and longed for the day when she could remain with her son. She had an obligation, however, and with each adventure her share in the profits brought her closer to her goal. With Adam's counsel she had invested her earnings wisely, and her wealth continued to grow at a very satisfactory rate.

Jason was a happy, healthy child. His resemblance to Jonathan grew so pronounced with the passing of time, that Katherine could barely look at him without being reminded of the man she had once loved; but even though she now hated Jonathan with every fibre of her being, it was his child who brought to her life the greatest joy.

The bond between Katherine and Adam grew stronger as the years passed. He was a constant source of admiration to her, and under his careful tutelage her natural abilities were developed to the fullest as she matured physically as well as emotionally. Her figure grew more voluptuous without losing its youthfulness; her coppery hair darkened to a rich auburn, and her emerald eyes acquired a look of veiled mystery. Fulfilling the promise of the naive young girl was a beautiful, striking woman who during those years captured many an aristocratic heart.

Adam never seemed to change; he was always the handsome, charming rogue she adored. Although in the course of their profession he came in contact with many lovely ladies, his heart was never involved. But there were times when he seemed lost in thought and a strange, wistful light appeared in his blue eyes that made Katherine wonder if there was hope for the love that she secretly carried in her heart.

She wasn't sure whether or not he returned those feelings; they never spoke of love, but she could feel its intangible presence between them. Yet she had borne the child of another man and realized that even for Adam this was a difficult barrier to surmount.

Perhaps in time — she hoped and prayed — his love for her would be strong enough to do so.

Eight

In his small and rather dusty Surete office, Inspector Maurice Furneaux read, for the umpteenth time, the report on the audacious theft that had taken place in Vouvray the year before. Once had finished, Furneaux removed his spectacles, set them down on top of his desk, and leaning back in his chair rubbed his tired eyes. In this position he remained staring at the ceiling for a few moments.

A neat and methodical man, the inspector was a thin and almost insignificant little man whose appearance had deceived many a criminal, for most of them underestimated his keen intelligence, his strong determination and unwavering perseverance. Once he took on a case, he would not rest until the criminals were safely behind bars, and that was the reason why he couldn't put this particular case aside even after all the time that had elapsed.

Having found no clues locally, he had contacted police organizations in other countries inquiring if they had received similar complaints. The answers had been slow in coming, but the last of the replies had arrived only that day.

Meditating with his eyes closed, Furneaux entwined his fingers and twirled his thumbs in slow motion as he usually did when in deep concentration. In the course of his inquiries he had learned that the number of jewelry and art thefts that had taken place in the last years was staggering. What was even more interesting, in those instances where entire collections had disappeared, the number of suspects had been always the same: a man, a beautiful young woman and their servants had been involved.

Although their nationalities and descriptions varied widely, the modus operandi was almost always identical; therefore, Inspector Furneaux was convinced that they were dealing with the same band of thieves operating at random throughout the Continent. But since each country in Europe was flooded with foreigners, he knew that it wouldn't be easy to detect the thieves, especially when they could so easily alter their descriptions.

With a small weary sigh, Furneaux replaced his wire-rimmed spectacles and carefully assembled his notes, placed them in a valise, and decided to consult his former chief and old-time friend, Eugene Francois Vidocq.

The son of a baker, Vidocq's criminal career had been interrupted when on occasion he had attempted other means of honest livelihood, sometimes as a showman, sailor, soldier, or puppetmaster. Time and time again apprehended and convicted, he became a daredevil prison breaker; but each time he was caught, and his sentence increased until finally he was put in chains.

After his last escape, back in 1799, for ten years Vidocq had lived in Paris in the disguise of an old-clothes dealer. During that time he received so many threats of exposure from former fellow convicts that one day, filled with hatred for them, he had gone to the police and offered his expertise of the criminal world in exchange for his freedom.

Desperate to contain the rising crime wave in the city, the Paris Prefect of Police had accepted Vidocq's offer. The former felon had then established offices in a gloomy building on the Petite Rue de Sainte-Anne and recruited his assistants among men who, like himself, were willing to trade their lives of crime in exchange for amnesty. In spite of the many attacks it received from many quarters, this extraordinary organization—which became known as the Surete—was able to clean out the criminal dens of Paris into which no police inspector had dared to venture before.

Things had gone well for Vidocq until 1833, when he had been forced into retirement by a new Prefect of Police who couldn't abide having an entire detective force made up of former criminals. It was then that Vidocq started his own private detective agency and also became a writer.

After reading the reports, M. Vidocq agreed with his friend:

"We're dealing with a very clever group of people," Inspector Furneaux commented. "Our informers have been unable to provide us with any clues, which leads me to believe they are not French."

Vidocq was thoughtful for a moment. "Have any of the stolen items been recovered?"

"No," the policeman shook his head. "And this in itself is most unusual. Even the paintings and *objets d'art* have disappeared without a trace."

Accentuating the wrinkles on his forehead, Vidocq looked at his friend. "And you say they have stolen entire collections?" he asked in a puzzled voice.

"In Vienna, Venice, and last year in Vouvray," the inspector nodded. "Unfortunately, all the victims have refused to publicize their losses, perhaps fearing ridicule for their own folly. It seems that they were so taken by the beauty of the young woman in question, that they invited the thieves into their homes."

"Which, of course, helps the thieves by not alerting other possible victims," Vidocq reflected wryly.

"It's so frustrating," Furneaux agreed glumly. "And since the thieves appear to have no known criminal connections, our informers are totally useless. I understand the police in Vienna and Venice came up with the same findings."

"Amazing!" Vidocq shook his head in bewilderment. A wistful note came to his voice when he added, "What I'd give to meet the brains behind this organization!" After a moment's silence, he pointed at the reports on his desk and asked, "May I keep these, Maurice? I'd like to study them in more detail. This is the most interesting case I've found in many a year."

"Of course, *mon ami,*" the policeman nodded readily. "As a matter of fact, that's why I came to you. I'd really appreciate any help you can give me in solving this mystery."

Inspector Furneaux rose from his chair, and Vidocq escorted him to the door.

Once he was alone, Vidocq poured himself a glass of Calvados and settled down to examine once more the papers his friend had given him. When he finished, he leaned back in his chair and stared thoughtfully at the ceiling. It had been some time since the theft in Vouvray, let alone the one in Vienna. He was getting on in years, and the investigation would entail a considerable amount of travel on his part—perhaps chasing a trail that was too cold to be of any use; but just the possibility of capturing the mastermind behind the capers, made Vidocq feel almost young again.

A few weeks later, Maurice Furneaux responded immediately to the note Vidocq sent him upon his return from Vienna. The former policeman took his friend into his office and showed him a board on which he had methodically listed all the details he had obtained during his travels. After a careful evaluation of the evidence, Furneaux nodded his agreement.

"I must say, they choose their victims well," Vidocq observed. "And since they strike at random, we have no idea where they'll turn up next. You know, Maurice," he went on with a pensive air, "I've been thinking. The only way to catch these thieves would be to set up a trap."

And for the next few hours, the two friends discussed the details of their plan.

Meanwhile, in London, Adam was attending a session at the Stock Exchange. His attention was drawn to the mercurial rise in the stock of *Minas de Rainha,* the Brazilian diamond mines on which both he and Katherine held a number of shares. And in the midst of the thriving activity, the seed of an idea began to germinate in his mind.

Until then, they had limited themselves to gambling and the theft of jewelry and *objets d'art.* But this perforce had established a pattern, and Adam was nagged by the danger this represented. The time had come to try something new.

Immediately he set to work on his idea, and at the end of two weeks and a considerable amount of research he was ready to present Daniel and Ronald with his new plan. His friends agreed that this would be by far the most daring exploit they had ever attempted, but the rewards and their sense of adventure made for an enthusiastic reception. After sending a letter to the Brissards to let them know that they would be in Paris in a month's time, Adam returned to Cornwall to alert Katherine to their new scheme.

Armed with actual figures on the flourishing mining operations on the other side of the world, a month later Adam and Katherine set out for Paris to meet the Brissards as had been previously arranged. Daniel had already gone ahead to prepare the ground at their final destination—the exclusive spa of Baden-Baden. Since his presence would not be required for several more weeks, Ronald remained in London awaiting word from Adam.

Angelique and Lazarus were carefully briefed on the Ferreiros—the illustrious Portuguese family living in Brazil who controlled the diamond mines—and all the information they had been able to gather regarding the Portuguese colony that for well over a century had replaced India as the main producer of the precious gems.

In due time a bearded and gray-haired Senhor Ferreiro appeared on the perfect scene of Baden-Baden to take the waters. He was accompanied by his golden-skinned, chestnut-haired daughter Gabrielle and a couple of faithful servants.

Adam's makeup made him appear pale and rather frail, while a change in the shape of her brows and the addition of an artificially turned-up nose completed Katherine's transformation.

Located on the east bank of the Rhine and halfway between Paris and Vienna, the famous spa was a gathering place for the bluebloods and the very rich of the world who went there not only for their health, but also to lose their money at the elegant casino built in imitation of Versailles.

In spite of his apparently failing health, the Brazilian mining potentate and his lovely young daughter soon became a part of the cosmopolitan society. Trying to find a suitable mark, they assiduously attended all the social functions and the casino; after meeting Count Walther von Driersch—whose considerable fortune had been greatly increased by two deceased wives—they had to look no further. Ambitious and cunning, the rotund and foppish count took an immediate interest in the heiress Katherine was playing.

Several weeks later, during one of his visits to the Ferreiros' elegant villa, Lazarus announced the arrival from Brazil of the geologist played by Ronald. Apologizing to his guest for the interruption, Senhor Ferreiro took his employee into the library and "carelessly" left the door ajar.

While Katherine found a pretext to leave the visitor alone for a few minutes, the count listened eagerly to the conversation going on in the other room. He could hear the excitement in the geologist's voice as he apprised his employer of the new diamond deposits recently discovered and of the need for additional capital to expand their exploitation.

Very calmly, Senhor Ferreiro stated that he was in favor of postponing such expansion. At the moment he did not wish to use his own capital and refused to issue new stock to the public, citing his failing health and his determination to keep control of the mines in the family. Again Ronald spoke of the enormous profits that could be expected from the promising new deposits, but Ferreiro remained unmoved by the convincing arguments. All this the count overheard while awaiting Gabrielle's return. By the time she did, he was bursting with suppressed excitement.

His mind still on the information he had just overheard, the count made very little conversation while walking in the gardens with Katherine. Full of self-importance as he was, the greedy man had no doubt that were he to ask for the girl's hand, Senhor Ferreiro would jump at the chance of such a brilliant marriage for his daughter. The alliance would not only provide him with the additional capital to expand his operations, but also to keep control of the mines in the family as well.

"My dear Count," Adam smiled, after the count had made his offer and asked for Gabrielle's hand. "I can't tell you how pleased I am. I must confess that my main concern during my illness has been my daughter's future. You have no idea how many suitors I've had to reject. My sweet Gabrielle is so naive that she doesn't realize how tempting her fortune can be to a certain kind of man." Then, playing on his victim's vanity, he sighed, "It's such a great comfort to know that she'll have someone of your maturity and position to care for her after I'm gone."

"I'm sure that won't be for many years yet," the count said reassuringly. Actually, he thought Senhor Ferreiro's appearance had deteriorated considerably since his arrival in Baden-Baden. With the old man out of the way, control of the mines would be in his own capable hands, he reflected with a surge of pleasure.

"Perhaps," Senhor Ferreiro smiled a little sadly. "But let's not talk about that now, my dear Count. This is too joyous an occasion." Following a small silence, he continued, "Now that you'll become part of our family, I shall be happy to turn over to you two hundred thousand shares on the mine at the current market price, and"—here his smile conveyed his pleasure—"I shall match that number of shares as my wedding present."

"That is most generous," the count said, a little startled.

"However, since you seem to be aware of the reason additional capital is needed, you must understand why I must ask you to pay for the shares in gold," Adam said then. "It is a considerable sum. Are you sure you can manage it?"

"Of course, Senhor Ferreiro," the count replied, "but it may take a little while."

"I don't have to tell you how important it is that this transaction be kept in the strictest of confidence," Adam went on. "I've always insisted in maintaining control over the mines and issued to the public only a small number of shares for corporate reasons, but until you and my daughter are married, not a word of this must be known." Until then, everything had seemed to be going in the count's favor. Now came the time to put a little impediment in his way so that he wouldn't become too suspicious of the ease with which he had won the hand of such an important heiress. Besides, it would take some time for the count to gather the gold, and they had to give him something else to distract him while he went about it. "Have you and my Gabrielle agreed on a wedding date?" Adam asked blandly.

The count looked startled. "Why, no," he stammered. "I haven't spoken to her yet."

"But, my dear Count, I had assumed that Gabrielle had accepted you already." Senhor Ferreiro looked quite concerned. "She's my only daughter and her happiness is what worries me the most," he said with an apologetic half smile. "I'm afraid that unless she agrees—" Giving a helpless shrug, he let his words trail.

The count gave him a look of astonishment.

"Gabrielle is a sweet girl and seems to be fond of you," Senhor Ferreiro said then in a voice full of kindness. "I'm sure she'll be pleased to know of your feelings for her. Just give her a little time to get to know you better." With a reassuring pat on the count's shoulder, he finished, "You have my permission to pay her court."

Once recovered from his initial astonishment, von Dreirsch was quite annoyed by this unexpected turn of events. Now, in addition to the gold, he also had to secure the silly girl's acceptance.

However, although he thought Ferreiro a fool because he would not immediately agree to the marriage, the girl seemed so pleased to see him again that the count was encouraged by her reception.

Determined to win her affections, during the time it took him to gather the gold Count von Drierch paid devoted court to the young heiress, lavishing on her flowers and expensive gifts that were accepted with charmingly demure grace.

To end the Oktoberfest celebrations, Franz Liszt was to appear in concert. Katherine had been filled with considerable anticipation, but nothing she had heard about the genius of the turbulent artist had prepared her for the actual experience. After watching the performance, and with the sound of the last chord still reverberating in the theater, she joined with the rest of the audience in a thunderous ovation and excited shouts of *"Bravo!"*

Later that evening she had occasion to meet the artist at

the party held in the grand ballroom of the hotel.

Tall and thin, Liszt had longish blond hair, magnetic green eyes, and a full, sensual mouth. He was immediately surrounded by admirers, particularly women attracted not only to his good looks and notoriety as a romantic figure, but also encouraged by the conspicuous absence of Marie d'Agoult, his mistress of many years.

Once introduced to the Brazilian beauty, the artist sought her company — much to the chagrin of the count, who had to sulk at Adam's side while at the other end of the salon Katherine and Liszt enjoyed what seemed an animated *tete a tete*.

"I must confess that watching your performance tonight was the fulfillment of a dream, M. Liszt," Katherine said, ignoring the scowling count across the room. "But the waiting was well worth it. It was magnificent!"

"I am flattered, Senhorita," Liszt smiled. "I had no idea my name was known in your country."

"Certainly your fame has reached us there," Katherine assured him, at the moment not caring whether that was true or not. "I, for one, have followed your career with great interest, which now that we've met will have new meaning."

A provocative gleam came to his eyes as he gazed at her, "Do you really mean that, Senhorita?"

Realizing that she had let herself be carried away by her excitement, Katherine felt her face suffuse with color.

"You're one of the loveliest women I've ever met," Liszt said in a caressing voice. In spite of her embarrassment, Katherine couldn't avert her eyes from his magnetic gaze. "I'd like to make love to you."

She gave an incredulous gasp. Then, recovering from her surprise, she smiled and retorted saucily, "M. Liszt, the newspapers have reported on more than your outstanding artistic talents, but even so I didn't expect such an offer from you so soon."

175

Liszt was amused. "Don't believe everything you read in the newspapers," he said with a sardonic smile. "I can assure you I'm not guilty of half the deeds attributed to me."

She gave him a humorous sidelong glance. "The price of fame?"

"You could say that," he chuckled in response. Wryly he added, "I suppose I've never been forgiven for some of my relationships."

There had been such an immediate rapport between them that she didn't hesitate to ask, "Are you referring to Countess d'Agoult?"

He looked wry. "I see you're indeed well informed." Following a brief but definite pause, he added, "Contrary to what you may have heard, I'm not a destroyer of homes or a master of seduction, senhorita. Marie had been unhappy in her marriage long before I entered the picture, and she had the right to find happiness. I never make promises I don't intend to keep. Marie knows this and doesn't expect me to remain faithful when we're apart."

"How very convenient," she chided him.

"It is," he replied, unperturbed by her mild reproach. "Of course, Marie enjoys the same freedom. It's only fair, don't you think?"

Katherine regarded him seriously. "You surprise me, M. Liszt. You're expressing ideas I never expected to hear from a man."

"I'm well aware of that," he nodded. "But why shouldn't a woman enjoy the same freedom as a man?"

"Because society not only condones, but even praises a man for the same deeds it condemns in a woman," she reminded him.

"Rubbish!" he gestured emphatically with his hands of long and sensitive fingers. "Women are made for love, and society is trying very hard to convince them that physical love is something to be endured, that only a man can enjoy its pleasures." His voice acquired an attractive huskiness when he added, "But we know better, don't we senhorita?"

Slightly taken aback, Katherine looked at him with startled eyes. "How can you tell?"

A light of devilry came to his green eyes as he laughed softly, "There is a certain — quality about you that tells me you have experienced the joys of love and passion."

For a few seconds all Katherine could do was stare at him. "Is it that obvious?" she asked at last.

He shook his head and smiled, "Only to me."

"I should hope so!" she laughed with a small quiver in her voice.

"Your secret is safe," he said, taking her hand warmly in his. "I only wish you would share some of those special moments with me."

Concealing a small sigh, Katherine replied, "The offer is quite tempting, M. Liszt, but . . ."

His brows rose humorously. "But?"

Katherine gave an almost imperceptible shrug. "What made such moments so special was something that went beyond physical attraction," she said, her quiet voice touched with nostalgia. "There was love, and tenderness, and friendship. Without those things, it would have no meaning, M. Liszt. At least, not for me."

Liszt regarded her intently for a moment. "You are a very special woman," he said, in his voice an undertone of admiration. "The man who has your love is indeed fortunate."

A movement behind the pianist made Katherine look over and past his shoulder. The count was advancing toward them, and the petulant scowl on his face was an indication that he was not at all pleased by her conduct. Oh, well, she shrugged inwardly, and tried to appease him by offering as engaging a smile as she could summon at the moment. This caused a sardonic twinkle to appear in the green eyes of the artist, who made his excuses and left as soon as it was polite to do so.

Although placated by her manner, the count remained by her side during the rest of the evening. When he asked to see her the next day, Katherine suspected that he was about to pop the question. Later, Adam confirmed that the count had told him earlier in the evening that the funds for their transaction were ready.

In anticipation of his arrival Katherine received baskets of flowers and a ruby brooch from the count.

Since she was supposed to be unaware of the arrangement between her father and her suitor, Katherine was absent when during his visit the geologist played by Ronald made a reappearance. Ronald presented Senhor Ferreiro with a voluminous report that he said had arrived from Brazil that day. Ferreiro introduced his employee, and the count was allowed a glimpse at the report. Before he could study it in more detail, however, Katherine appeared on cue and business matters had to be put momentarily aside.

As they strolled in the gardens, the count kept running through his greedy mind the figures he had just seen. What staggering profits were expected from the mines! If only this girl wouldn't delay in accepting the great honor he was about to confer on her!

Katherine left the count to his musings for a while and then decided that his appetite had been whetted enough by the report.

"I must thank you for your lovely gift, Walther," she said sweetly. The fact that she had called him by his given name for the first time was not lost on him. "Rubies are so beautiful, and I do tire of diamonds."

"You deserve only the best, my dear," he answered with what he must have thought to be a seductive glance.

Katherine had to catch her lower lip between her teeth in order to suppress a giggle.

The count cleared his throat. "My dear Gabrielle, by now you must know how great is my admiration for you," he said in a ponderous voice.

Demurely dropping her gaze, she murmured faintly, "I, too am very fond of you, Walther."

Again he cleared his throat. "Then, will you do me the honor of becoming my wife?"

She gave a small gasp of surprise, "Walther!"

The count suppressed a sigh of impatience. Would the stupid girl stop blushing and say yes! He waited a few seconds longer before demanding with ill-concealed exasperation, "Well, my dear?"

Fighting down laughter, she replied demurely, "I shall be honored to be your wife, dear Walther."

Beaming with excitement, Count von Driersch was so anxious to tell Ferreiro that his proposal had been accepted that he practically dragged Katherine back into the house.

Adam received the news calmly. After Katherine had left them to discuss the betrothal, he turned to the count with a pleasant smile. "Welcome to the family, my dear Count. You're a very fortunate man. My daughter is my greatest treasure, and I trust you will make her very happy."

"I shall do my best, Senhor Ferreiro," the count replied, impatient to get on with the subject of the shares.

But Ferreiro seemed more interested in discussing his daughter's happiness. "Have you and my Gabrielle set a wedding date?"

"Not yet, but I hope to persuade her to make it soon."

"Ah, the anxious bridegroom!" Adam exclaimed. The cynical gleam in his eyes escaped the count. "But we must allow the young lady to prepare for the wedding. It should be a magnificent affair, and we must take the time to make it so."

"Senhor Ferreiro, about our previous discussion regarding the shares . . ." the count began after a brief hesitation.

"Since it may take some time to prepare the wedding and I already have the sum you asked for in gold, why don't we conclude that part now so that our minds will be free to concentrate on the happy event?"

At first Adam feigned reluctance at the suggestion but eventually let himself be persuaded by the logic behind it. Finally it was agreed that the count would bring the gold the following day, and that Ferreiro should sign the shares over to him.

A deliriously happy count appeared the next day with two valises containing the stipulated amount in gold, which he turned over to Daniel. Daniel counted it carefully while Adam signed the documents.

"To simplify matters, I've decided to include in this transaction the shares I promised as my wedding present," he told von Driersch, who beamed at the news.

Daniel, whose baldness had disappeared under a gray wig, placed two sheets of paper on the table before Adam, who, in turn, took one and offered it to the count.

"My assistant, who's also my legal counsel, has insisted that we sign this document, my dear Count. It's just a formality stipulating that in the event the marriage between you and Gabrielle fails to take place for any reason, this transaction shall be canceled. You shall then return the shares to me, and I shall return to you the gold you have paid today. Would you have any objections to signing such an agreement?"

Since von Driersch had no intention of releasing the heiress from the promise, he rushed to answer, "No, of course not."

The documents were signed by both parties and witnessed by Daniel, who also provided the count with a copy.

Once the transaction was finished, Senhor Ferreiro sent for his daughter. A radiant Katherine appeared moments later, toasts were made, and a wedding date set for four weeks hence. She protested she needed more time to prepare but in the end allowed herself be persuaded by her anxious fiancé. Adam suggested a party to announce the engagement and they agreed that invitations should be sent out at once.

As soon as the count was gone, the friends rushed to change their costumes. Their luggage was packed and ready, and a carriage waiting.

Meanwhile, in Paris, M. Vidocq and Inspector Furneaux waited in a sumptuous drawing room for the Marquis d'Esterel to make his appearance.

If the rest of the palace bore any resemblance to the room they were in, they were on the right track, Vidocq reflected. Any of the items on display in that room alone was well worth the attention of the thieves they were after. A sculpture of a Chinese warrior on horseback, carved from a block of translucent green jade, in itself was probably worth more than the two detectives combined could earn in two lifetimes. Vidocq was no art expert, but the paintings on the walls required no elaborate explanations: Titian, Bellini, Tintoretto.

After compiling a list of possible targets to offer the criminals, the detectives had reached the conclusion that the Marquis had all the necessary attributes of the perfect decoy. All they had to do now was convince him to lend his cooperation, and they both knew that this wasn't going to be an easy task.

As Vidocq paced the floor, his steps were muffled by a thick Bukhara rug, and everywhere he looked, he saw another artistic treasure. He made an effort to suppress his growing irritation, for the Marquis had kept them waiting for almost an hour past the appointed time.

The ormolu clock on the mantel chimed another half

hour before the marquis made his entrance at last. Somewhere in his middle twenties and of medium height, his appearance did justice to his reputation of being a fastidious dandy. From the silver satin vest to his dark coat, his attire was a study in different shades of gray. His light brown hair was meticulously brushed, and the glance of his clear blue eyes made no attempt to disguise the distaste he felt for the visitors.

After the detectives had identified themselves, he addressed M. Vidocq.

"I believe I've heard the name before," he said.

Vidocq nodded. "It's quite possible, M. le Marquis," he replied. "I had the privilege of creating the Surete, the detective branch of the police which has been most successful in deterring crime in the city. I am now retired, but at the moment I'm acting as a special consultant to the police in an unofficial capacity."

"What do you want?" the marquis inquired bluntly.

"The reason for seeking this audience is that we would like to ask for your cooperation, M. le Marquis, in —"

"My help?" The Marquis interrupted, looking quite startled for a moment. Then his tone became annoyed when he said, "M. Vidocq, I've heard of your methods and am at a loss to understand your request. I have no criminal connections."

"Of course, M. le Marquis, I never meant to imply that you did," Vidocq rushed to assure him. "Please, allow me to explain. In this particular case we're not dealing with ordinary criminals. The fact is that we've been unable to find any underworld connections with a band of thieves who have been operating on the Continent for several years now, and that is why we need your help in setting up a trap for them. You see, these thieves prey on persons of quality such as yourself, and not only do they steal their jewels, but also extremely valuable *objets d'art* such as those we see around

182

you." As he paused, encompassing the room with a sweep on his hand, all eyes went to the paintings on the walls.

"Permit me, if you will, to give you a little background on the activities of the criminals," he went on. "I'm afraid we're not at liberty to disclose the names of the victims, but let it suffice to say that here in France, in Vienna and in Venice entire collections have been stolen, not to mention quite a few other thefts of lesser importance. You yourself could very well be their next victim, so, you see, it behooves you to see that those ciminals are apprehended."

The marquis was growing quite impatient. "So you want to use me as a decoy, is that it?"

Vidocq hesitated to put it so bluntly, and the marquis took this opportunity to add, "Why me? Surely there must be others who would do just as well."

"There are others, of course," Vidocq was reluctant to admit. "But after compiling a list of possible victims, the inspector and I have come to the conclusion that you are the most attractive potential victim we could offer the thieves. You see, we have studied the profiles of all the victims," he went on, aware of the marquis' growing displeasure. "All are men of great wealth such as yourself, who owned valuable collections of jewels as well as of *objets d'art*. One of the criminals is a beautiful young woman who . . ."

"A woman?" the marquis interrupted.

Vidocq nodded. "Yes, a very beautiful young woman who lures the victims with her charms and sets them up for her accomplices." He let the marquis ruminate on this information for a moment, and, as anticipated, his interest was now piqued.

"And what would you expect me to do?" inquired the marquis with caution.

"Simply to continue visiting your favorite places of entertainment, M. le Marquis," Vidocq replied, referring to the illegal gambling establishments which the marquis was known to frequent. Since this was a delicate subject, he went on to explain, "It is our belief that the thieves choose their victims at such places." Swiftly, he digressed, "And to make it even more attractive for the thieves, we've thought of planting an item in the newspapers about your fabulous art collection that we're sure will prove irresistible."

Looking quite sulky—although intrigued—the marquis didn't answer for a moment. "And what protection would I receive for my property?" he inquired at last. "What if the thieves succeed in robbing me?"

"With guards in the house disguised as servants, your property will be kept under complete security, M. le Marquis," replied Vidocq. "We'll lead the thieves to believe that your treasures could be easily stolen, and when they try to take them, we shall catch them in the act."

The marquis still remained unconvinced. "That sounds very well," he said testily, "but what assurances will you and the police give me that my property will be safe?"

Inspector Furneaux, who until then had let his friend take the lead, stepped in. "My detective force will watch your property twenty-four hours a day, M. le Marquis. I assure you that with your cooperation, the thieves will be apprehended."

After taking a moment to consider Furneaux's reply, the marquis said, "Tell me more about the thieves, Inspector. What information do you have on them?"

"We've learned that the woman works with a man who sometimes appears as her brother, her father, or even as her aging husband," Furneaux replied. "We've also been able to determine that another couple act as their servants, and that there are two other men involved. Since their descriptions vary from case to case, we must assume they use clever disguises. The only detail that remains unchanged is that the woman is young, extremely beautiful, and has green eyes."

The marquis looked wry. "That's not much to go on, is it, Inspector?

"It's all we have so far, M. le Marquis," Furneaux shrugged unhappily.

Shifting his attention to Vidocq, the young man said, "Tell me more about the woman."

"As all the others, she has presented different appearances," Vidocq began. "In Vienna she was dark, with raven black hair. In Venice she was a blonde, and here in France she had brown hair. Since skin tone can be darkened with cosmetics while a fair complexion is more difficult to attain by the same means, we must then deduce that she is fair, and according to all the victims, most alluring."

"A woman of mystery!" the marquis reflected with a tight smile. "A fascinating challenge, don't you think?"

A swift glance passed between the detectives, who in unspoken accord decided to play on the younger man's interest in the woman to gain his cooperation.

"Indeed it is, M. le Marquis," Vidocq nodded.

"And what do you propose to do with the thieves once they are caught?"

"Why, apprehend them, of course!" Furneaux replied. "Any court in the land would sentence them to life imprisonment with the evidence we shall have when we catch them *in flagrante delicto*."

"The woman, too?"

"But of course! She's just as guilty as the others!" assured Furneaux emphatically.

On his part, Vidocq remained silent. The marquis had something else in mind, and it concerned the woman.

The young marquis stood up and began pacing the floor. Then he paused and faced the detectives. "Very well, I will help you set the trap as you suggest, but under one condition." Again he paused, and the detectives waited expectantly for his next words. "After the thieves are caught, and before you put the woman in prison, I want her."

Inspector Furneaux opened his mouth to offer a protest, but Vidocq hushed him with a gesture.

The marquis waited.

"This is quite an extraordinary request, M. le Marquis," ventured Inspector Furneaux at last.

"What you're asking of me is also extraordinary, Inspector," the marquis countered mildly. "Those are my terms."

Vidocq and Furneaux exchanged glances again and remained silent, trying to reach a decision.

"M. le Marquis, this is a highly irregular request," Inspector Furneaux said at last. "I beg your forbearance, but M. Vidocq and I must discuss the matter with my superiors before we can give you an answer."

"Very well, Inspector, consult your superiors. But remember," the marquis said, wagging a finger at him, "unless my terms are met, I will not help you. Good day, gentlemen."

"Good day, M. le Marquis," the detectives answered in unison before they followed the servant who had been summoned to escort them to the front door.

Once they were out on the street, they walked quietly side by side, neither of them wanting to be the first to speak. Finally, it was Vidocq who broke the silence.

"Will the Prefect of Police agree to the request?"

Furneaux wearily shook his head. "I don't know, *mon ami*. Perhaps he will after I explain the importance of our plan. After all, the woman is a criminal, and we shall have her once the marquis is done with her." As an afterthought, he added, "Just in case, perhaps we should go over our list of possible decoys once more."

When they arrived at Vidocq's office, the two detectives consulted the list they had compiled.

"The only promising candidate is Count Brullard," Vidocq sighed, "and I've already ascertained that he's now out of France. In America, I believe. Who knows when he will return!"

Inspector Furneaux nodded thoughtfully. "It looks like we have no other choice but the marquis," he said unhappily. "I guess I shall have to discuss the matter with my superiors after all." With a shrug, he finished, "It's out of our hands now."

"Very well, Maurice. You will let me know the decision as soon as possible won't you?"

"Of course, *mon ami.*"

After his friend had gone, Vidocq ran through his mind the earlier interview with the marquis. In the process of investigating the man as a possible decoy, he had uncovered certain facts that augured nothing but grief for the woman if the request was granted.

"Why should I care what happens to her?" he asked himself out loud. "She's nothing but a criminal."

He tried to convince himself that her fate didn't matter, but his interrogations of the servants in Vouvray and Vienna came back to mind. All of them had remembered the young woman was a most charming and kind lady.

"You old fool!" he laughed out loud. "You're getting sentimental over a woman you haven't even met!"

It took two days for Inspector Furneaux to get an answer from his superiors. After much discussion, the Prefect of Police had agreed to grant — unofficially — the marquis' request as long as he turned the prisoner over to the police after three days.

The inspector communicated the news to Vidocq. Curiously, though, neither of them seemed very happy with the decision.

Again the marquis kept them waiting for a long time before he appeared. When he did, he went directly to the point.

"Well, gentlemen, I trust you have an answer for me today."

"Indeed we have, M. le Marquis," Inspector Furneaux answered. "My superiors agree to your request as long as you turn the prisoner over to us at the end of three days."

Wryly, the marquis eyed the two detectives who expectantly awaited his answer. "Very well, gentlemen," he said at last. Deliberately, he added, "Three days should be enough for what I have in mind for the lady in question."

The smile that accompanied his words sent chills up the spines of the two old men who had gained their expertise through their long years in the Paris underworld.

Nine

After the successful completion of the caper in Baden-Baden, Katherine and Adam stopped to visit their friends in Amsterdam before returning to Cornwall. The friendship between Natalie and Katherine had grown closer through the years and although brief, those visits were always enjoyable.

The evening before their planned departure, however, Katherine was feeling quite ill. She complained of chills and headaches, and when Natalie realized that her friend was also burning up with fever, she immediately sent for her physician.

After examining Katherine, the doctor diagnosed a severe case of influenza and offered to send a nurse. Natalie refused, saying that she would care for her friend, and only at the insistence of both Adam and Bernard that Katherine would receive better care from a competent professional did she relent from her purpose.

For almost a week Katherine burned up with fever while her friends feared for her life. The doctor visited her daily and reported on her condition. Finally, on the seventh day, the fever broke and Adam was allowed to visit the sick room.

He found her propped up by pillows and waiting for him anxiously.

"Adam!" she exclaimed, immediately cheered by the sight of him. "Oh, my dear, how nice it is to see you!"

Adam couldn't answer. He was appalled by her pallor; she had lost a great deal of weight, and the dark circles under her eyes made her look so frail that he almost felt like weeping.

Keeping his emotions from showing, he managed a smile as he bent over her to brush his lips to her brow. As he did, he tried to take comfort in the fact that her temperature seemed to be back to normal.

"Come and sit beside me," she invited, patting the edge of the bed.

At his hesitation, she took his hand and gently pulled at it. "I've missed you so much," she said, without releasing him.

He sat down, and there was an awkward silence while they stared at one another for a few seconds. She wishing he would take her in his arms and comfort her with words of love; he was immensely relieved that she was now out of danger, and suddenly realizing how very precious to him she had become.

"How are you feeling?" he asked at last in a voice altered by emotion.

"Much better," she replied with an awkward smile. "We'll be able to go home soon."

The thought of disappointing her made a contained look come to his eyes. "That won't be for a while, pet," he said carefully. "You're very weak, and the doctor said the trip would be too hard on you, especially at this time of the year."

Her mouth opened a little as she stared at him for a second. "But I want to go home!" she blurted out then. "Oh, Adam, it's been ages since I last saw Jason. Besides, Agatha and Jenny will worry if we don't get back."

"No, pet," Adam shook his head. "I'll write to them and explain that there'll be a delay. What is important now is for you to get better." Giving her hand a little squeeze, he said with unfeigned affection, "You've been a very sick girl, you know. I've—we've all been terribly worried about you."

Having noticed his slip of the tongue, Katherine smiled, "I'm sorry to have given you such a fright."

She asked about the others, and he answered all her questions with gentle humor to cheer her up.

"It won't be for long," he said when she brought up again the subject of going home. "Just a few more weeks. Besides, Natalie is looking forward to pampering you for a while. Surely you won't deny her that pleasure."

Katherine started to protest and then fell silent. She was very tired after spending only a few minutes in his company. "I guess you're right," she had to admit. "It's just that I can't wait to see Jason again."

"I know, pet." Leaning forward, he kissed her forehead again and rose to his feet. "Get some rest now. The doctor promised Natalie she'd be allowed to visit you this afternoon if you feel up to it."

"Oh, I will," she promised, hardly able to keep her eyes open by this time. "Give her and Bernard my love, won't you?"

"Of course, pet. Now, get some sleep," he commanded with a smile.

She drifted off the moment her eyes closed.

Adam's smile was touched with sadness as he watched her for a few seconds. Then, he stroked the silken cheek that had grown so pale and left the room.

While Katherine's recovery was going smoothly, Adam was growing increasingly restless after the second week of inactivity. It was then that an item in a Paris newspaper caught his eye. The article reported the purchase of an important painting by the Marquis d'Esterel and went on to describe his extensive collection in great detail.

"Most interesting," Adam reflected.

His next step was to consult the doctor attending

Katherine. When he was told that she shouldn't travel for at least another month, he immediately decided to visit Paris and investigate the situation there.

Angelique and Lazarus were surprised to see him so soon after their adventure in Baden-Baden, and he told them of Katherine's illness and their enforced stay in Amsterdam. Her youth and her warmth, as well as her wit and courage, had earned her a special place in their hearts, so the Brissards were relieved to hear that she was well on the way to recovery.

Adam showed them the newspaper clipping and told them of his intention to investigate the possibilities of relieving the Marquis of some of his treasures. That same evening he adopted one of his costumes and decided to pay a visit to the illegal gambling establishments of the medieval city.

It didn't take him long to run into the marquis, who was gambling for high stakes and throwing money around as if it were water. But something about his manner bothered Adam; although striving to appear unconcerned, the young man's manner betrayed alertness. This in itself was not unusual, since in such places one had to be on the lookout for any cutthroat intent on one's purse, but there was something else that Adam noticed and found very curious. Each time he was approached by a woman, the marquis seemed to become especially alert; then his interest faded quickly, as if the woman was not the one he had been expecting.

Adam didn't know exactly what it was about the marquis that made him uneasy, but he had learned to trust his instincts and they told him that something was definitely amiss.

When he expressed his doubts to the Brissards the next day, Lazarus inquired, "Do you think it might be a trap?"

"I couldn't say for sure," Adam shook his head thoughtfully. "But whatever it is, I'm going to find out. Tonight, our friend Bertrille will be paying a visit to his old cronies. If there's anything afoot, I'm sure Bertrille will find out what it is."

When Inspector Furneaux had concluded that our friends had no underworld connections, he had not counted on Adam's ingenuity. One of the most unsavory characters he portrayed was a man named Bertrille, who passed — but mostly collected — information. His supposedly occasional stints as a sailor made Bertrille's long absences seem plausible.

This character had frightened Katherine out of her wits one evening years before, after she had retired for the night. She had been reading in her room when it started to rain in the small hours of the morning. She got up to close her window, and as she had reached for the shutters to close them, she had seen a dark figure run stealthily into the garden. Lazarus being the only man in the house at the time, she had rushed to the Brissard's room and pounded on the door until he had appeared with his hair tousled and pulling a robe over his nightshirt. Her apparent agitation made him become immediately alert.

"Someone's trying to get inside the house!" Katherine told him. "I just saw a man run into the garden."

Having heard every word and becoming as alarmed as Katherine, Angelique appeared behind her husband. After trying to calm both of them down, Lazarus went back into the room and returned moments later with a pistol in hand. Both Katherine and Angelique had gone terribly pale and held each other protectively when they suddenly heard soft footsteps coming up the stairs. Hiding in the shadows, Lazarus cocked the pistol and waited for the intruder.

When the man came into view, Katherine had gasped with fright at his menacing appearance. There was a thick, whitish scar on the left side of his face running from above his eyebrow to the chin. His gray-streaked hair was covered by a sailor's cap; his thick brows and bushy mustache were also gray, his clothes dark and not too clean. They could smell rum even at the distance of ten paces.

At the top of the stairs, the man stopped cold in his tracks when he found himself looking into the muzzle of Lazarus' gun. Katherine had been startled when Lazarus put his gun down and let out a bellow of laughter, especially when he was joined in by Angelique and even the intruder—who removed his wig together with his cap.

"Adam!" Katherine had gasped to everyone's mirth. For a flick of an instant she had been angry at having been frightened half to death. Suddenly, the humor of the situation struck her, and she, also, burst out laughing.

Adam was thinking of that incident now as he applied the makeup that turned him into the ferocious-looking Bertrille. Imagining that a new scar would look appropriate for a man who supposedly got into many fights, he simulated a half-healed cut over his right eye.

"Very convincing," he congratulated himself when he finished.

After his long absence, Bertrille was made welcome by his criminal friends. Exchanging stories about their latest exploits, they each tried to impress the other with tall tales over several glasses of rum. Still bragging, Bertrille brought out of his pocket a gold crucifix and said he had stolen it from a passenger during his last voyage. Next, he asked the whereabouts of Antoine *le Ruise,* a fence of stolen jewelry. His friends directed him to Antoine, and he didn't have to look far.

A jolly little man, Antoine took the crucifix, examined it closely and offered Bertrille three hundred francs. Bertrille made a big pretense of being offended by such meager offer and they haggled back and forth over the price. In the end, Bertrille accepted five hundred francs and still feigned discontent.

"You've certainly earned your soubriquet of the Fox, Antoine." His voice was dry, sarcastic. "That crucifix is worth

194

at least three times that much. Next time, I'll take my business elsewhere."

Accustomed as he was to Bertrille's threats, Antoine laughed, "*Mais* don't be so put out, *mon ami*. After all, it's only a small matter."

"That well may be," Bertrille conceded gruffly, "only just wait and see what I bring you next time, *Ruise*."

Antoine chuckled. Bertrille was always boasting of large caches, only so far he had never seen any evidence. "Ah, *oui, mon ami*," he humored Bertrille. "Perhaps next time, you'll bring the jewels of the Marquis d'Esterel, eh?"

"And why not?" Bertrille replied assuming an injured air. "I might surprise you yet."

Much to Adam's puzzlement, Antoine slapped his thigh and laughed with such mirth that his paunch quivered and tears came to his eyes.

"Now, what's so amusing about that?" Bertrille asked with some belligerence. "Don't you believe I can do it?"

Still quivering with mirth, Antoine shook his hands in front of him. "Because," he got out between giggles, "if you even go near that house, you'll be the one getting the surprise!"

Bertrille looked puzzled. "How so?" he inquired. "What's been happening in my absence?"

Antoine wiped his eyes with the back of his hands, and after drawing a deep sigh paused to look at Bertrille with an air of promise. "You heard about the theft in Vouvray last year, didn't you?" he said at last.

Bertrille heaved a wistful sigh. "And how I wished I had a share on that one!"

"The police have been asking a lot of questions about the thieves," Antoine said, dropping his voice to a confidential level. "I've heard that the same gang pulled several jobs in other countries. Imagine, Bertrille, entire collections!" he drooled.

"*Sacre bleu!*" Bertrille exclaimed. "So tell me, have they found anything?"

"Not a thing," Antoine shook his head. "And they're going out of their minds, even Vidocq."

A gleam of caution came to Bertrille's eyes. "Vidocq?" he echoed. "But he's been out of the Surete for more than ten years!"

"Ah, but this is a very special case," Antoine said. Lowering his voice even more, he went on, "As I said, they have spies everywhere, but they have come up empty. Nobody knows anything about the thieves and someone, probably Vidocq, came up with the brilliant idea of setting up a trap with the marquis' cooperation. They've been extremely secretive about the whole affair, but the police aren't the only ones to have informers—" he finished with conspiratorial wink from his left eye.

Bertrille regarded him thoughtfully. "Are you sure no one knows who the thieves are?"

Antoine shook his head. "It's said that they are foreigners and wear disguises, but there's a great deal of talk about a green-eyed woman."

A flicker of surprise crossed Bertrille's blue eyes. "A green-eyed woman, you said?"

"That's how they got the marquis to cooperate with them," Antoine confided. "Rumor has it that they'll give her to the marquis when the thieves are caught."

Confusion joined the anger in Bertrille's eyes. "Why? What does he want with her?"

Antoine's smile faded and his face showed disgust. "It is said that the marquis has peculiar tastes," he said. "If he gets the woman—" with a shudder, he left the sentence unfinished.

"Thank you for the warning, *mon ami*," Bertrille said, and nothing in his demeanor revealed Adam's anger. "I guess I'll have to leave the marquis' jewels alone after all.

And next time I'll bring you my business even if you don't pay enough."

"So they set up a trap," Adam muttered as he removed his costume. He was seething with anger. The trap in itself was an interesting challenge, but the fact that the police was willing to turn Katherine over to the marquis as reward for his cooperation made him bristle.

The next day he met with the Brissards and told them what he had learned. "Under no circumstances is Katherine to return to Paris," he warned his friends. "If anything happens to me, Lazarus, I want you to go to Amsterdam and see her safely back to Cornwall."

Lazarus's gaze expressed his concern. "Why should anything happen to you? Surely you're not going to try robbing the marquis now!"

"I've no intentions of walking into the trap," Adam replied, his irritation showing in the tightness around his mouth. "But I'll teach him a lesson that he'll never forget. And Vidocq should benefit from it too," he added as an afterthought.

"What are you going to do?" Angelique inquired worriedly. They had never seen Adam so angry.

"I don't know yet, but I'll think of something," he said heavily. Refocusing his eyes on their faces, his anger seemed to abate when he saw their worried expressions. "Don't fret, my friends," he said with a tight-lipped smile. "I'm not a fool."

Following a constrained pause Lazarus asked, "Will you contact Ronald and Daniel?"

Adam shook his head. "This is something I want to do alone."

A worried glance passed between Angelique and Lazarus. "No, Adam," Lazarus said firmly. "We've always worked together, and we'll do so now. Whatever you decide to do, you must include Angelique and me, and I know Daniel and Ronald would say the same if they were here."

Lazarus' words seemed to take the edge off Adam's anger. "You're right," he admitted with a wry shake of his head. "Losing one's temper is the most dangerous mistake one can make in our profession. I promise I won't try anything on my own. I'll take some time to investigate the possibilities, and once I come up with something, I'll let you know."

"Good," Lazarus nodded.

"In the meantime," Adam went on, "I'll find a flat for Lord Ramsay, who'll arrive in Paris next Friday. Angelique, you may prefer to sit this one out."

"Nothing doing!" she protested immediately. "I'm going too. What about Daniel and Ronald?"

"I'll write to them today asking that they come down to Paris," Adam replied. A little wistfully, he added, "It's a good thing Katherine is not able to be with us, or she'd be here, too."

According to plan, Lord Ramsay arrived in Paris with two servants a few days later and occupied a flat his "agent" had already secured. As Lord Ramsay, Adam appeared portly and middle-aged, with iron-gray hair and mustache to match and carried himself with martial bearing. In his new disguise he began to frequent the gambling establishments of Paris, and in those nightly jaunts he often ran into the Marquis d'Esterel, who continued his extravagant behavior. They played at the same table so often that they even became nodding acquaintances.

Two weeks later both Vidocq and the Prefect of Police received identical letters. The words had been cut out from a local newspaper and pasted on a single sheet of paper. They read as follows:

Congratulations on your clever scheme, but we're wise to your plans. Better luck next time.

The International Gang

"How did they find out?" Vidocq asked with dismay.

"Someone must have talked," replied Inspector Furneaux dejectedly. After all the time they had spent on the investigation, someone's indiscretion had ruined their only chance to catch the thieves.

"I suppose we must tell the marquis," Vidocq reflected quite unhappily. "They won't try anything now, knowing that we have the house under surveillance."

The marquis was very angry when the detectives told him that their ruse had been discovered, and in silent frustration they had to listen to his furious epithets.

Later, back in his office, Vidocq offered a glass of Calvados to his friend and took one for himself. They sat slumped and in silence, nursing their drinks and pondering how they could set another trap for the slippery criminals.

"I wonder if they're still in Paris," Vidocq said finally.

"If they are, no thefts have been reported," Furneaux volunteered.

"Wait a moment, Maurice!" Vidocq cried, sitting up abruptly. In his excitement, he didn't notice that he had spilled some of the drink on his trousers. "Why would the thieves go to the trouble of letting us know that they are wise to our plans?"

Furneaux shrugged unhappily. "A matter of thumbing their noses at us, I suppose."

"But what if that's exactly what they want us to believe?" Vidocq proposed, his excitement increasing with every passing second. "And once we remove the guards —"

"Of course!" Inspector Furneaux became as excited as his friend.

Vidocq frowned then. "Are the guards still at the house?"

Furneaux shook his head in denial. "The Prefect of Police ordered them removed after he saw the letter."

Rising, excitedly, the old man said, "We must get them back immediately!"

"Yes!" Furneaux cried triumphantly, also leaping to his feet. "I'll see that they are sent back tonight, if possible."

"It must be tonight, Maurice," Vidocq warned him. "If I know my man, he'll try tonight."

Slowly, but steadily, Katherine's health continued to improve under Natalie's care, and the two women became closer than ever before. Their common bond to Adam had been the beginning of a lasting friendship.

Sometimes, watching Natalie with her husband, Bernard, Katherine was more aware than ever of all she and Adam could have if only he were able to surmount his scruples of her having borne the child of another man. For Katherine there was no other explanation for Adam's continued reticence when it came to their relationship. She was almost sure that he loved her as she loved him.

Still, there were always those times when she found herself reminiscing of moments shared with Jonathan that no matter how hard she tried, would not be exorcised from her memories.

Longing for the love she had once known, on several occasions she had caught herself wishing to be in Adam's bed. Only one reason had kept her away from it: the promise she had made to herself to never again become another man's mistress — not even Adam's. If he loved her, he would have to come to her.

Oh, the years they had wasted, Katherine reflected sadly as she watched Natalie and Bernard together and longed for the same happiness with someone of her own. It was then that she decided to speak to Adam when he returned from Paris.

By the middle of December she was fully recovered and anxiously awaiting his return. They had already missed the chance of spending Christmas in Cornwall; what could be keeping him? Every day she inquired if there were news of Adam only to receive negative answers. She began to worry, but with Daniel and Ronald back in England and herself here in Amsterdam, the idea that Adam would attempt anything on his own never entered her mind.

She was in the library one afternoon trying to occupy her restless mind with a book when, looking very somber, Natalie and Bernard came in with Ronald Lambert.

"Ronald!" Katherine bounced lithely to her feet and went to kiss him on the cheek. Ronald accepted the kiss, but rather than embracing her as he would have done other times, he remained stiff and uncertain. She drew back to look at him, and a feeling of dread invaded her when she noticed his uneasiness. "What are you doing here?"

Ronald regarded her uneasily. "I came to take you back to Cornwall," he replied.

Her mouth opened a little as she looked at him. "Where's Adam?"

"In Paris," Ronald replied, looking away from her probing gaze. His grim expression only served to increase her alarm.

Turning visibly pale she asked in a hushed voice, "Has anything happened to him?"

Dreading to tell her the news, Ronald avoided looking at her for a moment. Then, in a bleak voice replied, "Adam has been captured, Katherine."

There was a dismayed silence during which she looked at him as though she had failed to understand him. Then her pupils widened in shocked disbelief and her hands flew to her mouth to muffle a small cry of horror, "No!"

As though hit by a boulder, she slumped on the nearest chair when all her muscles went slack and her legs refused to support her.

Bernard rushed to hold his wife when Natalie wavered on her feet.

Witnessing the distress of the woman he had adored in silence for so long, made Ronald wish he had been caught instead of Adam, whom she loved. Sitting on his heels by the chair he took one of Katherine's hands. It was like ice. "We'll get him out, my dear," he said in a gentle, persuasive voice. "We've been unable to do anything so far because we don't know exactly where he's being held. Daniel and the Brissards are trying to find out where he is, but he made me promise to see you safely back to Cornwall if anything happened to him. I promise you that as soom as I get back to Paris, we'll get him out."

Katherine shook her head with anguish. "How can you even think that I'll go back to Cornwall without him?"

"But you must!" Ronald said quite emphatically. "Adam doesn't want you anywhere near Paris! It's too dangerous!"

The eyes she turned to him had misted. "Tell me what happened."

Ronald recounted the events that had led to Adam's capture. He told her of the plan concocted by Vidocq and the Surete with the marquis' participation.

"When Daniel and I arrived in Paris, Adam sent a letter to the police thumbing his nose at their efforts," he went on. "We were watching the house and saw the guards removed as he had expected, so we went in that same night. We had no problem in getting in and taking most of the paintings and sculptures—even some jewelry, but after we started to leave, Adam went back, I don't know why. We were a short distance away when we heard shots. I told Daniel to go on ahead and went back to see what had happened. There was nothing I could do, Katherine," he told her ruefully. "There were policemen everywhere, and Adam was being taken away."

"Was he hurt?"

"I don't think so," he shook his head.

Only Natalie's soft weeping broke the ensuing silence. Ronald remained by Katherine's side, still holding her hand

and not knowing how to console her. However, Katherine was the first to recover her composure.

"I'll be ready in one hour," she said, rising from the chair with vigorous purpose. "Except we won't be going to Cornwall."

"But you can't go to Paris!" Ronald exclaimed, determined to keep her from harm at all cost.

Pausing on her way out, Katherine half turned to give him a level glance from her green eyes. "If it were me in that prison, Adam wouldn't leave me, Ronald," she said with a touch of asperity. "What makes you think I'd abandon him?"

Ronald regarded her in silence. In spite of his apprehension for her safety, he had never admired Katherine more.

Natalie took a step toward her. "Katherine, I—"

"Nothing you can say will stop me, Natalie," Katherine cut her off with an uplifted hand.

"But I'm not trying to stop you," Natalie replied. "What I'm trying to tell you is that I'm going with you."

"What!" Katherine cried in surprise. "Oh, no, Natalie! You've been out of this for a long time. I can't possibly let you risk everything you have now."

"I wouldn't have any of that if it hadn't been for Adam," Natalie reminded her. "You may owe him a lot, but so do I." She turned to Bernard, who was regarding his wife with a mixture of admiration and apprehension. "You do understand, don't you, my love?"

Bernard came to her and lovingly put his arms around her. "Of course, my angel, and I'm going with you."

Natalie turned visibly pale. "But you can't!" she breathed bleakly. She reached out and touched his cheek. "You don't know anything about that world where Adam and I used to live, my love."

"But I want to help," Bernard insisted.

Natalie tried to persuade him, but nothing would make Bernard stay behind. Finally he agreed that once they were in Paris he would stay at a hotel without apparent ties to them. Natalie and Katherine embraced each other with emotion, and then it was Katherine who called everyone to order.

"We must have a plan," she said firmly. "Let's put our heads together and see what we can come up with. If by the time we get to Paris the Brissards and Daniel have not located Adam, the first step is to do so ourselves." She looked around at their somber faces. "Any ideas?"

It was Natalie who offered the first suggestion. "Since Ronald said they're looking for a green-eyed woman, perhaps it would be less conspicuous if we go as sisters," she ventured.

"Yes," Katherine readily agreed. Picking up the train of Natalie's thought, Katherine elaborated, "We could pretend to be two English sisters looking for their father. We could go to the police and ask for their assistance. If we don't let them know that we speak French, perhaps we might be able to pick up some leads while we are there."

And, in silent amazement, the two men listened as the two women formulated their daring plan.

Following a flurry of activity, their luggage was ready in short order and they were on their way to Paris that same day. Snow-covered roads made for a slow journey, but they set a grueling pace stopping only to change the tired horses for fresh ones. Daniel and the Brissards, who were astounded to see both Katherine and Natalie together, had discouraging news: Adam's fate was still unknown.

Without wasting any time, Natalie and Katherine got into their costumes. Wearing blond wigs and changing their faces, they became two English sisters who arrived and took rooms at an elegant Parisian hotel. Immediately they began their search for their missing father. Making their presence conspicuous they visited other hotels, hospitals, and every other place imaginable before they went to the police.

Meeting the inspector who was assigned to their case,

they discovered that at last fortune had smiled on them. Inspector Louis Rodin couldn't have been with the police very long, and the effect they had on him was quite devastating. Faced with the two most beautiful women he had ever seen, the young policeman was barely able to control his admiration while striving to retain his professional dignity. Once he was over his initial awkwardness, he was most anxious to be of service to such lovely ladies of obvious quality.

Taking the lead, Katherine introduced herself as Miss Rosalind Canning and Natalie as her sister Charlotte.

"Our plans were to come to Paris with Father," she began, "but when I became ill and he had to leave, we agreed to join him later." Anxiety deepened in her troubled face as she went on, "Inspector, no one has seen or even heard of him. We've made inquiries at every hotel in the city and even tried the hospitals without finding a trace of him." She paused to bring out a lacy handkerchief from her reticule, and dabbing at the tears that came to her lovely emerald eyes, she added in a tremulous voice, "I'm afraid, Inspector, that something dreadful has happened to him. Oh, I feel so responsible!"

Distressed by her tears, Inspector Rodin tried to offer comfort in the stilted and heavily accented English of which he was so proud. "Please believe that I will do my best to find your father, mademoiselle," he said, showing more confidence than he was feeling. "I shall make inquiries, and if your father came to Paris, I shall find him for you, I promise."

Katherine heaved a deep, tremulous sigh. "You're so very kind, Inspector," she said, her voice a breathy whisper. Eyes bright with unshed tears, she looked at him and attempted a brave smile that shook the poor young man to the core.

Clearing his throat, he tried to assume a professional manner. "Now, if you please, Miss Canning, may I have a description of your father and any other information that could help us find him?"

205

Both Katherine and Natalie offered a description of their imaginary father and invented all kinds of plausible information while Inspector Rodin took notes. Before they left, the young man assured them once more that he would endeavor to find their missing father.

Step number one of their plan had been completed.

Two days later, the Canning sisters reported the disappearance of their jewelry. The hotel management called the police, but the ladies insisted on speaking to "that nice Inspector Rodin," who was terribly flattered by their request.

"Unfortunately this matter is out of my jurisdiction," he regretted. "However, I shall be glad to speak to the inspector who is in charge of your case. What is his name?"

"Inspector Lichine," Katherine replied immediately. "But are you sure, my dear Inspector Rodin, you couldn't help us yourself?"

"I'm terribly sorry, mademoiselle," he replied, basking in the admiration he saw reflected in those marvelous emerald eyes. "But I assure you Inspector Lichine is most competent."

With a flutter of her long lashes, Katherine said in a husky voice, "My dear Inspector Rodin, aside from yourself, who, in your opinion, is the most competent detective?"

Looking deeply into those eyes that made his heart pound so wildly, he replied without hesitation, "Inspector Furneaux, without a doubt. But I'm afraid he'll be unable to take your case, mademoiselle. He's now very busy with a case involving a robbery that took place a few days ago."

Katherine's heart gave a tremendous bound, but the luminous gaze of her green eyes didn't waver as she said huskily, "It must be a very important case."

As long as she kept looking at him like that, Rodin would have told her anything. "Indeed, mademoiselle. The entire art collection and jewels of one of our leading citizens."

"Really?" Katherine was fascinated by the confidence. "And has he found the thief?"

"The matter has been kept from the press, but yes, one of the thieves was caught."

"Only one?" Her delicate brows rose quizzically. "Are you saying there were more?"

"Oh, yes, six of them," Rodin replied. "But we have the one we believe to be the leader."

"How exciting!" Katherine breathed. "You must be so thrilled, Inspector." Contracting her brow in a worried frown, she asked then, "But aren't you afraid the other thieves will try to rescue their leader?"

"Not to worry, mademoiselle," Rodin replied with a confident smile. "There hasn't been a single escape in the history of Lamartine Castle. Soon his accomplices will join him there, I assure you."

Only by calling upon all her acting ability was Katherine able to conceal her excitement as she breathed with apparent adoration, "Oh, Inspector, you men are so daring, fighting those awful criminals the way you do!"

Inspector Rodin's chest expanded, and under her careful prodding, he told of the security surrounding the criminal. Once they had their information, Katherine and Natalie expressed her confidence that he would see their jewelry and their father restored to them.

Meanwhile, unaware of the efforts of his friends, Adam cursed himself for his stupidity once again as he paced the stone floor of his cell. At least the frequent interrogations he was subjected to were an indication that no one else had been captured, he reflected moodily. He hoped that by this time Katherine was safely back in Cornwall, and that the others wouldn't be foolish enough to attempt to rescue him from this fortress.

Dim light filtered through the high barred casements as he

moved about the freezing chamber, trying to warm up and replaying in his mind the events that had led him to this cell.

For the first time in his career, he had let his emotions cloud his better judgment. He had brushed aside Daniel's objections to the danger and his reasoning that the marquis' treasures could be taken at any other time. It was more than the robbery he had wanted: to meet Vidocq's challenge and punish the marquis for his designs on Katherine. He had gone ahead against the counsel of his friends, and now he was grateful that at least no one but himself had to pay for his own folly.

Everything would have gone according to plan if he had not gone back into the house at the last minute. It had been a senseless thing to do wanting to frighten the marquis. He had gone to his room, taken one of the marquis' suits, and stuffing it with pillows made an effigy that he left on the floor after plunging a large kitchen knife in the spot where the heart would have been had a man been wearing the suit. He had also found some gold and jewelry that he also decided to take.

A short distance from the house he had been stopped by three policemen who had insisted on searching him, and shots had been fired when he tried to escape them. He had almost succeeded in eluding his pursuers when three other men cut off his escape. The search of his person yielded the jewels he had taken from the marquis' room at the last minute, and he had been taken back to the house. The robbery had been then discovered, and shackles placed on his wrists.

Vidocq and Inspector Furneaux had been dismayed at the news that the other thieves had already managed to escape with the marquis' property. Surrounded by guards Adam had been taken out of the house and pushed onto a wagon that had taken him to police headquarters, where he had undergone hours of grueling interrogation.

After several days of the same ordeal he had been taken

from his cell in the middle of the night and pushed onto another wagon. They had ridden for what seemed a long time; at first, the horses hooves pounded the cobblestones of the city streets, but later the muted sounds of the wheels told him that they had left the city behind. The carriage had stopped after a voice had shouted, "Halt!" There had been muffled sounds of voices, a gate creaking open, and then the carriage had resumed its journey, this time into a courtyard.

When he had been taken out of the wagon, Lamartine Castle had risen in the gloom before him like a specter from the Dark Ages. Torches illuminated the way as their footsteps disturbed the accumulated silence of centuries in the main hall.

His guards had followed a torch bearer through a passageway where a soldier unlocked an inner door. They had climbed the cold stone staircase to the upper floor, and the clashes of the locks and the creaks of the hinges he had heard there still seemed to echo in his ears. At last they had reached this turret where his cell was located.

Peeking out of the high barred casement Adam had seen that the sheer wall dropped into an open area where he could see patrols walking by. Beyond was a parapet, also patrolled. There was no way out of this fortress, he had told himself then. His only hope was to be taken to another prison, but after three weeks there were no signs of such transfer taking place.

Several days later, Adam was surprised when a guard he had never seen before secretly slipped a small package to him when he brought his meal of thin gruel and stale bread. After the guard left, Adam opened the parcel and found that it contained a portion of a soldier's uniform. What the devil? A small piece of paper folded inside one of the pockets clarified the mystery. *Be ready, K.* it read.

"Katherine!" he gasped. "Oh, my God, that crazy girl is in Paris!"

In the course of the following days, the same guard appeared and each time slipped other packages to him. After the uniform had been completed, he received still another parcel containing a razor, a bar of soap, a small mirror, a wig, and makeup.

"Good thinking, pet!"

He had grown a beard during his imprisonment, and by now his jailers were accustomed to it. No one would suspect a clean-shaven soldier of being an escaping convict. The note he found this time read, *Midnight tomorrow, K.*

Katherine and Natalie were very pleased with the efforts of their friends. For days Ronald and Daniel had haunted the taverns near Lamartine Castle until they had found a guard susceptible to the heavy bribe they had offered; now all that was left to do was to wait for the appointed time.

Adam waited in readiness as well. The time of his escape had been carefully arranged to coincide with the changing of the guard, and during the last few days he had kept an accurate count of the times his cell was checked. The last round for the night was at eleven thirty, and when the soldier appeared Adam called to him and asked for a drink of water. The guard laughed at his request and left.

As soon as the clatter of his heavy footsteps had faded away, Adam got out the razor and shaved his beard. Using the makeup and mirror, he changed his appearance. The wig and the uniform completed his transformation. Then, he waited.

As the familiar sounds of the changing of the guard were heard out in the courtyard, the guard his friends had bribed appeared to unlock his cell. Adam slipped out to the corridor, and with the man covered the distance to the main hall, where another guard was lounging against the wall. There was a tense moment when the man moved toward them, and

Adam knew relief mingled with surprise when he recognized that it was Ronald.

From there on the three of them continued to walk naturally—three off-duty soldiers on their way home—until they reached the outer door. Still expecting to be stopped at any moment, they passed the armed patrols and parapet unmolested.

Before boarding the coach concealed in the dark, Ronald paid the guard the balance of his bribe as promised, and the man quickly vanished in the shadows. Ronald and Adam embraced, thumping their backs heartily and laughing with relief as the coach sped into the night.

The escape would not be detected for hours, and by that time Adam would be safe in the flat they had rented under an assumed name.

Two days later, Bertrille reappeared and was able to learn that the police was scrutinizing very closely all foreigners coming into Paris or leaving the city, so they decided to lie low a little longer.

Angelique and Lazarus had returned to their normal lives, and Ronald and Daniel went back to London. Within a week, Mein Heer and Mevrouw Van Doorn traveled to Amsterdam in the company of their friends. There were a few moments of tension while their carriage was stopped and the guards carefully examined their papers, but Bernard's credentials got them through without a hitch.

Ten

More than ever, Katherine was glad to go home to Cornwall after their narrow escape from France. Not wanting to alarm Agatha and Jenny—who had been very worried over their delay—both she and Adam refrained from mentioning to them what had really happened.

The terrible danger they had faced, however, made Katherine realize one very important fact: that even though she loved Adam dearly, she really wasn't *in* love *with* him.

This discovery presented her with a dilemma. During all those years she had believed herself in love with Adam, she had also believed that her feelings were returned by him. Had this been her own fabrication as well, or was it true that Adam loved her? After all the kindness and affection he had shown her, the thought of causing him any sort of disappointment was a source of tremendous concern for her.

But there was more. She had also reached the point where she needed to put an end to the double life she had been leading. Each passing year had lessened her taste for the adventures she had to face and, moreover, she longed for the day when she wouldn't have to leave Jason again. Even before learning of Adam's capture, this had been one of the topics she and Natalie had discussed during her convalescence in Amsterdam.

As far as she was concerned, the trap set by the French police had been the *coup de grace* to their illegal activities. They had been extremely fortunate during that episode, but she was well aware of the terrible consequences it could have had for all of them. She hoped and prayed Adam had found the experience sobering enough to make him seriously consider retiring from such a dangerous profession as theirs. They had been operating on the Continent for too long, and sooner or later they were bound to get caught.

And last, but not least, her reasons for having embarked on a life of crime were still very much in Katherine's mind. She had vowed to pay Jonathan back for all the suffering he had caused her, and she now felt that the time had come to fulfill that promise.

However, making her decision was easier than facing Adam with it. It was knowing that he wouldn't try to hold her back that gave Katherine a sense of guilt as though she were abondoning him.

For the first time in many years the winter weeks spent in Cornwall were sad ones for her, knowing that she and Jason would soon have to leave those they had come to look upon as their only family.

"You've been very quiet," Adam observed one evening. "Is there something in your mind?"

Everyone else had retired for the night, leaving them alone in the small drawing room of the cottage. It was the time Katherine had chosen to tell Adam of her decision, but she was having a bit of trouble in broaching the subject.

"I was thinking that Jason's birthday will be here soon," she opened with hesitation. "He'll be six in another month."

Adam set down his empty glass on a nearby table and leaned back in his chair to regard her with a faint smile. "He's growing up, isn't he?"

"Yes," she nodded a little sadly. "Too quickly, I'm afraid."

"I remember when he was born, how tiny he was." He

gave a soft wry chuckle. "I was afraid to hold him for fear of hurting him."

Katherine removed her eyes from the flames burning in the small hearth, and when she looked at him, her soft gaze was troubled. "I don't want to leave him again, Adam," she said quietly.

He was slow to answer, "I know."

She gave a small gasp of surprise. "You do?"

He nodded ruefully. "I've also been doing a lot of thinking these past few weeks, pet. After that scrape in Paris, I think everyone is ready to call it quits."

"I'm so glad!" she exclaimed with an audible sigh of relief.

"Angelique and Lazarus have been talking of starting an acting school, something they've always wanted to do," he went on. "And when I saw Daniel in London last week, he was planning to open a jewelry shop. He'll do well, I know."

"And Ronald?"

"He still wants to paint. I imagine he'll be on his way to Florence soon." He paused briefly, his blue eyes becoming thoughtful. "And you, Katherine? What do you want?"

The flicker of her lashes was a sign of her inner stress when she replied, "I — I'm going to America."

A contained expression came to his eyes. "So you're going after Jonathan," he said in a reflective tone.

A tide of color rushed to her cheeks as she murmured faintly, "I've waited many years, Adam."

"You'll be treading on thin ice, my girl."

"I can take care of myself," she said with a deprecating gesture.

Adam gave a wry shake of his head. "I'm aware of that, Katherine. You've proven yourself very capable in dangerous situations, but this is different,"

"Different?" she repeated, defensively tipping her chin. Then her manner relaxed, and in a more reflective tone, she admitted, "You're right. It is different."

There was a pause. "You said you didn't want to leave Jason again," he observed then, grim faced and unsmiling. "Will you be taking him with you?"

"I can't just leave him behind," she shrugged unhappily. "I don't know how long I'll be in America."

After a moment's silence, Adam cleared his throat. "A few moments ago we were reminiscing of the day he was born," he said. "Do you still plan to keep his existence from Jonathan, or are you planning to use him in your revenge?"

Katherine went ghastly pale.

Unperturbed by the anger crackling in her eyes, he told her in a bland, reasonable tone, "You're making a mistake, pet. Why can't you forget the past and make a new life for yourself and Jason?"

"Forget the past?" She uttered a scornful laugh. How could she, when every time she looked at her son she saw a miniature version of Jonathan? Almost seven years of days—and nights—and despairing loneliness! "Jason is a bastard," she said in a voice tinged with bitterness. "How can I forget that? No, I won't find any peace until I find Jonathan again. I want him to know that I survived his treachery on my own terms. I want him to suffer the way he made me suffer. I want to see him crawl—" Pausing in her impassioned speech, she drew a deep breath in an effort to steady herself. When she spoke again, her tone was almost pleading, "Only then will I be able to start again, Adam. Can't you understand that?"

After sustaining her gaze for a few seconds, he uttered a heavy sigh. "Very well. Since you're dead set on this madness, I suppose there's nothing I can do to stop you," he said with wry shake of his head. "What are your plans?"

"I had thought of going to Baltimore, but I changed my mind after Natalie suggested New York."

"Why New York?" he asked in a curious tone.

"To begin with, it's the most important port on the East Coast," she replied. "Sooner or later Jonathan is bound to stop there. Besides, going to Baltimore doesn't necessarily mean that I'll find him, since he travels so much. But also New York should be safer for me, especially if by the time we meet again I've been able to establish myself there. Natalie was kind enough to offer to write to Bernard's cousins in my behalf, so I shouldn't have much trouble in that respect."

"I see you've thought the whole thing through," he commented wryly. "And you're right about avoiding Baltimore. That's Greenfield territory, and if I remember correctly, they are an influential family." He gave another wry shake of his head and smiled at her. "I should have known you had covered all the angles."

"I had a good teacher," she smiled back.

They sat in companionable silence for a few more minutes until Adam said, "New York, mmm. You know, pet, I've never been to America. I hear it's the land of opportunity."

Katherine shot him a warning glance. "No more of your projects, Adam. I'm through with all that."

"Very well, if you insist," he replied with an engaging grin. "But I've been almost everywhere there is to go in Europe. I like spending a few weeks in England now and then, but, honestly now, pet, can you see me leading the quiet life of landed gentry?" His brows rose humorously.

Although at first Katherine regarded him seriously, she couldn't resist his wicked charm. Still her voice held a note of mild reproach when she said, "Don't think you can fool me for a minute, Adam. I don't need a nursemaid. I'm a big girl now."

"A nursemaid!" he echoed, lifting both hands in a gesture of mock horror.

In spite of herself, Katherine laughed with delight, "Oh, Adam, you're such a rogue!" Leaning forward to reach for his hand, she blurted out unthinkingly, "A dear, sweet, wonderful rogue, and I do love you."

It wasn't until she had spoken those words that she remembered her earlier concern. Good Lord, what had she done? Awkwardly she let go of his hand.

As though aware of her confusion, Adam took her hand back and said gently, "And I love you, Katherine. You're the daughter I never had."

She turned slowly to regard him. His eyes were full of warmth and affection. Rising from the chair, she went to him and impulsively threw her arms around his neck. "Oh, Adam!" she said with emotion. "Thank you, my dear." She pressed her lips to his cheek in a fond kiss.

He put his arms around her for a moment and then, with his hands on her shoulders, held her away to look at her. "A nursemaid, eh?" he snorted through his nose.

They looked at each other for a second or two before they both burst out laughing.

To Katherine's surprise, Agatha and Jenny were excited at the prospect of traveling to America. But no one was more excited than Jason, who from a very early age had shown a marked interest in the sea and ships. He was bursting with excitement when in March the entire family traveled to Plymouth, where they boarded a clipper bound for New York.

In addition to Katherine and her entourage, there were only four other passengers aboard the *Seagull*: the Ramseys, a middle-aged couple from New York; Donald Baxter, a widower from Albany, was also middle-aged and very quiet; and finally Maxwell Chapman, an attractive bachelor apparently in his late thirties whose demeanor was polite, if somewhat aloof.

Dinner with the other passengers and officers was the highlight of each day; conversation was lively then, and Adam's easygoing, natural charm soon made him the most popular person aboard. At those times Chapman mainly watched and listened, contributing little to the repartee, while, on the other hand, Katherine joined the others with amusing stories. On occasion she would also take part in the friendly card games that took place after supper; at other times, however, she preferred to stroll the deck by herself, seeking moments of quiet solitude.

The ship was a clipper, and even though she had never sailed on a vessel of this type before it had a familiar feeling—perhaps because Jonathan had spoken of them so often. There were times when lifting her gaze to the billowing canvas, she could almost hear again the words he had used to describe the beauty of a clipper in full sail. *Half-poetry*—he had said—*all daring . . . the most beautiful sight in the world.*

Having found a spot that offered relative shelter from the icy winds of the North Atlantic, Katherine leaned against the railing. Cupping her chin in her hand, she absently stared at the white caps of the waves punctuating the darkness around them. This far north the mantle of stars appeared much brighter, and closer than she had ever seen them before.

Following the silver path penciled by the moon, the clipper glided through the waves leaving her past behind. There would be a new life for her after she had found Jonathan, she reflected. Her transformation from the serving girl he had known to the woman she had now become had taken years of work and careful development. She had prepared herself for the possibility that he wouldn't recognize her or even remember her. He had been her life; she had carried in her body the seed of their union, but to him she had been just one of many he had used and abandoned without a backward glance—a casual affair to satisfy his physical needs between voyages.

Would she ever find love again, Katherine asked herself then, or had Jonathan destroyed her capacity to love another man? Out there, almost suspended between sea and sky as though alone in the center of the universe, the future hovered before her as a dark unknown.

Suddenly, she was frightened.

Was Adam right in his warnings? Was she making a mistake in trying to exact her revenge? But she had to! As long as Jonathan walked the earth and sailed the seas without paying his debt to her, she would never be free to begin her life over again. And she wanted, desperately needed to love again—for her own sake as well as Jason's. Her greatest sorrow was to think of her son bearing the stigma of illegitimacy. Would he hate her for it when he was old enough to understand? She couldn't bear the thought of such possibility.

Even to begin her new life it was necessary to resort to deception, she thought with a touch of bitterness. Regardless of her wealth, doors which would open to the widow of a British officer killed in India she was now impersonating, would be closed to her if her real status of unwed mother were to be known. Therefore, she had agreed with some reluctance when Adam suggested that she should be known as Mrs. Cameron, and he as her father.

Stirring from her private thoughts, Katherine gave a sigh of resignation. The hour was advanced, and abandoning her post she returned to her cabin without taking notice of the tall figure who had been watching her from the shadows.

Maxwell Chapman had gone out on deck with the express intention of addressing her. He had looked for her until he found her standing alone by the railing; but her manner had been so absent, her gaze so remote, that he was reluctant to intrude on her reflections. From the very first moment he had been impressed by her beauty, but his admiration had increased as days passed and he had listened to her contributions to the general conversation. He found her quite intelligent and exciting, which he considered a remarkable combination for someone of her physical attributes.

The scion of a distinguished New York family and totally dedicated to his many business interests, Maxwell Chapman had never married. Black hair, slate-gray eyes, a patrician nose and a mouth of sensual lips complemented his elegant, slender fine figure of a man. All this combined with his name and his wealth to make him a prime target for the mothers of coy, giggling young girls who bored him to distraction, for he had found that his physical needs could be satisfied without demands on his emotions. His initial aloofness toward Katherine and her family was mostly due to his familiarity with Mrs. Ramsey's fondness for gossip.

Katherine was surprised when one evening during one of Mrs. Ramsey's bouts with *mal de mer,* Chapman offered to escort her on deck. She accepted graciously, and to her delight discovered that he could be quite charming. Like herself, Chapman was an avid reader and music lover, and that evening they remained on deck until the small hours of the morning engaged in animated conversation. She was pleased to learn that they shared similar tastes in music, and he was quite impressed by the knowledge she displayed on topics such as art and literature.

That evening marked the beginning of the companionable friendship that developed between them during the following days.

Even Jason took an immediate liking to Maxwell Chapman, who fascinated the little boy with his tales of the sea and its creatures, and patiently answered the spate of eager questions Katherine's son kept throwing at him.

Jason was particularly fascinated by the dolphins which from time to time raced alongside the ship. With the fresh wonder of youth he watched the sleek silver bodies riding the waves in graceful arcs executed in perfect unison, and listened to the strange sounds emitted by the animals — almost as if they were laughing, an impression that was heightened by their quizzically smiling faces.

It didn't take long for Mrs. Ramsey to notice the assiduous attention the very eligible bachelor was paying to the lovely young widow. Anxious to learn more about their budding romance, the garrulous lady redoubled her efforts to obtain further details from Agatha.

She found, however, that Agatha was busy elsewhere. Adam's sister seemed to have blossomed in the company of Mr. Baxter, who appered to lose all of his bashfulness in her presence. Most of her time was spent with the widower from Albany, and had Katherine not been so occupied herself with Maxwell Chapman, she would have been delighted to notice the relationship that was developing between them.

For Katherine, weeks seemed to fly by in Maxwell Chapman's pleasing company. She felt comfortable with his friendly, yet somewhat reserved manner, and his attentions toward Jason made him especially dear to her. Her instincts told her that his interest went beyond friendship; in unguarded moments she had caught a certain look of desire in his slate gray eyes. Yet she was pleased by the prospect, for she herself was attracted to his handsome dark looks. Neither of them, however, seemed ready to change the nature of their friendly relationship to a more intimate one.

The voyage had been a pleasant one, but it was nearing its end; the *Seagull* would be sailing into New York Harbor before the week was out. One evening while watching the sun set across the ocean, Katherine wondered if any of the friendships started aboard would survive their arrival in New York. She certainly wished to continue seeing Max Chapman.

As the ship neared its final destination, the balmier weather made their evening strolls more pleasant. Two days before reaching New York, they were standing in Katherine's favorite spot in the evening when, without a word, Max's arms suddenly went around Katherine's waist and he drew her to him.

"No, Max," she pleaded faintly.

Rather than releasing her, Max tightened his hold on her, and before she could stop him his lips covered hers in a long and passionate kiss that she tried to resist.

As his kiss grew more demanding, little by little her resistance faded, and she began to respond with hesitation at first that then became frantic hunger.

Her mouth left his abruptly, and for one shattering moment she looked at him with startled, frightened eyes. Her hands covered her mouth to muffle a groan of anguish.

Max took one step toward her when she started to turn away. "Katherine, wait," he said in a puzzled voice.

Katherine didn't listen, she didn't stop. Ignoring his call she ran away, back to her cabin where she leaned back against the closed door and pressed her hands to her breast as though to still the wild pounding of her heart. She felt like crying and didn't even know why.

She undressed and got into bed next to her son. And when at last the tears began to flow, she stifled her sobs on her pillow trying not to wake him.

Why had she been so disturbed by Max's kisses, she asked herself over and over. She had been aware that he desired her and found the idea appealing. Then why had she suddenly been so frightened? The answer came when she realized that the real reason for her state of agitation was her own response to his kisses.

She had been kissed many times and by different men in the course of the last years, but not even once had any of those kisses affected her at all. With Max it had been different.

Was it possible that she was falling in love with him?

For the first time since the inception of their friendship, Katherine felt ill at ease when she met with Max the next day.

Chapman couldn't help but notice her uneasiness. "Will you walk with me this evening?" he asked, still puzzled by her manner. "We must talk."

"Of course, Max," she replied after a brief hesitation.

For the rest of the day Katherine was on pins and needles.

Caught in a seething mass of conflicting emotions, she wanted, yet feared, the moment when she would be alone with him again. Over and over she told herself that she liked him, that she found him desirable; what, then, was the problem? Her emotions were so entangled, her desires so agonizingly confused, that she didn't know what to do.

No one but Max seemed to notice how strangely subdued she appeared during supper that evening. Anxious to be alone with her again, he kept throwing overt glances in her direction that she largely ignored.

After the meal was over and he was finally able to take her out on deck, she seemed a little distant as silently they stood side by side at the railing.

In all of his thirty-eight years, Max had never felt the strange sensations that he experienced as he contemplated Katherine's face bathed in moonlight. The slight tremor of her lower lip brought the memory of their kisses and an unfamiliar ache at the base of his throat. Craving, needing to touch her, he drew her in his arms once more. She came to him, yielding and trembling, and offering no resistance to the lips that claimed hers.

Her full, generous lips were soft, and they parted at the touch of his tongue to allow him access to the moist, warm recesses of her mouth that he explored with the wild intoxication of delight. Her hands crept up the front of his shirt with hesitation and finally entwined behind his neck as her tongue began responding to the caress of his.

Suddenly she drew back and abruptly turned away.

Torn between elation and disappointment, Max regarded her for a moment before he went to stand behind her. Encircling her waist, he bent forward a little to press a kiss on her temple.

"What's wrong, Katherine?"

The warmth of his breath on her skin made her close her eyes. "I'm frightened, Max," she said at last in a constricted voice. "There's so much you don't know about me."

223

He gave a small, wry chuckle. "It doesn't matter, darling."

"Oh, but it does!" Turning to face him, she looked at him gravely. "I care for you, Max, and I believe you care for me, too; but we still have time to break away without hurting each other."

His speculative glance made her eyes fall wretchedly. "There's a great deal I can't tell you because there are other people involved," she went on in a subdued voice. "I have no right to reveal their secret, Max. All I can tell you is that for the last few years, I've lived outside the law."

A mystified expression came to his face. "Are you— wanted by the police?" he asked at last in a shocked voice.

She shook her head. "I can't give you any details, Max, but no. Katherine Cameron is not wanted."

"Is that your real name?" he probed with unfeigned confusion.

"Yes," she assented in a low voice.

His eyes searched her face when he asked, "And your husband? Was he also involved?"

Her face flamed. "I was never married," she confessed, avoiding looking at him. "Jason is . . . illegitimate."

A note of disapproval was in his voice when he asked, "Is Adam Garfield your real father?"

She looked up at him and saw a dark, smoldering anger in his eyes. "He's my closest and dearest friend," she said quietly. "He and his sister came to my aid when I needed them, many years ago. They're my family now."

An uneasy silence spread between them as Max stared at her with a frown.

Breaking the constrained pause, she said, "Good night, Max." Slowly she turned and walked away.

His tense expression didn't change as his eyes followed her until she disappeared. She had offered no explanations, no excuses; she had simply stated the facts without seeking his sympathy.

For a second his eyes darkened. What he had just learned

explained the determination Katherine had shown to find a new life for herself and her son. Whatever the circumstances of his birth, it was obvious that she adored the boy. A new question came to mind: had she loved the father as much?

And, for the first time in his life, Maxwell Chapman knew jealousy.

Back in her cabin, Katherine quietly undressed in the dark. She got into bed, and lying on her back stared pensively at the ceiling. In spite of the loneliness she was feeling at the moment, she was surprised to find no lingering regrets in her mind. And, strangely enough, she was no longer afraid.

It was then that she understood that what she had been dreading all along had been telling Max the truth about herself. But she was sick and tired of lying.

Why had she told him now, she berated herself then. She knew she would never enter into a relationship under false pretenses, but why couldn't she have waited a little longer, until stronger feelings had developed between them? She called herself a fool; judging from his manner she had frightened Max away. She wouldn't be at all surprised if he never spoke to her again.

At this thought, the feeling of loneliness that had set in began to degenerate in disenchantment.

When Katherine saw no trace of Max during the last day on board, even though she had been half-expecting it, she felt disappointed and rather depressed. Deep in her heart she had hoped he would still want her, and it saddened her to discover that he didn't. In an effort to shake off her despondency, she told herself that it was better this way, before her own feelings for him became deeper. If there was something she didn't need in her life it was another heartbreak as the one she had already suffered at the hands of Jonathan.

Everyone was excited about their arrival the next day, those returning home as well as those reaching the American shores for the first time. Only Katherine and Max found it necessary to make an effort not to dampen the spirit of the evening.

At the end of the meal Max surprised her when he turned to her and with a studiously polite air inquired, "Would you care to take one last stroll on deck, Mrs. Cameron?"

"With pleasure, Mr. Chapman," she replied with a calmness she didn't altogether feel.

Neither of them spoke while he led her to their usual place. Once there, she managed to retain her serene expression as she looked up at him.

His eyes were dark as he gazed deeply into her green ones. He could easily get lost in those emerald pools, he thought. Beset by an emotion that was new and strange, he took her face in his hands and said huskily, "What an extraordinary woman you are, Katherine Cameron."

As his mouth came down to seek her own, a bright warmth flooded to her cheeks to fill her face with light. Her pulse beat quickened, and she returned his kisses imbued with an incredible joy.

Against a skyline of church spires, ships bearing flags from every corner of the world crowded the busy New York harbor when the *Seagull* discharged her passengers at the Battery.

Katherine, Adam and the rest of their group boarded a hotel stage that would take them to the Astor House, which Max had recommended as the finest in the city. Once they had breasted the traffic on Broadway — heavy with hackneys, wagons, carts and private vehicles — and reached their final destination, wryly they noticed that directly across the street from the pillared blue granite facade of the hotel was a graveyard.

Katherine found the decoration of the public rooms a bit too ostentatious for her taste, but to her immense relief the guest suites built around a handsome courtyard were bright, airy, and much to her liking.

Late that same afternoon they received a visit from a Mr. Lampson, a house agent sent to them by Maxwell Chapman to assist them in finding a suitable house.

After they had explained their requirements, Mr. Lampson warned them that the tremendous growth of the city had made housing terribly scarce. "But your arrival is most timely," he said cheerfully. "Moving Day is just around the corner."

"Moving Day?" Katherine inquired curiously. "What does that mean, Mr. Lampson?"

"Most leases expire on the first of May, Mrs. Cameron," the agent explained. "It's the time to change residences."

Her brows rose humorously. "Are you saying that all the people in the city move on the same day?"

"Only those who lease their homes," the agent nodded.

Katherine met Agatha's eyes in an amused, communicative side glance. "It must be quite confusing," she said with a half-smile.

"I'm sure you and your family will suffer no inconvenience, Mrs. Cameron," Mr. Lampson rushed to assure her.

The interview ended after Mr. Lampson promised to be back the next day with a list of properties for their inspection. After he left, the family decided to remain at the hotel for the evening.

In spite of her travels, hotel living was practically a new experience for Katherine. Although Jenny preferred to stay with Jason and take advantage of the room service offered by the hotel, Katherine, Agatha and Adam made use of the opulent restaurant and its splendid menu.

After supper, while Adam retired to the hotel's smoking room with the other gentlemen, Katherine and Agatha were introduced to the mysteries of the American rocking chair during their visit to the ladies' parlor. Thoroughly enjoying themselves, they swayed back and forth in rhythmic motion until the time came to rejoin the gentlemen.

Ensuing days were spent mostly inspecting properties, but all the houses Mr. Lampson had to show them were found unsuitable. By the end of the week, when they were beginning to think that they were going to miss the target date of the first of May, the house agent spoke of yet another property and of the efforts he had been making to secure permission for a visit. He finished by saying that he was expecting an answer soon, and that he would return when it came.

True to his word, he appeared two days later.

"Mistress Cameron, Mr. Garfield," he greeted them, looking very pleased with himself. "I truly believe you'll like this house. The owners are presently in Europe, where they're expected to remain for another two years," he went on excitedly once they were underway. "Their business manager consented to a lease—subject to your approval, of course—only after I invoked Mr. Chapman's name. As you will see, it's a beautiful house, and it even includes an excellent staff."

Looking out the carriage window, Katherine saw that the streets they were traveling were wide, lined with trees, and flanked on both sides by individual residences as well as rowhouses of harmonizing styles. A while later the carriage passed through tall wrought iron gates of intricate and painstaking design. On both sides of the graveled driveway, the well-tended lawn appeared as green and as smooth as a length of velvet.

The house was Grecian in style, with a marble facade and free-standing doorway porch with fluted columns. The rosewood-paneled door opened almost immediately after they rang the bell, and they were greeted by a distinguished-looking butler who admitted them as soon as Mr. Lampson identified himself and his companions.

In the spacious entrance hall, a Persian silk Kum carpet partially convered a tesselated floor in black and white marble. A large painting above the *meridienne* and a mirror-backed pier table supporting an enormous vase of fresh-cut flowers served as the foreground to a wide, majestic staircase.

Wide folding doors opened into a parlor where mahogany caned chairs and settees upholstered in blue and yellow lampas harmonized with the drapes to give the room an air of elegant simplicity. In the evenings argand lamps, wall sconces and crystal chandeliers would illuminate the room which at the moment was flooded with afternoon sunshine. Two fluted columns flanked the Italian marble mantlepiece supporting a porcelain ormolu clock which chimed the half hour while they were inspecting the room. The design of the exquisite Aubusson carpet repeated a pattern of medallions of flowers against a dark blue background that harmonized with the walls, which were painted a robin's egg blue. Small tables and etageres held a variety of *objets d'art* that their experienced eyes recognized as valuable, as were the excellent paintings hanging on the walls in elaborate gilt frames. A variety of plants and vases of flowers added color and fragrance to the charming room.

Bruce, as the butler had identified himself, threw open the double doors that separated the front parlor from the back one — which was used as a drawing room — and this merged two rooms into a larger one. Here the same colors prevailed, blue walls and satinwood furniture upholstered in yellow silk.

The tour continued through a richly wood-paneled and well-stocked library where Katherine lingered to admire an extensive collection of beautifully leather-bound books; a sun-filled music room where she saw a rosewood pianoforte with bands of carved, gilt molding; a dining room large enough to accommodate a great number of guests.

Of the several bedchambers on the second floor, she instantly fell in love with one where the paper on the walls had rows of muted yellow roses with soft tones of green and the faintest bit of pink. A great mahogany bed hung with crewel-embroidered curtains, a scalloped table set with English tea porcelain, a mahogany chair covered in pale green Italian brocatelle—these were some of the treasures she found there. She was surprised and quite delighted when Bruce opened the cherrywood base of a tall mirror with candle holders set at the corners, and uncovered a musical mechanism that, he explained, could play six different tunes. It was one of Mrs. Owen's prized possessions, he added, as was the French secretaire inlaid with lemonwood.

The french windows opened onto a small balcony overlooking the gardens, and the cool afternoon breeze brought in the sweet scent of the wisteria climbing on a trellis outside the window.

Once they had finished inspecting the premises, they were taken across a flagstone terrace to the grounds, where in addition to the rolling green lawns, there were wide hedges, colorful boxes of flowers and a greenhouse.

Jason was delighted with the visit to the carriage house and stables. Included in the lease was a luxurious landau, and there were four horses, each in its individual stall. The carriage horses were magnificent pair of matched Morgan Grays; the other two, a beautiful chestnut mare named Cindy, and a haughty black thoroughbred which answered to Sir Percival.

Katherine had fallen in love with the house at first sight, and at the end of the tour she knew they had to look no further. After discussing the matter with the others, they all agreed to go ahead and sign the lease.

Two dozen roses in a hand-painted vase were awaiting for Katherine at the hotel. In the accompanying note Max apologized for not having called on her, but a great deal of business requiring his immediate attention had accumulated during his absence. He asked if she would have supper with him the following evening and ended the missive by saying that he would be leaving New York in two days. *I've missed you,* read the brief postscript.

"And I've missed you, Max!" Katherine said out loud, merrily dancing about the room as she waved the note in her hand.

Immediately she set to compose a reply, accepting his invitation and telling him that she also had missed him.

Jason, who always insisted on doing for himself, was too sleepy this evening to offer a protest when she changed him into his nightshirt. He fell asleep as soon as his head touched the pillow, but Katherine was reluctant to leave her son so soon.

This was their special time of day, when after putting Jason to bed she would sit with him and read him stories. At other times they played their games or simply exchanged confidences. She had missed so much of his growing years, that now she wanted to make up for all the lost time. After watching him sleep for a few moments, she bent over the sleeping child and touched her lips to the warm, velvety cheek.

"Good night, my little man," she smiled and stroked his pale blond hair. Then she turned down the lamp and quietly went from the room.

The following day was a busy one, repacking their trunks and arranging for their transportation to their new home; still, Katherine was ready and waiting when Max arrived promptly at eight. She opened the door herself and stepped into his arms to answer his eager kiss.

Holding her close, he murmured into her hair, "Good Lord, how I've missed you!"

She returned his embrace, and then drew back a little to smile at him, "And I you, Max."

Reluctant to let her go, with his hands at her waist he regarded her lovingly. "You're even lovelier than I remembered," he said huskily.

She was breathtaking. Trimmed with frothy white lace at the neckline and sleeves, the shimmering pink taffeta gown lent a special lustre to her skin and left her shoulders bare. A double-strand pearl-and-diamond necklace matched the earrings sparkling in her small, pink earlobes. In spite of the current fashion of ringlets and elaborate frills, Katherine was confident enough to wear her own personal style. The one she had chosen this evening was simple yet elegant, and it served to accentuate the purity of her features.

She also regarded him with undisguised admiration. "Then we must make a very striking pair," she smiled at him, her eyes sparkling with pleasure. "You look devilishly handsome, Max."

He accepted her offer of a drink.

"Where are we going?" she asked as she handed him the glass.

"I'm taking you to a restaurant known for the best roast beef and Yorkshire pudding this side of the Atlantic," he replied.

"Lovely!" she grinned, sitting next to him on the Chesterfield settee. "A fare after my own English heart."

Their eyes met in a humorous glance that communicated affection. "I thought you'd approve," he said with a half-smile.

Dressed in his nightshirt, Jason burst into the parlor at that moment and was elated to see Max again.

"Max!" he cried, bubbling with excitement as he ran to him. "We're moving to a big house tomorrow, and I shall have ships in my room!"

Since Max was well acquainted with the Owens, owners of the house Katherine had leased, he knew that the ships Jason had mentioned were model ships that the youngest son of his friends — now a grown man — had collected during his childhood.

232

"Well now, young man," he said, setting his glass on the table to reach into his pocket. There was a small package in his hand when it came out. "Do you think you could find room for one more?"

Jason took the package Max offered and began unwrapping it with cheerful expectation. His face lit up with delight at the sight of the tiny replica of a clipper ship. He smiled, and impulsively throwing his chubby little arms around Max's neck cried, "Thank you, Max!"

Katherine's eyes became suspiciously bright as she watched them. She was touched and deeply grateful for Max's attentions toward her child, and this thoughtfulness endeared him to her even more.

"You're spoiling him," she chided him, yet her smile was full of warmth. She turned to Jason then. "Say good night to Max, darling,"

Before taking his mother's hand, Jason gave Max another quick but exuberant hug. Half-turning from the door leading into the bedchamber, Katherine said, "I shan't be long."

"Take your time," Max nodded, and picking up his glass again leaned back in the settee.

While awaiting Katherine's return, he thought of the glow that had come to her eyes at his gesture of bringing Jason a small gift. Smiling inwardly he told himself that a sure way to her heart was through her son. But he had to admit, it wasn't too difficult to like the ebullient little fellow.

Max rose to his feet when Katherine reappeared a short time later.

"He's so excited with your gift," she said coming toward him. "It was very sweet of you, Max. Thank you."

She stood on the tips of her toes to kiss him softly, but instead he pulled her to him, and folding her in his arms ardently sought her lips in a kiss that was long and deep. When he finally let go of her and she settled against his chest with a contented sigh, she could hear the pounding of his heart.

Max tried to disguise his emotion with a small jest, "What would I get for a big ship?"

"Oh, you!" she laughed, playfully pushing him away.

Jenny came in to stay with Jason as Max was helping Katherine with her pelisse. They said good night and went out.

His carriage was waiting in front of the hotel, and during the ride to the restaurant, Katherine told Max of their search for the house.

"Mr. Lampson was so patient, Max, and so helpful. I can't thank you enough for sending him to us."

"I'm glad he was able to help you," he replied, his gaze inexorably drawn to her lips. Her nearness and the soft fragrance emanating from her were too much for him to bear without wanting to touch her, crush her in his arms and taste her mouth once more. His loins were uncomfortably stirring with her proximity, and he tried to control his growing desire.

Great Scot! he groaned inwardly. No woman ever had affected him by just sitting there and talking of plain, ordinary things!

After their arrival in New York, Max had purposely stayed away from Katherine. Fighting the effect she had exerted over him during the voyage he had sought his mistress, who had been anxious to recover his affections after his prolonged absence. The gifts he had brought back from Europe had made Claire even more eager to please him, and after the long weeks of forced celibacy, in her body Max had found a welcome relief to his pent-up desires.

He had hoped that once back in New York, the pressures of business and the availability of Claire's charms would relegate Katherine to a not so prominent place in his mind. In fact, he had even hoped he would stop thinking about her altogether. A few days away from Katherine, however, had just made him wish the more to see her again. What was worse, his use of Claire only served to increase his longing for Katherine.

"The more I fight it, the worse it gets," he finally had to admit. He had sent the note and the flowers still hoping that when he saw her again, her effect on him would have diminished; but when she had opened the door, one look at her had convinced him to stop fighting windmills. Just holding her in his arms, kissing her sweet mouth, was far more thrilling to him than Claire's most expert handlings.

The restaurant was fashioned after the old English inns. There were burly benches, candles blazing on the tables, and jolly hubbub in the air. Mounted on the walls was a conglomeration of hunting horns, tankards and mugs, and pictures of hunts. The chill of the early spring evening warranted the cheerful log fire that was blazing in the enormous hearth. An obsequious waiter led them into a separate and more elegant dining area where benches gave way to individual table settings.

As they took their places, Max noticed how a few people looked away, a little embarrassed at having been caught staring. There were others, however, who continued to boldly examine Katherine from head to toe.

The stir created by their entrance didn't escape her, but Katherine made a pretense not to notice. Only after they were seated and the waiter gone for the wine Max had ordered, did she allow herself to look around the room and smiled at the staring ladies. The majority of them smiled back and returned their attention to their companions; one woman—who for a long time had been pushing her daughter at Max in vain—ignored her smile and continued to regard her with undisguised animosity.

"It's lovely, Max," she said, enchanted by the atmosphere of her homeland. "But I suppose we've created quite a stir. I told you we made a striking couple."

Max smiled and refrained from comment. He had enjoyed watching how she had handled the staring old biddies.

They sipped their wine and talked while waiting for the food to be served.

"What do you think of New York?" he inquired then. "Is it what you had expected?"

"It's much more, Max!" she replied, tipping her hand. "I haven't seen much of it as yet, but I've liked what I've seen." She paused and pensively toyed with the stem of her glass. "In Europe we hear a great deal about the American wilderness, about the savages and the people they kill. I've even heard them speak of New York as a large village, but they're so wrong!" Her voice quickened with enthusiasm to add, "There's so much energy out there!"

Her animation brought a sparkle of pleasure to his eyes. He loved this city where he had been born. Even after traveling to a great extent, no other place in the world gave him the exhilaration he felt in New York. Katherine had put it very aptly: *the energy,* she had said.

"I believe that in time New York will be the largest and most important city in the world," he confided. "I hope you'll let me show it to you when I return."

"I'd love that, Max," she said, a warm gaze accompanying her words. "To see it with you for the first time."

His hand started to reach for hers, but at that moment the waiter came to serve their meal and Max pulled back with a wry shake of his head.

Conversation ebbed while they did justice to the delicious Scotch broth that was followed by a delicate trout. After those dishes had been whisked away, Katherine's mouth watered at the sight of a slice of rare roast beef and the golden Yorkshire pudding that came with it. Roasted potatoes and sweet garden peas completed the fare.

"But this is grand, truly it is!" she exclaimed with unfeigned delight after tasting the succulent beef.

The waiter who was refilling their glasses beamed at her hearty approval.

Max had always been annoyed by girls who picked daintily at their food, but Katherine ate with relish, savoring every bite. As a man who enjoyed good food, good wines, and good cigars, her obvious pleasure made his own far more enjoyable.

During the course of their conversation after the delicious meal, Katherine learned that Max was well acquainted with Bernard's cousins, Frank and Johanna Benink.

"They'll introduce you to all the important people," he said a little wryly. "And I guess there'll be a lot of competition for your company when I get back from my trip."

"I'll be very happy when you return, Max," she said, her voice soft and gentle as a caress.

Through the entire evening Max had been anticipating the moment when he could be alone with Katherine; therefore, after escorting her to her suite, rather than saying good night at the door, he managed to get inside. It wasn't too difficult; knowing that it would be at least two more weeks before she saw him again, Katherine was reluctant to part from him so soon.

Once Jenny had gone, he wasted no time in taking Katherine in his arms. Willingly returning his kisses, she floated on a cloud of pleasing sensations while desire was mounting in his blood. As his kisses grew more demanding, his hands became bolder; seeking the warmth of her breasts, they gently stroked and fondled the satiny globes as his mouth traced the swelling column of her throat.

Katherine didn't realize that Max had eased her gown off her shoulders until it was too late.

"I want you so, Katherine!" he said huskily, firmly holding on to her when she tried to pull away.

"Max, please stop."

He still refused to let her go. "I want you so, my darling," he repeated between kisses. "Let me stay and make love to you."

Aroused by his caresses, Katherine was having difficulty in retaining her senses while her protests continued to go unheeded.

"My, God, you're so beautiful!" His mouth sought the soft mounds that cried to be fondled. She tried to push him away, but he wouldn't let her go. "Don't fight me, darling, please," he murmured as he teased her taut nipple with his tongue.

Struggling to resist the demands of the love-neglected flesh, Katherine was at the end of her rope; but when he lifted her skirts to caress her thighs she knew that if she didn't make him stop, they would soon reach the point of no return.

"Stop, Max. Stop *now!*"

Her tone brooked no room for argument, and with an agonized groan Max finally released her.

Bouncing to her feet, Katherine kept out of his reach while she covered herself with unsteady hands.

"I'm sorry, Max, I can't! Please don't ask me!" she pleaded, in a tremulous voice. She knew she was causing him pain; she herself felt the same.

A furrow deepened on his brow as he regarded her with an injured air, but the unfallen tears glistening in her pleading eyes made him take a moment to collect himself.

"Forgive me," he said hoarsely, his composure beginning to return. "I've behaved abominably. I'm sorry."

"I'm to blame, too, Max," she said with a tinge of regret in her voice. "I should have stopped you sooner, only I — I just couldn't."

With a rueful smile Max rose to his feet. Then collecting his hat and his cape he headed for the door.

"Good night, Katherine," he tossed over his shoulder before going out.

The door closed behind him — not with a slam, but quite emphatically.

Eleven

Once installed in the new residence, the family began to discuss their visit to Natalie's American cousins by marriage. Without wasting another minute, Adam sent a note apprising the Beninks of their arrival in New York, and the messenger came back with an invitation to tea for the following afternoon.

"Aha!" Adam said cheerfully. "At last we're beginning to make some progress!" Rubbing his hands together, he gave Katherine the flicker of a wink from his left eye when he added, "We'll be in the thick of things very shortly, pet."

Poor Adam, she mused wryly. The women had been quite thrilled with the search of the house and all the moving entailed, but the whole thing had been an utter bore to him. He was itching to get into action again; after all, an actor needs an audience.

However, Adam had not been idle. In the brief time that had elapsed since their arrival, he had already collected an impressive amount of information on people of interest.

"I've learned quite a bit about your friend Chapman," he told Katherine. "He's very wealthy, my girl!" After a moment's silence, he cautioned, "But be careful, pet. He's considered a confirmed bachelor who for years has maintained quite a string of mistresses."

239

Striving to look unimpressed, Katherine didn't look up from her embroidery.

"I understand that his current protege is a beautiful French-Canadian by the name of Claire," he went on at her lack of reaction. "Apparently, she's got quite a reputation for her — er, talents. Be sure that if you replace her in his affections, you have a wedding ring to show for it, pet."

A man like Max had strong physical needs to satisfy, Katherine told herself, and he certainly was rich enough to keep not one, but a dozen mistresses if he so desired. Even though she shouldn't be surprised by what she had just heard, she found herself frowning slightly. The discovery galled her, especially when only a few evenings before Max had tried to make love to her. But had not Jonathan admitted to loving his wife moments after having made passionate love to her? Men! There wasn't a single one of them who could be trusted!

"Don't you fret, Adam," she said with calm indifference. "I have no intention of becoming anyone's mistress, regardless of how rich he may be."

Adam knew her too well to be taken in by her affected nonchalance. He studied her carefully for a few seconds before asking with concern, "Katherine, are you falling in love with this Chapman fellow?"

Her first impulse was to deny it. Following a brief hesitation, however, she realized that it was foolish not to be honest with Adam — or with herself. "I don't know," she replied in a thoughtful voice. Avoiding his glance, she conceded with some reluctance, "He — he excites me. And he's been wonderful to all of us, especially to Jason, and Jason is very fond of him."

She fell silent. After a brief pause, she shrugged her shoulders. "At any rate, I don't know if I'll ever see him again."

"Oh?" He looked at her with raised eyebrows.

With a slight sense of guilt, Katherine told him of the episode at the hotel.

As she spoke, Adam's expression began to show amusement. Although Katherine had carefully omitted the juicier details, he could very well envision the scene.

"Not to worry, pet," he said with confidence at the end of her recount. "He'll be back."

She pensively shook her head. "I don't know, Adam. He was very angry when he left."

"Ah, pet, but I do know!" he chuckled, eyeing her with wry amusement. "Now, would you care to make a little bet to make it more interesting?"

One swift look at his face made Katherine burst out laughing, "You old rascal! You would bet on your own funeral, wouldn't you?"

A little while later, Katherine decided to change for dinner. At the bottom of the stairs she ran into Laurie, one of the downstairs maids who had just answered the door and was now carrying a bulky envelope in her hand.

"Is that for me, Laurie?" she inquired, hoping for a message from Max.

"No, mum," the girl shook her head. "It's for Mistress Agatha, mum."

"Agatha?" Katherine's brows rose quizzically. She put out her hand and said, "I'll take it to her, Laurie."

When Laurie handed over the letter, Katherine stole a brief glance at the return address on the envelope. The sender was a Mr. D. Baxter, in Albany. With a smug inward smile, Katherine told herself that Agatha had carefully avoided mentioning her friend. "On second thought, Laurie," she told the maid, returning the envelope, "perhaps it would be better if you deliver it yourself. And, please, don't mention I saw it unless she asks, all right?"

"Yes, mum."

Katherine's thoughtful gaze followed the girl as she went up the stairs. Agatha and Mr. Baxter? But why not? she reflected a little wryly. As she climbed the stairs, Katherine wished she had paid more attention to the widower from Albany. He had been such a quiet, self-effacing gentleman that she had taken little notice of him. Then, too, at that time she herself had been too busy with Max to notice much of anything else.

While in her bath, Katherine pondered on her discovery and decided to wait until Agatha herself brought up the subject of Mr. Baxter. Poor Agatha, she thought. She had been alone for so long!

Will I spend so many years alone too, she asked herself then. She thought of Max, and the memory of his kisses made her long for the comfort of his arms. Will she ever see him again, she wondered.

The following day, a warm reception by the Beninks marked the beginning of a pleasant afternoon. Johanna was a lovely, petite woman with dark brown hair and golden-brown eyes that sparkled with mischief. She was dressed in deep purple with a long rope of pearls as her only adornment. Her delicate, flawless complexion made it difficult to discern her age, which was anywhere from the mid-twenties to mid-thirties. Her husband, Frank, was a tall and pleasant fellow who bore a marked resemblance to his Dutch cousin, Bernard.

"How marvelous to meet you at last!" Johanna said with effusive cordiality in her voice. "We received a letter from Natalie and Bernard just a few weeks ago telling us that you were coming, and we've been dying to hear from you ever since."

Obviously, Johanna was the most extroverted of the pair.

"And how are they?" Katherine inquired with interest. "It's been a while since we last saw them in Amsterdam."

"Couldn't be happier," Johanna replied with an engaging

smile. She paused with an air of promise and then announced, "Natalie is with child."

Katherine's sensitive features lit up with pleasure. "How wonderful!" she cried, clasping her hands before her in delight.

"I knew you'd be pleased," Johanna said with a sparkle of pleasure in her golden-brown eyes. "Natalie mentioned that the two of you were very close friends. Oh, and by the way," she added as an afterthought while reaching for an envelope that lay on a nearby table, "She sent you this in our care. I'm sure she'll give you a detailed account."

"Thank you, Mrs. Benink," Katherine said as she eagerly reached for the letter.

"Please call me Johanna, my dear," the hostess invited with a friendly smile. "Natalie and Bernard have spoken so fondly of all of you, that we feel as though we've known you for ages."

Johanna kept the conversation flowing while they sipped their tea and munched on dainty little sandwiches and scrumptious pastries.

Her mouth opened in mild astonishment when she learned that they had leased the Owens' residence. "My dears, how on earth did you manage that?" she inquired with avid curiosity.

Tipping one hand, Katherine replied, "Well, during the crossing we met Maxwell Chapman and . . ."

Johanna gave an incredulous gasp. "*The* Maxwell Chapman?" she exclaimed, looking quite perplexed.

"So it seems," Katherine replied, her tone becoming cautious. "He mentioned that he's a friend of yours."

"That's right," the hostess nodded, "but we haven't seen him in ages." The gaze of her brown eyes betrayed alertness when she inquired, "So tell me, what happened?"

"Nothing, really." Katherine gave a deprecating shrug. "He sent a house agent who took us to see several properties, and when we saw the Owens', we knew it was the one we wanted." She fell silent, having caught the humorous, communicative side glance that crossed between the host and hostess.

"How nice of Max to send his house agent," Johanna observed, her tone wry and humorous. "I'm sure the man was very helpful."

"Oh, yes," Katherine smiled. By now she was secretly amused by the marked interest of her new friends on her acquaintance with Max. "And the house is quite lovely. As a matter of fact, even my son is delighted with it. He found a collection of model ships in his room, you see."

"Ah, yes," Johanna nodded pleasantly. "Natalie mentioned that you had a son. How old is he?"

Katherine's eyes glinted with fondness for her child as she replied, "He just turned six."

Katherine didn't mind the hostess' inquiries about her child, but in the back of her mind she was concerned that she would be questioned about her fictional husband. Although she had her story prepared, she hated having to lie to her new friend. Much to her relief, her fears didn't materialize.

"We didn't invite anyone else today so that we would have the opportunity to get acquainted properly," the hostess said after a while. "But, my dears, Natalie and Bernard asked us to see to it that all of you join our circle. We're planning a party next week and do hope you will attend. It'll be a marvelous opportunity to make new friends."

Katherine and Agatha exchanged glances and smiled, "How lovely, yes. We'll be happy to," Agatha replied for both of them.

"Katherine, my dear, be prepared," Johanna warned, her voice quickening with enthusiasm. "The men in this town will flock to your door in droves, you are so beautiful!" Looking to the older woman for confirmation, she added, "Isn't she, Agatha?"

Although Katherine had often been told by men that she

was beautiful, this was the first time a woman had paid her such a compliment. Consequently, a self-conscious blush suffused her cheeks when she said, "Thank you, Johanna. You're most gracious."

"Nonsense, my dear," Johanna dismissed with a blithe wave of her elegant hand. "I just speak the truth." Her pretty face cracked into another one of her mischievous smiles when she added, "I'm afraid we're going to give Max Chapman a little competition, which will be very good for him. By the way, where is he?"

Momentarily, Katherine was at a loss for words. "In Albany," she replied at last. "He may be gone two, perhaps three weeks."

"How splendid!" Johanna said cheerfully. "That means he'll miss the party, and by the time he gets back, you'll be surrounded by other young men. You know," she went on in a more conversational tone, "it's a shame that he keeps so much to himself, but he's been besieged by mothers pushing their daughters at him. I guess I can't blame him too much for avoiding the social scene. He's really very nice."

"Yes, he is," Katherine agreed in a soft voice.

Johanna gave her a speculative glance before turning her attention to Agatha. "And as I understand you're also a widow," she said. At Agatha's assent, she went on agreeably, "There are quite a few mature gentlemen who I'm sure will be very interested in knowing you, my dear Agatha." Again her tone quickened with enthusiasm when she added, "How wonderful to introduce two new beauties at the same time! The party will be a great success!" She stopped suddenly and quizzically regarded her guests. "But Natalie mentioned another girl," she said.

"That'll be Jenny," Agatha replied. "I'm afraid you'll have to meet her some other time. Perhaps at the party."

"Well, if she's another beauty, the ladies of New York will have quite a fit." With a devilish expression on her lovely face, Johanna clasped her hands together and grinned, "How perfectly marvelous!"

The three of them exchanged glances and then dissolved in gay, playful laughter.

Their mirth caught the attention of the men, who had eventually drifted apart from the women to become involved in their own discussions.

"I think we'd better rejoin the ladies, Adam," Frank said then. "To judge from their merriment, they must be planning something dreadful, if I know my wife!

The balance of the afternoon was spent in pleasant camaraderie. The Beninks showed themselves anxious to draw them into their social circle, and by the time they took their leave, the foundations for an excellent friendship had been established.

A few days before the party, Katherine went through her wardrobe trying to decide what to wear. She had an extensive collection of gowns and jewelry—necessary tools of her profession of the last years—and finally settled on a russet silk gown that was quite flattering to her hair and coloring. She put it on to see if any alterations were required, and finding that none were necessary handed it to Annie, who had become her personal maid. In the short span she had served Katherine, the girl had developed quite an attachment to her new mistress.

Donning a salmon-colored wrap over her undergarments, Katherine went to Agatha's bedchamber and knocked on the door. There was a little shuffling inside, and after a moment Agatha answered and asked her in.

"I just tried on the gown for the party," Katherine said as she walked into the room. "I decided on the russet silk. Have you decided yet what to wear?"

"The gown?" Agatha repeated. For a moment, she regarded her young friend with a blank, distant expression on her face. Refocusing her eyes on Katherine, she said then, "Ah, yes, the gown for the party. No, I haven't decided yet. Won't you help me, dear?"

Katherine's gaze betrayed a mild alertness when she replied, "Of course."

Agatha had seemed a little sad in the last days. Remembering the letter that had arrived for Adam's sister, Katherine thought, *I hope Mr. Baxter isn't giving her any trouble.* She wished there was something she could do to help her friend.

The two women began sorting through the gowns in the armoire, and after some deliberation chose a dark blue taffeta with long sleeves and a modest neckline. Katherine encouraged her friend to try it on, since she had never seen Agatha in it.

Once the older woman had changed into the new gown, Katherine examined her thoughtfully. The change was quite dramatic. "I'll be right back, Katherine said, and turning away rushed out of the bedchamber.

When she returned moments later, she was bringing with her a sapphire and diamond necklace as well as a set of matching earrings. "The minute I saw that dress I thought of these," she said, offering the jewels to her friend. "Why don't you try them on so we can see how they look?"

While Agatha sat at the dressing table, she proceeded to fasten the necklace around the older woman's throat. Once Adam's sister put on the earrings, both of them looked at the reflection the mirror returned.

"You look positively beautiful," Katherine smiled at her friend. "Johanna wasn't exaggerating one bit when she said you were going to find plenty of admirers here in New York."

A warm color rose to Agatha's cheeks. "You're teasing me," she said, self-consciously dropping her gaze.

"Teasing you!" Katherine protested with exaggerated innocence. "Don't be silly. Just look in that mirror and be honest. Don't you think you look simply grand?" As the older woman followed her advice, she went on in a light-hearted tone, "And I suggest that you get plenty of rest between now and the party because you, my dear, are going to be dancing your feet off that evening." Her smile increased when she added with mischievous twinkle in her eyes, "And who knows? You might find someone who will tickle your fancy."

Agatha looked a little startled for a moment. Then, her face flamed and she quickly dropped her gaze. In the brief, odd silence that followed, Katherine had the distinct impression that her friend was about to confide in her at last.

"Donald Baxter asked me to marry him," Agatha said without enthusiasm. She remained quite still, her shoulders slumped slightly forward and her eyes locked on the hands folded in her lap.

"Oh?" Katherine's brows rose in surprise. "And what did you say?"

"I said no."

Katherine studied her friend for a few seconds. It was plain to see that Agatha was suffering acutely with her decision. "Do you regret it?" she asked gently.

"I don't know," Agatha replied, her sensitive features reflecting her distress. "The first time he asked me was the night before we arrived in New York. I refused, but Daniel is a very persistent man. He's written to me again and again. I was just writing to him when you came in."

"And you were saying no again," Katherine reflected out loud. Her green eyes expressed concern as she asked, "Why, Agatha? Don't you love him?"

"Yes, I do," the older woman murmured faintly.

A mystified expression came to Katherine's face. "Then what's wrong? Don't you believe he loves you truly?"

Agatha removed her gaze from her hands to look at her with anguish. "I know he does, Katherine, but I'm afraid. You see, I've never told anyone about this before, but I was terribly unhappy while I was married." She paused and fell silent.

"After Mother died, I didn't want to be a burden to Adam," she went on with a distant, musing air. "He was working in London then and I knew it hadn't been easy for him to support both Mother and me, so when Jack proposed, I accepted. But I soon discovered that I had made a terrible mistake. Jack was a beast; he beat me when he was drunk, and he was drunk most of the time we were together."

"But why didn't you leave him?" Katherine asked with unfeigned compassion.

"I had nowhere to go," Agatha shrugged unhappily. "Adam had gone to the Continent then, and I was with child. Besides, during the three years of our marriage, Jack and I were together only a few months." Again she paused, and her eyes were troubled when she looked at her young friend. "When they told me he had drowned, God forgive me, but I couldn't mourn for him. All I could think of was that I was glad he wouldn't be coming back."

A tear slid slowly down her cheek as she continued, "My daughter was a sickly child, and she died, too. I was living in Plymouth when Adam came back from the Continent and convinced me to go back to our parents' home in Cornwall. He seemed more prosperous by that time, and I accepted. It was shortly afterwards that he began bringing girls from London to live with me.

"Not all of them were like you and Natalie and Jenny," she said with a rueful shake of her head. "A couple of them ran away with all the money I had in the house and we never saw them again, but most of them were happy to have a good home, and I was glad for their company."

"You still haven't told me why you won't marry Donald," Katherine prodded gently.

"I'm almost fifty years old," Agatha replied with a deprecating gesture. "Marriage entails things that — well, frighten

249

me. Donald is a wonderful man, and he deserves someone who can make him happy. I'm not sure I can."

Katherine concealed a small sigh of relief. Taking Agatha's hand, she said in a gentle voice, "Physical love with the right person can be a very beautiful experience, Agatha, and Donald Baxter seems quite different from the husband you described. If the two of you love each other, you shouldn't be afraid."

Agatha's gaze was probing, her smile tentative when she asked, "Don't you think I'm too old for that sort of thing?"

Hearing the note of hopefulness in her friend's voice, Katherine couldn't refrain from smiling. "Of course you're not. And, besides, it's never too late to grasp at happiness when it shows its face."

Agatha was thoughtful for a moment. Then, gradually, her brow began to clear and she pushed herself erect. When she raised her gaze to her young friend, her dark irises held a sparkle of excitement in their depths. "I'm going to tear up that letter I was writing and I'm going to say yes."

She bounced to her feet, and her step was charged with vigorous purpose as she strolled to the desk. She took the letter and tore it to shreds. "Yes," she said, and suddenly flung the handful of paper up in the air.

Agatha was smiling—glowing, actually—as she watched the tiny white pieces drift slowly through the air like snowflakes and then fall all around her.

Katherine was the first to burst out in delighted laughter; when Agatha joined in seconds later, her laughter was free and spontaneous.

"When do you plan to marry?" Katherine inquired after their mirth had subsided.

"The sooner the better," Agatha replied without hesitation. "Donald and I have already wasted too many years. We mustn't waste any more."

After giving her friend an affectionate hug, Katherine returned to her room. Once there, she thought over her conversation with Agatha and was surprised to discover that she was beginning to feel quite depressed. Her eyes were faintly brooding as she looked across the room with a pensive, contemplative air.

When she had spoken of the beauty of physical love between two people, she had been speaking of her own experiences with Jonathan. After so many years, she could still remember all the emotions, all the sensations his touch had evoked. In spite of herself, Katherine felt a ripple of warmth go through her body at the memory. Almost immediately a feeling of emptiness followed.

Determined to shake off the desolation that was threatening to overcome her, she sat at the dressing table and ran a brush briskly through her hair.

How long would it be before she came face to face with Jonathan again, she meditated darkly. Inquiring at the New York offices of the Greenfield line, Adam had learned that Jonathan's ship wasn't expected to arrive in the immediate future. Perhaps it was better this way, Katherine reflected. She needed a little more time to properly establish herself in New York society. Still, she was anxious for the confrontation.

Sitting there, she couldn't restrain her thoughts from drifting back to those days—and nights—she had spent with Jonathan in London. Gradually her actions slowed down, and as memories flooded back, her expression softened and her gaze grew remote and wistful.

Did he ever think of those evenings they had spent at that London inn, sitting in front of the fire to talk or sing or simply hold hands? Or of those nights of passion or gentle loving when nothing in the world existed or even mattered?

Would he even remember her?

Suddenly feeling quite foolish, Katherine shook her head and stared reproachfully at her own image. Clenching her hand around the brush handle, she breathed an irritated sigh at her own foolhardiness. How could she be so stupid as to think, even for a moment, that she had been more than a passing interest to a man who had taken her love and then betrayed her?

But the moment she had worked for and waited for was now close at hand. One day soon, Jonathan was going to pay his debt.

As Johanna Benink had anticipated, the introduction of the three English beauties made her party a resounding success. In her own mischievous way, she was delighted by the reception they received—gallantries and open admiration on the part of the males, as well as jealousy and a little envy from the young marriageable females.

Being a little shy, Jenny had been frightened at the prospect of meeting so many strangers, and it had taken quite a bit of doing on the part of her friends to make her attend the Benink's party. Looking very pretty in a gown of pink voile that set off her young blonde beauty to advantage, she was besieged by young admirers from the moment they walked into the ballroom.

Although Adam divided his attentions among the many ladies present, Johanna was delighted to observe that it was her good friend, Iris Cavanaugh, who seemed to interest him the most.

Chestnut haired, brown eyed and now in her middle thirties, the lovely Iris had been left childless and widowed after several years of what everyone thought to have been a reasonably happy marriage. Matchmaking being Johanna's vocation—and passion—over the years she had presented her friend with one candidate after another without much success, since Iris seemed to have no interest in re-entering the matrimonial state. In the beginning Johanna had been convinced that the memory of her late husband was cause for Iris' reluctance to accept a new man in her life; in due course she had learned that Iris had become quite fond of her independence.

This time, however, Johanna was sure Iris had met her match.

Although the men who showed a marked interest in Adam's sister were disappointed at the news of her impending marriage, both Katherine and Jenny fulfilled Johanna's predictions. Following the party, flowers and invitations arrived at their new home which, by that time, was buzzing with activity in preparation for Agatha's wedding.

It was amidst such confusion that a messenger delivered a basket of red roses and a note to Katherine. Maxwell Chapman was back in New York and asked if he could call on her that evening. She asked the young man to wait for a reply, in which she extended an invitation for supper.

Katherine was delighted to see Max again, and she didn't hesitate to tell him so when he arrived. Before they were joined by the rest of the family, she took him into the drawing room, where they sat close together in the settee.

"You look so tired, Max," she said in a voice full of warmth and affection. Impulsively she reached out to run her fingers over his creased brow.

"I just got back this afternoon," he replied, taking her hand. In a fluid motion, he drew her into his arms and began kissing her as a thirsty man drinks from a cool mountain spring. "Lord, how I've missed you!" he whispered hoarsely against her mouth. "I had to come back. I just couldn't stay away from you any longer."

She drank in every word. "I was so afraid you wouldn't come back," she confessed with a charming touch of shyness.

His glance touched her mouth as he said, "Never my love. I'll always come back to you."

He made to kiss her again but the sound of voices approaching made him realize that Katherine's friends were about to join them. He stood up at their entrance and was greeted with fondness by all of them, as well as immediately informed about the wedding. They hoped he would come, they added.

"I wouldn't miss it for the world," he smiled, and giving Adam's sister a kiss on the cheek added, "Much happiness, Agatha."

Agatha blushed, and once they were all comfortably seated, they sipped glasses of wine and discussed wedding plans until Bruce came and announced that supper was served.

While the others gathered in the drawing room again after supper for coffee and liquors, Katherine and Max, wanting to be alone, went out on the terrace.

The murmur of voices still reached them through the open french windows when Max drew her to him.

"Let's walk in the garden, Max," she said, leaning back a little before he could kiss her.

He released her with some reluctance, and arm in arm they walked in silence among the hedges, breathing the perfumed air.

"Quite a surprise the wedding, isn't it?" he finally commented.

"It all happened before our eyes, Max, only we were too busy to notice," she said with a small wry chuckle. "I'm very happy for Agatha. She deserves some happiness after being alone for so many years."

He was slow in asking, "And you, Katherine? You've been alone, too."

Katherine emitted a long sigh. "Yes, I have."

He stopped walking, and with his hand on her shoulders turned her to face him. "I'm here now, my darling."

Her eyes were full of thought as she looked at him in silence.

His voice was soft and pleading when he said, "Let me love you, Katherine."

Her face clouded slightly. "Max, I . . ."

He didn't let her finish, suddenly drawing her to him. "Let me love you, darling," he repeated over and over in a voice that shook a little with emotion. Raining kisses on her cheeks, on her eyes, on her brow, he continued pleading, "Let me love you."

His mouth found hers at last in a tender, yet passionate kiss to which she responded with longing.

"I love you so!" His voice grew husky as he continued to hold her, whispering words of love.

Her mouth left his abruptly, and taking a step back she turned away from him. For a moment she stood twisting her hands with anguish, her breast heaving.

Max came to stand behind her and encircled her waist. His breath was warm in her ear as he said time and time again, "I love you."

She felt safe in his arms and wanted to say, "I love you, Max," but somehow she couldn't bring out those words.

"I tried to forget you," he confessed, pressing a kiss on her temple. "I tried hard, but I couldn't. I want you, Katherine. I need you in my life."

Torn between longing and fear, Katherine heard the question, "Will you marry me?"

She let out her breath in a silent, whispering sigh as she turned around to face him. "Max, I . . ."

Looking at her intently he asked, "Do you love me?"

"I don't know, Max," she replied, shaking her head in unfeigned confusion. "I don't know."

The stricken expression that came over his features made her heart constrict painfully. Her tone changed to one of pleading when she said, "Please, Max, try to understand."

Max shot a pained look at her. "Understand what, Katherine?" he asked dispiritedly.

"Please, Max, will you give me some time?" she asked, her eyes hopefully fixed on his face.

"Time?" he repeated with an edge of bitterness.

"Please, Max," she said in a constricted voice. "I don't

know how I truly feel about you. I only know that I don't want to lose you."

His tense expression didn't change for a moment. Then his face relaxed. "All right, my love," he said at last. "Let's take some time." Tenderly, he touched her cheek and smiled wistfully. "All the time in the world. You see, I don't want to lose you, either."

Twelve

Letters from Europe began to arrive attesting that, as in their own case, the life of their adventurous friends had taken a normal pattern. The Brissards wrote that they were about to open their acting school and were very excited. In a postscript, Lazarus referred to the Marquis d'Esterel as "our friend Julian," and mentioned that after Adam's escape, "Julian" had disappeared from Paris for some time.

He's back now, Lazarus wrote, *but something must have frightened him very badly, because he seldom leaves his house. There are so many guards around the place that it resembles a fortress.*

Adam chuckled with amusement at this news and told Katherine what he had done to frighten the marquis.

"So that's why you went back after Daniel and Ronald had left!" she exclaimed, a little perplexed. "But why, Adam? What possessed you to take such a senseless risk?"

257

"More than stealing the marquis' treasures I wanted to frighten him," he replied with a deprecating shrug.

His affected nonchalance didn't fool Katherine, who regarded him with affection as she understood what his motives had been. Slipping her arm around his shoulders, she pressed her cheek to his and murmured, "Oh, my dear, the risks you took for me!"

Adam cleared his throat. "Everything turned out well thanks to you and Natalie," he dismissed gruffly.

"We couldn't have done much without the others," she reminded him gently. "We all love you very much, but then you already know that."

Even though Daniel's shop had been open for only a short time, it was such a tremendous success that he had hired two assistants.

Natalie's pregnancy was going well, and her letters were optimistic and cheerful.

Katherine and Adam commented on the lack of news from Ronald. Daniel had mentioned that Ronald had gone to Florence at about the same time they had embarked for America. They waited for news of him, but weeks passed, and then months, and a letter never came. Even though neither one of them voiced their thoughts, they were very worried; especially Katherine, who felt a deep and genuine affection for the big and burly man who was her friend.

After Agatha's wedding, Katherine found herself wondering more than ever about her true feelings for Max. She loved him, she thought at times, but remembering the glow of happiness on Agatha's face as she and Donald had exchanged their marriage vows, she had to admit that she wasn't quite sure.

Perhaps that kind of love came only once in a

lifetime, Katherine reflected. For Agatha it hadn't happened until she met Donald. As for herself . . . it had happened seven years before.

Still, that didn't necessarily mean that she didn't love Max, and his conduct left little doubt as to his love for her. Why, then, couldn't she make up her mind? There was also Jason to consider. Would Max be willing to accept the boy as his own and give him his name?

The activities after their arrival in New York, the wedding, Max—and most of all knowing that Jonathan wasn't due to arrive for a while—had made Katherine temporarily put aside her anxiety over the confrontation; still, deep in her heart she knew that this was the main reason that kept her from accepting Max's proposal.

Unless his business took him out of town, Max was always her escort to every social function, and their continued appearance in public gave rise to a great deal of speculation. Katherine chose to ignore a malicious rumor regarding their relationship when it reached her ears. Letting her conduct speak for itself, she dismissed it as petty jealousy.

On several occasions when Max had been absent, she accepted the company of Harry Webster, a young admirer of whom she was genuinely fond. More frequently, however, she was seen with Adam and Iris Cavanaugh—who had become quite close.

She had asked for time and Max had promised he would wait. Biding her time until the moment came to meet with Jonathan, Katherine let things happen of their own accord.

The opening of the French Ballet Company was a main event in the New York social circles. When

Katherine and Max arrived at the theater in the company of Johanna and Frank Benink, the four of them were greeted by the spectacle of acquaintances parading in their finery and exchanging lively bits of gossip.

At curtain call the gay crowd sought their seats, and the two couples occupied a box that commanded an excellent view of the stage as well as the audience. From this vantage point they could see how people looked about for familiar faces and waved at each other until the lights were dimmed and the orchestra began the overture.

Katherine was quite delighted with the occasion, since she had not seen the ballet since their visit to St. Petersburg two years before. Even though at that time she had seen the great ballerina Elena Andreyevna in the role of *Giselle* that had brought her to stardom, Katherine judged as excellent the performance of the very same ballet by the French company.

Aware that Max had returned from a business trip only that day, Johanna had not missed any of the wistful glances he had bestowed on Katherine while her attention had been on the stage. With a smug little smile, she turned to her husband just before the end of first act and whispered, "Let's give these two lovebirds a chance to be alone for a little while during the intermission, shall we, my darling?"

As soon as the curtain fell, she rose to her feet and said in a humorous tone, "I know the two of you have things to talk about, so I'm sure you won't mind too much if Frank and I leave you for a bit, don't you children?"

Without waiting for their answer, she and Frank went out of the box.

A feeling of warmth crept into Katherine's cheeks. A little shamefaced, she looked at Max and said lamely,

"We can go to the lobby if you like, Max."

Max gave a small wry chuckle. "As a matter of fact, for the last half hour I've been racking my brain for an excuse not to join them," he said. His eyes held hers in an intimate glance as he said, "You have no idea how I've missed you."

"And I've missed you," she said softly. "I wish you didn't have to travel so much."

He reached for her hand and pressed it to his lips. "I don't know what is worse," he said in a husky voice. "Being away from you, or being with you and unable to touch you, make love to you."

"Oh, Max!" she murmured with dismay.

She had carefully avoided situations where a repetition of the hotel episode could develop; on the other hand, knowing her to be a sensual woman, Max didn't miss an opportunity to bind her more to him by arousing her flesh. Theirs had almost become a struggle of wits.

"When are you going to say that you'll marry me, Katherine?" he asked bleakly.

The unhappiness in his voice made her reach out to touch his cheek. "You know I care for you, darling," she said in a voice altered by emotion. Her tone changed to one of pleading when she said, "I just need a little more time, please, Max."

He gazed at her heavily. "I don't know how much longer I can wait."

Her lips began to shape an answer, but before she could say anything, a couple of their acquaintances entered the box to say hello. Katherine breathed a sigh of immense relief at the interruption. More friends stopped by and stayed to chatter until the next curtain call, when Johanna and Frank returned.

The digression from their discussion had given Katherine a momentary respite, but shortly after the performance had resumed she was perturbed by a strange and uncomfortable sensation of being observed. In the beginning she tried to dismiss it as a product of her imagination and her conversation with Max, but try as she might to ignore it, the sensation persisted.

Her attention wandered from the stage, and in a rather absent manner her gaze traveled to the audience as though looking for the source of her discomfiture. Glancing up suddenly, she saw a pair of eyes staring at her intently from across the theater.

Her hand flew to her mouth to cover a small gasp of alarm. Jonathan!

As she went ghastly pale, her pupils dilated with shocked disbelief. Her heart gave a tremendous bound and stopped beating for a moment. She could feel those blue eyes boring into her, piercing her to the very marrow of her bones. Desperately she tried to look away, but the intensity of his gaze seemed to hold hers against her will.

She saw Jonathan bend down his head to listen to a remark from his companion. It was only at that moment that Katherine took notice of the young blonde woman sitting next to him. A shiver went through her as a panicky feeling invaded her stomach. His wife!

Max must have heard her gasp, because he leaned toward her and whispered, "Are you all right, darling?"

Unable to speak, she simply bobbed her head. Gulping down the lump in her throat to find her voice, she managed to say the first excuse that came to her mind, "It's just a headache, Max."

Her hand was clammy and as cold as ice when he took it in his own. "Would you like to go home?" he asked quietly.

At the moment she wanted nothing more than to flee

from the theater. "I think so, Max," she nodded. "I'm sorry."

"Don't worry, darling," he said, holding her hand a little tighter. He turned to Johanna and Frank and explained that Katherine wasn't feeling well and that he was taking her home.

A few seconds later they left the theater.

Still suffering from the effects of the shock of running into Jonathan so unexpectedly, Katherine began trembling so uncontrollably that her teeth were amost chattering. Max wrapped a protective arm around her shoulders and drew her to him as though trying to communicate to her some of his body warmth. Even after her trembling had subsided, she still remained huddled against him.

"Feeling better, darling?" he asked with concern.

She couldn't find her voice.

Feeling responsible for her state, Max blamed himself. "You'll be home soon, darling," he told her, pressing a kiss into her hair. "You should get to bed right away."

Since Adam and Iris had gone to the ballet with Jenny and her date, with the exception of Laurie, who was watching over Jason in the absence of the family, the house was quite deserted when they arrived.

Katherine dismissed her while Max poured a brandy for her. She drank it quickly in one gulp, and it burned her throat.

Max watched her with curiosity and alarm. "You must get to bed," he said, kissing her lightly on the pale cheek. "I'll see myself out."

He walked with her to the foot of the stairs and remained there to watch her as she started to go up. He waited until she was almost halfway and turned to leave.

"Max, wait!"

Abruptly he turned and saw her coming down almost

at a run. She stopped on the last step.

"Please don't leave me, Max!" She cried, throwing her arms around his neck. "Stay with me tonight, please!"

Max stared at her for one disbelieving moment. Unable to move, his hands hung lifeless at his sides.

"Please, Max!" she pleaded again in earnest. Her mouth sought his and clung to it in a desperate kiss.

Coming back to life, Max put his arms around her and held her tightly against him as they kissed. Without releasing her lips, he lifted her in his arms and started to climb the stairs. Neither one of them heard the coach that stopped in front of the house or realized that someone else had arrived until the door slammed shut. Max turned abruptly and was dismayed to find Adam rushing toward them.

"Max," Adam called as he came forward. "Is Katherine ill? I noticed you left the theater so suddenly."

Unable to hide his dismay, Max tried to explain. "She has a chill and a headache," he said, putting Katherine down. A little embarrassed by the situation, he blurted out, "I guess I should be leaving now, darling."

Katherine heaved a weary sigh. "Yes, I suppose it's best. Good night, Max."

There was nothing left for Max to do. "I'll stop by tomorrow to see how you're feeling," he said lamely.

"Yes, Max, thank you." She turned away and started to climb the stairs.

Adam had disappeared, and Max stood rather uncertainly at the bottom of the stairs for a few moments before he finally let himself out of the house.

Katherine was already in her bed when Adam came in carrying a glass on a tray. The glass contained one of his favorite remedies, warm milk laced with brandy and a bit of honey.

"Here you are, pet," he said cheerfully. "Drink it down while it's still hot."

Katherine refused the drink with a wave of her hand. "I'm all right, Adam. It's just nerves." She was silent while Adam set the glass on the night stand. "Jonathan was at the theater tonight," she said then. "With his wife."

"I know," Adam nodded, sitting down on the bed's edge.

She looked at him with surprise. "You saw him, too?"

Again he nodded. "And when I saw how suddenly you left the theater, I realized what must have happened. You panicked, didn't you?"

Katherine's face colored with mortification. "Oh, Adam, I'm so furious I could kick myself!" she said, her voice quivering with wrath. "For years I've been waiting to come face to face with him, and what do I do when it finally happens? Run like a frightened rabbit!"

Tears of angry frustration welled up in her eyes, and clenching her hand into a fist she punched the pillow.

"Easy, pet," Adam said, taking her clenched hand. "You'll be all right. You were taken by surprise, that's all."

"That's no excuse!" she cried with exasperation. "If I had lost my head when we were working the way I did tonight, it would have been the end of us all." She breathed an irritated sigh. "If I could do it then, how could I have made such a fool of myself tonight?"

"You're not as hard as you think you are, pet," Adam said with a rueful little laugh. "And I'm glad of it, even if you're not."

She shot him a sour look. "Is that supposed to make me feel better?" she asked with a touch of asperity.

He gave a wry chuckle. "What you did then you did because your heart and your emotions were not involved, can't you see? To run into Jonathan and his wife so unexpectedly after what happened in London, must have been quite a shock for you." Allowing for a reflective pause, he asked gently, "Are you sure you still want to go on with your plan of seeking revenge?"

"Of course I am!"

Adam sighed. "Now, what would it solve?"

"It'll make me feel a bloody hell better!" she almost shouted. She was instantly sorry for having lost her temper. Reaching for his hand, she held it tightly. "I'm sorry, my dear," she said with sincere regret. "Please don't be angry with me, but I have to do it, how can I make you understand?"

His blue eyes were thoughtful as he looked at her for a moment. "Jonathan Greenfield isn't one of those fops we met in Europe, Katherine," he said then. "He's not a fool or a man to be trifled with."

Katherine shrugged. "He's a man," she answered rather flippantly. "And I *know* how to handle men." Seeing that Adam remained unconvinced, she added with far more confidence than she was feeling, "I'll be all right, Adam, and I'll prove it the next time I meet Jonathan. That I promise you."

Unimpressed by her bravado, Adam leaned forward and said, "Just remember the most basic rule every gambler should follow, Katherine. When the cards are running against him, he must cut his losses and walk away from the game."

She made a deprecating gesture in response. "Will you find out for me how long Jonathan is expected to be in New York?"

"If that's your wish."

"Thank you Adam." She gave him a quick hug. "You're such a dear!" Suddenly she drew back and looked at him a little startled, realizing that Adam had left the ballet on her account. "Did you leave Iris at the theater?"

Wryly he nodded. "The way you left the theater, I was afraid you'd do something you might regret later. It seems to me that I arrived just in time."

A blush suffused her fair skin as she looked at him a little shamefaced.

"Would you like me to stay? I asked Jenny and Harry to take Iris home if I didn't get back in time."

She was deeply touched by his concern. "No, thank you, my dear. I'm sorry I spoiled your evening, too."

"Take care, pet," he said with a quick smile and giving her hand an affectionate squeeze.

He stood up, and Katherine watched him go out. A few moments later she heard a carriage ride away.

Once she was alone, her eyes fell on the glass that was left untouched on the bedside table. With a wry little smile she shook her head and reached for Adam's panacea. The milk was still warm, and she sipped it slowly with a pensive air.

What a fool she had made of herself, she reflected. Anger flared anew at the thought of how Jonathan would be laughing at her by now. During all those years she had been preparing for the moment of encounter, Katherine had envisioned the scene, imagined the words they would exchange. She would always appear cool and collected; she would smile indifferently at him, as though she had never seen him before or cared to. And Jonathan would simply pursue her, striving in vain to capture her attention and driven to despair by her indifference.

Well, she certainly hadn't smiled coolly, she mused a little wryly; and he knew without a doubt that she had recognized him. So much for her plans! Just seeing him across the theater with his wife had unhinged her. His wife. Oh, God, but it still hurts!

"It can't!" she said peremptorily. "I hate him!"

All through the night, Katherine ran the gamut of emotions ranging from fear of making a fool of herself again to anger directed in turns at herself and then at Jonathan. She wanted to wound him as deeply as she could, and in this she had to be careful which cards she used and how she used them.

The emotional stress and her anxiety over the coming confrontation were enough to exhaust her. A faint pearly light was brightening the sky when she fell asleep without even realizing it.

Katherine was rather pale, but calm when Max called on her the next day. She was feeling better, she told him, but still a little weak.

"Then I won't disturb you, darling," he said solicitously. "If you're not better by tomorrow, I'll send our regrets to the Raleighs."

"The Raleighs?" she repeated blankly. In her present state of mind, she had totally forgotten the ball they were supposed to attend. "I'm sure I'll be all right by then," she assured Max with a feeble smile.

"Katherine, about last night," Max opened with curious hesitation, "I'm sorry if I upset you."

A flicker of surprise crossed her eyes before they became green pools of understanding. "It wasn't your fault, darling," she assured him with a slight sense of guilt.

"I won't press you again, darling," he said with a subdued air. "I promise."

Katherine's throat constricted painfully. Swallowing the lump, she gave him a wavering smile. "Thank you, darling," she said in a hushed voice.

She had recovered her composure by the time Max called for her to take her to the ball. He never ceased to be amazed by her beauty, but this evening she looked specially delicious in an apple green gown and the glitter of diamonds at her creamy throat.

The Raleighs' mansion was reminiscent of a Venetian *palazzo*, a style of architecture that was becoming highly popular among those who could afford it. Marble steps led up to the portico, which was supported by majestic double pillars on each side of the front door. Thousands of lights were glittering when Katherine and Max passed the receiving line and continued on to a ballroom of impressive dimensions where a group of their friends had already assembled. Servants carrying trays of champagne glasses circulated among the elegant guests who waited for the hosts to open the dance. Meanwhile, in the minstrels gallery above, a small orchestra played a Mozart piece for their entertainment.

Several young women scowled their disapproval at the young men who rushed to list their name on Katherine's dance card. Most of them kept their distance whenever she was escorted by Max, but the more daring still approached her.

Susan and Tom Raleigh opened the dance at last, and the guests followed, among them Katherine and Max.

He was a marvelous dancer who made her feel weightless as they glided over the polished parquet floor. Soon after the first waltz, other partners whisked her away and Max stood on the sidelines with friends. Anxious to dance with Max again, Katherine began searching the room with her eyes. Instead, entering the ballroom with the same blonde woman she had seen with him at the theater, she saw Jonathan. At the sudden apparition she felt herself turning cold and missed a step. When her partner apologized, she gave him a perfunctory smile while inwardly repeating, *keep calm, keep calm*. But the years of training had not been wasted, and by the time the waltz ended Katherine had managed to regain control of herself.

The emerald irises held a sparkle of excitement in their depths, and the heightened color on her cheeks lent a special glow to her creamy complexion when her dancing partner returned her to Max, who regarded her with possessive pleasure as she stood beside him.

Determined to stop herself from looking anxiously around the room, Katherine was studiously attentive to the conversation between Max and another couple. Glancing up suddenly, she saw her enemy coming in her direction with an acquaintance. His wife wasn't with him. Hoping that her outward appearance didn't reflect the fact that she felt all tangled up inside, she braced herself for the confrontation.

As they were introduced she noted, somewhat to her dismay, how little he had changed. There were new lines around his eyes that hadn't been there before, but, if anything, they made his virile face even more attractive. His eyes were as deep blue, his chiseled mouth as determined as ever—yet, somehow, he also seemed different, she realized, sensing a new soberness in his manner.

"I believed we've already met, Captain Greenfield," she said in a rather detached fashion.

Jonathan gallantly kissed the hand she offered. "Indeed, Mrs. Cameron," he replied, taken a little by surprise. Recovering immediately, he added, "I didn't think you'd remember. I'm flattered."

His voice, as low and as husky as she remembered, caused an involuntary shiver to go through her limbs.

Forcing a smile, she inquired with a tinge of irony, "Mrs. Greenfield is well, I trust?"

For a second he looked at her with raised eyebrows. "She is, madam," he nodded at last. "I shall give her your regards."

With a tolerant smile, she said with acid sweetness, "Please do."

Quite satisfied with her performance thus far, Katherine turned to Max. "I believe this is our waltz, darling," she told him, linking her arm through his. At Jonathan she smiled and said lightly, "You will excuse us, won't you Captain Greenfield?"

His steady blue eyes reflected no warmth as they followed her slender figure and watched her step into Max's arms.

With a smug inward smile, Katherine congratulated herself for having caught Jonathan off balance. He had not expected her to acknowledge having met him or ask after his wife. Euphoria lightened her step while she danced with Max and then continued with other partners. Before she knew how it happened, it was Jonathan who was holding her in his arms.

Following a brief but intense silence, he said in a hushed voice, "Hello, Katie."

Momentarily, she was tempted to close her eyes and surrender to the inward thrill that just his voice could cause within her. Taking pains to conceal her thoughts, she looked into his eyes and replied lightly, "Hello, Jonathan."

She sustained his gaze for a few seconds and then, looking away, she tried to gather herself for a moment as they continued to dance in silence.

"We never did get a chance to dance in London, did we, love?"

"That was a long time ago, Jonathan," she replied in a

voice that, despite the beating of her heart, she managed to keep calm.

"It was," he nodded a little ruefully, "but I haven't forgotten."

She shrugged her shoulders with affected indifference. "I have."

Drawing her closer still, he held her until their bodies touched. "Have you, love?"

She drew away. With sharp little edge in her voice, she said, "Please don't call me that, Jonathan."

"Who calls you love now, Katie?" he asked after a moment's silence. "Chapman?"

Smiling into his brooding eyes, she replied, "Yes."

His mouth tightened, and when he spoke again, he did so between stiff, unwilling lips. "Is he your lover?"

"My relationship with him doesn't concern you," she said, in her voice a shade of reproach.

He looked sad for a moment, though it was quickly succeeded by a more determined expression. "How many others have there been, Katie?"

The anger in his voice made her smile. With a bright, provocative glance, she shook her head in mock dismay. "Do my ears deceive me? Why Jonathan, I do believe you're jealous! Could it be true?" Throwing her head back, she laughed throatily.

His tense expression didn't change when he rasped, "How many?"

The music had ceased, and they stood in the middle of the dance floor. "Darling," she said in a hushed, seductive voice, "I hope you don't expect me to discuss the details of my . . . love life with you now."

As the orchestra began the next waltz, a young man materialized at her side to claim his dance. Bestowing her new dancing partner with her most dazzling smile, Katherine turned away from Jonathan.

As she danced away, out of the corner of her eye she could see Jonathan looking after her. The way he stalked off the dance floor told her that he was ready to explode, and she was elated at the thought.

Although she studiously ignored him, through the rest of the evening Katherine was aware of Jonathan. She felt his eyes following her as she danced with Max and other men, and emotionally drained, it was with great relief that she left the party with Max.

The journey home was made in thoughtful silence.

Max had never questioned her about that past she had only hinted at, but she was now aware that he was thinking about her acquaintance with Jonathan.

And he was. There was something about the man that disturbed him, and he couldn't put his finger on what it was. Had he and Katherine met when she was, as she had said, living outside the law? She had not seemed alarmed at meeting him again, but Max had not missed the curious way they had parted on the dance floor.

Her voice interrupted his thoughts when she said, "Max?"

He half turned to look at her. "Yes, darling?"

"Please hold me."

Max smiled and drew her into his arms. Still, he continued to ponder on the question of Greenfield until he could no longer remain silent. "Darling, did you and Captain Greenfield meet when you were outside the law?"

"No, Max," she replied. After a brief hesitation she added, "It was before."

"Who is he, Katherine? Somehow he looks familiar, but I can't remember ever meeting him before."

He felt Katherine stiffen a second before she drew away. Following a long pause, she finally looked straight into his eyes and replied, "He's Jason's father."

She could hear the hiss of his indrawn breath. "Of course, that's it! The resemblance!" His expression became one of jealousy and anger when he muttered savagely, "Why didn't you tell me?"

Katherine concealed a small sigh. "You never asked me," she replied, laying her hand on his. "I'll tell you anything you want to know Max. I've never kept any secrets from you and I never will."

His brow contracted. "Did you love him?"

She looked away from the torment she saw etched on his grim face. "Yes, Max, I did," she conceded at last.

"Do you still?"

She faced him abruptly. "No!"

Her denial had been too swift, too vehement to satisfy him. Delving searchingly into her eyes, he asked in a bitter voice, "Is he your ghost, Katherine? Is he the reason why you haven't agreed to marry me?"

Her mouth began to shape a denial, but no sound came out.

"I'm not waiting any longer, Katherine," he said, genuinely angry. When she started to speak, he cut her off with an uplifted hand. "Just hear me out. I'm asking you, for the last time, to marry me. I'm going to Boston in the morning and won't be back for a couple of days. Think about it during that time, Katherine, because I'll expect your answer when I return."

Jenny had taken Jason to watch a performance by the Christy Minstrels when Bruce knocked on Katherine's door the following afternoon and announced that a Captain Greenfield was calling.

Immediately setting aside the letter she was writing, she replied, "Show him into the parlor, Bruce, please. I'll be right down."

"Very well, madam."

With her heart quivering in her throat, Katherine ran to the mirror and scanned her appearance. Her hands were shaking a little as she applied a few strokes of the brush to her hair. She started to leave her room and then decided that it wouldn't be a bad idea to keep Jonathan waiting for a little while. She didn't want to appear too anxious.

To put the time to good use, she also decided to change her dress. She searched through her wardrobe for something appropriate — something flattering without being too elegant or elaborate. After some deliberation she settled on a blue-green sprigged muslin dress that she knew was quite becoming to her figure. She changed at leisure and again looked in the mirror to brush her hair. Noticing how pale she was, she pinched her cheeks to heighten their color before going to meet her visitor.

Jonathan was standing by the window looking out when she came into the parlor.

"Hello, Jonathan," she said with cordiality.

He turned slowly to regard her. In her simple, yet elegant dress, she looked very much like the young girl he had known in London. Her carriage and the seductive smile she was smiling at him were new to him, however.

"Hello, Katie."

"This is a pleasant surprise."

His blue eyes were speculative and observant when he asked with a touch of irony, "Is it?"

She gave an almost imperceptible shrug. "Well, I'll confess I didn't expect to see you again so soon. Won't you have a seat?" she invited with a graceful gesture of her hand. "May I offer you some refreshment?"

He shook his head. "Nothing, thank you."

He occupied the chair she had indicated while Katherine sat on the sofa and waited for him to speak.

When they did, they began in unison.

"Katie . . ."

"Jonathan . . ." She smiled and fell silent.

"I want you back," he told her bluntly.

She could almost hear the pounding of her own heart. This was what she had been waiting to hear for seven long years! Dropping her gaze to conceal her excitement, she waited for him to continue. Without another word, however, he handed her a velvet case.

Giving him a curious glance, she opened the box. Inside the black velvet nest was the most exquisite necklace she had ever seen, a delicate mesh of gold where diamonds and rubies glittered full of fire and light. She looked at it fascinated, yet a little apprehensive.

"I've noticed that you have acquired a taste for expensive trinkets," he said moodily.

"It's beautiful," she admitted, schooling her features to remain impassive. "But this is hardly the gift to an old friend, Jonathan. Why are you giving this to me?"

"As I said, I want you back," he replied, and the grin warping his determined mouth was thin and humorless.

Katherine looked at him with a bemused expression. "And I suppose you expect me to fall right into your arms because of this?" she said, her excitement vanishing. This was not at all what she had expected to hear. Bouncing to her feet, she went to stand in front of the cold fireplace trying to keep her anger in check before she turned to face him again. Crossing her arms across her chest, she smiled loftily, "Do you really think you can buy me, Jonathan?" She uttered a scornful little laugh.

"I'll give you anything you want for a few days of your time, Katherine," he said, his expression temporarily shut and unyielding. "You'll be free to do as you please after I'm gone. Just name your price."

Holding her breath and face coloring with mortification, she listened to his proposition. Her indignation had become rage as he spoke. "Get out," she said, breathing violently as she came to stand before him. Flinging the case at him, she ground out through gritted teeth, "Get out and stay out." Abruptly she spun around and started to ring for the butler.

Undeterred by her fury, Jonathan rose slowly to his feet. "I'll find my way out, Katherine," he said with a tight-lipped smile. "Just think about what I said. I'll be back for your answer later."

"Get out! I never want to see you again for as long as I live!" she screamed at his retreating back.

It was only after he had gone that she noticed the jewelry case lying on the carpet. Abruptly turning away, she ran from the parlor and up the stairs to her room, where she flung herself across the bed to cry tears of frustrated anger.

Thirteen

Through a long and restless night Katherine played the scene with Jonathan over and over in her mind. Each time she berated herself for being such a fool. Had she played her cards right, she could have kept Jonathan dangling until she had had enough of her revenge. As it was, in a matter of minutes she had let her pride destroy her chance at the goal she had lived for for so many years.

She tried to derive some satisfaction from the knowledge that despite her failure to bring him to his knees, Jonathan still desired her; but this also made her uneasily aware that he might use other means to get what he wanted from her — even Jason, if he ever found out.

Adam had been right all along; Jonathan was unlike those other men she had dealt with as a professional enchantress. She had ignored the warnings once, but this time she wouldn't make the same mistake again. She had too much to lose. Now that the cards had turned against her, it would be sheer folly to stay in the game. The time had come to cut her losses.

Jonathan wasn't aware of the existence of their child, and she'd be a fool to give him another weapon to use against her. The first order of things would be for her and Jason to leave New York immediately. The only place she could think of at the moment was Albany. She hated to intrude on Agatha and her new husband, but this was no time to be fussy.

Having decided on this course of action, Katherine began worrying again. The new turn of events made her marrying Max of vast importance; however, after the ultimatum he had given her, she wasn't sure what he'd do if he came back from Boston and found her gone. Oh, damn! Why did he have to be away at a time like this!

By morning her plans had changed, but only slightly. The trip to Albany would have to be postponed for a day. Then, after she had told Max that she was ready to marry him, she and Jason could be on the next boat to Albany and out of Jonathan's reach.

Katherine was up and about even before the household began stirring to the new day. She wasted no time in seeking Bruce and instructed him to keep the gates locked; she also told him not to admit Captain Greenfield again under any circumstances. The other servants were informed that Jason had been slightly ill during the night, and that he would be kept indoors for the day. She couldn't run the risk of letting Jonathan get a glimpse of his son if he came around—as he was sure to do.

It was easier to convince the servants of Jason's imaginary illness than the active little boy himself. Keeping him indoors and entertained was quite an ordeal for Katherine, who didn't leave his side for a moment.

Later in the day Bruce informed her that Jonathan had called once more. Angered by her refusal to receive him, he had told Bruce that he would be back again.

Let him try, she said inwardly, let him beg. This is what I've been waiting for all these years.

Yet he had not begged, she reflected moodily. Instead, he had been insulting and infuriating. With renewed anger she repeated her earlier instructions to the butler, who accepted them without turning a hair.

Except for another attempt to see her on the part of Jonathan, there was nothing more to disturb her day, which she spent reading to Jason and playing games with him. Adam and Jenny had other engagements that evening, and since Max wouldn't return until the following day, there was no point for Katherine to dress for dinner. She tried to soothe her edginess in a long, relaxing bath and remained in deshabille for an early supper with her son.

Once she had put Jason to bed, Katherine went downstairs. With Adam and Jenny out for the evening she had dismissed the servants early, and the house was strangely quiet. Restlessly, she prowled the empty rooms wishing Adam or Jenny were there. She attempted reading a book, and failing miserably, she stepped out on the terrace for a breath of fresh air.

The August night was sultry with silence, and a huge Oriental lantern of a moon bathed the quiet grounds with a dim yellow light. The trees huddled dark and somber as she strolled among the hedges oblivious to the soft, earthy fragrance that floated about her like a tenuous veil.

Idly, she plucked a flower and absently toyed with it while her thoughts wandered once more to her earlier encounters with Jonathan.

Closing her eyes, for a moment she could almost feel around her the arms that had so recently held her if only in dance. With an inward thrill she could almost see her own reflection in those sapphire eyes so expressive that they mirrored his emotions like the windows of his soul: laughing eyes when he was happy; hard and frightening in his anger; dark with passion . . .

Gradually, the glow inside her faded. Was he with his wife now, she asked herself wretchedly, unable to shake the image of Jonathan holding the faceless woman in his arms.

Breathing an irritated sigh, Katherine asked herself why couldn't she stop tormenting herself like this. Purposely she nursed the memory of his betrayal, and a few seconds later she found herself staring in surprise at the flower that lay crushed in her hands. Angrily she flung the wilted blossom to the lawn, where she ground it with the heel of her slipper in the same manner she wanted to crush Jonathan's black heart.

She tried to derive some pleasure from the fact that she had accomplished her goal . . . after a fashion. Even though it hadn't happened the way she had envisioned it, Jonathan still desired her and she had refused him. Victory was hers at last, even more so when she married Max. Once she and Max were married, there was nothing Jonathan could do to her or their child. That would really be her final triumph over Jonathan!

Summoning the image of Max, she longed for his presence and the comfort of his love. With a slight sense of guilt she realized how her indecision had tortured him; she had seen the pain in his eyes at her confession that Jonathan had been her lover.

For a fraction of an instant she was frightened at the thought of losing Max; but no, she brought herself up short, she wouldn't lose him. Max loved her. She was sure of his love, and as soon as she saw him again, she would tell him that she was ready to become his wife. She did love him. Perhaps not with the same intensity she had once loved Jonathan, but that would come in time. In Max's arms, she would never think of Jonathan again.

Suddenly she was dropping with fatigue. There had been little sleep for her the last two nights, and she wanted to start preparations for her trip to Albany early in the morning. Going back inside the house, she made up her mind to send a message to Max, so that rather than waiting for the evening he would come to see her as soon as he got back from Boston. That way, she and Jason could leave for Albany without wasting another day.

Katherine mounted the stairs slowly. Before retiring, however, she went into Jason's room. Even in his sleep the little boy clutched in his hand the miniature ship Max had given him. Jason was quite fond of Max, and in time he would love him as a father. Yes, she had made the right decision, Katherine thought as she adjusted the covers in which Jason was entangled. She felt a little sad as she stroked the soft flaxed hair that so reminded her of Jonathan's.

Adam had been mistaken in his belief that she would use her son to seek revenge against the father; Jonathan would never know that his seed had flourished into such a sweet and wonderful child as Jason. He probably wouldn't even care anyway. He might still desire the mother, but he had another child — or perhaps more by now — with the woman he truly loved.

Emitting a weary sigh, Katherine tiptoed out of the room. As was her custom, she left the door slightly ajar so that she could hear if Jason woke and called for her during the night.

Just a trace a wisteria-scented breeze made the lacy curtains in her bedchamber billow sightly. Moonlight spilling through the open window made every detail clear as she ambled to the table to light the lamp.

She had reached the middle of the room when the door closed softly behind her.

"Good evening, Katie," said a low, husky voice.

Abruptly she spun around. A look of sheer disbelief illuminated her features at the sight of the tall figure leaning lazily against the door.

"Jonathan!" The name came out in a startled hiss of breath. "How — how did you get in?"

He gave a small, wry chuckle. "You wouldn't let me past the gate," he replied. Even in the dimness she saw the accompanying shrug and the gesture of his hand toward the window. "Did you really think that would keep me away?"

Her thoughts tumbled incoherently as they stared at one another across the room. Then, striving to gather herself, Katherine turned away. Her hands were trembling as she lit the lamp. Drawing in her breath, she schooled her features into a semblance of composure before she faced him again.

Hiding her disquiet behind a sharply annoyed tone she demanded, "What do you want?"

Jonathan returned her frownlike glance with amusement. Deliberately his eyes wandered over the long auburn hair clustered around her slender neck and followed the pure lines of her white throat. She was pale, but outwardly calm as his gaze shifted to the curve of her swelling bosom and lingered there for a few moments before he looked up into her eyes again. The hint of a sardonic smile appeared at the corners of his mouth when he said huskily, "I want *you,* Katie."

An involuntary shiver went through her. Lifting her hands before her as if to fend him off, she shrank back crying, "No, Jonathan, no!"

He responded with a laugh that was short and mirthless. "Don't tell me you're being faithful to your current lover."

The irony in his voice made her snap her head back as she retorted forcefully, "Max isn't my lover! We are to marry!"

He shook his head slowly. "No, Katherine, you are not."

Looking quite startled, her mouth partly opened before she closed it again and said, "Are you out of your mind?"

As though in a trance, she watched him move away from the door. Slowly, deliberately, he came to stand before her. Looking down at her thoughtfully, he asked softly, "Am I?"

Her stomach tightened, and a fluttering breathlessness took possession of her as he drew her to him. A deep soft laughter gurgled in his throat as he put an arm around her neck and gently pulled her head back. The warmth of his breath caressed her skin as he leaned over her to kiss the curve of her vulnerable throat. She gave a small whimper, trying to resist the wave of dizziness that washed over her as his lips traced the slender column of her neck and moved seductively along her jawline.

A pervasive warmth rippled through her as his tongue probed and explored the contours of her mouth. His hands moved along her back, pressing her body as though to meld them together as he possessed her yielding, pliant lips.

The imbuing surge of pleasure, all the trembling feelings, all the churning emotions she had felt so long ago came back in a tumultuous rush to make the world spin about her. Her body was responding to his caresses, and she could no longer withhold her responses; melting in his arms she clung to him, returning kiss by intoxicating kiss with desperate, frantic hunger.

Their mouths clinging to each other, he swept her up in his arms and carried her to the bed.

"My God, Katie, it's been so long!" he whispered, his voice made hoarse by passion, his hands parting her gown to seek the warmth of her flesh. "So very long!"

The words he had so fervently spoken filtered through to her conscious mind, jerking Katherine back to reality. The anger she had carried within her for so long flared anew, lending her the strength to push him away.

"Let me go!" Almost violently she freed herself from his embrace, shouting, "Don't touch me!"

Surprised and taken aback by he sudden outburst, Jonathan then abruptly backed away.

"It's been over for a long time, Jonathan," she said, her voice quivering with wrath. "I hate you. I told you yesterday that I never wanted to see you again, and I meant it. Just go away! Let me be!"

His frontal muscles constricted faintly. "Why is it so important for you to marry Chapman?" he demanded with a snort. "Is it because of his money?"

The disapproval in his voice made her glare at him with defiance. "I love him." She said it cuttingly.

His expression became so set that the muscles of his jaw were drawn tightly under his skin. "I won't let you go, Katie," he said in a strange tone of voice. "Not this time."

Her voice rose hysterically, "I won't be your whore again!"

A contained expression came to his eyes as he said softly, "I'll marry you, Katie."

Katherine looked at him with astonishment. Then her expression changed, and she uttered a scornful little laugh. "Don't tell me bigamy is legal in Baltimore," she said with sarcastic bitterness. "You already have a wife, remember? Or have you conveniently forgotten—as you forgot to mention when we were in London?"

Jonathan shot a pained look at her. His face was grim, his voice tight when he replied, "Mary Beth is dead, Katie. She died in childbirth seven years ago."

Katherine drew in a long, startled breath. Even her anger couldn't blind her to the unspeakable sorrow that came to his eyes. "I—I'm sorry, Jonathan," she said with genuine regret. "The child?"

He wearily shook his head. "Stillborn." Following a small, bleak silence, his voice became low and intent when he said, "I've been told that you have a child."

A gleam of caution came to her eyes. "Who told you?" she asked in a hushed voice.

"Come now, *Mrs*. Cameron," he said acidly. "You haven't exactly kept it a secret. Who was the father?"

All Katherine could do for a moment was glare at him in helpless silence. Then, removing her eyes from the glittering anger of his gaze, she tipped her chin slightly as she said defiantly, "That's none of your business."

She started to turn away, but seizing her by the shoulders, he muttered savagely, "I'm making it my business. Tell me, who was he?"

Katherine looked sulky and didn't answer.

"Who was he, Katherine? Who?"

"Let me go!" she cried, struggling to get away.

Jonathan wouldn't let her go. His hands clamped on her shoulders like bands of steel as he continued to torment her.

Neither one of them heard the door open. In unison they

turned abruptly toward the young voice that called, "Mommie?"

"Jason!" Katherine gasped in alarm.

A vast silence fell in the room. Holding her breath with apprehension, she shifted a swift glance at Jonathan's face.

For a second, it seemed frozen. Then a slow look of astonishment spread over his features. "My God!" she heard him murmur under his breath.

His hands no longer tried to retain her when she moved away and went to Jason. Dropping to her knees to come to his eye level, she made an effort to speak lightly as she inquired, "What is it, darling? Are you thirsty?"

Jason shook his head. "I heard you crying, mommie," he said putting his small hand to her cheek. "Are you all right?"

"Of course I am, darling," she replied with a bright smile that quickly came and went. She took him by the hand and started to get up. "Come, I'll take you back to bed."

Jonathan's voice froze her. "One moment," he said.

There was a knot of tension in her stomach as she turned to him. "Jonathan, please," she begged, her voice unsteady.

With a puzzled glance, Jason looked up at his father as he came to him slowly, eyes steadily fixed on him as though he were almost in a trance. "Who are you?" the boy asked with candor when Jonathan stopped before him.

The question made Katherine hold her breath as she sent an imploring glance to Jonathan. But Jonathan didn't see it; his eyes were intent on his son.

"Someone who's been waiting to meet you for a long time, son," Jonathan replied in a voice made even huskier by emotion. When he fell silent, Katherine realized that he was struggling for control so as to not frighten the boy. "My name is Jonathan Greenfield," he said at last, putting out his hand. Katherine noticed that it was trembling slightly.

"How do you do, sir," Jason said, politely shaking his father's hand.

Her throat constricted painfully, Katherine witnessed the scene through a haze of tears.

Jonathan's eyes searched the child's face with intense hunger. He had to swallow in order to ask, "How old are you, Jason?"

"Six," Jason replied showing the appropriate number of fingers. Even to do this he refused to let go of the toy he had in his hand.

Seizing on this, Jonathan asked, "What have you got there, son?"

"It's a ship," Jason grinned, proudly displaying his prized possession. "A clipper like the one we sailed from Cornwall."

"Cornwall?" Jonathan asked casually. "Is that where you used to live?"

"Yes, sir," Jason nodded. Looking to Katherine for confirmation, he added, "We all did, didn't we, mommie?"

Unable to speak, she gave an affirmative sign.

The boy shifted his attention back to his father. "They had lots of boats there, but mommie wouldn't let me sail in any of them," he said.

"Why not?" Jonathan inquired, raptly watching his son's face.

Jason shrugged. "She said I was too little," he replied, slightly downcast.

Jonathan couldn't refrain from smiling. "I have a clipper ship just like this one here, only she's a real one," he told the boy. "Would you like to see her?"

"A real one?" Jason's eyes—so much like his father's—widened in surprise. His young face was tight with eagerness as he turned to his mother and asked, "Could I, mommie? Please?"

"Of course, darling," she agreed unwillingly.

Jason turned a beaming face to his father.

"I'll tell you what," Jonathan said them. "Why don't you

287

let me take you back to your room, and we'll talk about it. All right?"

"Yes, sir!" Jason replied, bobbing his head in earnest.

Jonathan smiled. When he ruffled the child's flaxen hair, the action was meant to disguise a gentler caress. His hand was on Jason's shoulder as they left the room together.

Consumed with apprehension, Katherine watched them go.

With every shrinking nerve painfully on edge, she paced the floor while waiting for Jonathan to come back. What was going to happen now that he had learned of Jason's existence? Oh, why hadn't she taken him to Albany as she had originally planned instead of waiting for Max, she lamented.

When she finally saw Jonathan coming through the door again, one look at his face told her that he was still in the grip of a powerful emotion.

His expression swiftly changed to one of outrage. "How could you?" he roared. "How could you leave without even telling me you were carrying my child?"

Katherine looked at him almost fearfully. "I didn't know!" she defended herself hurriedly. Suddenly, she began weeping softly. "I didn't know," she wept.

Her distress seemed to take the edge off his anger. His face softened, and he took her in his arms. "You could have written to me when you found out, Katie. You always knew where to reach me. Why didn't you?"

At this question a flood of painful memories came rushing back; her desolation at his betrayal; the intense desperation she had known at the discovery that she was carrying the child of the man she had come to hate with every fiber of her being. Anger and resentment mingled with her pain, and at that moment she wanted to wound him as deeply as she could. Drawing away from his embrace, she looked at him with eyes glittering with resentment.

"Because I didn't want anything from you, Jonathan,"

she replied in a voice that was low and deliberate. "Not then, not now, not ever. You may be his sire, but he's my child. Mine, you hear me? He's mine!"

In the tense, breathless silence that followed, she saw Jonathan turn pale. She turned away.

"We're getting married, Katherine," she heard him say a few seconds later. "At once."

She turned slowly to regard him. For a few seconds she simply looked at him with contempt. Then, drawing herself up, she replied in a calm tone of voice. "I won't marry you, Jonathan."

He leaned over and gently held her by the shoulders. "I want you with me, Katie, and I want my son. He needs a father."

She was unmoved by the persuasion in his voice or by the grim set of his face.

"You have no claim on either one of us, Jonathan. And as for Jason needing a father, you're right, he does. But don't worry. He'll have one very soon when I marry Max."

Jonathan's fingers tightened on her shoulders. His blue eyes were blazing when he ground out, "I won't let you do it, Katherine."

Mocking him with a slight shrug of her shoulders, she challenged, "And how are you going to stop me? By claiming me as your property because years ago you won me in a game of cards? Or are you going to use force? It wouldn't be the first time, would it?"

Her scathing words made him turn his head aside as though she had physically struck him. His hands dropped away from her shoulders.

She stood before him, proud and defiant, as she said cuttingly, "Get out!"

His expression closed like a trap shutting. "Very well, Katherine, I'll go. But the matter is far from being closed." With that he stalked out of the room and left her standing there.

All the strength she had summoned deserted her then. A dry, convulsive sob rose in her throat and she collapsed on the bed trembling in every limb.

Finally, after all those years, her revenge was total, complete. Jonathan wanted to marry her, he wanted his son, and she had denied him both. She should be jumping for joy; and yet, all she could feel at this moment of victory was . . . desolation.

Refusing to face the new day, Katherine turned on her side and pulled a pillow over her head to block out the sound of a fast, persistent rapping penetrating her consciousness. At last the rapping ceased, but seconds later someone began shaking her gently, but urgently by the shoulder.

"Mum, wake up, mum!" an urgent voice insisted.

"Go away!" Katherine mumbled, gesturing blindly with her hand.

"Mum, please wake up!" the voice kept repeating.

Finally, Katherine pushed the pillow aside and squinted her eyes at the maid. "Yes, Annie, what is it?" she inquired with ill-concealed impatience.

Annie regarded her with apprehension. "I'm sorry, mum, but it's Master Jason," she blurted out. "He's not in his room, and we can't find him anywhere."

Katherine sat up suddenly, almost jerkily. "Jason!" she exclaimed, now instantly awake. She gave Annie a startled look. "Did you say he's missing?" Receiving an affirmative sign, she inquired, "Have you searched the grounds?"

Annie bobbed her head emphatically. "We're all searching now, mum."

Was Jason up to his old tricks again, Katherine thought with some annoyance as she pushed the covers aside. The adventurous little boy had a marked predilection for mischievous escapades. Once, while living in Cornwall, the entire village had participated in a wide search for him during one of those episodes. In the end Jason had been found hiding in one of the fishing boats, waiting for morning to go out to sea with the men.

While drawing on her robe, Katherine noticed that Annie was wringing her hands with anxiety. Katherine gave her a searching look. "Is there something else you haven't told me?"

"Yes, mum," the girl admitted with apparent reluctance. "The gate was wide open this morning."

Katherine's face reflected her bemusement. "The gate?" she repeated numbly.

"Yes, mum, and some of Master Jason's clothes are missing. I've already looked."

Katherine's brow creased in a puzzled frown. "But Jason wouldn't take his clothes unless — " Suddenly, her body went stiff and cold with fear. Jonathan! Had he taken Jason? The words they had spoken came rushing back to her, and she gave a low cry that she smothered with her hand.

Having rushed out of the room and practically flown down the stairs, she burst out on the terrace and frantically looked for Adam among those combing the grounds. Finally spotting him, she ran to him.

She stopped breathless at his side. "I think Jonathan took Jason," she told him, much agitated.

Adam was stunned for a moment. "But how? He was turned away!"

"He was in my room last night," she whispered hurriedly. "He came through the window, and he saw Jason."

Briefly, she related her conversation with Jonathan.

"Have you any idea where he could have taken him?" Adam inquired at the end of her recount.

"I don't know!" she replied, her voice rising. Realizing she was on the verge of becoming hysterical, for a moment she pressed the tips of her fingers to her temples as though trying to extract a clear thought. Looking up at Adam, she offered, "His ship, maybe."

Adam's anxiety over Jason's safety had lessened somewhat after learning that it might have been Jonathan who had taken him. "Easy, pet. At least we know he's all right." He tried to soothe her, yet a worried look crossed his face as he added, "But you know what that means, don't you? Shouldn't we call Max?"

She shook her head. "He isn't back from Boston yet." Tears were lurking in the eyes she turned to him when she asked, "What are we going to do?"

Adam became thoughtful. "I'll try to find Jonathan," he said after a moment. "Perhaps I might be able to persuade him to bring Jason back."

"I'll go with you," she said, immediately starting to turn away.

He reached out and stilled her. "No, Katherine. Stay here in case he comes back."

"But what if he's already on his way to Baltimore with Jason?"

"From what you told me, I have a feeling he's coming back for you, pet."

Katherine shook her head emphatically. "I told him that I was going to marry Max."

"Yes, but now that he has Jason, he may try to force you to marry him instead," Adam pointed out.

Katherine blinked, flushed, and looked frantic. "I will not!"

"On second thought," Adam reflected, "it may be better if I stayed and waited for Jonathan to show up."

Her alarm increased. "No, Adam, no!" she cried, urgently clinging to his arm. "Please find him before he takes Jason away."

Her anxiety made Adam relent against his better judgement. Katherine urged him to hurry.

She paced the floor after he had gone, waiting impatiently for what seemed an eternity and blaming herself incessantly for her stupidity. She should never have waited for

Max to return. If she had gone to Albany, Jonathan wouldn't have found out about Jason, and this situation would have been avoided.

All these years she had been convinced that Jonathan would have scorned his bastard even if he had known of his existence. His reaction had been completely different from what she had expected. Then, too, she had also believed that he had a legitimate child when, in reality, the child had been lost. She had been mistaken on both counts and now was paying for it.

But not with Jason, please, Lord! Not with Jason!

She was devastated by the idea that Jonathan would take her son away, never to see her child again. Oh, how she hated Jonathan!

She was near hysteria when Bruce came in and announced the arrival of Captain Greenfield with three other men. Katherine urged him to show them in, and expectantly faced the door.

It was Jonathan who came in alone.

"How dare you take Jason!" she demanded, furious.

"You left me no other choice," he replied blandly.

"Where is he?" she inquired anxiously. "Is he all right? Is he frightened? Oh, how could you!"

"Calm down, Katherine," Jonathan said quietly. "To answer your questions: yes, he's all right, and no, he's not frightened. As a matter of fact, he was quite delighted to be aboard."

"So you did take him to your ship," she said with dismay.

Jonathan nodded slightly. "I had promised last night, when I took him back to his room that I would take him," he explained. "I hadn't intended for it to be this way, Katie, but after what you said, I simply couldn't let you take him from me again. When I went back to his room, he came with me most willingly. He was never frightened."

"So that's how you got him to go with you!" she accused him. "I want him back!"

293

"And you shall have him, my love," he replied, holding her with a faint, calm smile. "As soon as you and I are married. I've already taken care of all the legalities and the minister is outside, so there won't be any delays."

Her pupils dilated in shocked disbelief. "You can't force me to marry you!" she exclaimed then, aghast. "I'll call the constable!"

Jonathan gave an almost imperceptible shrug. "Go right ahead, but let me warn you that he won't do you any good." He paused briefly before adding, "Jason is already on his way to Baltimore."

Her face went pale and taut at the cheekbones as she closed her eyes in dismay. When she opened them again and regarded him with a stricken expression, tears were trembling in her lashes. "How could you steal that child and send him away all alone on a long voyage?" she asked bleakly. "Have you no heart?"

"He's not alone, Katie, and you can be with him again soon," he said gently. "Just say you'll marry me." He paused, waiting for her to speak. When she had not replied after a few seconds, his voice turned solemn and determined. "If you don't, then there is no way on earth I'm going to let you have him back, you know."

She stared at him reproachfully. "You have no legal right to him," she snapped with sudden anger at his threat. "His name is Cameron!"

"He's a Greenfield," he countered mildly. "And he'll be where he belongs, where he should have been a long time ago if—" Letting his words trail away, he shook his head. "Never mind that, Katie. We can set things to rights now. Marry, and we can all be together once and for all."

Undeterred by her reticence he continued in his attempts to persuade her, but Katherine wouldn't listen. They were in the midst of an argument when Adam walked into the room. A flash of suspicious resentment crossed Jonathan's eyes.

"Who is he, Katherine?" he asked caustically. "Another one of your lovers?"

"Oh, you're insufferable!" she shot at him before turning to Adam expectantly. "Did you find him?"

Adam shook his head heavily, his expression somber.

Katherine turned to Jonathan in defeat. "Then it's true, isn't it? You really did sent him to Baltimore?" Deep in her heart, there had been a glimmer of hope that Jonathan had been bluffing.

"Look here, Greenfield," Adam began.

"I repeat, sir," Jonathan cut him off with a stern look. "Who are you?"

Katherine realized that Jonathan had never seen Adam without his disguise. "Adam Garfield," she replied, making no attempt to disguise her impatience. "You knew him as Professor Stuyvesant."

A look of complete surprise came over Jonathan's features as he regarded Adam.

Without bothering with further explanations, her tone changed to one of pleading when she said, "Jonathan, please let me have my son back, I beg of you."

Looking down at her seriously he said quietly, "He's my son, too."

The implicit reproach in his voice made Katherine stare at him in helpless silence. "You have no right to him," she still tried to argue.

"How can you say that, love?" Jonathan said gently. "Marry me, Katie."

Troubled, yet peevish, she replied forcefully, "I will not!"

Jonathan heaved a weary sigh. "Very well, Katie. If that's what you want, so be it. Goodbye."

A panicky feeling invaded her stomach as she saw him start for the door. "Wait!" she called, running after him.

Jonathan paused and turned to look at her, his expression cold.

"All right, Jonathan," she said bleakly, "I'll marry you."

"Don't do it, Katherine," Adam protested. "Wait until Max returns. He has enough influence to get your son back."

"Not in Baltimore," Jonathan pointed out dryly without taking his eyes off Katherine.

"He's right," Katherine admitted with a gesture of discouragement. Abjectly she shook her heard. "I can't let him take my son away from me, Adam." Slowly, she turned to Jonathan and said in a low voice, "Very well, Jonathan. You win. Call the minister."

"A wise decision, my love," Jonathan said with a grim little smile.

The ceremony was brief. The minister appeared quite jittery, the bride was gloomy, and only the bridegroom seemed satisfied.

A far cry from Agatha's wedding, Katherine reflected as the minister read the service in a jerky, high-pitched voice. That had been a joyous occasion for two people who loved each other deeply. This was a mockery; Jonathan didn't love her, and she hated him.

Adam and Bruce served as reluctant witnesses with the two officers Jonathan had brought along with him. When the ceremony was over, the butler escorted the three men to the door.

For once having lost his customary calm, Bruce returned moments later and hovered at the door.

"What is it, Bruce?" Adam inquired.

The poor man couldn't hide his dismay as he replied, "Mr. Chapman is here, sir,"

It was Jonathan who told him, "By all means show him in." To Katherine he said with irony, "He may be the first to offer his congratulations to the happy new couple."

Her response was to slant him a quick, angry glance.

Max came in and stopped short when he saw Jonathan standing next to Katherine, one arm possessively around her shoulders.

"Max!" she cried, rushing to him before Jonathan could stop her.

Still a little stunned, Max took her protectively in his arms.

There was cold anger in Jonathan's voice when he said, "Take your hands off my wife, Chapman."

"Your wife?" Max repeated, looking quite perplexed.

Jonathan gave him a wolfish grin. "You just missed the wedding, I'm afraid."

Swiftly, Max shifted his bemused glance from Jonathan to Katherine. "Is that true?"

Unable to speak, she bobbed her head in assent and burst into tears.

Max faced Jonathan angrily. "Look here, Greenfield, you can't get away with this. Katherine is engaged to me!"

Jonathan gave a small, humorless grunt. "Sorry, old man, but she's my wife now."

Releasing Katherine, Max went to confront Jonathan. "I'll kill you for this, Greenfield," he ground out through clenched teeth.

Abandoning his casual stance, Jonathan adopted a more belligerent attitude to reply with equal anger, "It's the only way you'd take her from me, Chapman."

Katherine followed the exchange with a feeling of terror. Before they could come to blows, she ran to stand between them. "No, Max, don't," she pleaded in earnest. "Please!"

The expression on his face was tight when Max looked down at her. The anguish written on her lovely countenance, the tears filling her eyes made him hesitate for just a moment. With compressed lips, he turned on his heel and stalked out of the room.

Katherine's heart constricted painfully as she saw him go through the doorway. After he had disappeared, she turned to Jonathan and cried, "Oh, how I hate you!"

Abruptly she turned and ran from the room.

Grim-faced, Jonathan watched her go.

* * *

Impervious to the voices shouting commands and to the crew members who rushed to obey them, Katherine stood at the railing of the ship indulging her discontent as she watched the city recede in the distance.

New York. They had been so happy there! She remembered their arrival only a few months before, when she and Max had been filled with the wonder of their love and hopes for the future. A tear slid slowly down her pale cheek as she said fervently, "Forgive me, Max."

All her plans had gone awry. Once again, Jonathan had won, and this time he had both she and Jason.

Jonathan had lied to her when he had told her that he had already sent Jason to Baltimore. Her son had been waiting for her aboard his ship, and bubbling with excitement had informed her that his father had promised he could take the helm once they were out to sea. Jonathan had done his job well; even if she could take Jason back, she wasn't sure he would want to go away with her.

Yet Jonathan's victory was only partial; as far as she was concerned, this mockery of a marriage would be in name only. If he wanted his marital rights, he would have to take them by force. She would never concede defeat; and now, as his wife, she was in a position to exact her revenge every day of their lives. It wasn't what she had sought, but what she had to accept. She shuddered at the prospect of having to live the rest of her life with only hatred and vengeance in her heart. God in Heaven, hadn't she suffered enough?

The sun had already set when Katherine turned away from the railing with a weary sigh and prepared to go below to the cabin. She had seen little of Jason since coming aboard; all his attention had been centered on his newly discovered father and the excitement of going out to sea again—this time aboard his very own ship.

Once the marriage had taken place, Katherine's concern

298

had turned to how she would explain the situation to her son. Even though Jason was very bright for his age, he was too young to understand the truth; on the other hand, she wouldn't lie to him.

Before boarding the ship, however, Jonathan had informed her that he and Jason had already cleared the air in that respect, and that she wasn't to worry. Although this had made Katherine wonder about the version he had given, she wouldn't dream of discrediting Jonathan to his child.

Once they were alone, Jonathan attempted to strike up a conversation by saying casually, "If the winds hold, we should make Baltimore soon."

She didn't bother to answer. It was only a while later that she asked the question that was bearing heavily on her mind. "How are you going to explain Jason and me to your family?"

"Explain?" Jonathan frowned slightly as he looked at her. "You're my wife, and he's my son. There's nothing else to explain."

"May I remind you that you were married to someone else when he was born?" she said a trifle dryly.

"I don't have to explain anything," he insisted quite stubbornly.

She looked at him skeptically and then heaved a weary sigh. Moments later, she said, "I'm rather tired, Jonathan."

Taking the implication, Jonathan rose to his feet. He seemed about to say something and then changed his mind. He turned away and went from the cabin.

Katherine undressed and slipped into bed next to Jason. She felt tired and emotionally drained.

She slept.

Fourteen

On the morning they were to arrive at their destination, Katherine emerged on deck and was greeted by a dark, overcast sky. Taking the miserable weather as an ominous prelude to the reception awaiting them, she mentally reviled Jonathan for placing her and Jason in such a situation.

Baltimore came into view shortly before noon.

A light rain was falling, and there was little chance for conversation while they disembarked. It wasn't until they were about to board the carriage that Jonathan said, "I sent a message ahead advising my parents of our arrival."

Flicking a wary glance at him she inquired, "Did you mention that you were not alone?"

He answered with a terse, "Yes," as he helped her into the carriage.

Jason kept excitedly chattering away with his father while the carriage traveled the city streets under a steady drizzle. Tense and silent, Katherine looked out the window with an unhappy sense of exclusion. After what seemed like miles and miles of rowhouses fronted by white marble steps, private mansions set back from the the road began to appear. At long last the carriage entered a driveway that was flanked on both sides by venerable shade trees, and stopped in front of a Georgian three-story mansion of red brick with doors and windows trimmed in white. Two one-story wings rose on each side of the structure.

The front door opened suddenly and a woman came out of the house. A few steps behind her came a very tall man whose marked resemblance to Jonathan proclaimed a close relationship between them.

Jonathan was the first to alight, and the woman rushed to him, her face eager, her arms extended in welcome. "Oh, Jon, you're home at last!" she cried, throwing her arms around him.

Jonathan caught his mother in his arms and kissed her with unfeigned affection and swept her off her feet in a powerful embrace. He set her down and turned to his father. The men pumped hands and heartily thumped each other's back.

Alicia Greenfield was tall and blue eyed. Although her blonde hair was beginning to turn gray, her complexion was still as smooth as that of a girl. Francis was almost as tall as Jonathan. His hair the color of gray iron, but despite the difference in coloring the resemblance between father and son was startling, down to the sparkling blue eyes and the disarming smile.

All eyes turned expectantly to the new arrivals.

Noticing how pale Katherine was, Jonathan gave her a reassuring smile as he helped her alight from the carriage. Taking both her and Jason by the hand, he turned to his parents to say with an unmistakable note of pride, "Mother, father, this is my wife, Katherine, and my son, Jason."

An odd silence fell.

For the flick of an instant, Alicia and Francis Greenfield were unable to do anything more than stare first at Jason, then at Katherine, and back at Jason again.

At their astonished expressions, a shiver of apprehension went through Katherine like ripples on the surface of a pond.

Alicia was the first to recover her composure. She smiled

301

and affably said, "My dear, how nice to have you with us. Welcome."

Katherine willed herself to relax in the warm, affectionate embrace that immediately followed the greeting.

Francis echoed his wife's words and gave Katherine a kiss on the cheek. Her smiling response came out a bit more tremulous than she had intended.

Next their attention shifted to Jason, who until then had been holding tightly to his father's hand while witnessing the reception extended to his mother. A little frown had formed on his brow, knowing that he was in line for more of the same. The prospect didn't make him very happy. Although a warm and affectionate child by nature, he was at that age when such effusive demonstrations were highly embarrassing to him. Even Katherine was allowed to hug him and kiss him only in strict privacy.

Aware of his uneasiness, she sent a glance and a reassuring smile at her son. She was never more proud of him as he submitted to the hugs and kisses a little stiffly, but without squirming out of the affectionate grasp of his grandparents.

"It's damp out here," Alicia said, turning to Jonathan and his family. "Shall we go inside?"

She turned and led the way.

Jonathan took his son by the hand. His other arm went around Katherine's waist as they followed his parents into the house. Once they were inside, the two newcomers looked around at their new home. The house was spacious and elegant.

At the bottom of the majestic staircase leading up to the upper levels, Alicia turned to her son and said, "Jonathan, we must give Katherine a chance to catch her breath. You know how overwhelming we Greenfields can be at times." Her voice was full of kindness when she addressed her new daughter-in-law. "Your rooms are ready if you wish to freshen up, my dear. You must be tired after your journey, so don't worry about us now. We can get properly acquainted after you've rested. Just let us know if there's anything you need."

"Thank you," Katherine nodded with a grateful smile.

While Jonathan took his wife and son to their rooms, Alicia and Francis stood at the bottom of the stairs silently watching their ascent. A communicative glance passed between them, and in silent accord they went into the drawing room.

"Katherine is quite lovely, isn't she?" Alicia commented.

"Yes, dear," Francis agreed readily. His tone quickened with enthusiasm when he added, "But that Jason! He looks just like Jonathan did at that age, doesn't he? There's no question, he's a chip off the old block."

A little frown wrinkled Alicia's forehead as she nodded thoughtfully. "There are going to be many raised eyebrows around here, I can tell you," she said then, her voice troubled. "However, my main concern is Felicity. I know she's going to resent Katherine, especially after she sees the boy."

Francis studied her worried face. His tone was placid when he said, "Don't you worry about Felicity, my dear. I know Mary Beth was her best friend, but she loves her brother and wants to see him happy again. She wouldn't do anything to hurt him."

A contained expression came to Alicia's eyes as she regarded her husband. Felicity had her father wrapped around her little finger. Francis had a blind spot where his daughter was concerned, but she knew better. And she was uneasy.

Standing in the middle of the room where Jonathan had left her, Katherine gazed at the four-poster bed with ill-concealed resentment as she removed her bonnet and flung it on a nearby chair. Every detail in the room proclaimed it as a woman's domain. Was this the same bed where Jonathan had made love to his first wife, conceived a child with her? she asked herself wretchedly.

"Why should I care?" she asked herself out loud. "I hate him!"

But she did care. She wanted to weep.

"I mustn't!" she told herself sternly.

Suddenly, she wanted to get out of that room where she could almost feel the ghost of Mary Beth lurking in every corner.

"Oh, Adam, help me!"

She thought of Adam, of his warnings not to panic, to keep her head. Drawing in her breath, Katherine fought to take control of her churning emotions.

Jonathan came back minutes later and found her staring moodily out the window.

"I put Jason in my old room," he said pleasantly. "Is there anything you need, love?"

His endearment sounded like such a mockery to her ears that she compressed her lips in annoyance. She turned slowly and glared at him. With a sharp edge in her voice she replied, "Yes, Jonathan, I need to leave this house. I can't stay here!"

In the constrained silence that fell, they stared at one another across the room.

"Please calm down, Katie," he said at last, coming toward her. "I realize how difficult this situation must be for you, but —"

"I am calm, Jonathan," she interrupted him, expelling an indignant sigh. "But I refuse to stay in this house. This is the same room you and Mary Beth shared, isn't it?" Before he could answer, she went on with passionate conviction, her voice rising with every sentence, "I can feel her presence here. I don't want to stay in this room, sleep in that bed. I just want out!"

An expression of regret came to his features. "I'm sorry, Katie. I should have considered your feelings . . ."

"Consider my feelings!" she scoffed with a laugh that was short and mirthless. "Don't make me laugh, Jonathan. You've never considered anyone's feelings but your own! Else, you would have let me go on with my life instead of forcing me into this miserable marriage and brought me here against my will."

He gazed at her heavily. "All right, Katie. If it will make you feel better, we'll get a house of our own."

"When?"

"Tomorrow, Katie. We'll start looking for one tomorrow." With careful gentility, he added, "You're tired now, honey. Why don't you get some rest? Don't worry about Jason, I'll look after him. Someone will call you when it's time to dress for dinner. In the meantime, call if you need anything, all right?"

When the door had closed behind him, Katherine glared after him and angrily stamped her foot. Then, without bothering to undress, she flung herself down on the chaise lounge.

A blush suffused her fair skin as she thought of those terribly embarrassing moments when Jonathan's parents had looked at Jason and immediately realized that she had been Jonathan's mistress at the time when he was still married to Mary Beth. What must they be thinking, she reflected angrily, getting gloomy. Of me, of Jason—Jonathan's bastard? She wouldn't be at all surprised if he was telling them right at this moment that she had been a prize won at a gaming table.

She felt unsettled, ill at ease at the thought of confronting Alicia and Francis again after they had learned the truth about her.

As usual, it was her pride that made Katherine determined to present her best front to the situation. Regardless of what they might think of her, or how they treated her, she would conduct herself with utmost dignity.

But, oh, why couldn't Jonathan have left her alone!

After a nap and a long bath had helped improve her disposition, Katherine dressed with care in preparation for the ordeal that lay ahead.

Standing at the bottom of the stairs, Jonathan looked up as his wife came down to meet him. Katherine had changed, he reflected, still finding it hard to believe how much.

Her movements were erect, graceful, and every one of her gestures evidenced distinction and perfect poise. She was no longer the frightened girl he had once known. This new Katherine was not only far more bewitchingly beautiful than he remembered, but also a strong-willed woman who had fought him every step of the way from the moment they had met again.

Offering his arm, he said in a hushed voice, "You look absolutely dazzling, love."

The intimate glance from his eyes gave Katherine a curious warm feeling inside. Doing her best to disregard it she smoothed the ample skirt of her fawn-colored silk gown and asked in a rather detached fashion, "Will there be anyone else for dinner besides your parents?"

"My sister, Felicity, is here with her husband," he replied, taking her hand and linking it through his arm. "I'm sure you'll like them."

While she concentrated all her efforts on concealing from him how very frightened she was, they covered the distance to the drawing room where the family had assembled. Before entering, she paused for a second to draw in a deep breath. "The performance begins," she said wryly, and fixing a smile on her face nodded, "I'm ready."

Squaring her shoulders and holding her head up, she went in. Instinctively, her fingers tightened slightly on Jonathan's arm as conversations ceased, heads turned, and all eyes fastened on her. She could feel many undercurrents in that room.

Jonathan laid a warm, reassuring hand over hers as he made the introductions.

306

Felicity and her husband, Ned Parker, had rushed to the ancestral home as soon as they had heard of Jonathan's arrival with a new wife. In the Greenfield fashion, Felicity was tall—much taller than Katherine. Her figure was slender and well formed, and on this particular evening her dark blonde hair was elaborately coiffed to frame her perfect oval face. No one could deny she was a beauty, but the long-lashed blue eyes she turned to Katherine reflected no warmth as she critically examined her new sister-in-law from head to toe.

Katherine was unaware that her name and her face were not strangers to Felicity. Although they had never met, Jonathan's sister made frequent trips to New York. One of her best friends in that city was Crystal Gaynor, the same blonde woman Jonathan had escorted to the ballet and to the ball at the Raleighs' where he and Katherine had met again after their long separation.

Having despaired of trapping Maxwell Chapman, Crystal had entered into a marriage of convenience with an older man. After a short time her husband had conveniently departed, leaving her in rather comfortable circumstances although the bulk of his estate had gone to his children from a previous marriage. This had been quite a disappointment to Crystal. She had expected to inherit far more than the annuity she received, and reviling the memory of her dear departed, she again entertained hopes of catching the elusive Max. Her hopes in that respect were dashed by Katherine's appearance on the scene.

During Felicity's last visit to New York, an ugly rumor had been circulating regarding Katherine's relationship with Max. Her attraction to the opposite sex had earned her much envy from many young marriageable females, but it had been Chapman's dedication to her the sin for which the jealous Crystal couldn't forgive her. She had painted for Felicity a bleak portrait of Katherine's character—just as she had done for Jonathan in answer to his seemingly casual inquiries as to Katherine's identity after the theater performance.

Katherine immediately sensed Felicity's hostility, but her husband's greeting was warm and genuinely friendly. Ned Parker was a tall and gangly man somewhere in his middle thirties who, at first blush, seemed like a pleasant and good-natured fellow. His eloquent brown eyes sparkled with pleasure at meeting the new member of the family. In this room full of Greenfields, Ned appeared to Katherine as an unexpected ally.

With her suspicions still lurking in the back of her mind, Katherine put on a marvelous performance. At least on the surface she charmed everyone but her sister-in-law. When dinner was announced, Francis graciously offered his arm to her, while Jonathan paired up with his sister and Ned escorted Alicia.

Conversation at the table was animated, and Katherine participated with outward ease. On the other hand, Jonathan's apparent fascination with his wife made his contribution to the repartee rather limited. His eyes seldom left her face for more than a few seconds, and he seemed to hang on each and every one of her words. His attention was abruptly jerked back to the general conversation by an unexpected statement from his sister.

"I understand that you were . . . engaged to Maxwell Chapman when you were in New York, Katherine. What happened?"

In spite of her surprise, Katherine managed not to lose her poise. Wondering how Felicity had learned so much about her, she turned a tolerant smile on Jonathan's sister as she repeated with feigned surprise, "Engaged?" The little laugh she gave then sounded quite unconcerned. "I'm afraid, my dear Felicity, that whoever told you that was trying to pull your leg. Max and I are very good friends, but there's never been more to it than that. He's such a charming man. Have you ever met him?"

She had no need to glance in Jonathan's direction to sense that his reaction to her praise of Max was resentment. With an inward little smile, she derived perverse pleasure from his discomfiture.

Brushing aside Katherine's question, Felicity said with malice, "But I heard you came with him from Europe."

With each passing second Katherine was growing more impatient and angry at Felicity's determination to embarrass her. She was sorely tempted to tell the truth and let Jonathan take the consequences. Pride and a touch of her spirit of adventure prompted her to match wits with her current opponent.

"In a way you could say that," she said with a calm, confident smile. "Actually, that's how we met, on the crossing to New York. He was such a charming companion that what could have been a long and boring trip, became most enjoyable thanks to him. He was wonderful to all of us, especially to Jason, who became very fond of him. He simply treasures a miniature ship Max gave him as a gift."

A mischievous glint came to her green eyes as she looked around the table with a confidential air and digressed swiftly, "However, there *was* a romance aboard. Between my aunt, Agatha, and the man who recently became her husband."

She went on to narrate an embellished version of Agatha's romance and subsequent marriage, therefore silencing Felicity, who fumed in her seat. At the end of her tale, conversation drifted to other topics.

Alicia had listened with concerned interest. The hostility Felicity had shown Katherine from the start had confirmed her earlier fears. She knew her daughter well enough to know that such feelings stemmed from more than her devotion to the memory of Jonathan's first wife. The real reason was that Felicity craved being the center of attention, and she deeply resented anyone who would take that position away from her. She had married a man who worshipped the

309

ground she walked on. Mary Beth had been her best friend simply because she had been a sweet-tempered young woman who had danced to Felicity's tune and followed her lead without question. Also, she had been pretty enough without posing a threat to Felicity's own beauty. Yet here was Katherine, not only a fascinating beauty herself, but also a woman of remarkable poise and self-assurance, and capable of standing up to Felicity's attacks without batting an eye.

There was bound to be trouble between them.

Alicia had studied her new daughter-in-law since the moment she had stepped into the drawing room that evening. How different she had looked then from the pale young woman who had arrived earlier in the day! Also, Alicia had observed her son during supper. His eyes had never left his wife. On the other hand, not even once had Katherine glanced in his direction, not even for support during Felicity's attacks. She had also seen Jonathan's face turn somber at Katherine's praises of Max Chapman, whoever the man was.

Did Katherine love Jonathan, Alicia wondered with genuine concern. Judging by Jason's age, they must have been together in London at the time he had taken the *Mary Beth* on its maiden voyage to England.

Alicia had good reason to remember that time very well.

Jonathan had sailed away unaware that his wife had been with child. Mary Beth had jealously guarded the secret from everyone because of her doctor's warnings that another pregnancy could endanger her life.

Alicia had been terrified at the discovery when Mary Beth could no longer hide her condition. She waited for Jonathan to return, but for some unexplained reason he had extended his stay in London. She had then written to him, and he had come back just in time to be at the side of Mary Beth during the ordeal of delivering a stillborn child.

At her death, Jonathan had been beside himself with

grief. He had gone out to sea, and since then it was only rarely that he came back to stay at home in Baltimore for more than a few days. During those brief visits Alicia had seen that he had not yet recovered from his loss. That warm, winning smile of his had been replaced by a dry sort of grimace that never reached his eyes.

Now, all of a sudden, he reappeared with a wife and a grown child that was unmistakably his. From what she had just heard, Alicia surmised that he and Katherine had recently married in New York, and that they had not been together during the intervening years since the birth of their son.

What was the true story behind their strange marriage?

The mystery of Katherine fascinated Alicia as much as the young woman herself. Who was she?

Oh, well, sooner or later the truth would come out, Alicia reflected. All she needed was a little patience.

And Alicia Greenfield was a very patient woman.

After dismissing the maid, Katherine felt too restless to get into the bed that had been invitingly turned down to receive her. Rising from the dressing table, she went to the window.

Although the rain had stopped hours before, she could still smell the scent of damp earth in the soft warm air. They sky, still overcast, was bereft of moon and stars.

Keenly aware of the muffled sounds she could hear in the adjacent room, she wondered if Jonathan would come to her this night and claim his marital rights. Jason's presence in the cabin had served as a shield between them during the voyage from New York; but once in this house, and as his legal wife, she was totally in his power.

A shiver of fear went up her spine at the remembrance of how easily she had almost capitulated to him when he had slipped into her room that night in New York. Fear because she had no delusions as to what her response would be if he came to her determined to possess her. He had already proven that she had no resistance to his kisses, and this powerlessness against his passion made her hate him even more.

"Katie."

At the sound of his voice, she turned around to face him. The dreaded moment of confrontation was now at hand.

Her body felt stiff and cold as she watched him advance toward her.

Stopping just a pace away, Jonathan reached into the pocket of his dark blue velvet robe. "I wanted to give you this," he said as he brought out a small object in his hand. "It's your wedding ring."

Blinking in confusion, Katherine swallowed. "But you already gave me this one," she said, lifting her hand to show the narrow gold band he had placed on her finger at their makeshift wedding.

"That was the best I could do at the moment," he replied, an undertone of wryness in his voice. "But this is the one I wanted you to have. It belonged to my maternal grandmother." His gaze was probing, his smile tentative when he put out his hand and asked, "May I?"

Not trusting herself to speak, Katherine gave a silent assent and held out her hand.

She couldn't tear her gaze away from his blue eyes as Jonathan removed the narrow band. After slipping the other ring onto her finger, he continued to hold her hand as though reluctant to let it go. He leaned over a little and at the same time lifted her hand to his lips. Holding her breath, Katherine felt a fluttering feeling within her as his warm lips kissed each finger and then moved to caress the sensitized skin of her inner wrist.

Gently, lovingly, he drew her to him. She could offer no resistance as he held her in his arms and planted small tender kisses on her cheeks, her brow, her temples, her eyelids, her nose. Katherine's heart was pounding wildly as his lips slowly moved down the side of her neck to the curve of her shoulder and then began a slow ascent toward her mouth.

With a breathless feeling, she found herself longing for the taste of his kisses. Such was the intensity of her longing, that it triggered the resurgence of fear that momentarily had subsided under Jonathan's tender assault.

"Stop it!" she cried, pushing him away.

He made no effort to retain her.

Her cheeks had flushed with color, her breast was heaving when she stepped back and said vehemently, "You're not going to touch me again, Jonathan! I don't love you!"

There was a silence as they stared at one another for several moments, neither yielding an inch.

Imperceptibly, his eyes dimmed. His face was motionless, expressionless, as he said in a voice totally devoid of emotion, "You're my wife, Katie."

"Against my will!" she half-shouted, throwing her hands up in exasperation. "You forced me into this situation, but I'll be damned if I'm going to crawl into your bed! Oh, how I hate you!"

Angrily, she turned away.

He reached out and spun her around to face him. "Now you listen to me," he said, his voice low and intense. "If you think this marriage is going to be a farce, you're mistaken, Katie. You're my wife, and I want you. And by God, I've waited long enough. I want you now."

Before Katherine could react, he reached out and took her in his arms.

With her hands splayed on his chest, she leaned back when he tried to kiss her. Tightening his arms around her, Jonathan's lips sought and found the pulse of her vulnerable throat. In spite of her resistance, she was powerless against the waves of intoxicating warmth that rippled through her as he continued his inexorable assault on her senses.

She twisted her head to escape his lips, but his hand came

up behind her to hold her still. His mouth clung to hers avidly, hungrily, compelling her lips to part and yield the sweetness within to the invasion of his tongue. She felt overpowered, overwhelmed, possessed as he explored her mouth, demanding responses that she tried, yet couldn't withhold. Of their own volition her hands came up to his chest and entwined behind his neck as she returned his kisses with a hunger of her own.

A frightful weakness came over her. Her legs were about to buckle under her when he swept her up in his arms. Their mouths still clung to each other as he carried her across the room and gently put her down on his own bed.

He removed her gown, and leaning over her for a moment let his eyes wander with possessive pleasure over her naked body. With trembling fingers he touched her face and traced the contours of her lips. "You're so beautiful," he whispered, his voice made huskier by desire. He pressed swift, small kisses on her face, her neck, her shoulders; and gently rubbing his cheek against the swell of her bosom, he murmured, "I need you Katie."

A throbbing wave of tenderness brought tears to her eyes, and for a moment she held his head to her breast. She gave out a long, shuddering sigh as his mouth touched and gently sucked each rosy nipple. He stroked and kissed and nibbled each one of her voluptuous breasts until their tips had crested with maddening, pulsating desire. His hands moved slowly, caressingly over her belly, over the curve of her hips, over her thighs, which parted willingly to receive his fondling of her most intimate places.

Passion licked at her as a searing flame, and arching her body she moaned with intense pleasure as his lips and his tongue followed the path forged by his hands and savored her delights. Her entire body was quivering with the intensity of her feelings when he sought her mouth again and the hardness of his pulsating flesh was at last within her, filling her with pleasure and satisfying her yearnings.

With thrilling, joyous intoxication she clung to him as their bodies, so deeply joined, moved in the old familiar rhythm that made all the years, all the heartaches vanish from her memory. Nothing existed, nothing mattered but this moment when time hung suspended and they became one flesh, one heart, one spirit. The glowing heat within her womb spread through her, imbuing every corner of her being with a sense of maddening delight that grew and grew as he continued to move within her until the passion burst forth in wave after wave of shattering, overwhelming climax.

Tears of joy, of tenderness, of love sprang from her eyes to moisten Jonathan's skin as their juices mingled and she hugged with fervor his tense, shivering body.

Then they were still, breathlessly still, before he took her in his arms again and held her tightly. The pounding of their hearts grew quieter.

She felt wet, spent and languid when he drew back at last and leaned on an elbow to look at her. A frown came to his brow at the sight of the tears still moistening her cheeks.

"Honey, don't," he said, softly touching the tips of his fingers to her cheek.

Turning her face away Katherine began to weep, softly at first, and then more copiously at the realization that in spite of his betrayal, her love for Jonathan was still intact.

She had never hated him. Regardless of how much she had professed to despise him, all she had done had been prompted by love, not a thirst for revenge. She had broken the law, risked her life and gone half across the world in order to find him, to be in his arms again.

Suddenly, she couldn't bear to have him witness her tears of shame and weakness. Abruptly, she rose from his bed and ran to her room to hug her secret.

Once there, still unable to use the bed that had belonged to Mary Beth, she stood for a moment, naked, uncertain and shivering with nerves, not knowing what to do. Then, she peeled the covers from it and carried them to the chase lounge she had used earlier, where she lay down and gave free rein to her grief.

What was she going to do now, she asked herself wretchedly. How could she continue living with Jonathan and sharing his bed knowing that all he felt in return for her love was just desire? How could she live day in and day out with the constant fear that at any moment he would find someone else and turn away from her?

As though in answer to her questions, she heard a door close, and steps she recognized as Jonathan's passed by her bedroom door. She rose from the chaise and went to the window. A few moments later, she saw Jonathan walking away from the house.

Where could he be going at this hour? To another woman perhaps? She remembered how often, while in London, they had made love through the night. They had been constantly together for days, and she knew that he had had no other woman during that time. Could it be that he was still seeking satisfaction in someone else's bed moments after having made love to her?

Oh, what a joke he would find it if he only knew how much she still loved him! Stupid, stupid Katherine! Longing for him even after he had used her and tried to hand her down to other men! How very amusing!

But she wasn't the same stupid girl who had mistaken his lust for love, not any more! The tender passion he had shown would not deceive her as it had done before. No matter what it cost her, he would never learn that she still loved him.

Katherine was about to dress the next morning when there was a soft knock on her door.

"*Entrez*," she said, bracing herself to confront her husband.

To her surprise, it was Felicity who came in.

"I'm sorry to intrude on you this early," she said with an apologetic little smile.

"It's all right," Katherine replied with a deprecating gesture. "What can I do for you?"

"I — I came to apologize for the things I said to you last night," she confessed, a little shamefaced.

Katherine took pains to conceal her surprise. "There was no need," she replied in a conciliatory tone.

"Oh, but there is," Felicity replied with apparent distress. "I'm afraid Jonathan is very upset with me."

Katherine's brows rose quizzically. "Oh?"

"Yes," Felicity nodded. "But that's not the only reason," she went on. "I also realize how selfish I've been. I'm truly sorry, Katherine."

After the malice Felicity had shown, Katherine wasn't entirely convinced by such display of humility. Still, she decided to give her the benefit of the doubt.

"Don't give it another thought," she dismissed with a blithe gesture of her hand.

Felicity gave her a winning smile. "You're so very kind," she said. "I do hope you forgive me and we can be friends. Better yet, sisters."

Katherine returned the smile. "Of course."

"Are you comfortable?" Felicity inquired then with solicitude. "Is there anything you need?"

"Thank you, but Jonathan and I are going out today to look for a house."

"Yes, I imagine this situation must be very difficult for you," Felicity said in an ingratiating tone.

Katherine's brow constricted faintly as she repeated, "Difficult?"

"Why — yes," Felicity said diffidently. Her tone became more ingratiating when she added, "Really, Katherine, we are family now. You can trust me. I know that under the circumstances, it can't possibly be easy for you being here in this house, especially staying in this room that belonged to Jonathan's wife."

Katherine didn't miss the intended barb, but because the estimation was so accurate, she remained silent.

Without an invitation, Felicity sat down on the edge of a chair. "This room is still just the way she left it," she went on at Katherine's silence. "Jonathan wouldn't have anything in it changed after she died. He was devastated when it happened. He loved her very much, you know."

"Yes, I know," Katherine assented quietly.

"Still, he's a man," Felicity added with a touch of feigned regret in her voice. "And men are different, well — you must know what I mean. No matter how much they might care for someone, they have — er — needs to fulfill, and I'm afraid Mary Beth was much too frail to satisfy someone like my brother. Poor darling, she never said a word, but she must have been aware that there were other women, although he was very discreet about it. Oh, please, don't get me wrong," she rushed to add. "I love him dearly, but that doesn't blind me to his faults."

Having figured out by this time Felicity's new strategy, Katherine looked at her with an ironic twist to her lips and said, "Faults? Jonathan?"

For a second, Felicity didn't know exactly how to interpret the remark. Dismissing it, she forged ahead to plant her venomous seeds in the mind of Jonathan's new wife.

"Well, I suppose he's no worse than any other man, and they are selfish creatures," she shrugged imperceptibly. "He wanted a son more than anything. Mary Beth loved him too much to deny him what he wanted, even though the doctors had warned her that she could lose her life if she got with child again."

Katherine frowned slightly. "Again?"

"Yes, she had two miscarriages in the course of their marriage, didn't you know?"

Katherine shook her head. "No, I didn't know."

318

"It was a sad situation, but I must admit that he did try to stay away from her bed. That's why they had separate chambers. This one was hers, his is through that door," she pointed at the inner door. "But I suppose even that didn't help poor Mary Beth much, poor darling. Oh, men can be such beasts!"

Felicity emitted a long, soulful sigh. "Anyway, I'm glad that now he has you and the son he always wanted. I'm sure things will be different this time."

Considering that her mission had been accomplished, Felicity looked at the small time piece she wore on a long gold chain around her neck. Rising to her feet, she exclaimed, "My goodness, I hadn't realized the time! Please forgive me, but I'm running late for an appointment. I just felt so guilty for the way I behaved, that I couldn't sleep a wink last night. I just had to see you and apologize as soon as possible."

She leaned over Katherine and kissed her cheek. "Goodbye for now, dear sister. I do hope you'll let me know if there's anything I can to do help you get settled."

She turned and walked away.

As she closed the door behind her, a smug little smile was on Felicity's lovely face. Katherine's ability to deflect her arrows during the course of the evening had made her very angry, and she had spent a good portion of the night trying to figure out a way to get even.

It had been a mistake on her part to bring up Katherine's relationship with Maxwell Chapman. It would only embarrass the family to have it known that Jonathan had married a woman who was no better than a slut. Because the frontal attack had only served to alienate Jonathan—and Alicia—without even putting a dent on Katherine's armor, she had realized that a more devious approach would be far more effective.

After looking at the situation from every angle, Felicity had come to the conclusion that her best card at the moment was to use the memory of Mary Beth to torment Katherine.

During her last visit to New York, Katherine and Jonathan had not yet married; therefore, it was simple to assume that after having an illicit affair with her, Jonathan had abandoned her in order to come back to his wife.

Knowing her brother, she had no doubt that he had been unaware of the existence of the child until he had run into Katherine again in New York, and that he had married his former mistress in order to give the boy his name.

Jonathan had been out of his mind with grief over the loss of his wife and child. And since Katherine had already experienced his desertion in favor of Mary Beth, what better weapon to use against her than Jonathan's devotion to the memory of Mary Beth and his desire for a son?

Even though Katherine had been aware of Felicity's motives, she still couldn't help but feel more depressed than she already was before her visit. Everything had turned against her, even her own emotions.

After witnessing Jonathan's departure, she had teetered between bouts of angry jealousy and overwhelming despair. The sudden arrival of the morning had found her exhausted, but wide-eyed and still waiting for her husband's return.

During that time she had constantly reviled herself for not having married Max while she had had the chance; for delaying her departure to Albany; for all the mistakes she had made — all except her determination to seek Jonathan again. She had ceased in her self-recriminations at the realization that none of those actions had been mistakes. She had made herself willfully blind to her real purpose in order to bring about the end result — to be with Jonathan again.

It was her goal that had been a mistake, and now that she had achieved it, there was no one to blame but herself. Once she had admitted to that, she was resigned to the fact that there was nothing to do now but to accept the situation and make the best of it. Perhaps finding a house of their own would help.

Determined to present her best front, Katherine took pains to conceal her weariness and used every trick she had learned to erase the redness a night of sleeplessness and tears had left in her eyes. A discreet application of powder and a touch of rouge concealed the circles that were beginning to show under her eyes and the pallor of her cheeks. She had learned the art of makeup so expertly, that when she appeared downstairs that morning no one but the most discerning eye could even to begin to guess that her radiant looks were due to artifice.

Jonathan and Francis were playing with Jason out in the garden when she came through the door. Undetected by them, she stood for a few moments watching the group at play.

Jason had always been a happy child, but he seemed to be in seventh heaven since finding his father. Now there were also grandparents who seemed to genuinely care for him despite his illegitimacy.

Once, Jonathan had stopped short of accusing her of having robbed their child of his rightful place. Since she herself had lacked a family of her own, at the time she had sincerely believed that having Max for a father would have been a solution. Now, seeing the warmth and affection lavished on her son by Jonathan's parents, she was no longer sure.

It was Jason who saw her first.

"Mommie, look!" the boy called, running to her with a big red ball in his hands. "Look at the ball Grandfather gave me."

Katherine smiled. "It's beautiful, darling," she said through her constricted throat. She had to swallow in order to say, "Daddy and I are going out to look for a new house. Would you like to come with us?"

Jason's bright smile began to fade. "Must I, mommie?"

"Of course not, darling. You may stay and play with your grandfather if you prefer."

"Good morning, my dear," Francis said, coming toward her.

Katherine noticed that although Jonathan had not made a move, he was watching her. "Good morning, Mr. Greenfield," she replied pleasantly.

"I'll have none of that *Mr. Greenfield*," Francis said with an undertone of reproach. "It's too formal. Francis will do until you find it more comfortable to call me father, all right?"

Katherine stood on the tips of her toes to kiss his cheek with a heart-felt, "Thank you, Francis."

He cleared his throat and smiled. "Jonathan tells me that you're going out today to look for a house," he said. Without waiting for her confirmation, he added, "We're going to miss having you and Jason around, Katie, but we do understand your wanting a home of your own."

How very kind he was, Katherine thought with a slight sense of guilt over the suspicions she had entertained. Her eyes were suspiciously bright as she reached for his hand and gave it an affectionate squeeze.

"Grandfather, can we play ball some more?" Jason inquired then.

"Sure can, my boy," Francis replied, tousling Jason's hair with unfeigned affection. He started to follow the boy, who was running ahead, and then half-turned to look at Katherine. "You and Jonathan go ahead and don't you worry about Jason, my dear. We'll keep him busy . . . or vice versa."

He smiled and waved at her, and turning to his grandson called, "Hey, Jason! Catch!"

Katherine watched her son run for the ball his grandfather had thrown. The big red balloon bounced twice on the ground before Jason caught it and grinned, "I've got it!"

"Great catch!" Francis applauded.

She refused to look at Jonathan as he came to stand beside her. They both watched the players for a few more moments, and then he asked, "Should we go now?"

She hesitated for a second. "Yes," she said at last. "I'll get my things."

As they were walking back to the house, she observed, "Jason seems quite taken with your father."

"Are you surprised?"

"A little."

"I'm not." Following a brief silence, he went on to say, "You're a good mother, Katie, and Jason simply adores you. You've done well by him, but a boy needs more than that. Grandfathers are very special, Katie. Even though I had my grandparents on the Greenfield side nearby, when I was Jason's age I went crazy whenever Grandpa Hansen came for a visit. He was sea captain, you know."

"I remember," she nodded.

Jonathan glanced at her in surprise. "You do?"

"Yes, you told me about him when we were in London. He was a privateer during the War of 1812, wasn't he?"

He gave her a long, searching look. "Yes, we did a lot of talking then, didn't we?" he said with a half-hinted smile.

A flash of resentment crossed through her eyes. "But you didn't say much, did you?"

He stopped walking and reached out to take her arm. "Couldn't we start over again, Katie?"

"Start over?" she repeated, glancing up warily. "And where do you suggest we start, Jonathan? London, or New York?"

Hearing the implicit reproach in her voice, he said gently, "We were happy in London, Katie."

"London was a long time ago, Jonathan. We can't bring it back. Too much has happened."

She started to walk away, but he stopped her. "Yes, Katie, we can bring it back if we try. Please, love, give us a chance!"

For a few seconds she was tempted to believe the plea in

his blue eyes. More than anything in the world she wanted to believe in his sincerity. Then she remembered her anguish when she had seen him go out in the night, and she knew that she couldn't live through another betrayal.

"I'm sorry, Jonathan," she said, shaking her head abjectly as she pulled away. "I can't."

Fifteen

A party had been planned for the following Sunday afternoon to introduce Katherine and Jason to all the members of the Greenfield clan. The summer squall had passed, leaving in its wake clear, azure skies and the land clean and fresh smelling — perfect weather for a barbecue on the grounds of the manor.

With enormous quantities of food being readied for the occasion, the kitchen bustled with activity, and the tantalizing aroma of fresh-baked breads, tortes and pies pervading the house made taste buds water. Alicia didn't hesitate for a moment when Katherine volunteered to help in the preparations; with so much to do and so little time in which to do it, no offer was turned down. She was immediately put to work.

For Katherine this proved a welcome distraction from her mental ravings. Knowing from personal experience that Jonathan was a lusty man, she had seen her suspicions of there being another woman become certainty when he refrained from coming to her again. Moreover, she heard him go out every night shortly after they had retired. He seldom returned before it was almost daybreak and there were times when he didn't come back at all; therefore, these nightly escapades served to remove from her mind any doubt she might still have had as to his having a mistress.

She was going over a list of last-minute chores with one of the servants on Saturday afternoon when she turned her head unexpectedly and caught sight of Jonathan watching her from the doorway. His gaze was so warm, so tender and possessive that for an instant she was immobilized by those hypnotic eyes that were touching her with the intimacy of a caress.

Her pulsebeat quickened, and an old familiar ache came to the base of her throat as his eyes moved caressingly over her face to touch her mouth, where they lingered for a few moments as though with fascination. A feeling of warmth rippled through her, and with a fresh sense of excitement she found herself yearning to touch him, to love him, to have his hard and urgent body close to hers again.

A light of devilry came to his eyes when their gazes met as though he could read her thoughts, and with blood hot on her cheeks she blinked in confusion and quickly dropped her lashes.

She was feeling so unsettled, so tangled up inside when she forced her attention back to the task at hand, that she would have been unable, if asked, to repeat the instructions she had given to the servant. All she knew was that when her gaze reluctantly slid back to the door moments later, Jonathan was gone.

Once she was alone, Katherine sank down on the nearest chair berating herself for being so weak where Jonathan was concerned. How could she have so little pride as to yearn so strongly for his arms when she knew that his lovemaking was just an act to satisfy his physical needs?

Her inward discourse of self-deprecation was suddenly interrupted when Jason burst into the room bubbling with excitement. "Mommie!" he cried. "Daddy is going to take us out for a ride!"

Swiftly her gaze shifted from the beaming little face to the tall figure who came strolling casually through the door, and Jonathan's guileless grin made her temper rise. Striving not to show it, she managed to make herself smile as she turned to her son. "That'd be lovely, darling, but I'm afraid you and Daddy will have to go without me this time. I promised to help your grandmother for the party tomorrow."

Jason turned a questioning glance at his father, who said in a cajoling tone, "Ah, come on, Katie. It'll be more fun if you come along. Won't it, son?"

How dare you use him, was the message in her eyes as she glared at her husband. "I'm sorry, Jonathan," she said, on her lips a tight little smile. "I really am very busy."

Regarding her with a flicker of amusement, Jonathan took both her hands and gently hoisted her from the chair. "I'm afraid you're out of excuses, my love. I've already consulted Mother, and she assured me that she can manage without you for the rest of the afternoon." Slipping his arms around her he held her close for a moment to plant a swift kiss on the tip of her nose and turned on his persuasive charm. "Come on, honey. Go get your hat and meet us out in front in five minutes, all right? There's something I want to show you."

Katherine's oblique glance was bemused as he turned her around. Pointing her toward the door, Jonathan gave her a gentle pat on her fanny as he said, "Hurry up!"

"Ooooff!" she hissed as she mounted the stairs, her back stiff, her step charged with indignation.

Muttering under her breath, Katherine went into her room to collect her bonnet. However, as she stood in front of the mirror tying the ribbons under her chin, she realized that her anger was more willful than spontaneous, and her expression began to show amusement at the thought of Jonathan's actions of moments earlier. He had treated her the way an affectionate husband would in cajoling his reluctant wife into an outing.

But willingly or not, she *was* his wife, she reflected. And since she had already made up her mind to make the best of the situation, why couldn't she simply accept it and stop tormenting herself over something she couldn't have?

Perhaps Jonathan's idea of starting over again wasn't so far fetched after all. Thinking back to that moment when he had been watching her, Katherine told herself that the longing that had swirled between them then couldn't have stemmed from her alone. He had wanted to make love to her then just as much as she had wanted him to. And if she became again his willing lover, maybe—just maybe—one day he would come to love her . . . truly love her.

Her expression softened at the prospect of spending the afternoon with Jonathan and their son like any other ordinary family would, and with a wistful little sigh she turned away from the mirror and went to meet the two men she loved most in the world.

The lovely weather, the lighthearted mood of the afternoon combined to make her feel a little giddy with joy as the hooded phaeton traveled the narrow country road that ran uphill beneath a canopy of evergreens. Sunlight filtered through the leaves; the air was warm and as gentle as a caress.

"Where are we going, daddy?" Jason inquired with curiosity.

Jonathan's mouth turned up at the corners as though trying to hide a humorous secret. "Mmm, it's a surprise," he replied, stealing a sidelong glance at Katherine.

Tilting her head to one side, she returned his glance with one of unfeigned curiosity. "What is it?"

"You'll find out soon enough, my darling," he answered with an air of promise. Returning his eyes front he popped the reins, and the horses sped up their pace.

Some five minutes later the phaeton reached the clearing at the top of the rise, where the terrain expanded in gentle slopes and the view extended as far as the sea, which appeared as a misty blue line in the distance. Jonathan pulled at the reins and halted the horses.

They sat in silence for a few moments until he turned to his wife and inquired, "Well, what do you think?"

"It's lovely," she replied in a breath of rapture.

Having caught sight of a squirrel, Jason gave an impatient tug at his father's arm. "Can we get off now, daddy?"

"Sure, son," Jonathan replied.

Without waiting for his father, the boy simply leaped out and ran after the squirrel, which immediately sought refuge among the branches of one of the trees surrounding the clearing.

Jonathan set the reins aside, got out, and turned to help Katherine. Taking her by the waist, he lifted her with ease and held her close as he put her down.

Her heart began to pound as she looked up and saw the way his eyes were fastened on her mouth. She willed him to kiss her and for a moment it seemed as though she was going to get her wish; all he did, however, was rub his knuckles gently on her cheek, and then, smiling a little wistfully, drew back. Wrapping one arm around her waist, he led her through the clearing to the other side.

"How would you like to wake up each morning to this view from our bedroom window?" he asked casually.

Stopping abruptly, she glanced up suddenly and caught him looking down at her with an expectant expression on his face. Blinking in surprise, she swallowed and asked, "*Our* bedroom window?"

A frown had formed on his forehead when he looked away. "I bought this land years ago with the idea of building a house," he told her after a moment's silence. "I want to do it now, Katherine. For us, for Jason. Perhaps for other children, if we ever have them."

The exhilaration she had felt until then suddenly degenerated into a deep sense of disenchantment. Although he had left it unsaid, he had just told her that the house had not really been meant for her, but for Mary Beth and her children.

"Building will take too long," she said in a toneless voice, her eyes faintly brooding as they gazed into the distance.

He looked at her with an ironic twist to his lips. "And the chaise you've been using isn't very comfortable, is it, my love?" he commented with a small, wry chuckle.

A swift surge of irritation showed in the tightness that came to her mouth as she turned to glare at him. What did you expect from me, she wanted to shout.

Did he imagine for a moment that she had no feelings? First, he had tried to buy her favors by tossing her a jewel; failing that, he had forced her to marry him against her will. And now, to top it all, he was telling her that all she could expect from their marriage were Mary Beth's leavings — her bed, her room, her house — even a bereaved husband who worshipped her memory and was still trying to find her in someone else.

Oh, what a fool she had been to believe that there was a chance to win his love, that they could start all over and be happy together!

Her tone was chilly, her manner distant when she said, "Go ahead and build your house, but in the meantime, I still want to lease the one we saw the other day." She started to walk away and then, half-turning to him she added, "And yes, the chaise *is* uncomfortable, but even so I still prefer it to your bed."

By noon on Sunday, the servants were busy setting up

long tables on the lawn; a good number of chairs had already been carefully arranged beneath the branches of the shade trees. Columns of steam rose from the huge pots of water boiling in readiness to receive the buckets of clams, and live blue crabs and lobsters that would feed the expected guests. A steer turning slowly over a pit fire was occasionally brushed with a red sauce by an attending servant, and by the time the relatives began to arrive the warm September air was filled with the delicious aroma of the roasting meat.

The Greenfields were numerous, and together with their extended families they formed an imposing crowd. By three o'clock the lawn was crowded with the bevy of aunts, uncles, and cousins of various degrees of proximity, all anxious to meet the new additions to the family.

In their crisp white dresses and blue ribbons in their hair, Felicity's two young daughters sat primly in their chairs. Since their mother had forbidden them to play so as not to dirty themselves, the glances they cast at the children who were free to romp and gambol on the grass were wistful and forlorn.

There were children ranging in ages from two to sixteen, and Jason was having the time of his life with so many cousins to play with.

Looking quite lovely in a pale yellow dress, Katherine circulated among the guests with Jonathan assiduously at her side. All the time she was conscious of the way his hand slipped casually around her waist or absently stroked her arm as they paused to talk to the various relatives.

She had been uneasy before the party, dreading to face so many people who would probably ask her innumerable questions she had little inclination to answer. Uppermost in her mind was the fear of a slight, or of any remark concerning her liaison with Jonathan at the time of his first marriage; but if the Greenfields thought about it — as she was

331

sure they did—they all seemed willing to accept her in their midst without a qualm.

To her immense relief Jonathan was called back into the house and she was left with Aunt Jossie, a plump, matronly lady in her fifties, and a Greenfield by marriage.

"Oh, dear!" Aunt Jossie said a few minutes later, looking past Katherine's shoulder. "Penny is here."

Katherine half-turned to look at the tall, regal-looking lady who was advancing in her direction. The woman carried herself with a proud bearing, and the energy of her springy step belied the whiteness of her hair.

Penelope Greenfield Hammond paused before Katherine to examine her haughtily. "So you're Jonathan's new wife," she said at last.

Her emphasis hushed the conversation around them, and silence spread as eyes turned to the confrontation between Katherine and Francis' older sister. From a distance, Felicity watched the scene with a smirk on her face.

Katherine realized that the moment she had been dreading had finally arrived. Following her initial surprise she was infuriated by the old woman's hauteur, but almost immediately she recovered her presence of mind. A calm, confident smile came to her lips as she held the woman silently, but steadily, for a few seconds.

"And you must be Aunt Penelope," she said evenly, almost pleasantly. "My name is Katherine."

Penelope's cold eyes were speculative and observant as they stared back at her for a full minute, but as she sustained her gaze, Katherine saw a flicker of amusement begin to appear in their blue depths.

The quiver that came to the lips of the older woman gave way to a smile that soon expanded into a hearty laugh. "Now you know why they call me *The Terror* behind my back," she said, laughing. "You'll do, my girl. You'll do well indeed. I'm glad to see that Jonathan showed more sense this time."

"Why?" Katherine inquired with curiosity. "Was there anything wrong with Mary Beth?"

Penelope gave an almost imperceptible shrug as she replied, "She was a sweet child who had adored Jonathan from the time they were children."

"Did they grow up together?" Katherine inquired, wrinkling her forehead.

"Practically," Penelope nodded. "The families were close friends and she and Felicity were of the same age, so they did spend a great deal of time together."

"Then she and Jonathan were childhood sweethearts," Katherine reflected.

"Not really," Penelope shook her head. "He was more interested in the sea and ships than anything else while he was growing up. Girls held little attraction for him until he was, mmm, maybe fourteen, when he stowed away on one of our ships. My guess is that he must have made some pleasant discoveries in that respect while he was away."

"At any rate," she continued after a moment, "he never did pay much attention to Mary Beth. Then, about ten years ago, he was seriously wounded during a fight with Chinese pirates on a voyage to Canton, and during his convalescence at home she was always there, helping to care for him. They became engaged and were married in no time, and then he was off again. Francis had hoped that once they were married he'd stay on and take over some of the family business, but Jonathan wouldn't hear of it. Mary Beth accepted his leaving her so soon just as she accepted everything else he did. As far as she was concerned, he could do no wrong. She worshipped him."

"He loved her too," Katherine observed somewhat sadly.

"Oh, I'm sure he did," Penelope replied. "As you must already know, he has a warm, affectionate nature. I suppose that in many respects, Jonathan is very much like his father. They are the kind of man who's very protective toward his women — mother, wife, sister, daughter — whoever they might be, and one of their favorite ways of showing affection is to pamper them and give them everything their little hearts desire. Mary Beth was the type of woman who brings out the best in them, sweet-tempered, delicate, frail."

"And I'm none of those things," Katherine observed wryly.

"Thank God for that," Penelope scoffed mildly. "I'd have been very disappointed if you had dissolved into tears a few moments ago. I like a woman with backbone, and you have that, my dear."

Katherine's face showed wry amusement as she repeated, "Backbone?" She gave a little laugh. "I hope so, because I have a feeling that, under the circumstances, I may have need of it."

"Don't worry too much about it, child," Penelope said, affectionately linking her arm through Katherine's. As they started to walk together, the older woman continued, "We Greenfields are an impetuous, lusty lot, and we have caused more eyebrows to raise than I'd care to count. But one thing, though; we're a close-knit group, and we stand by our own. As long as there's a Greenfield around, no one would dare say a word against you or your child, you can take my word on that. Besides, Jonathan's been away for so long, that no one can be sure as to the hows and whens of your relationship; but even if your arrival causes a bit of a stir, it will pass soon enough, you'll see."

She paused to watch Jason at play with the other children. Her eyes still followed the boy's antics while she smiled and said, "Just count your blessings, my dear. You have a beautiful, healthy child and a good man for whom many women would give their eye teeth, I assure you." She turned her blue gaze at the younger woman, who saw the gleam of caution that had come to her eyes as she said, "Don't let anyone spoil it for you, do you understand? No one."

Deeply moved, Katherine planted a kiss on the withered cheek that smelled faintly of sandalwood. "Thank you, Aunt Penny. You really are a dear."

Felicity had watched the scene through lowered lashes. "So," she muttered under her breath, "that tramp has charmed even Aunt Penny."

She felt cheated. Aunt Penny was the undisputed female social leader of the Greenfields, and her approval of Katherine—in addition to the support of Jonathan's parents—had sealed her triumph.

But Felicity would never accept her, just as she had never accepted taking second place to Jonathan.

A bitter taste rose in her throat when she thought of her brother with resentment. He was the eldest, the male, the heir; he sailed the seas and built their ships while she, the daughter, remained at home to lead a humdrum existence. Mary Beth had been a fool, a spineless little creature with no other thought in her head than bearing her husband's brats, and who felt guilty and inadequate because she couldn't.

Katherine, however, was a different story. From what Felicity had heard about her, she had traveled extensively, could carry on an intelligent conversation on many topics of which Felicity herself knew practically nothing about. Even Francis—the father who had always done whatever she wanted to please his little princess—now regarded her enemy with frank and open admiration.

Why not, Felicity thought bitterly. Katherine was not only beautiful enough to have the most pursued man in New York at her feet, but she had also given Jonathan a son, an heir to carry on the Greenfield bloodline. In only a matter of days, that snotty little brat had stolen Francis' affections from her own daughters.

Now that Aunt Penny had stamped her seal of approval

335

on Jonathan's new wife, there was no question in Felicity's mind that as long as Katherine was around, she was to play second fiddle not only to Jonathan, but also to his wife as well.

And the prospect made Felicity quite unhappy.

As the leaves began piling on the lawn in little heaps of autumn, Jonathan startled his wife by launching an earnest campaign to woo her by courting her as an ardent admirer and becoming again the man she had known—and loved— in London.

Even though she could see through his scheme, it was difficult for Katherine to show resentment toward this warm, gentle, and amusing Jonathan who plied her with thoughtful or silly little gifts; who took her for long rides in the country with their son or sailing in the bay; who gazed at her so lovingly with those sparkling blue eyes that seemed to reach deep into her soul.

Her response was to disregard his efforts toward a reconciliation; regardless of how much she wanted to believe it possible, his nightly escapes continued without interruption.

One afternoon, during a picnic, she was watching Jason at play with his cousin Billy when she heard the sound of familiar chords from Jonathan's guitar. Her glance met his tender gaze as his husky voice rose softly above the music.

> Alas, my love you do me wrong
> to cast me off so discourteously
> and I have loved you for so long
> delighting in your company
> Green eyes are my desire
> Green eyes are my delight
> Green eyes fill my heart with joy

Years before, while sharing the intimacy of a cozy fire, he had sung to her his own version of that old, haunting love song. And now, as he continued to lazily strum his guitar and hum the melody, Katherine was painfully reminded of those magic moments they had shared so long ago.

Why did he have to continue torturing her this way, she asked herself wretchedly. There were times when she could almost believe in his love, yet she knew that for him it was just a game to bring her willingly to his bed.

Pride prevented her from allowing Jonathan to witness her grief, and becoming aware of the tears welling up in her eyes, Katherine rose from the blanket they had spread on the grass and ran away.

Jonathan also rose and made to follow, but seemed to think better of it. Shaking his head a little wryly he sat down again chuckling to himself, "Ah, Katie, my love, I think you're beginning to soften up a bit."

The first evening spent in their new home went rather smoothly.

Since she had been unwilling to wait until the entire house had been furnished, only a few of the rooms contained some pieces of furniture by the time they moved in. Therefore, after she had put Jason to bed, Katherine settled down to read in the same room where Jonathan was still working on the scale model of a clipper ship that he and his son were putting together. Needless to say, Jason was delighted with the enterprise.

Katherine looked up from her book when she heard her husband muttering something unintelligible under his breath.

Jonathan also glanced up suddenly and when he caught

337

her staring at him, she blinked in confusion and quickly dropped her gaze.

"Honey, could you come here for a second and help me with this?" he said after a moment.

Following a brief hesitation, Katherine put her book aside and went to stand beside him.

"What do you want me to do?"

"Put your finger right here and hold it down while I tie the knot, all right?"

She nodded.

"Wait," he said, covering her hand with his under the pretense of directing her. "Right about there. Good."

Again he directed his attention to tying the knot.

Intent on his work, how much like Jason he looked, she thought with a warm feeling. At that very moment what she wanted most was to throw her arms around his neck and hug him tightly, and her fingers itched to run through that thick mane of silver blond hair catching the light from the lamp.

Easy, Katherine, watch yourself, she cautioned inwardly, and concealing a small sigh she held her position until he looked up at her and grinned, "Thanks, love."

"You're welcome," she replied and went back to her chair.

Although she tried to concentrate her attention on the book, she couldn't read; her eyes kept wandering in Jonathan's direction much too often. She sat there for a few moments longer, holding the book in front of her with a pretense of interest until she realized how dangerously close she was to falling into his trap.

Mentally reviling herself for being such a goose, she closed the book and decided to retire. At long last she would be able to sleep in her own bed. How nice, she thought ruefully, my own lonely bed.

Before leaving the room, she half-turned toward her husband and said, "Good night, Jonathan."

Glancing quickly upwards he smiled, "Good night, honey."

I wish he would stop calling me *honey*, she thought with a little vexation as she mounted the stairs.

She went into her room and changed into her nightdress. While the maid was putting her clothes away, Katherine sat at the dressing table and unpinned her hair. As she started to brush it, however, her action was arrested by a knock on the door. Jonathan came in without waiting for her invitation, and standing by the door gave a discreet cough.

"Good night, Louise," he said to the maid, who made a hasty retreat and left them.

Warily, Katherine watched through the looking-glass as he crossed the room and came to stand behind her. With his hands on her shoulders, he leaned over and put his smooth-shaven cheek against hers.

"First night in our new home, love," he said, studying their faces in the mirror.

With a knot of tension in her stomach, Katherine sat stiff and erect as his hands moved caressingly over the curves of her shoulders and came down to stroke her upper arms.

At her lack of response, Jonathan took the brush from her hand and began running it through her hair.

Intent on his task, after a moment he said, "It's been a long time since I brushed your hair. Remember?"

How could she forget?

Memories of another time and another place tumbled through her mind: similar scenes of quiet intimacy that had culminated in the sweetest, most wonderful lovemaking she had ever known.

Keenly aware of his touch, Katherine forced herself to remain motionless as she tried to marshal her chaotic thoughts. Her heart was pounding erratically when he finished brushing her hair and set the brush down on the dressing table. He sat down beside her and his arm went around her as he softly kissed her on the lips. Terrified of betraying her emotions, she didn't dare return the caress regardless of how much she wanted to.

The warmth flowing through her increased as his lips traced the column of her neck, and his hand cupped her breast when he kissed her mouth again.

When she still withheld her response, he drew back and said, "Good night, my love." He rose and left the room.

Katherine sat there for a few seconds blinking in astonishment. She had been terrified that he would make love to her, and now she was quite frustrated because he had not. Her whole body was longing for more of his touch. Abruptly, she rose from the seat and stamped her foot angrily.

"Ooff!" was all she could say, shaking a fist at the door through which he had disappeared. "Ooff!"

Flinging herself on her bed, she pounded the pillows with her fists crying, "Damn him! Damn him!"

A quiet, distant sound made her cease in her tantrum; straining her ears to identify it all she could hear was silence. A few seconds later suspicion that Jonathan had gone out made her get up and go to the door that connected their rooms. Pressing her ear to the wood, she listened for sounds of activity on the other side. There was nothing. Careful not to make a sound, she opened the door and looked in. The room was empty.

"That does it!" she muttered, closing the door again.

She got into bed and tried to sleep; however, certainty that Jonathan had sought his mistress made her run the gamut of emotions ranging from anger to despair while the grandfather clock in the hallway chimed hour after hour of a long, lonely night.

As dawn was breaking, she heard Jonathan moving about in his room. He was there for a little while and then left again.

Where had he spent the night? And with whom?

All his efforts during the day were meant to deceive her into believing that he loved her. But what kind of a fool did he take her for when every night he sought another woman's arms?

Katherine had hoped that it wouldn't be long before Jonathan announced that he was sailing away again. She had decided that with him absent from Baltimore, her life there could be rather pleasant, since Jason was very happy with his new family and she herself had become quite fond of Alicia and Francis. Her hopes were dashed, however, when shortly after signing the lease for their house she discovered that Jonathan had taken over the running of the Greenfield Shipyards.

When he came home for dinner that day, as he had taken to do of late, she tried to gauge his mood and found him as pleasant and attentive as ever. For some strange reason she felt rather disappointed, and while he and Jason talked and laughed together during the midday meal, she sat at the table toying with her food in silence.

"Katie?"

Hearing her name, she glanced up swiftly. "Yes?"

"Is it all right with you if I take Jason with me this afternoon? I promised to show him the shipyards and now would be a good time to do it."

"Will there be any danger?" she asked, unable to think of anything else to say.

"Of course not, honey," he smiled indulgently. "I wouldn't take him there otherwise. I'll take good care of him."

"Then I suppose it's all right," she replied, lowering her gaze and feeling rather foolish.

Impatient to be on the way, Jason asked, "May I be excused, daddy?"

"Ask your mother," Jonathan replied.

Jason looked anxiously at his mother. "May I, mommie?"

"Don't you want your dessert? It's chocolate pudding."

Even his favorite treat failed to tempt Jason, who shook his head and said, "I'm not hungry, mommie."

Katherine sighed, "Very well then."

Jason rewarded her with a grin before he rushed upstairs to change his clothes, and left alone with her husband, Katherine directed all her attention to the food on her plate.

"Honey, are you feeling all right?"

She nodded without looking at him.

After a moment's silence he asked, "What's the matter, love?"

That I love you, she wanted to say. That I want you to love me and no one else. Instead, she shrugged her shoulders and quietly replied, "Nothing."

Suddenly finding herself very near to tears, she rose abruptly from the table and left the room.

Feeling the need to reach for someone dear, after Jonathan and their son had gone Katherine sat down to write a letter to Adam. When she finished that one, she wrote another to Natalie, and then to Agatha, and to Jenny. She thought of Max and wondered how he was doing. On impulse she started a letter to him and then changed her mind. No, she had hurt him enough already, she reasoned. It would be better if he never heard from her again.

And crumpling the sheet of paper into a ball, she threw it into the wastebasket.

In their preoccupation with the move, neither Katherine nor Alicia had been able to give much thought to Katherine's introduction to Baltimore society, but once the new family had settled in their own home, Alicia announced the party that would increase her daughter-in-law's circle of friends.

Greenfield Manor was the stage for the festive occasion,

and it sparkled and shone with lights and polish the night Katherine was to be introduced to Baltimore's elite.

Invitations from the Greenfields had always been a mark of distinction, but on this occasion they carried the added attraction of meeting the foreign beauty who had captured the elusive Jonathan Greenfield. For the past several weeks the drawing rooms of Baltimore had been buzzing with speculation about his unexpected arrival with a wife and a child, and the mystery surrounding the beautiful second wife of the heir to the Greenfield empire have given rise to numerous rumors.

Katherine's radiance that night belied her inner apprehension. The experience she had earned during those years in a precarious occupation came to her aid as she faced the curious crowd with outward aplomb. In a rustling green taffeta gown and emeralds sparkling at her creamy throat, she appeared like a queen receiving the homage of her subjects. And at her side was Jonathan, the crown prince.

Felicity was burning with envy, watching her new sister-in-law draw the attention of the guests. As a child, she had loved her big, handsome brother. While growing to young womanhood, however, the pride their parents had displayed over his achievements had added a measure of jealousy and resentment to her emotions toward him. She longed for the life of excitement he led and to bask in the admiration of their elders as he did. But a woman's lot is quite different from that of a man, and this Felicity could not accept. She loathed playing second fiddle to Jonathan, and especially now to Katherine, who could turn heads with her beauty, her worldliness, her charm.

But everyone had a weakness of some kind of another, Felicity had told herself time and time again during those weeks when she had feigned affection toward her rival. Somehow, somewhere, there had to be a chink in that armor Katherine wore with such apparent ease. But no matter how carefully she studied her opponent, it had been to no avail thus far. Still, there had to be a weakness; and regardless of how slight, anything that would annoy Katherine and obstruct her triumph would satisfy her.

When the dancing started, Jonathan waltzed with his wife until good manners made him relinquish her to other partners. He then danced with other guests, and Katherine had to smile at his roguish wink when he danced by with a plump matron in his arms. Later on she saw him dancing with a pretty blonde woman who seemed to hang on his every word. This time, when they danced nearby, he didn't have a glance to spare for his wife.

The waltz ended and another began, and Jonathan continued to dance with the same woman whose name she couldn't remember because she had met so many people that evening.

Katherine felt her heart constricting with jealousy as a touch of suspicion colored her thoughts. Was that, perhaps, the woman with whom he spent his nights, she asked herself wretchedly.

She didn't know how she could bear to be in the same room with them. For the rest of the evening her smile became fixed, and she tried to keep herself from looking at the woman again.

Even though Katherine tried to hide her distress, Felicity was quick to notice that something had spoiled her sister-in-law's enjoyment of the evening. Hoping that sooner or later she would discover the cause she watched her closely, and at last her patience was rewarded. It was for just an instant that Katherine's mask fell, exposing all her pain and jealousy as she saw Jonathan dance with the same blonde woman again; just for an instant, but it had been enough for Felicity.

She had found the chink in Katherine's armor!

Sixteen

Following Katherine's introduction to Baltimore society an abundance of invitations to teas, dinner parties, and soirees began to pour in. Jonathan escorted his wife to most of those social functions and in public they appeared as a normal, happy couple; in private, however, their relationship continued as estranged as it had always been.

Jonathan was attentive and patient as he continued to court her, and this behavior on his part was driving Katherine to distraction. If in truth she had hated him as much as she professed, she would have been hard put to maintain that hatred alive: loving him as she did, her life became a constant struggle against her own emotions.

She had been surprised by the ease with which Jonathan had assumed his role as a father; he had instantly won Jason's affection, and no matter how busy he might have been at any moment he would set everything aside to listen to his son and solve his little problems.

But he had always been gentle, and loving, and warm, Katherine reminded herself wistfully. By taking her away from Langford he had probably saved her life; when she had awakened in the night with her nightmares, he had chased away her terrors rocking her in his arms back to sleep; he had soothed the pains of her bruised body and of her battered soul. It was his way . . . until he had practically raped her and tried to sell her to someone else as though she were no more than a slave.

No, he had broken her heart once; to let him do it again would be sheer folly on her part.

Katherine lived in terror of revealing her feelings and continuously rejected his advances, because she knew how easily all her resistance crumbled when Jonathan touched her. Listening for her husband's footsteps, each night she lay in the darkness, longing for his arms. She cried herself to sleep, and when she finally slept, she did it fitfully; her nerves were on always edge, irritation her constant companion. For all those reasons she began looking for ways to purposely vex him; but all her efforts proved useless, since he seemed quite determined to outwait her tantrums.

As Penelope had stated, he was generous to a fault. Katherine could acquire anything her heart desired, but it was he who paid all the bills. Her personal allowance, however, was very small, and before long this extraordinary contrast made her realize the reason behind it: that Jonathan suspected she would flee from him if she had the funds to pay her way.

He had no idea that he had married a rich woman, and she had no intention of enlightening him in that respect.

Forced into the marriage against her will, Katherine had refused to burn all her bridges behind her. She had retained enough presence of mind to realize that her situation in Baltimore could very easily become untenable, and if her fears materialized and she had to make her escape, she had no desire to find herself penniless again; consequently, before leaving New York she had given Adam all the necessary powers to handle her finances.

Having become accustomed to being financially independent, Katherine found her present lack of coin a source of frequent irritation, but since she was determined not to ask Jonathan to raise her allowance, she decided, instead, to sell one of her jewels. For this purpose she chose a ruby ring she didn't particularly fancy, since it had been given to her by one of her admirers in Europe.

She felt much better when she left the jewelry shop with a considerable sum of money in her purse. Her improved state of mind would not have been such, however, had she been aware that the transaction had been witnessed by unfriendly forces.

As she watched Katherine drive away in her carriage, Felicity asked herself what could have possibly made her new sister-in-law part with her jewelry. Could it be that she had some secret vice—such as gambling—that she wished to keep from her husband? Or perhaps she was being blackmailed by someone from her lurid past. The possibilities were endless, but of one thing she was sure: whatever the reason, Jonathan would be unhappy to learn that his wife was selling her jewelry behind his back, and he was sure to manifest his displeasure.

Felicity detested the smell, the noise, and dirt of the shipyards; these were things to be avoided. At this moment, however, she had no hesitation in ordering her coachman to take her there. It was only a small sacrifice compared to the satisfaction of causing friction between her brother and the English intruder.

Katherine was answering invitations that same afternoon when, without knocking, Jonathan burst into her bedchamber. His face was set in a frown as he stood before her and without a word set the ruby ring on her writing desk. So unexpectedly confronted with the jewel she had just disposed of, Katherine went pale.

"Why, Katherine?" he demanded harshly.

He had spoken so sharply that she jumped in surprise and was, momentarily, at a loss for words. How could he have found out so quickly? Could it be that he had someone watching her, spying on her? The suspicion made her bristle with anger.

At her silence, Jonathan slammed his fist on the desk and roared, "Why, Katie?"

She compressed her lips briefly before answering with obvious reluctance, "I needed the money."

"To do what?" he demanded, glowering at her. "Run away?"

Adopting an injured air, she replied in a sharply annoyed tone, "It was my ring. I had every right to sell it anytime I wanted to."

So angered was Jonathan by her reply that a vein in his temple began to pulse. "You didn't answer me, Katherine," he said, making a visible effort to control his temper. "Why did you need the money?"

Katherine blinked, pursed her lips, and looked angry. "Because you don't give me enough for my expenses!" she blurted out, and rising abruptly from the chair she turned away from him.

A deep sigh of exasperation seemed to dissolve Jonathan's anger. "Then why couldn't you tell me that you needed more?" he demanded in a tone less sharp.

Boiling with indignation at the thought that she was being spied upon, all Katherine wanted at the moment was to strike back at him. Her voice was low, deliberate, when she turned to face him and replied, "I told you once that I didn't want anything from you. I still don't."

The effect of her scathing words was the same as that of a physical slap on his face. His eyes opened in surprise as the color went out of his face.

Covering her mouth with her hands and instantly regretting her words, she looked at him through eyes widened in shocked disbelief.

Jonathan stared back at her silently for a few seconds before he turned and stalked out of the room.

He didn't come home for two days, and during that time Katherine was torn with indecision. With all her heart she wanted to go after him and beg his forgiveness, but she knew that following her impulse would put her at his mercy.

It was late on the third night when she was surprised to see him coming out of Jason's room. By this time she had been going quietly out of her mind with worry over his absence.

They stood a few paces apart in the hallway, looking at each other as though not knowing what to say. His face looked so haggard that her heart constricted painfully. His clothes were rumpled, as though he had been sleeping in them, and the golden stubble on his face indicated that he had not shaved in the last few days.

Looking at him with a stricken expression and quivering lips, Katherine struggled with an overwhelming desire to burst into tears. She ached to beg his forgiveness, to run to him and cover his weary face with kisses.

"Hello Katie," he said at last.

His small, grim smile that faded almost instantly undid her. Her lower lip stuck out in a pout and she burst out crying, "I'm sorry!" she hiccuped, "I—I didn't mean it!"

Crossing the distance between them, Jonathan came to her and put his arms around her.

"It's all right, love," he said quietly, holding her close. He gently stroked her hair and she purged her sorrow and her guilt in a flood of tears. When at last her sobs subsided, he drew back a little. Looking at her sadly, he brushed her hair from her tear-ravaged face and kissed her softly on the lips. Then he turned away and went into his room.

Touching the tips of her fingers to her colorless lips,

Katherine gazed with longing at the door that closed behind him.

In the days that followed Jonathan's manner was polite, yet somewhat distant, and Katherine tried to ease her conscience by telling herself that the change offered a relief from the emotional turmoil she had been suffering. However, she found herself unconsciously trying to make up to him for the words she had spoken in anger. She was more pleasant, and her smile became warmer when directed at him; she even consulted him on matters such as the furnishings for their new home, which until then she had acquired on her own.

It was during that time that a letter from Adam arrived, announcing that he and Iris were planning to marry on the Saturday following Thanksgiving. They hoped that she and her family would come for the holiday and the wedding.

Adam then referred to the two clippings he had enclosed, and Katherine put the letter aside to discover that they were from London newspapers. The first one was an obituary: Charles Langford was dead.

She read of the death of her former tormentor with a strange feeling of detachment. At one time in her life—in those days when he had kept her prisoner—her hate for him had been so strong that she had felt almost capable of killing him herself. Now, after all those years, she felt absolutely nothing.

The man had been an instrument of fate, she realized now without rancor. Without his intervention, she might have never met any of the people who had turned her life around so completely.

Heaving a wistful little sigh, she put the first clipping aside and addressed her attention to the other one. As it turned out, it was the ray of sunshine that she needed at the moment.

The clipping was an article singing praises to the work of a new artist who had been holding an exhibit that month. Apparently, Ronald Lambert had taken London by storm. The critic not only extolled his impeccable technique, but also the sensitivity of his art.

A smile came to illuminate Katherine's face as she continued reading about Ronald's "overnight" success. At the end, her eyes were brimming with tears at the remembrance of the confidences of her dear friend, of his struggle through the years, and she uttered a prayer of thanks before returning her attention to Adam's letter.

There was more uplifting news. Jenny, who had gone to Albany for a brief visit with Agatha, had extended her stay because of a young man she had met there. Adam went on to suggest that there might be another wedding in the not too distant future.

The rest of the letter was entertaining gossip, and Katherine was filled with longing for New York and for all those who had been her family until Jonathan had taken her away—and yes, even for Max. She fervently hoped Jonathan would agree to take her and Jason to New York. She seriously doubted it, though, especially after their terrible argument over the sale of the ring; but since she wasn't the type to concede defeat without even trying, Katherine immediately turned her efforts to find the best way to present her request to her husband.

She began by changing the dinner menu for that evening to include all of Jonathan's favorite dishes and wines; then she washed her hair and took a long bath before dressing with special care in one of her most flattering gowns and jewelry he had given her after their wedding. To crown her efforts she applied a touch of the seductive scent she had

351

brought with her from France that she usually saved for very special occasions.

And all those efforts were rewarded by the admiration she read in Jonathan's eyes when she came to meet him.

Their meals were usually taken *en famille,* but this evening Katherine wanted nothing to interfere with her plans and Jason had already been fed by the time Jonathan came home. Supper was delayed until he had had a chance to play with their son, and then the boy was put to bed early.

Katherine was attentive and witty during dinner, and as the evening progressed and Jonathan seemed to be warming up to her, she decided that the food and the wine would have mellowed him enough by the end of the meal, when she planned to broach the subject uppermost in her mind.

Once they had retired to the drawing room, while pouring the coffee she asked, "Should we have some brandy?"

"If you like." He started to rise from the divan saying, "I'll get it."

"Let me," Katherine said, getting quickly to her feet.

Jonathan sat back and let his gaze follow her movements as she served the drinks.

She came back and smiled as she handed him the glass.

"A few invitations came in today," she said casually as she sat beside him. "The Mitchells are having a party next week. Should we accept?"

When he didn't reply after a few seconds, she half-turned to look at him. Her heart began to pound when she met his blue gaze.

Jonathan smiled slightly and asked affably, "When is it?"

"On Friday," she replied in a voice huskier than she had intended.

His glance dropped to her mouth as he asked quietly, "Would you like to go, love?"

"I don't know," she murmured absently. The warmth flowing through her came to her cheeks when his arm came around her shoulders and he began to play with a tendril of her hair, coiling and uncoiling the curl around his finger. A little breathless, she added, "I can't remember who they are."

"Who?" Jonathan asked, leaning over to press a kiss on her shoulder.

"The — Mitchells," she replied, closing her eyes as his lips began to trail small, gentle kisses from her shoulder to the curve of her neck and continued upward to her ear. As he gently nipped her earlobe, the fingers of his other hand came up to give a breast a soft squeeze.

Her heart was pounding like mad, and she disregarded the warnings of her mind by telling herself that she couldn't risk his temper now by pulling away. She sat quite still, her breast rising and falling more rapidly as his tongue and his teeth continued to lick and nibble her ear and the sensitive area behind it.

She drew in a long sigh as his hand slipped beneath her chemise to caress her breast.

The giddiness, the delicious weakness spreading through her limbs made Katherine realize that unless she did something soon, she would be snared in her own trap.

In a hushed voice she said, "Jonathan."

"Mmm, yes?"

"The party," she reminded him, pulling back a little.

Gazing into her eyes, he sighed wistfully, "Ah, yes, the party."

He took her in his arms, and for a moment she was lost in the sensations his kisses could stir within her. She was breathless when he drew back at last, and knowing that if she didn't speak up quickly, that if she let him kiss her again he would make her forget her purpose, she forced herself to say, "Darling, what should I do about the invitations?"

"Whatever you want, love," he said huskily as he stroked her cheek, his eyes intent on her mouth.

"Anything?"

Looking into her eyes, he smiled and said huskily, "Anything."

Now was the time, she decided. "Then may I tell Adam that we'll be at his wedding?"

A flash of surprise crossed his eyes. "Adam is getting married?" he asked, drawing back. He looked at her silently for a few seconds before adding, "When?"

"At the end of next month," she replied diffidently. "The Saturday after Thanksgiving."

"Oh?"

Not knowing what to make of the bland expression that had come to his face, Katherine made a valiant effort to summon her courage. "Agatha and Donald will be there for the holiday and the wedding," she got out as he reached for the snifter of brandy. "Do you think we could go, Jonathan? Could we go to the wedding, please?"

Jonathan drained the brandy remaining in the glass and got up. Sitting on the edge of the divan, Katherine clasped her hands tightly on her lap as she watched him get up and cross the room. He refilled his glass from the decanter and turned to face her. Her stomach was tied in knots of tension as she waited for his reply.

Swirling the amber liquid in the snifter, he asked in a deceptively mild tone, "You miss New York, don't you?"

"Oh, yes!"

The words were out of her mouth before she could stop them, and she jumped in surprise when he angrily set his glass down on the table. "So that's the reason for all this sweetness, isn't it?"

Guiltily, Katherine dropped her gaze to her hands.

"All you want is to go back to New York," he accused her. "To your lover!"

She gave him a look of astonishment. Bouncing to her feet, she went to stand before him. "Max wasn't my lover!"

He gave a short, humorless laugh, "Liar!"

She raised her hand to strike him, but Jonathan grabbed her arms and held them behind her. His voice rasped with anger when he demanded, "You'd do anything to go back to New York, wouldn't you?"

By now much too angry to be frightened, she shouted, "Yes!"

The rage she saw on his face made her realize too late that she had pushed him much too far this time. Only once before had she seen him this angry, and closing her eyes tightly, Katherine waited for the blow that would probably end her life right then and there. Instead, she was swept up in his arms, and realizing his intentions as he started for the door she began to struggle, crying, "No Jonathan, don't!"

Mounting the stairs three steps at the time, he was heedless to her pleas, and once in her room he roughly set her down on the bed. Leaning over her, he held both her flailing arms above her head with one hand, immobilizing her, as with the other he tore at her dress. The delicate fabrics of her garments offered little resistance, and in a matter of seconds she was lying naked and helpless beneath him.

"No, please!"

His mouth silenced her pleas as it crashed savagely onto hers. His kiss was punishing, almost bruising as it ravished her mouth, as it compelled her lips to part and yield to the assault of his tongue. Katherine's squirms began to weaken; her enemy, her flesh, betrayed her as it began responding to the rough caresses of his urgent hands. Before she knew it, she was responding to the dizzying, drugging kisses that devoured her, that consumed her, that inflamed her mind and her flesh until the need to be a part of him was overwhelming.

Her tense body was aflame, shivering with the intensity of her desire for him when he plunged into her depths at last. Locked in tight embrace they moved in savage rhythm, until

355

the rippling sensations within her became wild tremors that burst forth in a maelstrom of feelings. He was her love, her life, now and forever; and lying in his arms, fulfilled and breathless, she listened to the pounding of his heart waiting, waiting for a tender word, a gentle touch that would unlock the secret of the love she carried in her heart.

And although the word never came, she still melted in his arms and responded to his passion when he claimed her and possessed her again and again through the night.

In the morning, he was gone.

When he came home again, Katherine remained withdrawn and silent and refrained from asking about the trip. That night he came to her again, and after an initial struggle she succumbed to his embraces.

Ensuing days and nights were a repetition of the same. They hardly spoke to each other, and Katherine bitterly resented his use of her. She tried to submit without a response, but Jonathan knew her body too well; after all, it had been he who had initiated her to the delights of passion, and even against her will knew how to bring her to fulfillment.

As his lovemaking became more leisured, even her resentment couldn't survive for long after his hands and his mouth caressed and kissed every curve and cleft of her body, as he fondled and nibbled until she was tingling all over and could no longer withhold her moans of pleasure. Yet Katherine wouldn't admit total defeat. Although she was powerless against his passion, she still refused to become the generous lover she had once been and never lifted a finger to touch him.

One night, after he had made love to her, Katherine lay still with her eyes closed while Jonathan propped himself on an elbow to watch the firelight play on her naked body. As his fingers gently stroked her cheek he asked suddenly, "When is Adam's wedding?"

Her eyes opened and she blinked in surprise. "The Saturday after Thanksgiving."

Continuing to caress her cheek, he smiled at her a little ruefully. "If you still want to go, you may write to him that we'll be there."

Suddenly, she felt like crying.

Bursting with the warm colors of autumn, the countryside went unnoticed by the silent passengers of the carriage riding north. A terrible scene had preceded their departure from Baltimore because although Jonathan had agreed to take her to New York, he had flatly refused to bring Jason with them.

"Honey, the overland trip is too long for a child his age," he had said.

"We could have gone by sea, but that's not the real reason, is it, Jonathan?" she had demanded.

"He'll be fine with my parents," he had tried to pacify her. "And, besides, this way we can be alone together for a little while, Katie."

"You're holding him hostage!"

He had not even bothered to deny her accusation, and she was still smarting from their argument when they stopped at a roadside inn just before sundown. Actually, Katherine had intended to only pick at her food; when it was served, however, she found that she was too hungry to sulk and ate everything on her plate, and this only served to augment her indignation.

Their room wasn't large, but it was very pleasant, and there was a log fire crackling cheerfully in the hearth when they went in. Tired of being jolted in the carriage all day,

Katherine inwardly prayed that the bed would be comfortable.

As though reading her mind, Jonathan went to the bed and lay down on it. "Mmm, it's nice and soft," he said, giving her a wicked grin. Putting out his hand, he beckoned to her, "Come, love, see for yourself."

Tipping her chin, Katherine stuck out her lower lip in a pout and said dryly, "I want a bath."

"And I've anticipated your wishes, madam," he replied, getting up to give her a rakish bow. A knock on the door punctuated his action, and straightening up he winked at her and said, "Ah, there it is now."

He went to answer the door and spent the next few minutes helping the innkeeper carry the tub and place it in front of the fire. After it had been filled, he dipped a finger to test the temperature of the water and adopted a stiff British accent to announce, "Your bath is ready, madam."

Katherine paused in her unpacking to give him a sour look. "I'd like some privacy, if you don't mind."

He came to stand behind her and encircled her waist. "I remember a time when you didn't mind if I watched you," he said, dropping a kiss on top of her head and turning her around to face him lifted her chin to make her look at him. "You even let me bathe you, remember?"

Suffocating with embarrassment, Katherine dropped her gaze. "Please, Jonathan," she said in a hushed voice.

The blush that came to her cheeks made her look so sweet and vulnerable, that he didn't have the heart to tease her further. "All right, Katie, I'll go." He leaned over her and kissed her softly on the lips before he turned and went to the door. With his hand on the knob, he half-turned and said, "Save me some hot water, will you, honey?"

Katherine expelled a long sigh of relief as the door closed behind him. Then, she undressed, pinned up her hair and stepped into her bath.

She lay back in the tub for a while, letting the hot water ease the tension of her muscles before reaching for the cake of soap. She was lathering a leg when Jonathan returned, and casting an appreciative glance at her shapely limb, he couldn't help but tease her. "Need any help?"

She glowered at him, and pursing her lips continued lathering her foot with a vengeance.

"Come on, Katie," he laughed. "Are you planning on spending the night in the tub? You're going to be all shriveled up, sweetheart. Besides, I could use a bath, too, you know."

Infuriated by his lighthearted mood, Katherine shot him a peevish glare as she rinsed her foot. She started to get up then, but when she looked around for the towel, she discovered that it was beyond her reach. Covering her breasts with her hands she sat frowning for a few seconds, galled by the prospect of having to ask for his help, but not knowing what else to do.

Smothering a laugh at her predicament, Jonathan finally took pity on her. He took the linen towel and held it up for her.

Katherine rose from the tub and quickly wrapped herself in the cloth before stepping out of the bath.

While she dried herself, Jonathan divested himself of his clothes and went into the tub. Humming *Greensleeves* while splashing merrily, he seemed totally unaware of her indignant glares. When she reached for her nightdress, however, he interrupted his singing to say, "Don't bother, Katie. You know I prefer you in the buff."

Katherine opened her mouth to give him a piece of her mind and then closed it again, knowing that it would have been useless. Breathing an irritated sigh, she slipped the gown over her head.

"It's coming off in a moment, love. Why bother?"

The amusement in his voice made her choke with fury as

she drew back the covers and prepared to get into bed.

"Come over here and scrub my back, won't you, love?"

"Scrub it yourself!"

"Tsk, tsk, tsk, temper, temper," he shook his head in mock reproach, adding fuel to her indignation.

She got into bed and turned her back to him.

Jonathan finished his bath, and seeing that the towel was lying on the floor by the bed where she had dropped it, he called, "Honey, would you mind handing me the towel?"

Trying to ignore him, Katherine didn't move.

"Honey?" he persisted goodhumoredly, "The towel? Please?"

Katherine was in a huff as she shoved the covers aside, got up, picked up the towel, and flung it at him. He caught it in the air with a good-humored, "Thanks, love."

As he started to get up, she turned away abruptly and got quickly back into bed, pulling the covers all the way up to her chin.

Jonathan continued humming as he dried himself, and when he finished he doused the candle and slipped into bed beside her. The sheets were cold against his bare skin.

"Brrr!" he shivered, seeking the warmth of her body. He embraced her, and knowing the futility of a struggle she held herself stiff and unresponsive in his arms as he brushed her hair back and began covering her face with gentle kisses. His lips explored and nibbled the column of her throat, the lobe of her ear.

"Mmm, you smell so sweet," he whispered softly. "Love me, Katie."

She turned her face away to deny her kisses, but he gently forced it back toward him and his lips moved enticingly over her own. "Yield to me, love," he said huskily when she clamped her teeth to keep his tongue from penetrating her mouth. When she wouldn't yield, he began licking her lips and tracing the contours of her mouth with the tip of his tongue.

Even though in her mind she refused to yield, her lips parted to the kiss that left her breathless.

Drawing back a little to look at her, he whispered, "Make love to me, Katie. The way you used to."

She wanted to, but that would have been her final defeat. Closing her eyes to his blue gaze, she shook her head and said, "No."

He didn't stop her when she turned away, but his arms went around her and his hands cupped her breasts as his mouth began an exploration of her nape and shoulders. His hands slipped beneath the nightdress to caress the front of her body while his mouth continued moving down her back. He turned her around and caressed every inch of her, and her will to resist crumbled under his unrelenting attack on her senses: the sound of his husky voice murmuring to her, the feel of his roughened hands gliding smoothly over her body or gently stroking, kneading, massaging, caressing. Her gown had slipped away at some point in time she couldn't remember, and she was lost in a world of sensation, aware only of the heat of his body against her naked skin, of the sensuous feeling of the fur on his chest as feathers brushing against her hardened nipples as he rubbed against her, and she shivered with anticipation at the hardness she could feel pressing against her.

Arching her body to offer her breasts, she heard his soft indrawn breath before his lips and teeth nibbled and gently pulled at the engorged nipples. The warm glow rising inside her reached new heights as he sucked them into his mouth, first one and then the other, and his fingers found that nucleus of sensations that was her inner core and relentlessly explored and fondled until she was moaning with over-whelming desire that he fill the void that was inside her.

She felt whole again when he plunged into her depths at

last, and thrashing, moaning, she dug her nails into his back and clasped him with her legs, urging him to increase his tempo as he moved within her. He was still filling her as she was shaken with the tremors of passion, and unrelentingly brought her to new heights again and again before allowing his own release, in unison with her final climax.

Weeping, Katherine clutched him to her, reluctant to let him go even in the aftermath of love.

In the days that followed, Katherine was unable to maintain her anger in the face of Jonathan's attitude. He refused to rise to her needlings and, instead, teased her out of her tantrums with his humor, wooed her into his arms with his tenderness, and assaulted her senses with his passion. Little by little, her will to resist him faded, and she began to allow herself to believe in his love.

No longer did she sit in sullen silence during their journey. Everything was changing. The air was crisper and the sky had taken a different hue; even though winter was blowing near, her heart was filling with springtime. Dusk brought promises of quiet evenings listening to the songs a fire can sing, and of moments of exquisite rapture by its golden glow.

Wishing to prolong this interlude Jonathan set a more leisurely pace to their journey, and by the time they stopped at the inn in Philadelphia, Katherine was almost ready to put aside her caution.

Once Jonathan had left her in their room, Katherine discovered that one of her valises had been left in the carriage. She waited for a while, but patience had never been one of her strongest virtues; when time passed and he had not returned, she decided to find the innkeeper herself and ask him to fetch her luggage.

She went out of the room and down the stairs. Finding no

one in the main hall she continued her search, and the faint sound of voices pointed her in the direction of the dining room. She looked uncertainly around the room, and even with his back to her, she immediately recognized Jonathan's familiar figure at a corner table.

As she started to enter, he moved a little to one side, and this revealed that he wasn't alone. Katherine stopped cold in her tracks when she saw the buxom blonde who was sharing his table.

Although not very young, the woman was rather pretty, Katherine admitted with a stab of jealousy as she hesitated at the entrance. She didn't know whether to turn and walk away or join her husband and his companion, but what happened next did away with her indecision. The woman began kissing Jonathan's hand, and he put an arm around her.

Smothering a gasp, Katherine abruptly turned away and ran up the stairs, gasping for breath and clutching at her bosom with both hands as though to still the pounding of her heart and ease the pain that was choking her. Finally she reached her room and closed the door behind her.

Leaning against the door, she covered her face with her hands crying, "Stupid, stupid, stupid!"

Struck by a terrible wave of desolation, she sank down to the floor when her legs refused to support her any longer. How could she have been so stupid as to fall in his trap again? It was clear that for Jonathan, winning her love was just a game, a matter of pride. He was so accustomed to have women fall into his arms, that her own resistance was nothing more than a challenge.

Her grief was too brutal, too violent for tears; all she wanted at that moment was to die. Unaware of her actions, Katherine rose from the floor and walked stiffly toward the bed. Lying on top of the quilt with her eyes closed she felt lifeless and completely hollow, as if someone had ripped her breast open and torn out her heart.

She had not moved when some time later she heard Jonathan's footsteps outside the door and he came in.

"Katie!" he exclaimed, rushing to her side. "Honey, what's the matter? Are you ill?"

His features were tight with worry when he lay a hand on her forehead to feel her temperature. It was cold, as was the hand that he took and held in both of his. "Darling, what's wrong?"

The anxiety in his voice sounded almost genuine, and she couldn't bear the feel of his warm fingers on her face a moment longer. "Migraine," she lied.

"Is there anything I can do?"

His voice was so gentle that she wanted to scream at him like a fishwife. Instead, she said quietly, "Please leave me alone."

Jonathan stood there undecided for a few seconds and then went to the dresser, poured water over a cloth and brought her a cold compress. She didn't offer a protest when he laid it gently on her forehead.

"Should I send for a doctor?" he asked anxiously.

"Just go. I'll be all right."

This time, against his wish, he complied.

Although she was still pale and unwell in the morning, Katherine flatly refused Jonathan's suggestion that they remain at the inn until she had recovered from her sudden malaise. All she could think of at the moment was to reach New York.

She clung to her pretense to avoid Jonathan's attempts at conversation when they took to the road again and his lovemaking when they stopped for the night.

Seventeen

Only at the sight of the outskirts of New York did Katherine begin to come out of her lethargy, and by the time the carriage passed through the gates of the Owen's house her mood had swiftly changed to one of ill-concealed excitement.

Adam came out to meet them, and before the coach had come to a complete halt she practically leaped into his arms. "How good to see you again!" she exclaimed, hugging him with fervor. "Oh, my dear, I've missed you so much!"

He held her tightly for a moment and then drew back a little to regard her with a mixture of concern and fondness. "Let me look at you," he said, his voice husky with an emotion that he tried to mask behind a quick smile. "As lovely as ever, pet." Expectantly, he looked past her and asked, "Where's Jason?"

"He's staying with Jonathan's parents," she replied in a light tone that she hoped didn't betray her uneasiness. "We thought the journey overland would have been too long for him."

Adam's expression reflected his lack of conviction at her explanation, and a sudden angry sparkle came to his eyes when his gaze met Jonathan's. A look of active dislike passed between the two men, but the arrival of Agatha and Jenny prevented a more disagreeable scene. The next few minutes were full of hugs and kisses as they all talked excitedly at the same time, and then Katherine introduced her husband to her friends.

Although Jenny made no attempt to conceal her hostility toward Jonathan, Agatha's greeting was considerably warmer and friendlier.

The house servants had quickly gathered in the portico to welcome their former mistress, and an older man came running hat in hand to offer a bunch of flowers to her. Kurt, the head gardener, spoke very little English, and when Katherine expressed her appreciation and delight for his gift, Jonathan was surprised that she did it in fluent German. But even more revealing to him of how she truly felt was her exclamation when she walked into the house.

"What a nice homecoming!" she said.

The presence of Iris Cavanaugh and Donald Baxter at dinnertime completed the family reunion, but there was also a new addition to the group. Robert Talbert was only slightly taller than Jenny herself. His figure was slim and his face angular and bony, but although it couldn't be said that he was a handsome young man, his smile possessed such an extraordinarily attractive and spontaneous quality that made it easy to understand why he had captured Jenny's heart.

Iris's warm, outgoing personality was well-suited to Adam's own nature, and Katherine was glad that at last her dearest friend had found the happiness he so well deserved. That Agatha had found the same with Donald was plain for all to see.

That only left she and Jonathan, Katherine reflected, feeling herself getting gloomy as she watched her husband in conversation with Agatha's husband. Before the scene she had witnessed in Philadelphia, she had hoped that they, too, could find happiness together; now she knew that would never be possible.

Her eyes lost their abstraction when, as though sensing her mood, Jonathan half-turned and stared at her thoughtfully for a few seconds. Self-consciously, she looked away from his probing gaze and forced her attention back to the general conversation, which at the moment concerned the entertainment planned for the length of their visit. There were numerous festivities to attend, beginning with the dinner party the Beninks were throwing in their honor the following evening.

"Johanna is dying to see you, pet," Adam told Katherine. "Which reminds me, a letter came from Natalie just a couple of days ago. She and Bernard are now the proud parents of a healthy son."

"Thank God!" Katherine smiled, feeling her gloom lighten at the good news. "I've written several letters to her from Baltimore but am still waiting for the replies. I must admit I was getting a little worried."

Iris gossiped about people Katherine had met that summer, and Adam added his witty and amusing remarks. Katherine remembered some of those mentioned and had forgotten others; there was only one person she really wanted to know about, but she couldn't ask after Max in Jonathan's presence.

Dear Max! Had he forgiven her? Did he still love her? These and other questions crowded her mind as her attention wandered off again. How different her life would have been if she had married Max! But then she thought of Jason. Even if Max had given the boy his name and accepted him as his own, now that she had seen Jason's delight with his real father and those of his own blood, she was aware that, in itself, wouldn't have been enough.

As the evening progressed, Katherine's thoughts turned to

the moment she would find herself alone with Jonathan in their room. By feigning illness she had avoided his embraces, but now that she had dropped her pretense she was sure that he would make love to her again. With the memory of the episode in Philadelphia still fresh in her mind, she dreaded the moment. She was so nervous about it, in fact, that she drank too much wine during the sumptuous dinner, which she barely touched; consequently, she was quite tipsy by the time she retired.

Annie had just finished putting her mistress to bed when Jonathan came into the bedchamber. Katherine had fallen asleep almost instantly, and the girl said good night to him and left.

Before undressing, he stood by the bed for a moment looking down at his wife. His suspicions that the illness she had pleaded during last few days of their journey had been feigned had been confirmed by swift change in her mood upon their arrival in New York. The nights they had spent together before reaching Philadelphia had encouraged his belief that, at long last, she had been well disposed to reconcile their differences. He had believed to be so close to winning her that the sudden change in her manner had left him quite baffled, but his efforts to clear the mystery had been indifferently brushed aside by her.

The soft shadows her long lashes cast upon the bloom of her cheeks gave her a charming, vulnerable quality in her sleep, and he continued to look at her as though fascinated by her exquisite beauty. The curve of her breast, rising and falling gently as her breath came soft and even through her slightly parted lips made desire stir in his loins. Regardless of how much she professed to hate him, he knew he could make her body respond to his touch, yet that wasn't enough. He would never be satisfied until he possessed her heart as well as her body, and since she had proved such a strong opponent, the duel between them would have to go on.

Jonathan undressed, and after getting into bed he gently drew his sleeping wife into his arms. Her body was soft, relaxed as he held her, and giving a contented sigh she snuggled against him. Inwardly smiling at her purring sighs, he stroked her hair spread over the pillow, delighting in its silken texture and delicate fragrance. Emitting another long sigh, Katherine parted her lips in an unconscious invitation.

Even in her sleep she responded to the kiss that became less tentative and more demanding as it grew in intensity. Her fingers caressed the nape of his neck as he leaned over her and drank the heady wine of her kisses and trailed his lips along her throat. Still without awakening, Katherine took his hand and placed it on her breast. Jonathan stroked it gently through the diaphanous fabric and then eased the gown from her shoulders.

The rosy nipples tautened at the touch of his lips, and as she held his head to her breast in an unspoken plea for his caresses, a delicious weakness spread through her limbs as he complied.

"Make love to me, Katie," he said then, lifting her over him when he turned on his back.

Raising herself on an elbow, she leaned over him and covered his face with kisses, lingering on his mouth, invading it with her tongue, exploring and savoring the taste of it. Letting her hair brush his skin as she kissed and nibbled his flesh, she continued to give him the pleasure that until then she had denied him.

He drew in his breath when she lowered herself on his erect sex and offered her breasts to him. He sucked them into his mouth, first one and then the other, as she continued moving her hips, bringing them both to the brink of ultimate pleasure only to stop in order to prolong the moment of fulfillment.

His hands were urgent on her flesh as she continued her bittersweet torment, and when at last she could no longer contain her own need, with a cry of joy she increased the tempo of her thrusts until she collapsed with the tremors of her climax.

Holding her against him for a few moments, Jonathan stroked her gently, murmuring tender words of love. Then, realizing that she had fallen asleep again, he laid her down by his side and held her until sleep also overcame him.

Katherine was still sleeping soundly when Annie came in with her morning coffee. When she didn't stir at her entrance, the girl set down the tray and drew the drapes open to let the pale sunshine in, since her instructions were to awaken her mistress.

"Good morning, mum," she said cheerfully.

Katherine stretched and made to sit up, but immediately fell back on the pillows, groaning, "Oh, good Lord!" The moment she tried to open her eyes, the brightness in the room made a sharp pain stab her behind the lids. The entire room seemed to be spinning about her at a maddening speed. Her mouth felt full of cotton, and a thousand hammers were pounding inside her head with a vengeance. Never in her life had she felt so miserable.

Squinting her eyes, she saw Annie bend down from the waist to pick up something from the floor. When the girl straightened up again, she recognized the article of clothing the girl was carefully folding as her own nightdress.

Discovering that she was naked beneath the covers, Katherine was struck by the sudden realization that what she had believed a dream had really happened. She had made love to Jonathan!

"Oh, my God!" she groaned, closing her eyes again.

Uttering a sigh, Annie helped her mistress to a sitting position and covered her nakedness with a robe de chambre before she set the bed tray on her knees. The nightdress on the floor and the state of the bed were indications that in addition to being handsome, the mistress's new husband was a vigorous lover. Romantic, too, if the red rose he had asked her to give his wife with her morning coffee was anything to go by.

Katherine ceased holding her head between her hands in order to accept the cup of coffee Annie had poured for her. Her hand was shaking as she raised it to her lips. *I'll never drink champagne again for as long as I live*, she vowed inwardly, trying to shut off the sound of Annie's voice. All she longed for at the moment was complete and blissful silence.

Although the hot coffee provided some relief to her discomfort, she still felt awful even after finishing a second cup. It was only then that her eyes fell on the single red rose on the tray. Automatically, she started to reach for it.

"It's from Captain Greenfield, mum," Annie said when she noticed the gesture.

Katherine's hand remained suspended for a moment over the flower. Then, taking the rose so as not to make the girl suspicious, she made an effort to make her tone sound casual when she inquired, "Is he still at home?"

"Yes, mum," Annie nodded. "The Captain is in the drawing room entertaining Mrs. Benink while you dress."

"Johanna is here?" Katherine inquired, startled. "Why didn't you say so!" she exclaimed, pushing the covers aside.

"But I did, mum," Annie sighed.

Sitting on the bed's edge, Katherine put a hand to her head. "I'm sorry, Annie. I guess I wasn't really listening," she apologized sincerely. "My head is just killing me. Please set out my blue dress and ask Mrs. Benink to come up, will you?"

"Yes, mum."

Annie laid out her mistress's garments and left while Katherine was washing.

Katherine was about to sit at her dressing table when Johanna breezed into the room, and the two women embraced and exchanged friendly kisses.

"Please forgive me for barging in on you like this, dear Katherine, but I simply couldn't wait until this evening to see you again," Johanna said in her flighty, cheerful manner. "I knew we wouldn't have much chance to talk in private then."

"I'm glad you came," Katherine smiled at her friend. "I've been dying to see you, too. How's Frank?"

"He sends his love. Did you hear the good news about Natalie's child?"

"Adam told me last night," Katherine nodded. "I'm so happy for them. Would you like some coffee?"

"No thanks," Johanna waved her hand as she sat down in an armchair. "I already drank gallons of it with that charming husband of yours. What a dreamy man! He's simply gorgeous! No wonder you were so hesitant about Max!" Her eyes widened, and pressing her hand to her mouth she said "Oops!"

"It's all right, Johanna," Katherine replied, realizing that the resemblance between her new husband and her son had made Johanna put two and two together. Since they had become such good friends, she had always hated the lie that existed between them and now said quite sincerely, "I'm glad that now you know the truth." Digressing swiftly, she inquired anxiously, "Have you seen Max lately? How is he, Johanna?"

Johanna shook her head unhappily. "We haven't seen or heard from him since you left New York," she replied. "You were the only reason he became more sociable, and now he has vanished again. Your marriage must have been quite a shock to him."

"Yes, I think it was," Katherine nodded with regret. "He arrived a few minutes after Jonathan and I were married,

372

and I can't tell you how horrible it was. I thought they were going to kill each other."

"I can imagine," Johanna said in a subdued tone. Then, immediately dropping her seriousness, she added with affectionate irony, "Oh, well, nobody dies of a broken heart, least of all men. Let's not talk about it any more. How are you and Jason getting along in Baltimore?"

While she finished dressing, Katherine told her friend of how happy Jason was with his father, and although she also spoke fondly of Jonathan's parents she refrained from mentioning her initial difficulties with Felicity. In fact, for the benefit of her friend, she painted a rosy picture of her existence.

After her friend had left, Katherine was relieved to discover that Jonathan had gone out. She was free to spend the afternoon with Agatha, who confirmed that Jenny was giving serious consideration to marrying Robert Talbert.

Katherine inquired, "Has he proposed yet?"

"Not yet," Agatha replied, "but Jenny hasn't told him that she's thinking of going to live with us in Albany. Perhaps if he believes she'll stay in New York, he might pop the question before going back home. He seems quite taken with her, you know."

"What do you think of him, Agatha?"

"He's a very nice young man and from a good family. I've known him for only a few months, but I do like him."

And she likes Jonathan, too, Katherine thought with some impatience. "On the surface so do I," she said. "But the question is, will he be good to our Jenny? What sort of man is he? Is he kind-hearted? Is he generous? And I'm not referring to his money."

"I'm aware of your concern, my dear," Agatha replied. "And Jenny's been worried about it too. Sooner or later she'll have to tell him what her life was like before she came to us, but there's no point in saying anything until the occasion arises, don't you agree?"

"I suppose you're right," Katherine replied, remembering how she had berated herself for telling Max the truth about herself when it was still too early in their relationship.

"I'm almost sure he won't hold it against her," Agatha said placidly. "After all, she wasn't to blame."

"Oh, I do hope so, but I'll feel much better when the matter is resolved," Katherine said fervently. "Poor Jenny. I know from experience how difficult it is having to confess one's past."

Agatha's sensitive features reflected her empathy as she reached for her young friend's hand and said, "But Jonathan understood, didn't he?"

After a brief moment of hesitation, Katherine answered, "I haven't told him."

"You haven't?" Agatha said with a startled gasp. "But why, my dear?"

Katherine shrugged her shoulders slightly. "He hasn't asked, and I haven't volunteered the information," she replied evasively. "Besides, the situation is quite different. Jenny will have to explain to her husband why she isn't a virgin, but I owe Jonathan no explanations of what I had to do in order to survive."

"I thought you had forgiven him," Agatha said, shaking her head half-reproachfully. "He loves you, Katherine."

Poor, gullible Agatha, Katherine thought containing a bitter laugh. But, she wasn't alone; Jonathan had a knack for deceiving women.

"And I love him," Katherine admitted, since she didn't want her friend to worry over her marital troubles. Hiding her unhappiness behind a quick smile, she added, "I'll tell him when the time is right, Agatha. I promise."

* * *

It wasn't until Katherine was dressing for the dinner party at the Beninks' that Jonathan returned in a very cheerful mood. As soon as Annie was out the door so that he could change, he came to her and put his arms around her.

"Don't," Katherine protested, wedging her hands between them when he tried to kiss her.

He hugged her playfully. "Are you cross because I was gone all day?"

Turning away from him, she replied dryly, "I'm not cross."

He came to stand behind her and encircled her waist. "I had an errand to run and some shopping to do. Would you like to see what I bought?"

"Not particularly," she shrugged indifferently and tried to get away.

He turned her around to face him. "Honey, what's the matter? After last night, I thought . . ."

"Please!" she interrupted him. "I don't want to talk about it. Last night I had too much champagne and didn't know what I was doing."

A deep frown came to his forehead. "Is that all it was?"

"Of course," she replied, tipping her chin slightly. "Don't read any more into what happened, Jonathan. Nothing has changed."

As soon as his hands relaxed their grasp and fell from her shoulders, Katherine turned away and went to sit at the dressing table.

While brushing her hair, she tried to keep herself from following Jonathan's movements through the mirror as he dressed. When he was ready, without another word he went out to let her finish her preparations.

Meeting old acquaintances at the dinner party held little joy for Katherine, who went through the evening with a fixed smile on her face and feigning a gaiety that she was far from feeling. That Jonathan seemed to be enjoying the great deal of attention he was drawing from the ladies only added to her misery, but she wouldn't give him the satisfaction of revealing how she felt.

"My dear, what a delicious man you've married," Susan Raleigh said with a girlish giggle. "Every woman in the room would gladly trade places with you, he's so charming, not to mention handsome. And I understand he's got a fortune to boot! We all thought that you and Max were a sure thing, but had I known about Jonathan I would have put my money on him. As much as I like Max, compared to Jonathan he's such a cold fish that believe me, I wouldn't have hesitated either!"

"Max isn't a cold fish," Katherine defended her former suitor. "He's a very nice man."

"That may be true," Susan agreed with good humor, "But, my dear Katherine, he was always so aloof that he never gave anyone the chance to discover his better nature. It's good of you to defend him, but I still think you made the right choice. I'm only sorry that you had to leave New York. I'm looking forward to having you and your husband come to my ball before you go back to Baltimore. And don't worry about running into Max," she added as an afterthought. "We sent him an invitation before we knew you were coming, but we were informed that he's out of town."

"Thanks, Susan," Katherine smiled. "We'll be there."

"Good," Susan smiled back. "I see that Tom is trying to catch my eye, so he must be ready to go home. Good bye, dear. I hope to see you again soon. Happy Thanksgiving."

Katherine returned the good wishes and soon the party came to an end.

Once they had arrived at home, Jonathan came to their bedchamber for only a few moments before he went out again. When time passed and he failed to return, Katherine realized that he must have planned to spend the night with someone else.

Mid-morning brought an unexpected caller. Katherine

read the calling card Bruce had given her, and even though she carefully searched her memory she failed to recognize the name of Mrs. Crystal Gaynor. Upon entering the parlor, however, she immediately recognized the pretty blonde woman as the same one who had been Jonathan's companion to the ballet and the Raleighs' ball before their marriage.

The two women stared at one another for a few seconds as though trying to gauge each other's strengths and weaknesses.

"It's good of you to receive me, Mrs. Greenfield," the woman said at last with a smile that made Katherine feel rather uneasy. "Actually, I came to see Jonathan, but your man said that he wasn't at home."

Katherine nodded. "I'm sure he'll be sorry to have missed your visit," she replied as politely as she could, although with a marked lack of enthusiasm. "Is there anything I can do for you?"

"I don't think so," Crystal replied. Then she seemed to change her mind. "On second thought, yes. I think you can help." Reaching into her reticule, she brought out a folded piece of white cloth that she tended to Katherine and added, "I'm afraid he left this cravat at my house when he came to see me. His initials are embroidered, so I'm sure he'll want it back."

To see Katherine turn visibly pale with shock was a welcome sight for Crystal Gaynor. At long last she had the chance to humiliate the woman who had robbed her not only once, but twice, of making a brilliant marriage. Although their motives were different, she was glad that in sharing her antipathy for Katherine, Felicity had given her the means to exact revenge from her rival.

Although Crystal was well aware that in taking this step she was running the risk of compromising her reputation, she found the satisfaction she derived from humiliating Katherine was a small compensation for what she had lost

377

on her account. Jonathan would have made a far more generous husband than Max, Crystal thought with renewed spite.

Felicity's assurances that the hated Englishwoman would keep the secret had echoed Crystal's own beliefs. Accustomed as Katherine was to being at the receiving end of male adoration, she would surely find it a bitter pill to swallow having to admit that so soon after their marriage the man she had chosen over another had found her charms insufficient to keep him faithful.

Katherine rose abruptly to her feet and went to pull the cord to summon a servant. It took a superhuman effort on her part to keep her voice steady when she said evenly, "Get out of my house."

Crystal's smug smile did not falter as she also rose from her seat and replied, "With pleasure."

Now that her mission had been accomplished, Crystal was sure that she had nothing to worry about. Katherine's pride wouldn't allow her husband's alleged philandering to become public knowledge.

Once her visitor had departed, Katherine flung Jonathan's cravat into the fire burning in the fireplace. Sick at heart, she watched as it was consumed by the flames.

Caught in a whirl of shopping, parties, and wedding preparations, Katherine struggled to present a cheerful countenance to her friends even though she was more unhappy than ever before. She had little to be thankful for when Thanksgiving Day arrived at last and the family celebrated their first such holiday to the applause of the "natives," as Adam kept referring to the American members of their group. In a brief but moving prayer, Agatha gave thanks for the blessings bestowed upon them and the happiness they had found in the new land.

And most of them had found happiness with someone to share their lives with, Katherine reflected. As for herself and

Jonathan—how much longer could she continue to live with him, loving him and knowing that there was no hope that her love would ever be returned?

Adam's wedding to Iris was a joyful affair with many friends in attendance, and following a gay reception and a superb wedding feast, the newlyweds departed on their honeymoon amidst cheers and good wishes.

Coming back to a quiet, almost deserted house, Katherine was possessed by a sudden attack of melancholia as well as a deep sense of loss. Even after Iris had entered Adam's life, she herself had never felt that her place in his heart had changed. The wedding had made her realize that even though he still loved her and always would, things could never be the same now that he had a wife.

And with the wedding being over, she and Jonathan would soon be going back to Baltimore, she reflected with mixed feelings. She missed Jason and wanted to see him again, but she was depressed at the thought of going back to the same situation they had left behind. No, not the same situation, she corrected herself. It would be even worse, because now her suspicions of Jonathan's infidelities had been confirmed.

The last ball they were to attend was at the Raleighs—where she and Jonathan had met again after their initial estrangement—and, as before, the mansion was like a gleaming jewel.

When they made their entrance a gay and elegant crowd had already assembled in the ballroom, where she was greeted effusively by many acquaintances of old that she had not had occasion to see until that time. As soon as dancing began, Jonathan took her around the floor twice and then she was claimed by other partners.

Suddenly Max was there, and it was with a feeling of un
reality that she stepped into his arms. Following the music ir
silence, they gazed into each other's eyes for moments tha
seemed suspended.

"I've missed you," he said at last.

So choked with emotion was she, that all Katherine coulc
do was to gaze into the gray eyes that held her so lovingly.

"You look more beautiful than ever, my darling."

The wistful note in his voice made tears come to her eyes
All she could articulate through her constricted throat was
"Oh, Max!"

His smile was wistful as he said, "Hush, darling. Don'
say anything. Just let me hold you."

Unaware of the many pairs of eyes that followed thei
movements, they danced on.

"Are you happy?" he asked huskily.

She couldn't answer. She wanted to say yes so that the li
would help him to put her out of his heart forever, but some
how she couldn't bring out the words.

"I see," he said thoughtfully at her silence. "I still lov
you, Katherine, and always will. When I heard abou
Adam's wedding, I hurried back to New York because
knew that nothing could keep you from attending."

"You shouldn't have, Max."

"Shouldn't I?" His soft laughter was tinged with bitter
ness. "You have no idea how hard it's been for me to sta
away from Baltimore. The only reason I haven't gone ther
is because I knew I wouldn't have been able to leave withou
you." After a moment's silence, he asked, "Will you come t
me, darling?"

Sharply she drew in her breath. Going away with Ma
would have been a solution to her current predicament. Fo
an instant, she was sorely tempted to take advantage of hi
offer. But that instant passed quickly. "I can't, Max," sh

380

shook her head at last. "You know I can't."

His eyes were probing as he held her gaze steadily. "If I could find a way . . . would you come to me then?"

Sadly she shook her head. "No, Max."

"You still love him, don't you?"

She looked away from the pain in his eyes. "Yes, I do," she admitted ruefully. "I don't want to, but somehow I can't stop loving him."

Suddenly taking her by the hand, Max drew her into an empty room off the ballroom.

"But you did love me," he protested, holding her hand tightly. "I know you did."

"Yes, Max, I loved you and I still do, but it's not quite the same." She paused, aware of the pain she was inflicting and searching for the right words to explain her feelings. "I didn't know why I couldn't marry you before, but I do now. I care for you, Max, very much, but it's Jonathan that I love with all my heart and soul. It will always be him, even if we make each other miserable," she finished with bitterness. She looked up at him and reached out to touch his cheek. "I'm sorry, darling. I never meant to hurt you."

He caught her hand and fervently pressed it to his lips. "I know, darling."

A third voice rose in anger, "How very touching!"

Katherine jumped, and she and Max whirled around in unison toward the voice. She gave a terrified hiss of breath at the sight of Jonathan advancing toward them. He was in a rage, and realizing that a matter of honor such as this could easily end up in a duel — and a death on her account — Katherine rushed to stand in front of Max as though to protect him with her body.

"Jonathan, please, don't!" she cried, fear clutching her heart. "It's not what you think!"

In a voice rasping with anger, Jonathan ordered, "Step aside, Katherine."

"No, I won't!"

Jonathan's face was white and pinched with anger as he glared down at her, and knowing that there was no reasoning with him in this state, it was to Max that she appealed. "Please go, Max. Do it for me, please!"

Briefly, Max held her pleading gaze before he turned on his heel and walked away. Jonathan made to follow him, but Katherine clung to his arm. "Take me home, Jonathan, please."

Angrily, he took her by the arm and steered her toward the door. The small group that had assembled there to watch the scene parted to let them through. The music stopped playing at the precise moment they emerged, and a flush of embarrassment suffused Katherine's cheeks as they crossed the ballroom with the eyes of a curious crowd fixed upon them. She was grateful to reach the foyer, where a servant handed them their coats.

Once they were inside the coach, she turned to Jonathan angrily. "How could you! How could you humiliate me like that!"

"Humiliate you!" he rasped. "You were the one parading with your lover!"

"He's not my lover! I've told you a million times!"

"I don't believe you!"

Breathing an indignant sigh Katherine turned away, and the journey home was completed in stony silence. When the carriage stopped before the front door, Jonathan helped her down and then walked away without another word.

Alarmed, she called after him, "Where are you going at this hour?"

He continued on his way without bothering to answer, and filled with apprehension she saw him disappear in the darkness.

Tension and fear continued to grow within her as hours passed and Jonathan failed to return. Where could he have gone, she kept asking herself, sick with worry as she paced the floor. Could he have gone to settle accounts with Max? "Please, God, don't let anything happen to either one of them!"

Her frayed nerves were about to give out when Jonathan came back at last, and her relief swiftly turned to anger.

"Where have you been?" she demanded. "I've been going out of my mind with worry!"

Her anger evaporated just as swiftly, however, when she noticed the blood stains on his clothes. Feeling quite faint, she grasped the back of a chair for support as she asked feebly, "What happened?"

Jonathan glared at her briefly, and without answering began to take off his coat. To Katherine's horror, she saw that his shirt was also stained with blood, as was the hand he pressed to his side with a grimace of pain. Covering her mouth with her hand, she turned even paler and cried, "You're hurt!"

The sight of his wound when he took off his shirt left her incapable of movement for the space of a few seconds. Then, mentally shaking herself, she went to him. "What happened?" she asked again, helping him ease the shirt from his shoulders.

"Someone took a shot at me," he replied while examining the wound. "Get me some bandages, a bowl of water, and a bottle of whiskey."

"But you need a doctor!"

"There's no need," he shook his head briefly. "Looks like the wound is clean. The bullet did little more than graze me."

"Then let me fetch Agatha. I'm sure she can help."

He shook his head. "I don't want to alarm her. Just go and get what I asked for."

Undecided, Katherine hovered for a moment before she ran to find the articles he had requested. When she came

383

back a few minutes later, she set the bowl down on a table and began to cleanse the wound. Her hands were shaking.

"A few inches more and you could have been killed," she said, unable to control the tears that were running down her cheeks.

"And that would have saddened you greatly, wouldn't it, my darling wife?"

The caustic tone of his voice made Katherine's heart thump with apprehension. She looked at him as though unable to understand him.

Jonathan gave a short, mirthless laugh. "Did you think that after tonight you'd be free to run to your lover?"

Eyes wide with horror, Katherine shook her head, unable to summon her voice to deny his accusations.

His fingers were like bands of steel as they closed around her wrist. "Tell me, whose idea was it, Katherine? Yours, or that coward's?"

"No!" Katherine gave an incredulous gasp. "How can you say that?"

Releasing her wrist, Jonathan pushed it away from him. "It doesn't matter. You're not getting rid of me that easily. I keep what's mine, and you better get through your head once and for all that you belong to me, Katherine. I don't give a damn how much you hate me."

"But I don't . . ."

Lifting a hand, he cut her off. "Spare me your lies, will you? Just do me a favor and don't say any more."

As though dismissing her from his mind, he turned his attention to his injury. Katherine poured the whiskey on the wound at his direction, and he took a swig straight from the bottle as she applied the dressing with unsteady fingers.

"I wish you'd let me call a doctor, Jonathan," she insisted when he leaned his head back in the chair and closed his eyes. "You must have lost a lot of blood."

"Forget it," he stated flatly. Following a brief, but definite pause he added, "We're going home tomorrow."

"But you're in no condition to travel!"

He looked at her with a jaundiced eye. "So what do you want me to do? Break your precious Max's neck, or stick around so that his henchman can finish the job? Either way you'd be rid of me, wouldn't you?" Before she could deny it, he added acidly, "Not a chance, my darling wife."

Later, while lying in the dark, Katherine couldn't get her mind off the attack. Had it been a robbery attempt, or had Max really tried to have Jonathan killed? No, it couldn't be true! Not Max! Yet the day of her wedding he had threatened to kill Jonathan, and the words he had spoken only this evening came back to haunt her over and over again. "If I could find a way . . ."

Jonathan is convinced that I hate him, she thought wretchedly, that it's Max I love. But after all I've said and done, how could I expect him to believe me now if I tell him the truth?

Eighteen

Not even being with her son again could bring Katherine out of the gloom that had settled over her after returning to Baltimore.

The journey from New York had been a nightmare. Time and time again she had been on the brink of confessing her devotion to Jonathan, but each time she had been deterred by the frightening coldness he had adopted toward her following the shooting incident. Soon she discarded the idea. No longer did he pretend to make love to her; now, when he took her, he simply possessed her, and there were moments when she felt like a trapped animal subject to the whims of a cruel master.

Perhaps if earlier in their marriage she had put pride aside and admitted her love, all this heartbreak they were both going through could have been avoided. Now it was too late, and she had no one but herself to blame if her whole life was in shambles.

They spoke little to each other and only of ordinary, everyday things; and it was during one of these brief and impersonal exchanges that Jonathan asked her to decline social engagements for the following week, and to cancel any she might have already accepted.

"We'll be going to the country with my parents next week," he informed her.

"For how long?" she inquired.

"Until Christmas. It's been sort of an established tradition to celebrate Christmas there, just the immediate family. I'm sure Jason will enjoy it."

"I'm sure he will, " she replied. But will I, she asked herself.

Felicity, Ned, and their two young daughters had already taken residence by the time Katherine and Jonathan arrived at the country estate with their son, and although they tried to behave normally in the presence of others, Felicity was quick to notice that her brother didn't seem as entranced with his wife as he had been in the past.

Congratulating herself over the apparent success of her secret campaign against Katherine thus far, under the guise of sisterly affection Felicity took every opportunity to twist the knife in her sister-in-law's wound. It didn't matter how small or insignificant the detail as long as it served to mortify her.

Sending Jonathan's cravat to Crystal had been a stroke of genius. Because of her friend's resentment against Katherine over Maxwell Chapman she had been sure of her cooperation, and the report in the letter Jonathan himself had brought back from New York had confirmed the success of their scheme. However, it was a second missive from Crystal, telling of the angry scene between Jonathan and Max at the Raleighs' ball, that had inspired Felicity with an idea that was sure to rid her of Katherine for good one way or another.

Although Katherine had never been completely deceived by the specious sisterly affection professed by Felicity, she had no inkling as to the extent of her jealousy. Perhaps under ordinary circumstances she would have taken her insidious remarks in stride; however, at the moment her emotional state was much too fragile, and this made her more vulnerable to her sister-in-law's venom. And caught between Felicity's camouflaged hostility and Jonathan's cold, suppressed anger, she was on the brink of despair.

Among the entertainment planned for the season was a hunt organized by a neighbor, and it was on a chilly December morning that Katherine found herself in the midst of an excited group of riders partaking of the morning drink. She had never participated in a hunt before, and the patches of frost on the ground and a leaden sky above did nothing to lighten the apprehension she felt. After Jonathan's early lessons, horseback riding had soon become one of her favorite pastimes; however, chasing after a poor, defenseless animal with the express intent of putting an end to its life in the name of sport was another matter altogether.

Conversation and laughter were all around her as the servants offered trays of drinks to the already mounted riders, and the barking and growling of the dogs in the background added to the din. A shiver went through her limbs when two of the excited hounds started a fight and had to be pulled apart before they could inflict serious damage to each other. Imagining what they could do to the prey, she elevated a prayer that none could be found, or that the poor creature could elude its pursuers. The whole exercise was repugnant to her but, apparently, she was the only one who felt such qualms; everyone else seemed to be having a jolly good time.

"Don't look so grim, my dear sister," Felicity said with a laugh. Pulling at the reins of her black hunter, she maneuvered the powerful animal alongside of Katherine's own gray and gestured toward Jonathan, who was laughing with Rosemary Wills—the pretty daughter of the neighbor who had organized the hunt—as though he had not a care in the world. "Does that bother you so much?"

Katherine's denial was obscured by the strident notes

from a horn stabbing the frosty air. At the signal, the hounds were released from their leashes and the riders, laughing and joking with each other, urged their horses into motion.

Reluctantly, Katherine turned the mare's head around and began to follow. Although the excited animal tried to rebel against the slower pace imposed by its rider, it was quickly subdued with a firm hand.

While lagging behind, Katherine tried to put the distressing thought of death out of her mind and, instead, strove to derive pleasure from the early morning ride across the misty countryside that somehow made her think of England. Little by little she eased her hold on the reins, and the steadily increasing speed of the run, the motion of the mare beneath her and the feel of hooves pounding the frozen ground began to communicate some of the excitement of the beast to its rider.

Even though her veiled hat afforded some protection, the icy wind stung her face and made her eyes water as she flew over fences and hedges. A while later, through her blurred vision and the wintry mist, she could see that the riders had stopped among some stark naked trees, and somewhat apprehensive at what she would find, Katherine forged ahead.

A male figure came to meet her as she rode in.

"Ah, there you are!" Francis said, putting out his hands to help her down. "We were beginning to wonder if you were lost. Jonathan went looking for you." Drawing a silver flask from a pocket in his jacket, he uncapped it and filled the tiny cup with brandy. "Here, my dear, better drink this. It will warm you up a bit."

His breath formed little jets of steam in the cold air as he spoke, Katherine noticed, and lifting her veil she gratefully accepted the cup. While taking small sips of the brandy she looked at the faces around her, searching for the young woman who had been with Jonathan earlier. She couldn't find her.

Having finished the brandy, she returned the cup to her father-in-law, who screwed it back on the flask. "Thank you, Francis."

"Jonathan should be coming back soon," he said, returning the silver flask to his pocket. "I hope he does before the hounds pick up the scent again." Following a brief, odd silence, he added, "Are you enjoying yourself?"

Managing a smile, she replied, "Yes, of course."

"You sit well on the saddle," Francis observed. "Have you done a great deal of riding?"

"Some," she replied with an evasive shrug. Sensing his curiosity over her background, she tried to divert him from the subject. "I've always enjoyed it, and so does Jason. He's been improving steadily now that he's been riding every day. We should get him a pony of his own."

A twinkle of merriment came to Francis's blue eyes. "Mother and I had the same idea," he said with a confidential air. "We think he'll be very surprised come Christmas morning."

This time the smile came easily to Katherine's face. "He'll be overjoyed," she said, and covering his gloved hand with her own, she added warmly, "Thank you, Francis."

"Not at all, my dear. He's been a delight, and I can't tell you how much we enjoyed having him with us while you and Jonathan went to New York. It's uncanny how much like his father he is when Jonathan was at that age. Even his interests are similar."

"Yes, he does have a fondness for ships," Katherine said cautiously, suddenly struck by the uneasy feeling that Francis was leading up to something—she had no idea what it could be. "Jonathan has taken him to the shipyards several times."

"Jonathan has always been partial to the shipyards, but

they're only a part of our interests," Francis said carefully.

Immediately, Katherine picked up the clue to what her father-in-law had in mind. Remembering her conversation with Aunt Penny, she was now sure that Francis wasn't sure as to Jonathan's plans. What he was really asking from her was to influence her husband into staying in Baltimore to take over control of their many business concerns. The way things stood between them, however, the sooner Jonathan sailed away, the better it would be for both of them. And for her a respite from their constant struggle.

She was reprieved from the discussion by the sudden stirring of excitement caused by the hounds again picking up the scent of their prey, as well as the arrival of two riders. Jonathan and Rosemary Wills didn't have time to dismount, because everyone else was remounting to continue the chase. He stared at Katherine for a few seconds after his father had helped her remount and, as though immediately dismissing her from his mind, turned his horse around and went off with the other riders.

"Do try and stay with the rest of us," Francis told her from his saddle. "We don't want you getting lost."

"I will," Katherine assured him, and took off at a gallop flicking her riding crop over the mare's rump.

This time the excitement of the run failed to touch her, and the tears that were trembling in her lashes were not caused by the icy wind whistling past her ears.

It was now clear that Jonathan despised her. His only reason for hanging on to her was their son — and his pride. But what if at any moment he decided to rid himself of her and keep Jason? How could she stop him?

The barking and growling of the hounds became louder, and pulling at the reins Katherine abruptly halted her horse. The gray reared, and for the next few seconds her hands were full just trying to control the animal. Then she was frozen by the cruel spectacle unfolding before her eyes: that of a magnificent antlered deer kicking and swinging his head in a desperate attempt to repel the frenzied hounds circling around it. The dogs would back away from the sharp horns as they swept by, only to close in again and again on the doomed beast to bring it down.

Damp and exhausted the buck continued his struggle for survival, but it soon became apparent that it was flagging. Sensing their victory the dogs went in for the kill, and as the deer was being pulled down, as the majestic head was being inexorably drawn into the mass of snarling beasts, Katherine caught a glimpse of the terror in its eyes.

It was at that moment that Jonathan looked away from the spectacle and saw his wife. She had lifted her veil and her face was totally drained of color, her mouth open as though she was gasping for air. Then, with a sob, she turned her mount around, plunging her heel in the mare's flanks, and the gray took off like a flash.

"Katie, wait!" Jonathan called after her.

But she couldn't hear him. Whipping her horse into a mad race, she was fleeing from the scene.

Jonathan spurred his horse and started after her. His mouth went dry when he saw her approaching a fence. Holding his breath, he watched her sail over the obstacle without a mishap.

As they landed on the other side of the fence, the impact of the hooves on the hard ground sent Katherine's hat flying from her head, and deprived from this protection her hair escaped the pins and fluttered behind her like a burnished banner as she continued her flight.

Jonathan could tell that the gray was tiring as the distance between them grew shorter. Suddenly he felt himself turning cold. Ahead was another fence, and even at a glance he could see that it was too high. "My God, she's going to kill herself!" he muttered under his breath.

His heart ceased beating as the mare's front hooves

cleared the fence, and for the flick of an instant it seemed as though nothing would go wrong. Perhaps when fresh, the horse could have taken the fence, but a whitish foam was already forming on the gray flanks of Katherine's mount.

It happened quickly, almost in the time it takes to blink an eye. One moment horse and rider were sailing through the air; the next, both were tumbling to the ground.

An anguished cry escaped Jonathan's throat, "Katie!"

Having reached the fence, he jumped off his horse and bounded over the obstacle. Katherine was lying prone on the ground, and with eyes only for his wife as he knelt down beside her, he didn't see the two riders who were approaching at a gallop. Gingerly, her turned her over on her back.

A flood of relief went through him when he saw that she was still breathing, and subduing an impulse to hold her tightly, he brushed with his fingers the dirt and strands of hair that clung to her damp cheeks. "Katie, honey, wake up," he called to her.

"How is she?" Francis inquired as he came up on foot. Pale and tense, Alicia was at his side.

"She's unconscious," Jonathan replied. "I'm afraid to move her until we know the extent of the damage. We must get a doctor."

Quickly recovering her presence of mind, Alicia turned to her husband and said, "Francis, I believe one of Leonard's houseguests is a doctor. Why don't you ride back and find out."

Francis started to turn away, but a groan from Katherine made him pause.

"She's coming to," Jonathan said. "Katie, honey, wake up."

When at last Katherine's eyes fluttered open, the first sight they met was her husband's troubled face.

"How do you feel, love?" he asked, his voice anxious.

She seemed a little disoriented for a moment and then replied, "I'm all right." She made to sit up. "Oh, my shoulder hurts!'

"Do you hurt anywhere else?" Jonathan inquired anxiously as he helped her to a sitting position.

Katherine shook her head. "No, I don't think so."

"You took quite a tumble, young lady," Francis admonished, although his expression was one of relief. "Consider yourself lucky it's only your shoulder that is hurt. You could have very easily broken your neck."

"The mare!" Katherine exclaimed, turning her head to look around. Seeing no trace of the horse, she inquired anxiously, "Was she all right? Oh, I hope I didn't hurt her!"

In his concern over his wife, Jonathan had neglected to spare a thought for the horse she had been riding. Now he tried to calm her down. "We'll find her, honey. The fact that she's gone is an indication that she wasn't badly hurt, if at all. Come, love. Let me take you home."

Francis said, "I'll see if I can find that doctor."

"But I'm all right," Katherine protested weakly.

"Hush up," her husband ordered, regarding her tenderly. "I still want him to look you over."

There was a warm feeling inside her when he carefully lifted her in his arms and carried her to his horse. Was he putting on an act for the benefit of his parents, or was he truly concerned, she was asking herself when he mounted behind her and held her in front of him across the saddle. Or perhaps he was reacting so protectively toward her during the accident because it was the only way he knew how.

Regardless of the reason, for the moment, it was enough. She was afraid to hope for more.

Jonathan's manner toward his wife took a different turn after the accident, and this started Katherine believing that perhaps he no longer suspected her of plotting his death.

Felicity, however, was quite peeved at their apparent reconciliation.

"Enjoy it while you can, you slut," she muttered to herself one day, watching from her bedroom window Katherine and Jonathan go out for a walk. A few paces ahead of them was Jason. "You have exactly seven days left."

"For what?" a voice asked behind her.

Startled, Felicity whirled about. "Mother!" she gasped. "I didn't hear you knock."

Waving her hand in an impatient gesture, Alicia looked at her daughter sternly. "Answer my question, Felicity. Who has seven days left?"

"Why, the old year, of course," she replied, rounding her eyes in feigned innocence.

"Don't try to fool me, Felicity. I'm your mother, remember? I know you too well. You're cooking up something, and I demand that you tell me what it is."

When Felicity still refused to answer, Alicia went to the window and looked out. Seeing the three figures walking away from the house, she turned to face her daughter. "It's Katherine, isn't it?"

Felicity pursed her lips and looked sullen.

"Good Lord, Felicity, why do you resent her so much? She hasn't done anything to you, has she?"

"She's a slut!" Felicity exploded. "She was his mistress while Jonathan was still married to Mary Beth! Are you so blind, or don't you even care?"

Alicia expelled an impatient sigh. "For heaven's sakes, what does that matter now?" Her tone became gentler, more persuasive when she added, "Mary Beth is dead, my darling. Nothing can hurt her now. Katherine *is* Jonathan's wife and he loves her, any fool can see that."

"Oh, Mother!" Felicity scoffed.

"It's a fact you must accept, Felicity."

In a voice filled with contempt, Felicity replied, "Never!"

Alicia heaved another sigh. "Honey, don't you see that by going against Katherine you'll only be hurting your own brother?"

"And what about her, mother? She's a tramp, an adventuress, and she's already hurting him even more than any of us ever could. Can't you see it?"

Thoughtfully, Alicia returned her daughter's glance. Perhaps there was some truth in what Felicity was saying. She and Francis had noticed the underlying tension between their son and his wife upon their first arrival, and then following their visit to New York.

During the time Jason had been with them, the boy had unwittingly provided Alicia with answers to some of the questions that had been nagging her since Katherine's arrival. In her own mind she had put together as much of the puzzle as she could figure out, but there were still many blanks left to be filled. She had discreetly drawn out of Jason that the first time he had seen his father had been in New York; and, furthermore, according to the boy, Katherine had traveled a great deal while they had lived in Cornwall. All Jason had said about those trips was that his mother had been working, and, although curious, Alicia had refrained from pressing the boy for more information.

There was much more to Katherine than outward beauty and superficial charm. Francis had been immediately captivated by her, and despite the apparently unfavorable circumstances of her involvement with Jonathan, Alicia found herself inclined in her favor even though she had been unable to penetrate the underlying reserve — more a defensiveness — on Katherine's part.

Alicia loved her children fiercely, but even though she had made herself never to favor one over the other, it was Jonathan, her first born, who held a special place in her heart. He was strong and courageous, a man of the sea, a leader of men; yet she had been a witness to his overwhelming grief over the loss of his first wife. Only after he had brought back Katherine and Jason with him had he begun to resemble again the Jonathan he had once been.

Thus far Alicia had successfully refrained from becoming a meddling mother-in-law; since neither Katherine nor Jonathan had asked for her advice she had stood by, hoping that they would be able to reconcile their marital differences. But if there was nothing she could do to actively help them, the least she could do was to keep Felicity from adding to their troubles.

It took only a few seconds for those thoughts to pass through Alicia's mind, and following the brief silence she said, "Every marriage goes through difficult times now and then, honey, and the worst we can do is interfere when that happens. I want you to leave them alone, Felicity. Do you understand?"

"But, Mother—"

Lifting a hand to forestall her protest, Alicia said firmly, "Now listen to me, Felicity. I don't know what you've been planning, but whatever it is, I want you to call it off right now. I won't have any more of this war of nerves under my roof. I mean it."

Dropping her gaze meekly, Felicity replied, "Very well, Mother."

Alicia studied her daughter for a few seconds and then, apparently convinced of her sincerity, she said with a lenient smile, "Darling, you and Jonathan are the greatest treasures your father and I have. I can't think of anything that would grieve us more than to see our children at odds with each other. Being a mother yourself, you should be able to understand how that would make us feel."

Felicity's lush lashes had captured tremulous tears as she looked up at her mother and said, "And I love you and Daddy too, Mommie."

Her fears now assuaged, the older woman put her arms

397

around her daughter and hugged her tightly. "I'm sure you do darling."

Once the door had closed behind her mother. Felicity dried her eyes and went to stand before the mirror to repair the damage her tears had caused.

"Seven more days, Katherine," she said to her reflection with a malicious, disquieting smile. "That's all you've got left."

The wheels of her plan had already been set in motion; she couldn't stop them even if she had wanted to. And she didn't.

Hopes for a white Christmas materialized the next day, and looking out from the drawing room window Katherine watched as three generations of Greenfield males went out in search of a Christmas tree.

Jason was bounding jubilantly ahead of his elders when she noticed that Jonathan paused and bent down to collect a handful of snow. Realizing his intent when he began shaping it into a ball, she touched the tips of her fingers to her lips to hide a smile and watched him pitch it at Jason's back, where if shattered to smithereens.

Startled by the unexpected attack, Jason turned around to find his father and grandfather roaring with laughter. Immediately entering into the spirit of things, the boy wasted no time in making his own snowball and retaliating. Although he had aimed at his father, the target hit was his grandfather, and in a matter of minutes the three of them were engaged in an exuberant and uproarious snowball fight. From her observation post Katherine could hear the hearty laughter of the men, as well as Jason's shrieks of glee when his projectiles found their target. Who was having the most fun she didn't know: the child or the adults.

One of the qualities she had always enjoyed in Jonathan

was his spirit of fun, and this was a gift that Francis also possessed. It was as if in spite of the importance of their positions and responsibilities, locked inside these Greenfield men was a small mischievous child ready to surface at any moment. Watching the group frolicking in the snow, Katherine found herself smiling.

When at last the battle was over, Jonathan hoisted his son to his shoulders and headed for the woods. Merrily swinging an ax in his hand, Francis followed behind.
ax in his hand, Francis followed behind.

Watching them disappear at the bend of the lane, Katherine reflected on how much her happiness and unhappiness depended on Jonathan and his moods. The last two days, after her accident, the change in his manner had given her something to hope for. Her shoulder was still tender and bruised, but she didn't mind the pain. She would bear that and more if it helped her to reach her husband.

Was she deluding herself again, she wondered. Perhaps. But all the misery she had gone through in the last weeks had taught her one valuable lesson: even if she could no longer hope for his love, if she and Jonathan were to reach any kind of understanding for a tolerable relationship — and they had to, if they were to live together — she would have to put all her cards on the table.

The next seven days would dictate whether she admitted to Jonathan that she loved him and always had, so that they could start a new life with the new year — or if she had to make her escape.

Fervently she prayed for the first of the two options.

The entire family spent a good part of Christmas Eve in the joyful task of trimming the tree the men had brought back from their earlier expedition.

Although Jason found more pleasure in the company of

his male cousins, Katherine was rather amused by his tolerance of Felicity's daughters, Stephanie and Ruthanne. If, as Aunt Penny had told her, Jonathan took after his father in his attitude toward women, it soon became apparent that Jason was a chip carved from the same block.

Pretty—and aware of it—at the age of eight Stephanie was a miniature version of her mother. Ruthanne, on the other hand, was rather tomboyish and as easygoing as her father. Needless to say, her personality, as well as her being older than Jason by only two months, made her his favorite of the two.

To avoid showing any preference among the children, Francis suggested that they draw straws for the privilege of setting the star at the very top of the tree. Ruthanne was disappointed over losing, but she was glad that Jason had won. Although all she did was roll her eyes into her head when her sister went crying to her mother, Jason's smile of triumph faded from his face as he looked after Stephanie.

Francis handed him the star, and Jonathan was about to lift him up to the tree when, after a moment's hesitation, the boy turned away and went to his older cousin.

"Please, don't cry, Stephanie," he said in a troubled voice. "You can have the star. I don't mind."

Immediately, Stephanie ceased weeping. Her eyes were dry, however, when she turned to her cousin and rewarding him with a radiant smile, she accepted the star he proffered. "Oh, thank you, dearest cousin!" she said, and giving him a swift peck on the cheek. "You're such a sweet boy!"

Blushing scarlet at the unexpected kiss, Jason self-consciously backed away and went to sit with his mother to watch Stephanie being lifted by Jonathan so that she could set the star atop the tree.

Katherine had watched how her son had been maneuvered by his cousin with a mixture of emotions: admiration and pride for his thoughtfulness and generosity, amusement over his naivete; and a little irritation, too, for allowing Stephanie to make a fool of him.

He definitely had a great deal to learn about girls!

Not feeling a bit sleepy after preparing for bed, Katherine sat in front of the fire in their bedchamber.

"How's your shoulder?" he asked, and having added a log to the fire, he came to sit beside her. "Does it still hurt?"

"Just a little," she replied.

Cautiously, as though with hesitation, he stretched out one arm on the backrest of the sofa behind her, but didn't touch her until Katherine moved closer to lean against him.

After they had been sitting in silence for a few moments, she said quietly, "It was a very nice Christmas Eve, wasn't it?"

"Yes, it was," he replied, pressing a kiss to her hair. "And I was very proud of Jason."

"So was I," she replied pensively. Suddenly, turning her head, she giggled against his shoulder, "But, Jonathan, you're going to have to talk to that boy. Stephanie made a perfect fool out of him."

"He'll learn," he chuckled wryly. "Just give him time."

Again they fell silent, and sitting close together, his arm around her, her head on his shoulder, they seemed to be listening to the crackling of the flames leaping in the fireplace.

"Mmm, it's so nice to sit here like this," she said after some time had gone by. "It's late and the children will be up early tomorrow morning, but if I go to bed now, I know I won't be able to sleep. I guess I'm excited about Christmas. I can't wait for Jason to see what your parents are giving him." Turning her head a little to look at his face, she asked, "Do you know what it is?"

With a half-smile he nodded, "The pony?"

"Oh, he's going to be so happy! He always loved Christmas, but I do believe this is the happiest one he's ever had."

"And for you?"

She sustained his probing gaze for a few seconds and then, dropping her lashes, she leaned against him and admitted quietly, "Yes, for me too."

His arm tightened slightly around her shoulders and for a moment he said nothing. Then, he started telling her of other Christmases he had spent in this house as a boy; of the treehouse his grandfather had built and where he and Felicity had played with their friends. Having little to contribute because of her lack of family ties, for the first time since their marriage she told him of Jason's escapades in Cornwall, of how he liked climbing trees; and he listened avidly to her narration of their son's first growing years.

Yes, there was hope, she told herself, and moments like this, when he was warm and gentle and loving, erased the pain his past cruelty had caused.

An excited little voice saying, "Mommie, daddy, wake up!" pierced the deep silence.

Startled out of a pleasant dream, Katherine drew away from the warm arms that held her to sit up abruptly. The fire had gone out and the bedchamber was steeped in darkness.

"Jason!" she exclaimed at the ghostly little figure standing beside the bed in the gloom. "Are you all right? What's the matter, darling?"

"It's Christmas morning, mommie! Let's go see our presents!"

"Are you sure it's morning already?" she laughed, drawing her son onto the bed between herself and Jonathan. "It's still awfully dark."

Jonathan, now also awake, lit the lamp on his side of the bed to look at the clock. "He's right," he chuckled. "It's almost six."

"It's also freezing in here, and he didn't even stop to put on his robe and slippers," she observed, pulling the covers over her son. "You're going to catch your death of cold, young man."

"Aw, mommie, it's not so cold!" the boy protested.

"I'll make a fire," Jonathan said, easing out of bed.

Katherine and Jason remained snugly warm in bed while he went to the fireplace, where he piled up some logs on the grate and touched a match to the kindling. An orange glow was spreading slowly through the room when he came back to bed.

"Can we look into the stockings now, daddy?" Jason asked with the impatience of youth.

"We're going to have to wait until everybody else is up and about, son," he replied. To distract the boy, he inquired, "Were you hoping for anything in particular?"

"Yes, daddy," Jason nodded. "A spinning top."

"Well, now," his father said, suppressing a smile. "Have you been good enough to deserve one?"

A little worried frown came to the young forehead as Jason shifted his glance from his father to his mother and asked in a small voice, "Was I, mommie?"

"Mmm." Aware of her son's diffidence, Katherine pretended to think hard for a moment. Then, unable to keep him on edge any longer, she hugged him, laughing, "Of course you were, darling! You've been a very good boy, and both Daddy and I are so proud of you!"

With his confidence restored, Jason smiled at his father, who tickled his belly.

The three of them remained abed for a while longer, talking and playing, until Jason asked again if it was time yet to go look in the stockings. A communicative glance passed between the parents and then, pushing the covers aside, Jonathan said to his son, "All right, I'll see if anyone else is up. You stay here with your mother while I go fetch your robe and slippers."

Hugging their child and with a dreamy expression on her

403

face, Katherine watched him get up, pull on his robe, and leave the room. How wonderful it would be if they could always enjoy the sweet contentment of this warm, peaceful intimacy, she sighed wistfully.

"The girls are up," Jonathan said when he returned moments later, and so anxious was Jason to be on the way downstairs that he let his mother help him with the robe while his father put the slippers on his feet.

"Hurry up, mommie!" he said as Katherine started to get up.

"I'm coming, I'm coming!" Katherine laughed happily. She drew on her robe and quickly ran a brush through her hair before rushing out of the room after her son and her husband.

In the hallway they ran into Ned and the girls, who were as anxious as Jason to open their presents. As soon as they entered the parlor, the children ran, crying with excitement at the sight of the many gifts piled up under the tree.

The stockings that they had hung up on the mantel the night before, were now filled with candy.

Stephanie was pleased with the beautiful china-faced doll, but even more delighted with a pretty locket on a gold chain that she immediately decided to wear. Ruthanne, however seemed more interested in Jason's red spinning top than in her own doll.

Pointing at a large box tied with a red ribbon, Francis said, "Look, Jason, that one is also for you."

"For me?" the boy said, and a little bemused went to the box and pulled at the ribbon. He lifted the lid and peered inside. His bewilderment was apparent when he looked up at his grandfather. "A saddle?"

"Huhumm," Francis nodded, suppressing a smile. "Of course, it won't be much good without a something to put it on, right?"

Slowly, a look of dawning understanding came to Jason's

404

eyes, and with an enormous grin splitting his face he exclaimed, "A pony!" He ran to his grandfather and threw his arms around his neck. Then, drawing back, he asked excitedly, "May I see it, grandpa?"

"Of course, my boy," Francis replied, ruffling his hair with affection. "Go get your coat and we'll take you to the stables." As Jason started to run, he added as an afterthought, "And don't forget your boots!"

After the children had finished opening presents, it was time for the adults to exchange gifts. Except for Felicity, who came in last with her hair already carefully dressed everyone else seemed to have just stumbled out of bed.

In his robe and slippers, gray hair in disarray, Francis made a funny picture leaning on his elegant walking stick. Jonathan's hat also looked so out of place that it made everyone laugh with good humor.

There was a fur muff for Katherine from Jonathan.

"It's lovely, darling, thank you," she smiled at him, putting her hands inside it to lift it to her face. Her eyes registered surprise when her fingers touched a hard object inside. She drew it out. It was a small velvet case. She looked at her husband. Suspecting what she would find inside, for some strange reason she couldn't explain she wished he had refrained from buying her another jewel.

"Well, aren't you going to open it?" Felicity inquired when she hesitated.

Katherine blinked and smiled, "Yes, of course."

It was a bracelet of diamonds and emeralds.

"It'll go beautifully with your necklace, dear," Alicia said, admiring the jewel.

"And with her earrings," Felicity pointed out with acid sweetness. "Katherine, my dear sister, at this rate you'll soon be able to start your own jewelry shop."

Alicia shot a warning glance at her daughter, who returned it with one of perfect innocence. Luckily, Jason returned at that moment and Francis said, "Well, who wants to go to the stables to look at Jason's pony?"

Ruthanne jumped to her feet, saying, "I do!"

"Well, go on, then," Francis smiled. "Go get into some warm clothing."

Rising from the chair, Katherine said, "I think I'll come along, too."

And in the end everyone went, except Felicity and Stephanie.

Nineteen

It was New Year's Eve and, outside, snow was falling.

Jonathan came into her bedchamber dressed in elegant evening clothes, and Katherine turned away from the mirror to say with a smile of pleasure, "Darling, you look positively smashing!"

He looked at her strangely for a moment.

Her smile faded and she returned the look almost fearfully. With undertone of bewilderment in her voice she asked, "Is anything the matter?"

"Should there be?" he returned with raised brows.

Inwardly alarmed, she drew her breath in softly. With the uneasy feeling that he wasn't being truthful, she shook her head and turned slowly to face the mirror. Her hands were rather unsteady as she finished putting on the drop earrings—two large emeralds surrounded by small diamonds— that matched the necklace at her throat and bracelet on her wrist.

The new bracelet had provoked the only bleak moment on Christmas Day, and looking at her reflection now she wondered if those jewels were cursed with bad luck.

After spending such a delightful Christmas, Katherine had found that going back to Baltimore was something she no longer dreaded. In fact, with the change in their relationship, for the first time she began to think of the house as their home.

Back in the city, the busy social activities of the holiday season had made the days go swiftly by, and each one that had ended without a change in her relationship with her husband had encouraged her to believe that, at long last, happiness was close at hand.

Could it be that her own fear that something would go wrong at the eleventh hour was making her see ghosts where none existed? she wondered now as she put the last touches to her toilette.

Perhaps it was all in her mind. Following her riding accident, Jonathan's manner couldn't have been more loving. They were now on their way to the New Year's ball, and when they came back home again she would lay all her cards on the table so that there would be no more secrets between them. They would be able to start all over again—with the new year.

Please don't let anything go wrong now, Katherine prayed as she went to Jason's room to kiss her son good night. She found the boy playing with his spinning top.

"You look so pretty, mommie," Jason said, touching her face.

"Thank you, kind sir," Katherine replied lightly, and hugged the sturdy little body in her arms. Drawing back to look at him she said, "Come, darling. Let's get you into bed."

Jason grimaced. "Aw, mommie, couldn't I stay up a little longer?"

"It's past your bedtime, my love. Besides, with Daddy and I out for the evening, I'll feel much better knowing that you're safely tucked in bed, rather than getting into some kind of mischief." She tweaked his nose.

Holding her face between his hands Jason insisted, "I'll

be good, mommie, I promise. Please let me stay up a little longer. I'm not a babe any more."

Katherine gave a sigh. "Very well," she nodded with reluctance. Wagging a finger at her son, she added, "But only for half an hour, you understand? I'll ask Mrs. Fordham to send you to bed then, so don't try to talk her into letting you stay up any later than that."

Jason grinned, "I won't, mommie."

"Good night, darling."

She gave him another hug before leaving the room, and after she had given her instructions to Mrs. Fordham, Katherine went to find Jonathan.

It had been snowing steadily since morning, but her velvet gown, the soft hooded pelisse, and the blanket covering her knees kept her comfortably warm during the carriage ride to the ball.

Katherine wasn't yet accustomed to leaving her son totally in the hands of servants. When necessity had made her leave him so soon after his birth, Agatha and Jenny had already become her family—and, therefore, Jason's; but even so, it had taken Katherine a long time to reconcile herself to the situation. Since this evening was the first she had gone out without leaving Jason asleep in bed, she was a little worried. Mrs. Fordham was a good, dependable woman who had come highly recommended, but it hadn't taken long for Jason to discover that he could charm his nanny into almost anything he wanted.

Telling herself that she was making too much of her worries, Katherine made an effort to bring her attention to the present. Suddenly realizing that Jonathan had hardly spoken while she had been involved in her own musings, she again felt a prick of apprehension.

What was wrong with her this evening, she mentally reviled herself, refusing to succumb to the impending sense of doom that she couldn't shake.

To break the heavy silence, she asked the first thing that came to her mind. "Darling, when will the architect finish the plans for the new house?"

Since she had always been reluctant to discuss the subject, her own question surprised her.

He half-turned to look at her. "Probably next month. Why?"

"I was just wondering," she shrugged slightly, keeping her tone light. "I don't know the first thing about building houses, but perhaps it wouldn't be a bad idea to let me take a look at them."

"Yes, of course."

There was such lack of enthusiasm in his reply, that it only served to renew her bemusement. Fortunately, they were arriving at the ball.

Alicia and Francis were already there when they made their entrance, and it was her still-handsome father-in-law who claimed Katherine's first dance.

"You seem a little worried," he said while they danced. "Is anything wrong, my dear?"

"It's nothing, really," she tried to shrug it off, and summoning a smile went on to explain, "Jason is usually in bed when Jonathan and I go out in the evenings, but he was still up when we left tonight. I suppose you'll think I'm rather foolish, but I can't help worrying about leaving him alone with the servants."

"You sound like Alicia when the children were young," he said, shaking his head with a wry smile. "Even with a houseful of servants to look after them, she couldn't be out for one evening without worrying about them. Especially over Jonathan. He could get away with murder and the maids wouldn't breathe a word to us. Not that he ever did anything really bad; he just had a propensity to get into a lot of mischief."

"I'm afraid I'm finding the same thing with Jason," she

replied wryly. "He has poor Mrs. Fordham wrapped around his little finger."

"It must be the Greenfield charm," Francis observed, keeping a perfectly straight face although his blue eyes were twinkling with laughter.

"What else?" she laughed, and with a sudden rush of tenderness for the older man she said, "I love you, father."

It was the first time she hadn't addressed him by his given name, and slightly increasing the pressure of his hand holding hers to communicate his own emotion over the step she had taken, Francis smiled into her eyes. "We love you, too, Katie." He was the only other person besides Jonathan who addressed her by that affectionate name. Clearing his throat, he added, "And don't worry so much about Jason, my dear. He's not a babe any more."

"Those were his exact words!" she said, and burst out laughing.

Francis was caught in her laughter, and they went on dancing.

Suddenly she found that her mood had lightened. There was nothing to fear, and she had been a fool to let her imagination run away with her! When the waltz ended and she danced with Jonathan, her eyes were bright, her smile warm and spontaneous as they whirled around the floor.

Feeling as though a great weight had been lifted from her shoulders, for the first time since she had been in Baltimore Katherine allowed her true vibrant personality to come to the surface. She was at her magnificent best as she danced every waltz and joined in the many conversations with great elan. Like a shining star, she dazzled everyone.

Everyone, that is, except Felicity.

Shortly before midnight, during a break in the dance, Katherine went upstairs to freshen up a bit. She was returning to the ballroom moments later when she ran into Felicity, who was coming up the stairs.

411

"Enjoying yourself, Katherine dear?"

A little disturbed by the overly sweet smile accompanying the question, Katherine replied, "Yes, it's a lovely party, don't you think?"

"Of course." There was a trace of malice in Felicity's laughter when she added, "Ah, but the best is yet to come."

Katherine's sensitive features registered something very like fear. She licked her lips and swallowed, but even so her voice came almost in a whisper. "What do you mean?"

Derision lurking behind her indulgent smile, Felicity replied, "Why, dear sister, haven't you heard that your former traveling companion is here in Baltimore? As a matter of fact, he arrived just a few minutes ago. I'm surprised he didn't write to let you know that he was coming."

"We — we don't correspond," Katherine managed to get out.

"Tsk, tsk," Felicity shook her head wryly. "Well, that's men for you. For most of them out of sight means out of mind," she mocked with a slight shrug of her shoulders. "But don't be concerned, dearest Katherine. Now that he's here, I'm sure you'll both find occasion to reminisce over old times."

Katherine had turned quite pale, and satisfied with the effect of her news, Felicity said, "Cheerio, dear sister. I'll see you later." She gathered her voluminous skirts and continued up the stairs with a smile on her face.

A few moments earlier, just before Maxwell Chapman had finally made his appearance, Felicity had begun to worry about the success of her plan. She had feared that perhaps after the scene with Jonathan in New York, Chapman had decided to ignore the letter that — using an imitation of Katherine's handwriting — she herself had sent him. She had even managed to obtain an invitation to the ball for him.

But now that he was at the ball and Jonathan had been

412

alerted to his presence in Baltimore by means of an anonymous letter, her part was done. The rest was up to the protagonists of the drama that was about to unfold. Katherine was frightened; Jonathan was angry; and Maxwell Chapman was hopeful of getting back his former mistress.

Let's see Katherine get out of that, Felicity chuckled to herself. At the top of the stairs she turned and saw that Katherine was still at the same place where she had left her, except that now she was clinging to the handrail as though she was about to faint.

And, indeed, Katherine was on the brink of passing out on the stairs, because the news she had just learned had hit her with the force of a physical blow.

Through her jumbled thoughts came images of Jonathan, bleeding as he had been in New York. And even if she lived to be a thousand, she could never forget the accusation in his eyes. All that horror that she had thought behind them came back to haunt her again.

Why couldn't Max have stayed away from Baltimore when she had made it clear that she didn't love him?

But perhaps she was overreacting, Katherine admonished herself in an effort to regain her presence of mind. Max traveled to many parts of the country in the course of his business, and perhaps his presence in Baltimore had nothing to do with her. But even as she repeated this inwardly, Katherine couldn't make herself believe it.

What could she do? Her first impulse was to turn around, go up the stairs again, and hide there until the ball was over. Except perhaps that wouldn't stop a confrontation between Jonathan and Max. Then she thought that with so many people at the party, it might be possible for her to plead a headache or some other discomfort and ask Jonathan to take her home before he noticed that Max was also there.

At the sound of feminine voices approaching, Katherine made an effort to set her features into some semblance of

413

composure and proceeded slowly down the stairs. When the ladies passed her by, she was able to return their smiles without calling attention to herself.

By the time she reached the foot of the stairs, Katherine had made up her mind to ask Jonathan to take her home, and elevating a mental prayer that Max wouldn't see her, she stepped into the ballroom.

He was there, standing with a group of people near the entrance, and immediately caught sight of her. She looked at him as though he was a stranger, and then she looked away quickly—although not quickly enough to miss the flicker of surprise that crossed his eyes—and continued on her way. Somewhere in that crowd was Jonathan, and she had to find him. Anxiously she searched the faces of those around her.

"Katherine," a familiar voice said behind her.

Abruptly, she swung around to face him. "Please, go away before Jonathan sees us, Max," she said, flicking a wary glance about her.

A crease formed between his brows as he looked down at her and said, "You're frightened."

Her face was flushed, her voice eager when again she pleaded, "Please, Max!"

Looking genuinely annoyed, Max glowered for a few seconds that for Katherine seemed to last a lifetime. "Very well," he nodded at last. "Where can we meet?"

"We can't!" she gasped, distressfully twisting her hands together.

Her dismay failed to move him. "We must!" he insisted firmly. "I'm not leaving until we talk."

All she could think of at the moment was to get away, and to curtail their conversation inquired, "Where can I reach you?"

"At the Lord Baltimore Hotel."

"I'll send for you when I can," she said hurriedly. "But

please don't try to reach me until then."

She turned away and was swallowed by the crowd.

A few moments later she caught a glimpse of Alicia and Francis and headed in their direction.

"There you are, my dear," Alicia said taking her hand. "It's almost midnight. Where's Jonathan?"

"I don't know," Katherine replied. "I went upstairs for a moment and haven't been able to find him."

Alicia looked at her with some concern. "Are you feeling well, Katherine? You look rather pale."

"Well, I do have a headache," Katherine admitted with apparent reluctance. "I was hoping Jonathan would take me home. If I could ever find him in this crowd, that is."

"I'm sure he's also looking for you," Alicia assured her. "Why don't you stay with us until he comes."

A few minutes later the music ceased, and Jonathan arrived at her side as the countdown began.

9—8—7—6—5—4—3—2—1—

The crowd cheered, "HAPPY NEW YEAR!"

All the people around them were laughing and kissing and hugging each other with considerable glee. Katherine put her arms around her husband, and looking up into his eyes said, "Happy New Year, darling."

She offered her lips for his kiss, and he brushed them lightly with his own without returning her embrace.

Katherine didn't have time to dwell on this because Francis folded her into an exuberant embrace and gave her a resounding kiss, saying, "Happy New Year, Katie!" and then Alicia followed suit.

The orchestra began playing, and all through the ballroom voices rose in song:

> Should auld acquaintance be forgot
> and never brought to min'?
> Should auld acquaintance be forgot

And auld lang syne?
For auld lang syne, my dear,
For auld lang syne
We'll take a cup of kindness yet,
For auld lang syne . . .

As she half-heartedly joined in the singing of the old familiar lines, Katherine's gaze was drawn to a pair of gray eyes across the room. Fear flashed in her eyes and she looked away quickly, but not before Jonathan noticed and caught a glimpse of his enemy as he melted away in the excited crowd.

Katherine asked him then to take her home, and they said their goodbyes to his parents.

Watching them make their way to the exit, Felicity smiled.

"Happy New Year, darling," Ned said, putting his arms around her.

"Yes, darling," she purred. "Happy New Year indeed!"

The silence inside the carriage was fraught with tension, and with nerves painfully on edge Katherine asked herself if—earlier in the evening—Jonathan had already been aware of Max's presence in Baltimore. If that was true, then it was possible that his suspicions had been renewed. She couldn't find any other explanation for such a swift change in his manner.

For almost a week she had run over and over through her mind the words she had wanted to say to Jonathan when confessing that she had never stopped loving him; but now, in a desperate attempt to salvage their future, all she could say while reaching for his hand was, "I love you, Jonathan."

Drawing his hand away, he looked out the window as though he hadn't heard.

Katherine didn't know which was more difficult for her to

bear: Jonathan's hot temper, or the icy indifference behind which he had retreated.

Fearful of making things worse, three days into the new year she still hadn't summoned enough courage to communicate with Max. It was on the fourth when she came to the painful conclusion that as long as he remained in Baltimore, there was always danger for the tense situation to explode in their faces. She had to send Max away, and she knew that a simple letter wouldn't accomplish her purpose. She would have to meet him in person.

The next obstacle was to find a suitable place to do so. Since she couldn't ask him into her house, she gave considerable thought to adopting a disguise to visit his rooms at the hotel, but this also presented too many problems. When she had sold the ring, Jonathan had found out too quickly, which could only have meant that someone had been watching her. And if that was the case, she now had to find a way of eluding her pursuer.

When the solution finally came to her, even in her present state of mind Katherine had to smile, because it reminded her so much of Adam's elaborate — and effective — schemes.

It took only a few minutes to compose a brief message that a carriage would be waiting later that afternoon at a certain time and place. She didn't sign her name, just her initial.

She sealed the note, addressed the envelope, and prepared to go out.

Katherine had her coachman drop her off not far from the hotel, and finding a boy willing to deliver a message in exchange of a coin wasn't a difficult task. She then went to a millinery shop she had never patronized before, and purchased a hat with a heavy veil to conceal her features.

She slipped out of the shop through the back door, and once she was reasonably confident that no one had followed her or recognized her, Katherine hailed an enclosed cab.

Disguising her voice, she directed the driver to the address she had given Max and told him that he was to wait for another passenger. He then was to drive around the city until further instructions were given.

If the cabbie suspected an illicit assignation between a married lady and her lover, the expression on his face didn't betray his thoughts.

The cab reached the designated corner much earlier than the appointed time, but this was also according to Katherine's plan. The cabbie wouldn't be able to recognize her, but neither did she want the man to get a good look at Max. Even so, she didn't have long to wait.

The cabbie was faithful to his instructions, and as soon as Max climbed aboard, the carriage set into motion.

Katherine drew the curtains and lifted her veil to look at him. "Max," she said quietly, choked with emotion by the naked adoration she found in his eyes.

"My darling," Max said huskily, taking her gloved hands in his and pressing fervent kisses on their backs. "I was beginning to fear this moment would never come!"

He drew her into his embrace and made to kiss her, but wedging her hands between them she reproached him softly. "You should never have come to Baltimore, Max. Why did you?"

"But you sent for me!" he exclaimed, regarding her with an expression of bemusement on his elegant features. "You said in your letter that—"

"What letter?" she cut him off. "I never sent you any letter."

"I have it right here," he said, reaching into his pocket. "I've been carrying it with me, read it so many times that I know it by heart."

Reaching for the envelope he had taken out of his pocket, she said, "Let me see that."

Her eyes widened in surprise as they scanned the lines

written in a hand that very much resembled her own. The wording was a impassioned plea regretting her decision to marry Jonathan, and begging Max to come and take her away with him.

Katherine finished reading the letter, and making an effort to restrain her indignation she folded it, and returned it to the envelope. "I'm sorry, Max," she said, raising her eyes at him while slipping the envelope into her reticule. "I never wrote that letter."

Seeing his hopes so cruelly dashed, Max gazed back at her dazedly for a few seconds. "Then, who?" he asked at last.

"I don't know, Max," she replied, and then a look of dawning intuition came to her eyes. "Unless . . . unless it was Felicity."

Max gazed at her heavily. "Who is she?"

"My sister-in-law," Katherine shrugged unhappily. "I was aware that she resented me, but until this very moment I never suspected how much she hates me." Following a brief silence, she reached for his hands and added, "I'm sorry she used you, Max."

For the next few seconds, the only sound was the clop-clop of the horses' hooves as they fell on the snow-covered street.

"You must leave Baltimore immediately, Max," she said at last. "Each moment you spend here makes it more difficult for me. You know how Jonathan feels about you."

"But he has you," he said bitterly. "I have nothing."

Deeply moved by his sadness, she said softly. "He's convinced that you and I were lovers, Max."

"I don't even have that to remember," he said, holding her beloved face between his hands. "I never knew the sweetness of your love, of holding you in my arms and making you mine! I've never loved another woman the way I love you, Katherine, and never will. I keep telling myself that if Jonathan hadn't interfered you'd be my wife now, not his. I know you're not happy with him, that you fear him. Leave him, darling! If you come away with me now he'll have to divorce you, and then we can be married."

Shutting her eyes tightly to the plea in his gray eyes, she shook her head and said raggedly, "I—I can't!"

Kisses rained upon her face as Max continued pleading with her, "Say you'll come away with me, darling. Say it."

Her soul, tormented by Jonathan, reached out for the balm of Max's love, and she offered no resistance to his lips as they traced her face, to his hands as they caressed her. "Oh, Max!" she breathed raggedly, throwing her arms around his neck and offering her lips, which he claimed in long, hungry kisses.

But suddenly it was all wrong. Even though she willed herself to respond, she couldn't feel anything. Max's kisses no longer thrilled her; his caresses left her cold.

Easing her hold on him, Katherine drew back. "I'm sorry, Max. I can't."

His urgent hands seized her by the shoulders. "Darling, please listen . . ."

"No, Max," she shook her head listlessly. "I don't love you. I—I'm sorry."

Max turned visibly pale, and unable to witness his distress, Katherine dropped her eyes. "I never meant to hurt you," she said softly. "I do care for you, but I don't love you." Her gaze rose to meet his as she added, "I shouldn't have let this happen. I know that it was cruel of me, but I was hurting, Max, still am, and I tried to reach out for your love to stop the pain. Can you ever forgive me?"

"Forgive you!" He gave a short bark of a laugh. His voice became a hoarse whisper, and with eyes fastened on hers with terrible intensity, he went on with passionate conviction, "I would go down on my knees and beg, I would cheat, steal, even kill, do anything you want if you'd only let me love you!"

420

Katherine's sharp intake of breath was accompanied by an expression of horrified disbelief. "It was you!" she said in a constricted voice. "It was really you who tried to kill Jonathan!"

Max gazed back at her defensively.

Dropping her face into her hands, she wept bitterly and with remorse, "Oh, Max, what have I done to you?"

Taking her hands away from her face, Max crooked a finger under her chin to make her look at him. "I've lost you, haven't I?" he asked, not really expecting an answer from her. He shook his head and smiled bleakly. "No, not even that, because I never had you."

Grim-faced, he dropped his hand and shrugged resignedly. When he spoke again, he did so in a monotonous tone. "Just remember that I love you, Katherine, and always will. If you ever need me, all you have to do is call."

He called to the driver to stop. Tenderly he touched his lips to hers before he opened the door; and then, as quiet as a whisper, he slipped out of the carriage and from her life.

Her secret encounter with Max left Katherine deeply shaken with remorse. It was she, with her ambivalence who had driven Max to such extremes. Regardless of her lack of malice, she should have known that a purposeful man such as he, who had willfully detached himself from love for most of his life, would be unable to cope with defeat when caught in the grip of such a powerful emotion.

It was in this state of mind that two days later, when she was answering her correspondence, her new butler, Preston, presented a calling card from a Mr. Stephen Crossland, who was requesting to be received.

The name was totally unfamiliar to her, but upon closer examination of the card she saw the message written on the reverse side of it. *A friend of Ronald Lambert, from London,* it read.

"Please show the gentleman to the drawing room and offer him some refreshment, Preston," she told the butler. "I'll be right down."

She took a moment to pinch her pale cheeks and smooth her hair before she went down to meet her visitor. Expectantly, she went into the drawing room and there, standing before the fireplace warming his hands, was a tall man elegantly dressed. He turned to face her at her entrance, and a flicker of surprise crossed his eyes before he smiled pleasantly.

"Mr. Crossland," she offered her hand with her most welcoming smile. "How nice of you to come."

"Mrs. Greenfield." The man kissed her hand with a courtly bow. "A pleasure to make your acquaintance, madam."

Katherine invited him to be seated and immediately said, "Please forgive my impatience, Mr. Crossland, but tell me, how is Ronald? It's been a long time since I've had news of him." Realizing that Stephen Crossland was staring at her in a very peculiar manner, she covered her mouth with her hand. "Oh, no! Something has happened to him, hasn't it?"

Crossland blinked and cleared his throat. "Please, don't be alarmed, Mrs. Greenfield. Ronald is in good health, I assure you. Forgive me, but it's just that meeting you in person has been quite a revelation to me."

"I'm afraid I don't understand what you mean, Mr. Crossland."

He rose from his seat and went to collect the large package that he had leaned against the wall, which until then had escaped her attention. Coming toward her, he said, "When you see this, you'll understand."

He placed the parcel next to her on the sofa, and at her quizzical expression explained, "It's a gift from Ronald, madam. When he learned that I was traveling this way, he asked me to deliver it into your hands."

Impatiently, Katherine tore at the wrapper and once the contents were revealed, her breath caught in her throat. She found herself staring into her own eyes as though in a mirror.

In the portrait, she stood with her head partly turned, her rich auburn hair cascading over one shoulder, her lips parted in a teasing half-smile. But it was the vibrant expression in the emerald eyes, long-lashed and mysterious, that lent the canvas a life of its own. Every stroke of the brush was an expression of love, the way Ronald saw her—and remembered her.

The revelation of Ronald's love left her unable to move or even speak. All she could do for the next few minutes was to sit there staring at the painting.

"You didn't know, did you?" Stephen asked quietly.

Slowly, Katherine shook her head.

"To answer your earlier question, Mrs. Greenfield, Ronald is doing very well. As you probably already know, that exhibit he held last year has made him the most sought-after artist in England today."

"Is he happy?"

"Happy?" Crossland repeated, gazing with fascination into emerald pools now misted with tears. "I believe he is. You mustn't worry about him, Mrs. Greenfield."

"Ronald is very dear to me, Mr. Crossland."

"And he's aware of it, madam," the man nodded. "I'm sure that is why he wanted you to have this now, so that you would know what loving you had done for him."

Dropping her gaze to her hands, Katherine remained silent.

"Ronald and I've been friends for a long time, Mrs. Greenfield, and you probably know as well as I that he had always been an excellent artist—technically speaking, that

423

is. He was a master at reproducing other artists, however, something very vital was missing from his original work. I don't know how to describe it — soul, spirit, sensitivity, feeling. But no matter what name one might give to it, there was no question that it was missing."

Katherine listened attentively while Crossland went on. "The reason for my surprise when I first saw you was that having seen the painting I was quite astonished, even though I'm very familiar with Ronald's work. I couldn't believe how perfectly he had captured you on canvas without having you there to pose for him. But I guess that, in a way, you did pose for him, because regardless of the distance that exists between you, you've never really been away from him at all. It's difficult, next to impossible, for anyone to express an emotion one has never experienced. And, apparently, those emotions you have inspired in his heart are what have given him that special touch that he was missing. So, in a word, what you have given Ronald is the most precious gift anyone could have given him: his art."

"I shall leave you now, madam," he said, and taking her limp hand in his bent from the waist to kiss it reverently. "It's been a privilege, Mrs. Greenfield."

He straightened up and walked away. It wasn't until he was almost at the door that Katherine recovered her voice and called after him, "Mr. Crossland?"

He turned to face her and waited.

"Thank you," she said, coming to him. "When you see Ronald again, please give him my love."

"I shall, madam."

Once her visitor had departed, Katherine returned to the drawing room to look at the painting.

"Dear, dearest Ronald!" she said, moved to tears by his gift of love across the sea. Perhaps it was just a coincidence that Ronald's message had arrived at a time when she needed it most, when she was grieving and remorseful for the pain she had inflicted on one man who had loved her. And then she realized that regardless of what Mr. Crossland had said to her, she had little to do with Ronald's success.

It was he who had the talent, and as to the missing ingredient — what the man had called sensitivity — that, too, had existed in Ronald's heart and soul all along. No one had put it there. It was a natural part of him just as was the color of his eyes. To believe otherwise would be terribly flattering to her vanity, but quite false. And, therefore, by the same token, it would also be a matter of vanity to make herself responsible for Max's actions.

Feeling cleansed of the remorse that had tormented her ever since her meeting with Chapman, she lovingly touched the painting and whispered, "Thank you, dearest Ronald."

Having finally regained her composure, Katherine summoned a servant and ordered the painting now hanging on the wall over the mantel to be removed, and stayed to see it replaced by Ronald's portrait.

Jonathan was spending more time than ever away from home, and she had seen little of him since the New Year's ball. Since her evenings had been spent alone since then, she was rather surprised when she walked into the drawing room before dinner and found him there.

"Jonathan!" she said with a hopeful note in her voice. "I didn't know you were home."

He didn't turn to face her immediately, but remained as he was, standing on feet planted firmly apart before the fireplace, with a glass of brandy in his hand while he looked up at the portrait.

He tossed his drink down in one gulp, and when he finally swung about to face her, his expression was so terribly grim that it made her heart give a tremendous bound and she shrank back a little. "When did you pose for this?" he asked in a hoarse whisper.

He had given her such a fright, that when her lips shaped

425

an answer no sound came out. Nervously, she licked her lips and swallowed to clear her throat in order to reply, "I — I never did."

"I see." His eyes were dark and brooding as they moved over her face, and then he turned to look at the portrait again.

"Jonathan!" Her hands flew to her mouth to cover her horrified gasp.

He had crushed the empty glass in his hand, and he didn't even seem to feel the pain.

Twenty

"Brr, it's freezing!" Alicia said, shivering, as she stepped out on the street. "I'm afraid we picked the worst day to goshopping for Ruthanne's birthday present. It was good of you to come with me, Katherine."

"I'm glad you asked me!" the younger woman replied affecting a lighthearted tone. "I've hardly been out of the house in the last couple of weeks, and I needed this outing. Besides, you know how fond Jason has become of little Ruthanne, even if she's only a girl," she finished with a laugh.

"Let's see how long that will last!" Alicia said, catching her laughter. "Give him a few more years, and girls will be all he'll think about. Well, mostly, anyway. Say, what would you say to a nice hot cup of tea? We could go into that shop and get warm."

Katherine glanced in the direction her mother-in-law had pointed and noticed that a new tea shop had opened at the locale formerly operated as a bakery. "Sounds like a marvelous idea," she said.

A little bell tinkled when the two women entered the tea shop. The small area, which contained a dozen or so tables covered with crisp white linen, was pervaded with a delicious aroma of bread baking somewhere on the premises, as well as that of cinnamon and other spices.

Alicia and Katherine selected a small table by the window from where they could watch the people going by, and a few moments later a woman came to take their order.

"Good afternoon, ladies," she said in a pleasant voice. "What would you like? A fresh batch of scones will be ready in a few minutes."

After ordering tea and scones Alicia turned her attention back to her young companion and discovered that Katherine had suddenly turned quite pale.

"What's the matter?" she inquired with visible concern. "My dear, are you unwell?"

Disbelief had dilated Katherine's pupils when she had recognized the waitress as the same woman with whom she had seen Jonathan at the Philadelphia inn. Forcing herself to look at her mother-in-law, she said in a rather unsteady voice, "I'm sorry. I—I didn't hear what you said."

"You look like you've just seen a ghost!" Alicia said. "Are you all right?"

I only wish it were a ghost, Katherine thought miserably. "I'm feeling a bit faint," she admitted truthfully.

"Oh, dear!" Alicia crooned with sympathy, reaching across the table to pat Katherine's hand. "You know, I didn't want to mention it when we met earlier this afternoon, but I thought you looked rather . . . well, sort of depressed."

Tipping her hand, Katherine replied, "I may be coming down with a chill."

"Or perhaps with a little companion for Jason?" Alicia suggested with a lenient smile.

Glancing swiftly upwards, Katherine denied, "No!"

The vehemence of her denial made Alicia's smile falter, and she stared back at her daughter-in-law with a puzzled expression on her face.

"I'm sorry," Katherine said, and with a deprecating shrug of her shoulders tried to smooth out her blunder. "I didn't mean to startle you, but you took me quite by surprise," she said, her tone returning to a normal conversational level as she began to remove her gloves. "I'm not with child. Not yet, anyway."

Alicia gazed at her probingly for a few seconds before she dared to inquire, "Would it displease you if you were?"

"Displease me?" Katherine repeated, taking her time to finish removing her gloves so as to gauge the degree of her mother-in-law's interest. "I don't know," she answered at last. "At this very moment, I would prefer to wait a little longer to have another child. There's plenty of time."

Alicia had often wondered who had been the instigator of the separate-bedrooms policy in Katherine's household. The frailty of Mary Beth's health had been the cause of such sleeping arrangements for the young couple during Jonathan's first marriage, and his long and frequent absences had helped to avoid the tension that normally occurs when a young man finds himself barred from his wife's bed. This time, however, Jonathan had remained in Baltimore, and even though Katherine seemed to enjoy the best of health the same arrangement still prevailed. Was Katherine reluctant to share her bed with her husband, Alicia had asked herself many a time. Could that perhaps be the reason for the tension that she could sense between them?

She remembered how concerned she had been in those first days of their stay at the country estate during the holidays. Even though they had made a valiant effort to conceal their difficulties, she had been aware that their apparent harmony was just a front. Katherine's riding accident had seemed to have brought them closer together, but from what little Alicia had seen of Katherine and Jonathan in the new year, it was obvious that the situation had again taken a turn for the worse. In the last few days Jonathan had been moody, and Katherine had lost her sparkle. Actually, the reason behind Alicia's invitation to go shopping had been to provide Jonathan's wife with an opportunity to confide her troubles if she felt so inclined.

Although their relationship had been a harmonious one until then, Alicia found Katherine's reserve like a wall she found difficult to penetrate; even more so because she hated to appear as a meddlesome mother-in-law.

"I imagine it must have been difficult for you when Jason was born," she opened with hesitation, "but it doesn't have to be the same next time."

"It was a normal birth," Katherine replied, sensing the questions Alicia wanted to ask and purposely evading the subject.

Concealing a sigh, Alicia had to postpone further queries until the tea was served and the woman went away again. "Giving birth the second time is usually easier than the first, my dear," she said then. "You shouldn't be afraid."

Although Katherine had been careful not to look at the woman serving the table, she was very distressed by her presence. If not for Alicia, she would have walked out of the shop. Stirring her tea, she replied without thinking, "I'm not afraid."

"Is Jonathan afraid?"

Katherine's eyes registered surprise for a second and then understanding. Having already lost a wife in childbirth, was Jonathan afraid to risk her life now for the sake of another child? Alicia couldn't know that the situation was entirely different, that where he had deeply loved Mary Beth, she herself meant next to nothing to him.

Stirring her cup thoughtfully so as to avoid looking at her mother-in-law, she replied, "I don't think so."

There was a long silence after which Alicia said, "Perhaps I shouldn't speak of this to you. I'm aware that it can't be easy to hear, but I believe you should know because what happened in the past may affect your future."

Katherine set down the spoon and prepared to listen.

"I don't know how much Jon has told you about his first marriage," Alicia began rather diffidently. "Perhaps nothing. He hasn't spoken of Mary Beth even to us after she passed away."

She paused briefly, and when Katherine remained silent, continued. "Francis and I were away when he came home after a long voyage. Mary Beth was alone in the house and apparently neglected to tell him that the doctor had warned her that another miscarriage would be dangerous—even fatal. At any rate, even after he had sailed away she kept her condition a secret until she could no longer hide it. She wanted a child so desperately!"

And he was with me in London during that time, Katherine reflected glumly.

"Francis and I had been very close to her parents, but her death left them so devastated that they broke off the friendship. She was their only child, and I'm afraid that, in their grief, they blamed Jon for her death."

After what she had just heard, Katherine reflected that there was a good chance remorse played an important role in Jonathan's veneration for the memory of his late

431

wife. Had he not been unfaithful while Mary Beth had knowingly risked her life to give him the child he so desired? Still, that didn't help her own situation.

To ease Alicia's mind, she said gently, "I understand what you're trying to tell me, Alicia, but I believe he's over that now. Jonathan has already mentioned that we might have other children. In fact, the new house we're planning is large enough for several of them." In a lighter tone she added, "Who knows? Maybe half a dozen!"

Taking her cue Alicia laughed, "Now, don't get carried away, my dear!"

Katherine was clever, Alicia reflected rather ruefully. Once again she had side-stepped the subject with ease. She still felt the need to make one more effort, however, and becoming serious said, "Just remember, my dear, that if you ever need someone to talk to, I'll be glad to listen."

Deeply moved by the offer she knew had been made with the best of intentions, Katherine regarded Alicia in silence for a few seconds. She wished she could confide her troubles to her mother-in-law, but what could she tell her without revealing that she had been sold to a rake by her aunt? That she was a prize Jonathan had once won in a card game? And if that wasn't enough, what would be her reaction if she learned that her son's wife was a criminal wanted by the police in every country in Europe? Shock? Horror? Disgust? Probably all of them.

And so, unable to take advantage of Alicia's generosity, with a faint smile Katherine said, "Thank you, Alicia."

The gaiety Katherine had affected was nothing but an act for Alicia's benefit. Whether or not Jonathan felt remorse over Mary Beth's demise didn't alter the fact that he had no love for his current wife.

After her visit to the tea shop with Alicia, Katherine made inquiries that uncovered not only that Theresa Martin—the woman who had served them—was the proprietress, but also that it had been Jonathan who had financed the business venture.

Any vestiges of hope were quickly wiped away by this discovery, and all she had left was a bleakness of spirit. She had confessed her love, and Jonathan had thrown it back at her face.

Each day that went by left her more weary of keeping up her guard, of the pretense she had to maintain in front of others, and the bleak prospect of years of more of the same that lay ahead made her sick at heart, depressed, and gloomy.

How could she continue to endure the torture when there was nothing left to hope for? In her mind she had planned her escape a thousand times, yet still she hesitated. What was she going to do about Jason? How could she, in good conscience, take him away from the father he had come to adore? From the loving grandparents, from the comfort, the security of being a Greenfield? What could she offer him besides her love? Would it be enough to compensate him for robbing him of his birthright?

She was perfectly aware that the negative answers to all those questions left her only one alternative; but how could she leave without her son?

Did she love her child enough to give him up?

"Mommie, isn't Daddy going to take us sailing again?" Jason inquired a few days later.

"I'm sure he will, my love," Katherine replied. "As

soon as the weather is nice again. It's awfully cold now."

"Because it's winter," Jason said in the manner of explanation. He had just learned about the seasons. "The teacher said that the snow melts in spring and everything turns green."

"That's right, darling. All the trees will have new leaves, and there'll be lots of pretty flowers."

"I think I like spring better," Jason reflected.

"So do I," Katherine nodded with a half-smile. "Probably everybody loves spring."

"Mrs. Martin likes winter best. She says it's good for business because people come into her shop to get warm and drink tea and chocolate."

"Mrs. Martin?" Katherine gave her son a look of astonishment. Then, taking pains to conceal her surprise, she strove to make her tone sound casual. "When did you meet her?"

"A long time ago," Jason shrugged, turning his attention to spinning his top. "Daddy takes me to her shop sometimes when we go out, and she gives me hot chocolate and cakes. She says I have to eat a lot because I'm a growing boy." He looked up at her and asked, "Is that true, Mommie?"

"Not if you don't want to," Katherine said with a trace of a snap. When Jason regarded her quizzically, she made an effort to restrain her indignation. "You shouldn't eat too many sweets when you go out, darling," she explained in a conversational tone of voice. "They can make your belly ache and, besides, they spoil your appetite for a good dinner, which is what you really need."

"My belly doesn't ache," Jason argued, frowning.

Katherine concealed a sigh. There was no point in arguing with her son. It was the father who had to be set straight, and she would see to it. Immediately.

434

Impatiently she waited for Jonathan to come home, knowing that it would be late, if at all. She rarely saw him these days. Apparently his new mistress demanded a good deal of his time.

As she paced the floor, Katherine wondered what was worse, knowing with whom Jonathan was betraying her, or being in the dark as to the other woman's identity. Either way, she couldn't bear the thought of him making love to someone else.

Once she had admitted her love, he had given up the pretense that until then he had maintained in order to win her. He felt no love for her and never had. Having already bent her to his will, she no longer presented a challenge. He had what he wanted: his son and her defeat.

It was then that Katherine experienced a return of her fear that if Jonathan decided to keep Jason and rid himself of her, there was nothing she could do. The Greenfields were powerful, and she would have no one to whom she could appeal her case.

Perhaps he had already taken the first step . . .

All the doubts she had entertained until then suddenly evaporated from her mind. She would make her escape, and she would take Jason with her.

Money was no object. Experience had taught her that she couldn't sell her jewelry without attracting attention; therefore, anticipating this very instance, during her visit to New York she had brought back with her more than sufficient funds to buy her way to freedom.

Once her mind was made up, Katherine turned her attention to the mode of escape. The first step was to get to New York and seek Adam's help; however, the Greenfield's maritime involvement would make it impossible for her to buy passage without Jonathan's knowledge. Even if she adopted a disguise and a different

435

name, she didn't doubt for a minute that Jason would be immediately recognized.

The roads were the only way left to her, but the inclement February weather would make them difficult — even dangerous — to travel. Alone, these conditions wouldn't have given her pause, but although there were many inns along the road, anything could happen; were they to be stranded in a blizzard, they could very well freeze to death before help could reach them. Not even her desperation would make Katherine expose Jason to such danger.

She would start making inquiries as to the possibility of finding a carriage to take them only if there was a break in the weather.

At a snail's pace days passed one after another without any improvement in the weather, and Katherine was almost at the end of her rope when Jonathan told her that he was planning a trip to Portsmouth — a city in New Hampshire — to inspect a shipyard whose owner was offering it for sale.

Much to her surprise he asked, "Would you like to come with me, Katie?"

Katherine was barely able to conceal her excitement. By now she had learned enough of American geography to know that New Hampshire was to the north and, therefore, probably more accessible to New York than Baltimore.

"Would Jason go with us?" she inquired casually, striving not to show how much depended on his answer.

"If you think he can make the voyage," Jonathan answered, avoiding to look at her. "There are some heavy seas at this time of the year."

"I'm sure he will be all right," she said, slowly releasing

her breath which, until that moment, she hadn't realized she had been holding. "When shall we leave?"

There was a long silence before Jonathan replied, "In a couple of days. Can you be ready by then?"

"Of course."

"Make sure you pack enough warm clothing," Jonathan said slowly. "We'll be sailing from here to Boston, where I have some business to do before going on to Portsmouth."

Because Max had often traveled between the two cities, she was aware that a railroad service existed between Boston and New York. And that's when Katherine decided that once they reached Boston, she and Jonathan wouldn't be traveling in the same direction.

* * *

Jason was overjoyed at the news of the voyage, but Katherine was surprised to find that now, when everything seemed to be favorable to her plans, she wasn't as happy about it as she had expected she would be. Although there was nothing else she could do, the thought of leaving Jonathan was not one that she could relish; in fact, it took a great deal of effort on her part to show enthusiasm over the proposed trip.

She made a point of taking Jason to visit his grandparents before their departure, and there were tears in her eyes when she said goodbye to Alicia and Francis.

For fear of endangering her escape with Jason, Katherine was reluctant to take along both Mrs. Fordham and Louise, but a refusal to bring the servants could make Jonathan suspect her intentions.

As it turned out it was the women, and not Jason, who suffered from the heavy seas during the voyage. Mrs.

Fordham became ill from the moment the ship set sail; Louise was also affected by the rolling motion of the ship, and with the servants out of commission, it was left to Jonathan to care for his sick wife. Katherine couldn't keep down any of the nourishment he forced into her, and she thought she would surely die before reaching Boston. She was still alive, however weak, when the ship finally sailed into the Bay of Massachusetts.

"I'll take Jason with me so that you can get some proper rest," Jonathan told her once they had been installed in an elegant hotel suite. "We won't be sailing for Portsmouth until next Friday."

Katherine couldn't hold back a groan at the thought of boarding another ship again.

"Would you prefer to stay here in Boston?" he inquired at her dismay. "I could go to Portsmouth alone and meet you back here next week."

Refusing to believe that he was willing to leave her behind, she stole a cautious side glance at him. "Will you be taking Jason with you?"

"If you want me to."

She stared up at him, wondering if she could believe him, and made a helpless little gesture with her hand to say, "I suppose we can decide later."

There had to be a catch somewhere, Katherine thought when she was alone. But the first thing she had to do was to get well quickly so that she and Jason could take the train to New York as soon as possible. Two days of rest and nourishment worked wonders on her excellent constitution, and as soon as she was on her feet again, she went to the train station to learn of the scheduled times of departure for New York. Once they got to New York, Adam would hide them where Jonathan couldn't find them.

This was as far as Katherine could plan at the moment.

Going back to England held little attraction for her, and she had already decided to wait a little longer—until she could think more clearly—to make up her mind as to where they would go next.

On Wednesday, before meeting Jonathan for lunch, she purchased tickets for the Friday morning train.

The thought of the railroad tickets she was carrying in her reticule kept Katherine's nerves on edge during the midday meal she shared with her husband and son. Each time Jonathan looked at her, she was afraid he would be able to read in her eyes the guilt she felt over her deception.

"Why don't you leave Jason with me this afternoon?" she said when lunch was over. Mrs. Fordham had not yet recovered from her ordeal at sea, and Louise spent most of her time caring for the older woman. When he hesitated, she added, "I'm well enough to take care of him now, and I'm sure it'll be much easier for you to conduct your business without him to worry about. In fact, I've thought it over and decided to follow your suggestion that we stay here while you visit the shipyard. I just can't bear the thought of another voyage right now."

For a second his eyes darkened, and the probing look that followed made her quite uneasy. "Are you sure?" he asked at last.

With a sudden warmth creeping into her cheeks, she dropped her gaze to reply, "I'm sure."

Jonathan rose from the table and, before leaving, put his hand on Jason's head to say, "Take good care of your mother, son. Remember she hasn't been well."

"I will, Daddy," Jason grinned.

Jonathan smiled at his son and affectionately ruffled his hair.

Watching the gesture with a sense of guilt, Katherine felt tears sting her eyes.

"Katie?"

Quickly, she blinked back the tears to look at him with suspiciously bright eyes. "Yes, Jonathan?"

"If you feel up to it, I thought perhaps tomorrow we could all spend the day together. This is your first visit to Boston and you've hardly seen anything of it."

"That would be lovely," she said sincerely.

"Then let's plan on it," he said, and quickly turned away.

* * *

Their last day was over, and realizing that she might never see him again, when Jonathan politely escorted her to her bedroom door Katherine was seized by an overwhelming need to be held in his arms one last time before they parted.

They had already said good night, and standing only a few paces apart, after a few moments they were still looking at each other in silence.

"Jonathan," she said when he started to turn away.

He turned to her quickly. "Yes?"

"It was a lovely day," she said with a melting softness in her gaze, wishing with all her might that he would reach for her and take her in his arms, and fearful of rejection if she made the first move. "I'll never forget it."

"I enjoyed it, too," he replied with a half-smile that went as quickly as it came. "Good night, Katie."

"Good night," she got out through her constricted throat and watched him walk away toward his own bedroom. Before he could disappear through the door she called again, "Jonathan."

With his hand on the doorknob he turned to look back. "Yes, Katie?"

Katherine nervously licked her lips and swallowed to clear her throat in order to ask, "Will you be leaving very early tomorrow morning?"

His eyes were faintly brooding as he looked at her across the room. "Yes, why?"

"I — I thought that perhaps I won't be seeing you then," she shrugged deprecatingly. Her voice lowered to a near whisper when she added, "I just wanted to . . . wish you a good trip."

"Thank you, Katie."

"You're welcome." There was a silence. "Good night, Jonathan."

"Good night, Katie."

Longing to touch him, she saw the door close behind him. She turned and went into her own bedchamber, carrying with her a sense of desolation that remained with her while she prepared for bed.

Katherine knew that she would always remember this last day they had together as one of the happiest — as well as the saddest — of her life. After tonight, she would never see him or ever hear the sound of his voice again.

She remembered little of the sights they had seen on that day, because in her state of mind every one of her senses had been filled by awareness of him and nothing else carried any importance. She clearly remembered his voice telling the story of the famous Boston Tea Party, but the story itself was a blur in her memory. The elegant houses on Beacon Hill had only reminded her of the home in Baltimore she would no longer share with him, and of the new one with a view from the hill that she would never see from her bedroom window.

She eased the robe de chambre off her shoulders and was about to get into bed when a soft knock on the door made her pause. Her heart bounded so violently that she had to press her hands against her breast to still its thumping.

"Yes?"

An involuntary shiver went through her when the door opened and Jonathan came in. He stood there for a moment, gazing at her as though fascinated, and with a trembling feeling she watched him slowly advance toward her.

Wordlessly he took her face between his hands. Her pupils were wide and dark as his intimate glance moved over her features. Softly she drew in her breath and closed her eyes as his head came down. He traced small, lingering kisses on her cheeks and her chin before seeking her parted, yielding lips with driving urgency. She drank the taste with greedy haste, relishing the warm, moist invasion of his tongue, as he hugged her tightly.

"Jonathan," she breathed when at last he drew back, but he wouldn't let her say more. Her mouth was captured again, and eagerly throwing her arms around his waist she returned his kisses with raw, feverish hunger, urgently pressing her body against his.

His lips left hers to track a path of fire down her neck, and she threw her head back to offer her white throat to his caresses as she stroked the back of his nape with her fingers.

Eased from her shoulders, her nightdress fell unheeded to the floor around her feet and he lifted her trembling, naked body in his arms. He set her down on the bed and sat on its edge for a moment, leaning over her and letting his eyes and his hands wander over her body with possessive pleasure, stroking, fondling, making her body melt under his touch. She lost all track of time, place, of everything, and she closed her eyes to best savor the rich

442

sensations evoked by the caresses she would never know again after this night.

A delicious weakness swiftly spread through her limbs as his mouth fastened on her swelling breast, and the warmth glowing in her loins flared into a searing flame of passion that licked at every fiber of her being. She moaned in a ragged, broken manner as his lips and his hands explored the curves and clefts of her body until she was overwhelmed by the need for fulfillment.

"Oh, please, please take me!" she moaned, almost wept, thrashing her head from side to side on the pillow.

Hot and hard his flesh plunged at last into her moist warmth, and arching her body to receive him fully she clung to him, wanton and urgent as they moved in sensuous rhythm. She cried and wept when they reached the summit of passion's pleasure, which exploded within her like a burst of flaming stars. For a moment they lay quietly, wet and spent, still deeply joined as though trying to prolong the moment when they were one.

They loved again, and slept to awake and make love one more time. And afterwards, wrapped in pleasant languor they slept in each other's arms.

Katherine awakened with a start and sat up abruptly.

"Jonathan," she said in a strangled voice, looking at the empty space beside her. It was morning and he was gone, but the imprint of his head on the pillow brought tears to her eyes. Closing her eyes, she lay back on the pillow and let the tears flow.

The night spent in Jonathan's arms had moved her deeply. In all the time they had been together, they had made love in many ways: sometimes with gentleness or in the heat of consuming passion; with joy and good humor; or as two adversaries in the field of battle. But

443

through it all, she had never felt the deep sense of desolation that had been so much a part of their embraces. Perhaps it was her own bleakness of spirit which had imparted such sentiment to the occasion; she had said goodbye, but had she been mistaken, or was the sensation that Jonathan had shared her feelings a product of her own reluctance to leave him?

Yet leave him she must, she told herself, feeling her determination beginning to falter.

She gave a faint sigh and with one last glance of resignation at the empty pillow beside her she shoved the covers aside and got up. She had to hurry if she was going to make the morning train to New York.

While still tying the belt of her robe around her waist, Katherine left her room and went to find Louise.

The servants presented her with an added complication. She wasn't sure if Mrs. Fordham had sufficiently recovered to undertake another trip, even if this one entailed no more than a few hours on a train. The poor ailing woman was her responsibility, and she simply couldn't abandon her in a strange city even if Louise remained to care for her.

"Louise, how's Mrs. Fordham this morning?"

"She's much better, ma'am."

"Well enough to travel, do you think?"

"To travel, ma'am?" Louise regarded her mistress with dismay. "Oh, I don't know."

Recognizing the maid's misgivings about boarding another ship, Katherine smiled and said, "This time it will be by train, Louise. Just for a few hours."

An expression of relief came to Louise's plain features. "I'll have to ask Mrs. Fordham, ma'am."

"It's all right, Louise," Katherine said. "I'll ask her myself. Why don't you start packing Jason's belongings and I'll join you as soon as I talk to Mrs. Fordham."

"Yes, ma'am."

Katherine watched the girl go and then went to Mrs. Fordham's room.

A flurry of activity followed Mrs. Fordham's assurances that she was perfectly able to undertake the train journey, and the packing was completed in short order.

"Where are we going, Mommie?" Jason inquired as they were leaving the hotel.

"For a ride on a train, darling," she replied, affecting a cheerful tone. "And then we're going to visit Adam. You remember Adam, don't you, my love?"

"Of course I do, Mommie." Jason was silent for a moment and then asked, "Is Daddy coming to see Adam, too?"

A lump suddenly developed in Katherine's throat and for a moment she didn't know what to answer. She hated having to lie to her son, yet she couldn't tell him the truth. "I'm sure he will, darling," she contemporized.

She tried to distract him until they reached the station, and then the excitement of seeing the train and getting aboard took care of the rest . . . momentarily, at least.

A voice cried, "All aboard!" A whistle blew, and with a hiss of steam the train set into motion.

Looking out the window, Jason waved back at the people on the platform.

"Good bye, Jonathan, my love," Katherine whispered quietly as the train pulled from the station.

Twenty-one

"Katherine!" Adam exclaimed rushing into the room where she waited, and giving her a mighty hug added, "Good heavens! I could hardly believe it when Hudson told me you had arrived!"

"Oh, Adam!" Katherine clung to him like a drowning man hangs on to a piece of flotsam.

Sensing her distress he drew back to regard her, and a concerned look came to his face. The tears he saw lurking in her eyes gave him a clue as to the reason for her presence in his house. He nodded in tacit understanding before turning to Jason. "Well, my boy, so you finally came to see Old Uncle Adam, eh?"

With a grin splitting his face, Jason rushed into his wide-open arms.

Tightly holding the sturdy little body, Adam straightened up saying, "My, you've grown! You're getting so big that I can hardly lift you up any more."

"I'm almost seven!" Jason said proudly.

"Just wait 'til Iris sees you. She won't be able to recognize you."

Echoing his words, Iris Cavanaugh Garfield walked

into the room, and the next few minutes were devoted to the amenities of the reunion.

"I'm sorry to have dropped in so unexpectedly," Katherine tried to apologize to Adam's wife.

"What nonsense, my dear!" Iris protested affably in her melodious voice. "Consider this house your home in New York where you're welcome any time and for as long as you want."

Unable to speak, Katherine gave her a grateful smile.

"Well, now," Iris said. "Where's that handsome husband of yours?"

Katherine sent Iris a look of caution as she replied, "Jonathan left us in Boston while he went to New Hampshire on business, so Jason and I decided to pay you a visit in the meantime. Mrs. Fordham was very ill during the voyage from Baltimore."

Iris's smile faded. A questioning look swiftly followed by a light of dawning understanding came to her eyes, and reaching for Katherine's hand she said warmly, "I'm glad you thought of us. We have plenty of room."

"I do appreciate your generosity, Iris, but I don't think we should stay here."

Iris's glance shifted from Katherine to Adam and then to Jason. "I'll bet that tummy of yours is quite empty after all those hours on the train," she said to the boy. "What would you say to a nice hot cup of chocolate and a slice of apple pie?"

Jason's eyes lit up at the offer. "Mmm, yes, Aunt Iris! I'm very hungry."

Taking him by the hand, Iris said to Katherine, "Take your time. I'll send you some tea and see that your servants are taken care of."

Both Katherine and Adam remained silent until Iris and Jason had disappeared through the door, and then, turning to her, he said quietly, "So you left him, didn't you?"

"Yes," she nodded heavily. Her voice was choked, her eyes brimming with tears.

He came to her and took her in his arms. "You still love him, don't you, pet?"

Again Katherine nodded, and the tears she had managed to hold back until then came forth in a cloudburst.

He stroked her hair, and handing her his handkerchief he let her cry until her sobs began to subside. "Are you sure you can't work things out?" he asked then.

She shook her head while drying her eyes.

"I'm sorry, pet."

"Where can we go, Adam?" she asked, her voice unsteady.

He started to reply, but the door opened at that moment and a white-gloved servant came in with a tea service.

"That will be all, Hudson, thank you," Adam said to the butler when the man set the tray down on the table.

"Yes, sir," the man said and went out again.

Adam poured a cup of tea, added a dash of cream and set it before Katherine saying, "Let's sit down and have some tea, pet. It'll make you feel better." Offering a plate of small sandwiches, he admonished gently, "And do eat something. If you lose any more weight you'll remind me of that time you had influenza. Remember?"

"Yes, I remember," she replied with a dismal sniff as she sank down on a chair. "However, what I remember best of that time was when Ronald came and told us you had been captured."

"That was a nasty piece of business, wasn't it?" His tone was gruff, yet at the same time gentle. "Well, at least something good came out of it."

448

She regarded him quizzically. "Something good?" she repeated in a puzzled voice.

He nodded. "We found out how we truly felt about each other, didn't we?"

Katherine lifted a flushed and confused face at him. "You knew all along, didn't you?"

"That you thought you were in love with me?" At her hesitant nod, he admitted wryly, "Well, I must confess I was having a problem of a similar nature myself."

Katherine's expressive brows arched in surprise. "You?"

He leaned forward in his chair and reached for her hand. "I was drawn to you from the very first moment I saw you at Langford's party, pet. After Greenfield took you away and I saw not only that he was being good to you, but also that you had fallen in love with him, I tried to put you out of my mind. Yet somehow I couldn't, and I suppose that was what made me impersonate Professor Stuyvesant, and everything else."

"And I suppose that if Jason had been a girl, I might have asked you to marry me," he sighed wryly, "which, of course, would have been a dreadful mistake for both of us. Thank God, he turned out to be a boy!"

All Katherine could do was stare at him in astonishment.

He made an apologetic little gesture with his hands and gazed at her affectionately. "There were times during those months you were carrying him, when I found myself almost believing that I had been granted a second chance with someone else, pet. Someone . . . I had loved very much."

After an odd silence that lasted a few seconds, he went on in a reflective fashion. "Her name was Caroline, and she was very young — about your age — when we met. She was beautiful, pet. Her hair was the color of the sky at sunset, when it becomes a flame. Her eyes were as green as emeralds . . . like yours. I fell in love with her from the moment I saw her even though she was way above my station and I knew I didn't have a prayer. I was just a poor young man trying to make it as an actor, you see, so you can imagine my surprise and delight when I discovered that she returned my love."

"More than anything I wanted to marry her, but that was impossible, so we became lovers and met in secret every time we could, always aware that if her father ever found out about us, it would be the end. Oh, Caroline, when one is young and in love like we were, nothing matters but those moments when we could be together."

Not realizing that he had called Katherine by the name of his beloved, he went on, "As you must have surmised, pet, we were found out, and her father was powerful enough to ruin what career I might have had. However, I could have lived with that; the worst part was that he forced Caroline to marry someone else, and then she died in childbirth. It wasn't until much later that I learned the child had been mine. When I went to visit Caroline's grave, there was another, a smaller one, next to hers. Our daughter's."

"Oh, my dear!" Katherine whispered, holding his hand a little tighter. "I'm so sorry."

"That was a long time ago, pet. Before you were born," he said, his voice wistful. Then he cleared his throat and attempted a smile as he added, "After all those years, having you around was almost like having Caroline back. But you were not Caroline, although you had her beauty, her dignity, her courage. Even some of her gestures, you know that certain way you tip your chin sometimes. You could very well have been her daughter. Our daughter."

He shook his head and gave her a smile that had a

450

touch of sadness. "That was what the plan concocted by Vidocq and the Marquis d'Esterel made me realize, Katherine. That my love for you was that of a father for a daughter. And after helping me escape, you learned that although you loved me, you were not in love with me. Am I right?"

"Yes," she nodded.

"So, you see, everything turned out for the best. It usually does."

"Not always," she said tonelessly.

"What happened, pet?" he asked, regarding her with indulgent affection. "How did you manage to escape Jonathan?"

She told him everything, and at the end of her narrative he said, "As Iris said, you and Jason are welcome to stay with us for as long as you want, pet."

"But this is the first place Jonathan will come to when he discovers that we left him!"

"You'll be under our protection, Katherine. You'll be safe from him."

"I'm afraid, Adam. I need to spend some time alone to pull myself together, to figure out what to do next, where Jason and I could go."

Following a thoughtful pause, Adam said, "Our lease on the Owens's house still has a couple of months to run. You were always fond of that house, and the staff is devoted to you. Would you like to go there?"

Katherine was aware that Adam had given up the lease and moved into Iris's house after their wedding, and since Jenny's romantic interest had made her move her residence to Albany, the Owens's house had been occupied only by the servants. It would be a safe place for her and Jason, Katherine reflected. "Yes, I'd like that," she replied at last.

"Very well," Adam nodded. "I'll send a message to

Bruce that you'll be there after dinner this evening."

It was only three days later that Hudson came into the drawing room where Adam and Iris were sitting and announced, "Captain Greenfield came asking for Mrs. Greenfield, sir. When I told him she wasn't here, he asked to see you."

Adam and his wife exchanged glances and he said, "Please show him to my study, Hudson."

The butler nodded and left the room.

Adam remained in his seat thoughtfully for a few moments and then got up. "This isn't going to be easy," he said to Iris, who watched him go with a concerned look on her lovely face.

Jonathan was facing the door when Adam came into the study and said with a marked lack of enthusiasm, "What do you want, Greenfield?"

"You know perfectly well what I want, Garfield. Where are they?"

"They're not here."

Jonathan's face was grim. "I saw them coming in here last Friday," he said.

Adam's well-controlled expression didn't betray his surprise. "I already told you that they're not here," he said acidly. "Do you want to search the house?"

Jonathan shook his head. "Where did they go?"

"Leave her alone, man!" Adam blustered forth, his face tight with anger. "Don't you think you've caused her enough grief?"

Jonathan's reply made Adam look at him in astonishment. Their conversation lasted for almost half an hour, and at the end Adam said, "Very well, I'll speak to Katherine, but I can't promise that she'll agree to see you. Where can I reach you?"

"At the Astor House."

Adam escorted his visitor to the front door and watched him disappear down the street. Then, he went out through the service entrance.

He made a stop at the Astor House, where he confirmed what Jonathan had told him, and then went on the Owens's house, where he was immediately taken to Katherine's presence.

"He's here," he said without further elaboration.

Turning visibly pale, Katherine murmured faintly, "So soon?"

"I must say, he surprised me a bit," Adam reflected, shaking his head.

"Why? We were expecting him, weren't we?"

"It's not that," Adam replied, flapping an impatient hand. "To tell the truth, the chap looks quite miserable." He looked at her speculatively. "As a matter of fact, pet, you don't look so good yourself, if you don't mind my saying so."

Katherine disregarded the observation he had made in a slightly humorous tone. "What did he want?"

"To see you, what else?" Adam shrugged.

"No!" she cried, abruptly turning away. "I don't want to see him! I can't!"

Adam came to stand behind her and put his hands on her shoulders. "But you must, pet. He told me that if you want to marry Chapman, he won't stand in your way."

Abruptly turning to face him again, Katherine cried, "He did what!"

Adam extended his hands, palms up, at his sides and smiled deprecatingly, "I told you he surprised me. And, by the way, he also gave me his word that he won't try to take Jason away from you."

Katherine's mouth fell open. "And you believed him?"

"Yes, I did," he nodded.

Katherine stared at him in astonishment for one full minute, and then was suddenly seized by the hysterical desire to burst out laughing. "We're all losing our minds!" she said between nervous giggles. Then, dropping her face in her hands she wept, "Oh, God! I think I'm the one who's going insane!"

Adam took her hands away from her face and made her look at him. "Now, don't get hysterical on me, Katherine!" he said peremptorily. "Pull yourself together and listen!"

Her face was so white and pinched that her eyes looked enormous as she stared back at him.

"Look, pet, I know it's not going to be easy, but you have to see Jonathan," he said in a more persuasive tone. "As your husband, and the father of your son, he deserves that much. Besides, you told me you had even considered leaving Jason with his father so as not to rob him of his birthright, didn't you? Well, who knows? Perhaps you might be able to reach some kind of agreement with Jonathan about that. There's so much to discuss between the two of you, and, as I said, he gave me his word he won't try anything."

"I suppose you're right," she admitted bleakly. She took a deep breath and said, "Very well, Adam. I'll see him."

"When?"

"I might as well get it over with soon," she shrugged unhappily. "Tonight, after dinner."

"Shall I tell him nine o'clock?"

"That'll be fine."

"Very well then. I'll send a message to him," Adam said, rising to his feet. "Do you want me here?"

Katherine took a moment to consider his offer. "Thank you, Adam, but perhaps I should see him alone."

Adam gave her an affectionate hug and kissed her on

454

the cheek. "Funny!" he said, shaking his head wryly as he started to take his leave.

"What is?"

"I was just thinking," he said. "Even though I've never been fond of the man, I never took Jonathan Greenfield for a fool."

Katherine's expressive brows rose quizzically. "What do you mean?"

A small, almost imperceptible smile formed on his lips.

"Oh, nothing," he said in a voice deceptively casual. "But did you ever stop to think how convenient that trip to Boston was? How easily you were able to get away from him? That was rather foolish of him, don't you think?"

And with that, he left.

Promptly at nine o'clock, Bruce escorted Jonathan into the drawing room where Katherine had been waiting for the last half hour.

She didn't move away from the window when he came in. At the sight of her husband, Katherine's heart constricted so painfully that she instantly regretted she hadn't asked Adam to be there. As usual, Jonathan was elegantly dressed, his hair was meticulously brushed, but there were lines of strain on his grim face, and his eyes were bloodshot as though he hadn't slept for several nights.

"Hello, Katie," he said, his voice huskier than it was ordinarily.

She found it astonishingly difficult to reply, "Hello, Jonathan." Trying to maintain a stolid attitude, she waved a hand toward a chair and had to swallow to clear her throat in order to ask, "Would you like a brandy?"

"Please," he nodded as he sank into the chair.

A crystal decanter and glasses were on a table next to her. Her hand was shaking as she started to pour the drinks, so the decanter rattled against the rim of the glass and some of the liquor spilled on to the silver tray beneath it. She managed to pour two fingers of brandy into one of the snifters without spilling more of it, and when she turned back to face Jonathan found that his eyes were intently fixed on her. Dropping her gaze, she advanced toward him and handed him the glass. Their fingers touched briefly and she jerked away abruptly. Determined not to show the tension that was building up within her she said, "Adam was right. You look terrible!"

"But you look beautiful, Katie. As always." He had tried to make light of it and failed.

Katherine looked back at him, struggling with an overwhelming desire to burst into tears. Please, don't let me break down now, she prayed, clenching her teeth to keep her jaw from trembling.

Jonathan drained the glass before inquiring, "How's Jason?"

"He—he's well. Asleep now."

"Could I see him?" he inquired in a tightly controlled voice.

"Why, yes, of course. But first . . ."

He cut her off. "You'll get your divorce, Katie, although it may take a while. These things take time. If you give me the name of your solicitor, I'll provide him with all the evidence you may need to use against me. In the meantime, I will open a bank account so that you won't lack for anything."

Quietly, she said, "I don't need your money, Jonathan."

His eyes remained fixed on the empty glass, and rubbing the tip of his finger over the edge he asked bitterly, "Do you still hate me that much?"

"No, Jonathan," she said gently. "It's just that I don't really need it."

"I suppose not, once you marry Chapman," he muttered, then looked at her sharply. "But Jason is my son. I'll provide for him even if you won't accept anything for yourself."

"I don't need your money or Max's!" Katherine snapped with a sudden flash of anger. "I have my own!"

Jonathan looked at her a little startled. "Your own?" he asked rather dubiously.

With arms akimbo and an angry sparkle in her eyes, Katherine lifted her chin to reply emphatically, "Yes, my own! Or did you think Adam supported us all those years?"

Jonathan's silence was his admission that he did.

"Well, he didn't!" said with a trace of a snap. "When I left you in London, I promised myself that I'd never be dependent on anyone else again. Adam gave me the chance to become financially independent, and I took it."

"And I thought . . ." Shaking his head wryly, Jonathan let the sentence trail off.

"That keeping money out of my reach would keep me in Baltimore?" she finished for him.

Wryly, he nodded, "Yes."

"Well, now you see how unnecessary that was."

"Ah, Katie, you're always full of surprises! I'll miss . . . Oh, never mind." He gazed at her wistfully. "All right, so you don't need a settlement, but what of Jason?"

"He's your son," she replied with a shrug. "I'm well aware that what I have to offer him can't compare to what you and your family can, Jonathan, and I don't want to rob him of what's rightfully his. But I can't bear

457

to lose him!" Her breath caught in a small sob.

Jonathan got up briskly and went to her. He started to put his arms around her and then dropped them at his sides.

"You won't lose him, Katie," he assured her, trying to calm her down. "He could come to Baltimore and spend some time with us, but I'll never take him away from you, honey. I give you my word."

Tears were trembling in her lashes when she looked up at him and said in a whisper, "Thank you, Jonathan."

He took one step back and cleared his throat to say, "Well, now, is there anything else we ought to discuss?"

"I suppose not," she said, her voice fading slightly.

Lifting his empty glass he asked, "May I have another brandy?"

"Yes, of course," she said, taking the glass from his hand, careful not to touch him.

This time she filled two glasses, and after handing him one she lifted her own and smiled weakly, "Here's to a friendly divorce!"

Jonathan raised his glass unenthusiastically and they finished their drinks in silence.

Katherine set her empty glass down on the table. "Would you like to see Jason now?" she asked nervously. At his nod, she led the way out of the drawing room and up the stairs. "I'm sorry he's asleep, but I thought it would be easier for everyone if he didn't know you were coming this evening." She stopped in front of the bedroom door and put her hand on his arm to say remorsefully, "You may see him tomorrow during the day, if you wish."

She went into the bedroom followed by Jonathan and went to light the lamp. As the light invaded the room, a sob caught in her throat when she turned to look at Jonathan and saw the expression on his face. Such was the sorrow reflected there as he watched his son, that she couldn't bear to watch any more.

"I'll wait for you downstairs," she got out through her constricted throat before she rushed from the room.

Blinded by tears she ran into her bedchamber and shut the door behind her. Pressing her hands to her mouth, she moaned deep in her throat, "Oh, darling, forgive me! Oh, God, I love you, Jonathan!"

Once it had broken, the dam of tears couldn't be contained regardless of how hard she tried. She blew her nose, drank a glass of water, held her breath, and splashed cold water on her face, and still she kept on sniffling. What she needed was stiff drink to steady her nerves, but all the liquor was downstairs.

Katherine splashed on more cold water and dried her face before she quietly went down the stairs.

In the drawing room she poured a hefty measure of brandy into the snifter and was drinking it when Jonathan came in. She took one look at his face and poured more brandy into his glass, which she offered to him without a word. Jonathan accepted it gratefully and gulped it down.

"Has he missed me, Katie?" he asked when he was able to speak again.

"Oh, yes, he has!"

"What did you tell him?"

"That you love him, that you miss him."

"I do, you know."

Instinctively, she reached for his hand. "Oh, darling, I'm so sorry!"

Touching him sent a shock through her, and she had to fight the impulse of throwing herself into his arms.

"I know, love, I know," he said, his voice hard and bitter. Wearily, he turned and started to walk away.

He was almost through the door when she called, "Jonathan!"

Swiftly, he turned to face her.

"That last night, in Boston, you knew, didn't you?"

"That you were planning to leave?" He nodded heavily. "Yes, I knew."

"And you didn't try to stop me?" She looked at him appealingly. "Why, Jonathan?"

He smiled wistfully. "Because I love you, Katie."

Sharply, she drew in her breath. "You . . . you love me?"

"I've always loved you, Katie. Always."

She still couldn't bring herself to believe him. "In London," she said, coming to him. "Did you love me then?"

"Yes, honey, only I didn't find out myself until it was too late."

"But you were leaving me!" she argued hotly. "You told me that you loved your wife!"

"I know what I said, honey. And I did care for Mary Beth. I cared for her deeply, but I didn't know what love really was until you came along."

"Everyone says that you couldn't forget her."

"Forget her! My God, Katie, she was my wife! And I killed her, just as surely as if I had put a bullet through her. No," he reflected bitterly. "A bullet would have been more merciful. No one should go through the agony she suffered before she died, Katie. I was there, I saw it with my own eyes. She was so small, so frail, and she died horribly because of me."

"Don't blame yourself, darling. It was her choice to have your child. You didn't know her life was in danger."

"But that's the point, can't you see? I should have known! I would have known had I been there, instead of gallivanting all over the globe, wrapped up in my own

460

interests. And do you know something, Katie?" He gave a short, mirthless bark of a laugh. "After she died, I went back to England and tried to find you. Even though I felt responsible for her death, I needed you more than ever. I couldn't stop loving you, wanting you."

"How can you say that you loved me when you were passing me to another man!" she snapped, fighting her desire to believe him.

He gave her a slow look of astonishment. "What do you mean, *I was passing you to another man*?"

"Were you not planning to sell me, or pass me on to Darby after you were gone?"

His eyebrows went up in puzzlement. "Darby?"

She nodded emphatically. "You told me I'd be protected after you were gone. Was Darby supposed to become my new *protector*, or did you have someone else in mind?"

When he finally understood, a look of sheer disbelief came to his sharp features. Seizing her by the shoulders he said emphatically, "When I said you'd be protected, I meant by me, no one else." He saw her eyes widen in surprise and her mouth open a little. "Honey, I had to get back to Baltimore quickly and I couldn't bring you with me, so I bought a house for you in the country. I also hired people to protect you in my absence, and provided for you so that you wouldn't lack for anything until I could get back to England."

"You never intended to sell me to Darby?" she asked in dismay.

He shot a pained look at her. "Good Lord, Katie! Just the idea of another man touching you tears me apart!"

"Oh, Jonathan, I thought . . ." Unable to finish the sentence, she covered her face with her hands and wept bitterly.

Jonathan took her hands away from her face and

461

crooked a finger under her chin to make her look at him. "Was that the reason you left me without a word?"

Unable to contain her weeping, Katherine nodded.

"Did you love me, Katie?"

"Love you? I worshipped you, Jonathan, but after what happened that night I thought . . ." shaking her head, she let her words trail.

"Honey, those two months I spent with you in London were the happiest of my life. I stayed much longer than I should have because I couldn't bring myself to leave you. I even thought of bringing you to America with me, but when I received a letter telling me that Mary Beth was with child again, I had to come back without delay. You had occupied every waking thought I had since we met, and when I learned that my wife was risking her life to have my child, I realized that as much as I wanted you with me, I had no choice but to leave you behind. You have no idea the hell I went through, Katie, and the total indifference you showed as to whether it was me or someone else in your bed as long as you were safe from Langford really tipped me over. Just the idea of you and another man . . . Good Lord, Katie, I hated you for making me love you!"

"It wasn't indifference," she wept softly. "Just my stupid pride that kept me from telling you how much I loved you, from begging you take me with you."

His arms tightened around her, and he pressed a kiss on her hair. "I spent years searching for you, my love. Once, when I felt that I had lost you forever, I went and bought that land on the hill. Every time I was in Baltimore feeling that I was losing hope of ever finding you again, I went there and told myself that one day I'd build you a house on that very spot, where we could live together."

She drew back to look at him. "It was for me?"

"Of course, my darling," he smiled at her. "Why else did you think I took you there and told you about it?"

"I thought it was meant for Mary Beth," she admitted guiltily.

"You little fool!" he gave her a playful squeeze. "But who am I to talk? For seven long years I yearned for you, and when I found you in New York and saw the way Chapman kissed you, the way you touched him and smiled at him, I felt like a perfect fool, pining away for a woman who, I thought, sold her favors to the highest bidder. Even then I still wanted you, and I figured that if I had you again I'd be able to get you out of my system once and for all. I was willing to pay whatever price you demanded."

"You were horrible!" she accused him.

"Yes, I was, wasn't I?" He laughed softly. "Of course, all it took was just one kiss to make me realize that I was wrong about forgetting you. The only way to get you out of my heart is by tearing it out."

"Oh, darling, I wish you had told me then!"

He gave a short laugh. "I tried to, honey, but you said that you hated me, remember? And you were very convincing. Besides, after what happened, I thought you had good reason to hate me. If there had been more time I wouldn't have forced you into marrying me, but when you told me you were going to marry Chapman, I was afraid I'd lose you forever. Even though you said you hated me, the way you kissed me that night made me hope that I could still win your love."

Holding her face between his hands, he looked into her eyes and said huskily. "I love you, Katie, I need you so, my love!"

"But you let me go," she chided him mildly.

"I had to, honey. I'd rather live with your hatred than without you, but that portrait of you made me realize what I was doing to you. In that painting you were as beautiful and as vibrantly alive as you were in London, or last autumn in New York. Then I saw you standing there, so pale and frightened, and the contrast was so sharp, that it made me face facts that I had willfully tried to ignore. That I was destroying you, killing you a little each day, and it was then that I realized that because I loved you, I had to let you go. Setting you free was the hardest thing I've ever done in my life, Katie, not only because I love you, but also because I knew you wouldn't leave without Jason."

"Oh, Jonathan!"

"I had been working up enough courage these past few weeks, hoping for a miracle, perhaps, so that I could keep you both with me, but when I learned that you had been making inquiries about a carriage to take you to New York, I was afraid you'd take to the road."

"So to ensure our safety you invented the trip to Portsmouth," she interposed. When he nodded, she asked, "Why didn't you just tell me that we were free to go?"

"I couldn't bring myself to do it," Jonathan replied wryly. "Even in Boston I kept hoping you would change your mind at the last minute."

"Did you really go to Portsmouth?"

"No," he shook his head. "I came to New York on the same train with you and followed you to Adam's house. When you went to him rather than straight to Chapman, I decided to give you a few days to think things over before trying to see you."

"Over the years I tried to convince myself that I hated you," she said. "But I never did. I loved you, and that was why I couldn't marry Max even before you came back into my life." Reaching out to touch his cheek she said, "I told you the truth, Jonathan. Max and I were

464

never lovers. You have been my one and only lover, darling. I've never loved anyone else. Never will. I thought my life was over when I finally got enough nerve to tell you that I loved you and you drew away from me. Why did you?"

"How could I believe you when I knew you had sent for Chapman?"

"But I didn't!" she protested emphatically. "Until Felicity told me that he was there at the ball, I had no idea he had come to Baltimore."

"Felicity?"

"Yes, Felicity saw him at the ball and told me," she replied, reviling herself for her slip. Regardless of how much damage Felicity had inflicted, she didn't want to set Jonathan against his sister. Now that she knew that he loved her, Felicity could never hurt them again.

"Why did you meet him?"

"You knew about that too?"

He nodded.

"I had to. He wouldn't go away unless I saw him. When he asked me to divorce you and marry him, I told him that I couldn't because I loved you, not him." She paused to say, "When I left you, I never intended to marry Max or anyone else, Jonathan. Please believe me, I didn't even think of a divorce until you mentioned it."

When he held her in his arms, she knew at last that she had exorcised the ghosts from the past. "My love," he said, burying his face into her hair.

She had cleared his doubts, but her own still remained. Drawing back from his embrace, she said, "Just one moment, Jonathan."

"What is it, honey?"

"I have to tell you that I'm not willing to share you with anyone."

He looked down at her, seemingly quite puzzled. "I

don't understand what you mean, Katie."

"What I mean is that as much as I love you, I won't put up with your other women!" she snapped waspishly.

"My . . ." His puzzlement dissolved into a rich and husky laugh as he threw back his head.

Making an effort to restrain her indignation, Katherine said drily, "I fail to see the humor."

Jonathan regarded her with indulgent affection. "And what makes you think I have other women?" he inquired with exaggerated innocence. Even after his mirth subsided, a flicker of amusement still danced in the blue depths of his eyes.

"Do you take me for a fool?" she accused him. "I heard you leave the house every night when you thought I was asleep! Sometimes you didn't come back until morning! And with my own eyes I saw you kissing that woman when we stopped in Philadelphia last November. It was disgusting!"

"Embarrassing is a more appropriate word, Katie," he mocked her mildly.

Katherine was not amused.

He heaved a weary sigh. "Katie, my love, we've been a couple of fools." At the sight of her pursed lips, he added, "I haven't even looked at another woman since we were married, honey."

When she still seemed unconvinced, he smiled wryly and said, "Katie, after seven long years longing to hold you in my arms, have you any idea of what it was like for me to have you so close and not being able to touch you? I felt like a criminal when you started crying after we made love that first time, so I promised myself to be patient, to wait until you wanted me to make love to you again. But it was hard, honey. I couldn't trust myself to stay away from your bed, so sometimes I went out, others I simply went downstairs just to put some distance between us. I never dreamed that you were jealous!"

"That's all very well, but you still haven't explained that woman in Philadelphia, who very conveniently appeared in Baltimore a few weeks later to operate a business you financed. And please don't tell me she's a long-lost cousin, because I won't believe you."

"Would you believe me if I told you she's the widow of an old shipmate of mine?"

Katherine blinked in astonishment.

"I was very surprised to find her serving tables at the inn," he continued. "I had served with her husband before he left Greenfield Lines several years ago to ship out on a whaler. He died after a long illness that ate up all their savings, and Theresa and her son were left destitute, Katie. When she told me what had happened, I suggested that she come down to Baltimore and offered to lend her the money to start a business. And by the way, you would have met her at that time in Philadelphia had you not developed such a sudden headache."

"Oh!" Katherine dropped her gaze, feeling a rush of warmth come to her cheeks.

Grinning, Jonathan regarded her fondly. "Have I forgotten anyone?"

Because she now believed his explanations, Katherine was rather reluctant to inquire, "Why did you call on Crystal Gaynor when we were in New York?"

"Crystal?" Rather puzzled, Jonathan stared at her for a few seconds before he said, "Now I remember! Felicity had asked me to deliver a package to her. They've been friends for a long time."

"Wasn't it a letter?"

"There was a letter inside when she opened it in front of me. The package itself was about so big," he confirmed, gesturing with his hands to indicate the size of the parcel.

"But you didn't see what was inside the package?"

"No, it was also wrapped, and she didn't open it Why?"

That explained how Jonathan's cravat had been in Crystal's possession, Katherine reflected, hoping that Jonathan would never be forced to learn of his sister' attempts to destroy their marriage. But if ever again Felicity interfered in their lives, she herself would have to settle accounts with her sister-in-law — in her own time, in her own way. With a deprecating shrug she replied, "Jus curious."

"Are there any more questions, my love?"

When she raised her gaze to him and saw all the love and tenderness reflected in his blue eyes, she shook her head and rushed into his encompassing arms. Jonathan loved her, deeply loved her. There had been no one else in spite of her constant refusals and the pain she had inflicted by denying him his child, not once but twice And if he could still love her after that, then nothing in her past would matter. She would have to tell him of that part of her life she had spent outside the law, living by her wits, but that could wait until later. All she wanted at this moment was to be in his arms again.

"No more doubts, my love?" he asked, and when she shook her head, their lips met in a long, searing kiss that made the world spin about her.

With their arms around each other they went out o the drawing room, but as they approached the staircase Bruce, appointed her protector, stepped out to block the way.

Katherine turned a radiant face to the servant and said, "It's all right, Bruce. Good night."

Her smile assured the servant that she wasn't being

forced, and without changing his impenetrable expression he simply replied, "Good night, madam, sir," and turned on his heel.

Epilogue

As Katherine lay fulfilled and naked beneath him, Jonathan brushed strands of tousled hair away from her face and gently traced the fingers of one hand along the contours of her lips, which were now slightly swollen from his kisses. "I love you," he murmured.

With a renewed sense of wonder, she lifted her soft gaze to say in a hushed voice, "And I love you, Jonathan. Let's never stop saying it to each other, darling."

"We'll make up for all those years we've waited, my love. On that you have my promise." He smiled, and the intimate glance accompanying the gesture added a warm glow to the pleasant languor that had taken possession of her.

"All those years," she murmured faintly. Following an odd silence she said quietly, "All those years you spent searching for me, I always knew where to find you, Jonathan. I had promised myself that I would, except I'm ashamed to admit that my motive was revenge."

"Revenge?" He regarded her with surprise.

"That's what I kept telling myself," she sighed. "I was so hurt by what I thought your betrayal that I vowed I'd make you pay. I hated you then, Jonathan. I hated you so much that when I discovered I was carrying your child, I prayed that . . ."

"Honey, don't," he said, placing the tips of his fingers over her lips. "Let's not dwell on the past. We have each other now, and we have our child. It's all that matters."

"I have to tell you because I think it's important that you know what I was doing during those years we were apart."

Her distress was so apparent that he was beginning to become quite concerned. "You couldn't have done anything so terrible," he said, trying to calm her down.

"I was a thief," she blurted out without more preamble.

He blinked and stared at her in astonishment. "A thief?" he echoed dumbly.

"Well, I was also a gambler," she nodded, "but mainly a thief. You see, aside from the fact that I had to earn a living, when I decided to get even with you I realized not only that in order to carry out my plan I had a great deal to learn, but also that I would need a fortune. Besides, I didn't want to be dependent on another man again. Adam had offered to help me whether or I worked with him or not, but . . ."

"Adam!" he interrupted angrily. "He was the one who put you up to it, wasn't he?" Before she could reply, he muttered savagely, "Damn it, I should have known! I'll break his miserable neck!"

"Wait, Jonathan! Please hear me out!" she pleaded in earnest. "Adam and his sister offered me a home when I had no one else to turn to. They cared for me and for your son and gave us not only their protection, but their deep affection as well. He didn't trick me or force me to

471

do anything I didn't want to do. I could have stayed with them even if I hadn't agreed to become his accomplice, but I didn't want charity however well intended, can't you understand that?" Her tone became more persuasive when she added, "It was my choice, darling. Please don't hold it against him. It would hurt me deeply to have the two of you at odds with each other. Who knows what would have become of me and Jason if it hadn't been for him."

When he managed to curb his anger, she went on to tell him of how carefully Adam had prepared her, and of their activities on the Continent. She concluded her narrative by saying, "So, you see, darling, although there was danger, I always had the protection of Adam and his friends. We were all very close, almost like a family."

"And this painter, Ronald Lambert, is he the one who sent you that portrait?"

"Yes," she nodded. "He's become quite famous."

"He's in love with you," he said, frowning.

Katherine reached for his hand. "Darling, does it matter? You're the only man I've ever loved. That first night when we made love I cried because it was then that I discovered that I still loved you, perhaps more than ever, although I still believed you had betrayed me. All that hatred I professed was a lie; a lie because I was ashamed to admit, even to myself, that I could be so weak where you were concerned. I love you, Jonathan, and I only hope that you won't stop loving me because of what I did."

"Come here, you little idiot," he chuckled, drawing her to him. Folding her in his arms he said, "Honey, I don't care if you robbed the Bank of England, if you stole all the money in Europe, or the whole world for that matter. All I care about is that you're back where

472

you belong, Katie. With me. We'll never be apart again, my love."

"You won't sail away?"

He shook his head. "Father has been after me for years to start taking over some of his business interests, which I should have done long ago. But I simply couldn't stay in Baltimore, Katie. Not as long as I had hopes of finding you."

"Darling, I'd hate to be without you, but I wouldn't want you to give up the sea because of me."

He smiled, and holding her hand against his cheek replied, "I've had my fill of sea adventures, honey. What I'm anticipating now is the adventure of our lives together. I've already missed the first years of our son, and I intend to see him grow. Besides, I've got a feeling that living with someone as unpredictable as you are may be the most exciting adventure of them all."

He leaned over and kissed her on the lips.

When the kiss ended, a little breathless she said, "Oh, my love, I was so afraid you wouldn't understand, that I didn't want to tell you of my past. But there shouldn't be any more secrets between us, Jonathan. Not ever again." Her voice dropped to a near whisper to add meekly, "Darling, are you still angry with Adam?"

"I ought to be for placing you in such danger," he replied in a voice that was gruff, yet soft at the same time. She gazed at him so appealingly that he burst out laughing. "All right, I'll make my peace with Adam for your sake, but don't think for a minute that I'm going to be fooled by that meekness you're feigning, you thieving wench. It may have worked on those victims you robbed blind, but I know you better than that."

"But, sire, it's not your purse I'm after!" she giggled, her green eyes dancing with mischief. And taking his face between her hands she pressed soft, lingering kisses upon his smooth-shaven cheeks and traced the contours of his mouth before claiming it at last.